CHAMP

THE GRAPHI

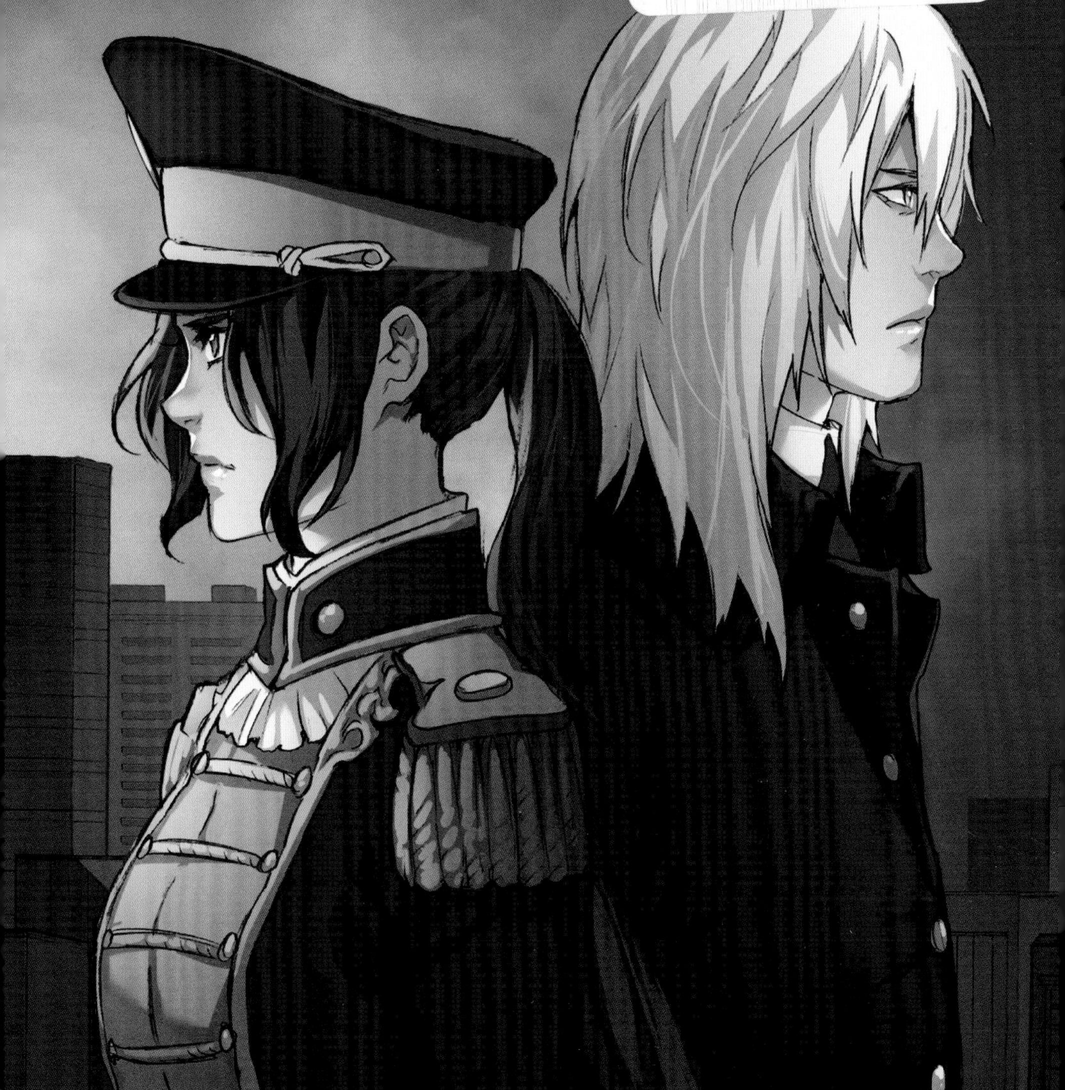

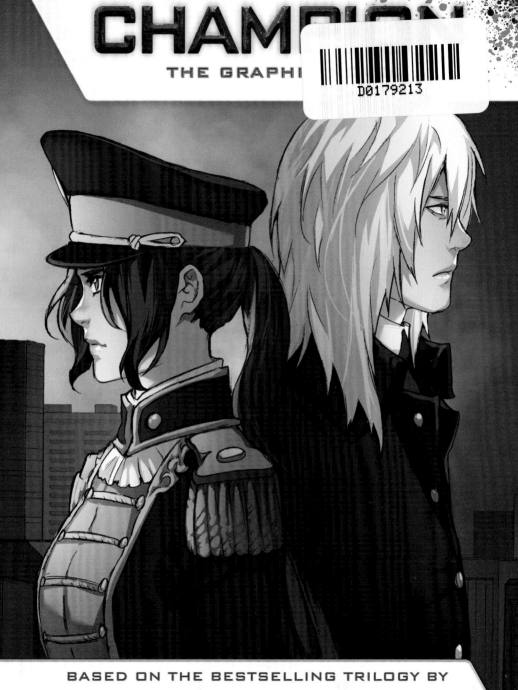

BASED ON THE BESTSELLING TRILOGY BY

MARIE LU

ADAPTED BY LEIGH DRAGOON · ILLUSTRATED BY KAARI

G.P. PUTNAM'S SONS
An Imprint of Penguin Random House LLC
375 Hudson Street
New York, NY 10014

G.P. Putnam's Sons is a registered trademark of
Penguin Random House LLC

Library of Congress Cataloging-in-Publication Data is available.

Pencils by Kaari
Colored by Kaari, Depinz, Angie, and Melina of Caravan Studio

Printed in Canada

ISBN 9780451534347

3 5 7 9 10 8 6 4 2

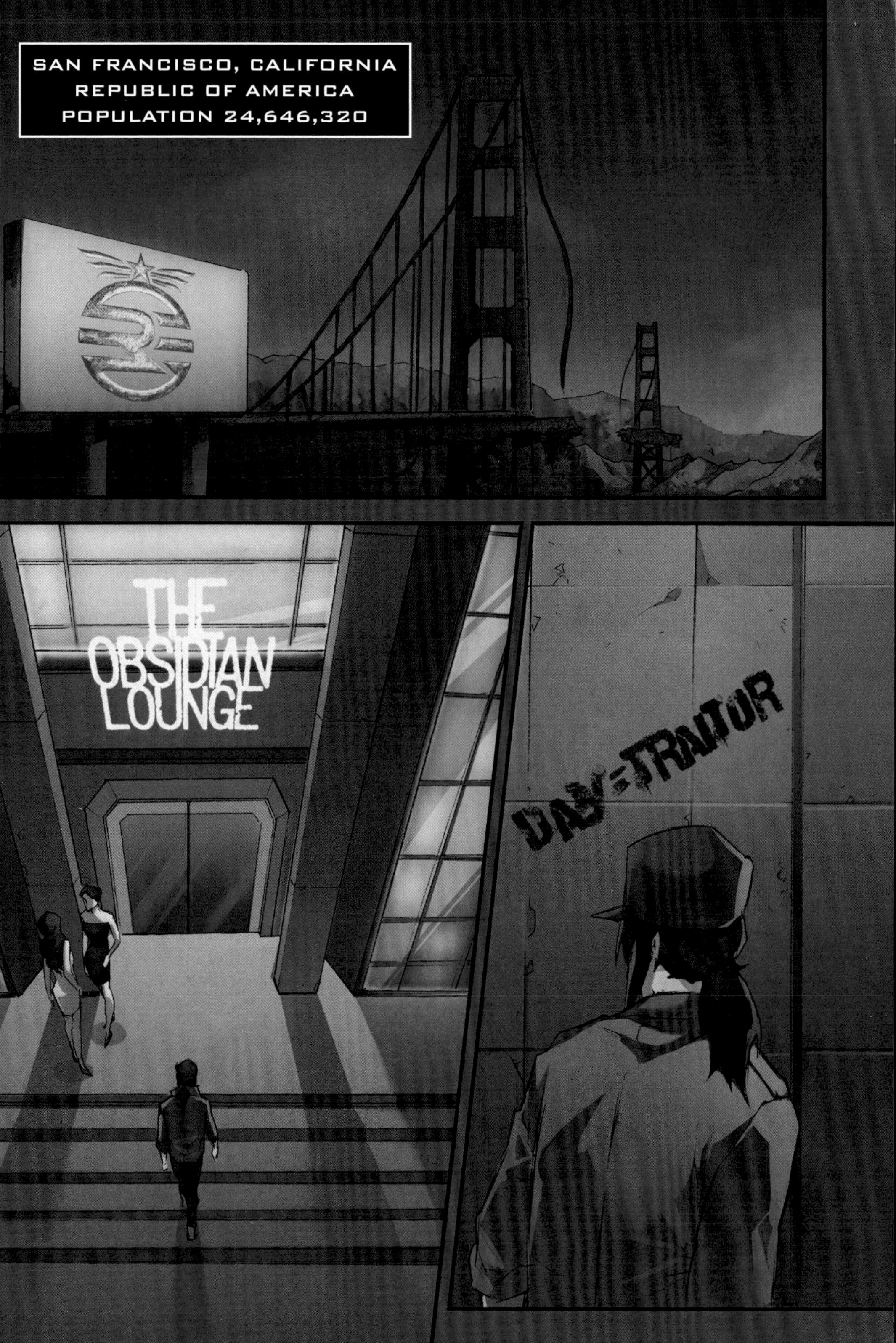
SAN FRANCISCO, CALIFORNIA
REPUBLIC OF AMERICA
POPULATION 24,646,320
THE OBSIDIAN LOUNGE
DAY=TRAITOR

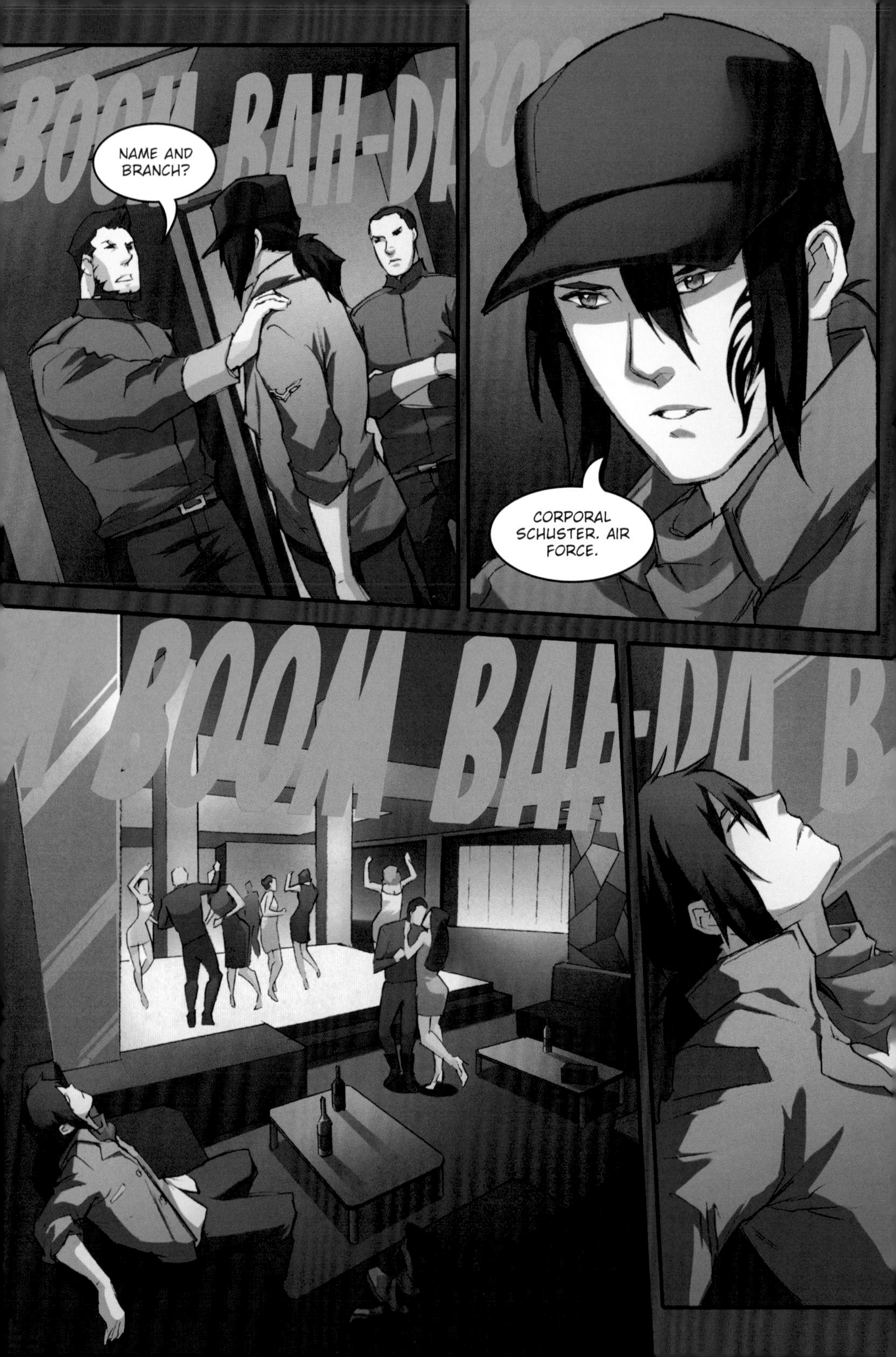
BOOM BAH-DA
NAME AND BRANCH?
BOOM BAH-DA
CORPORAL SCHUSTER. AIR FORCE.
BOOM BAH-DA B

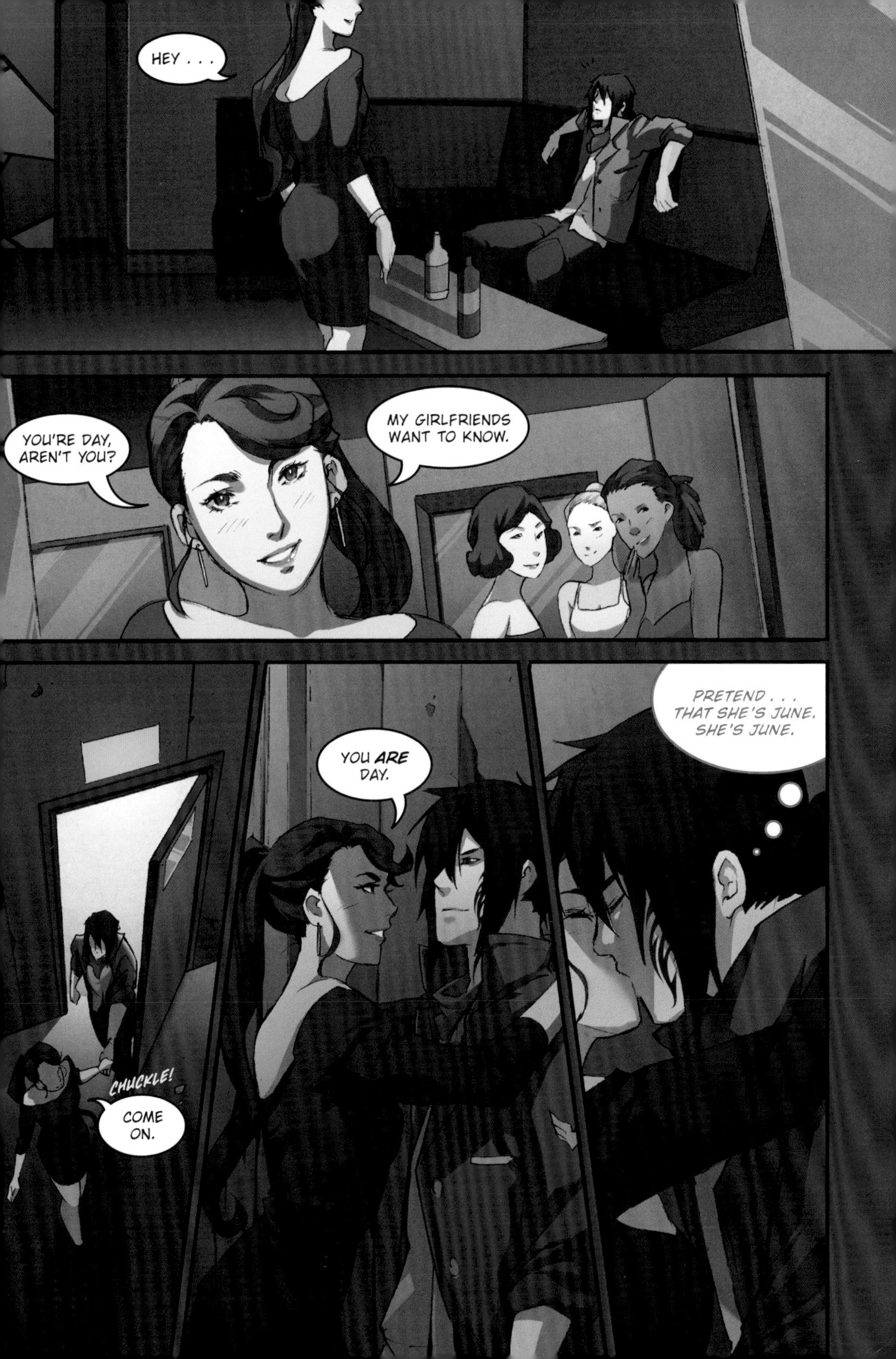
HEY . . .
YOU'RE DAY, AREN'T YOU?
MY GIRLFRIENDS WANT TO KNOW.
CHUCKLE!
COME ON.
YOU **ARE** DAY.
PRETEND . . . THAT SHE'S JUNE. SHE'S JUNE.

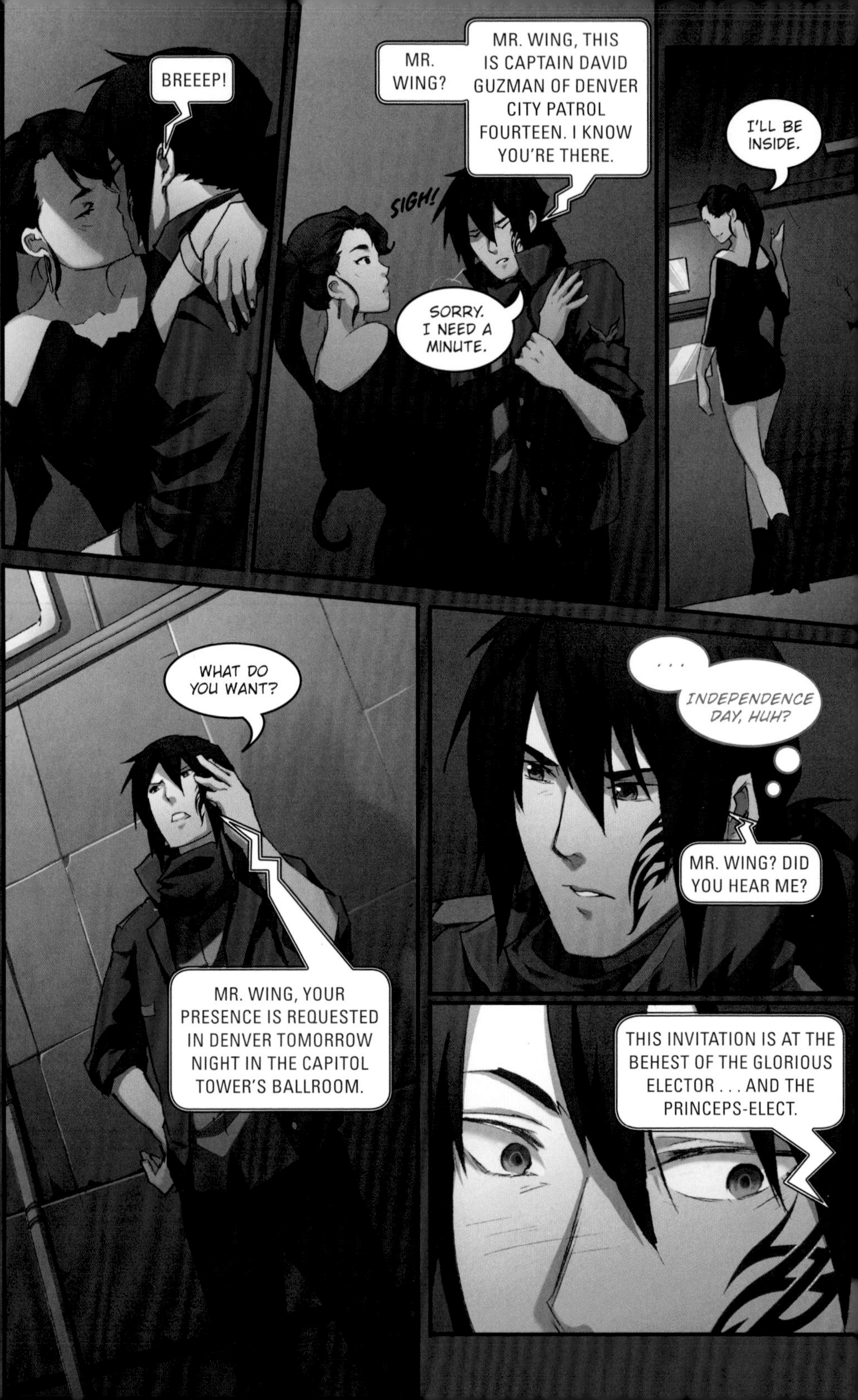
BREEEP!
MR. WING?
MR. WING, THIS IS CAPTAIN DAVID GUZMAN OF DENVER CITY PATROL FOURTEEN. I KNOW YOU'RE THERE.
SIGH!
SORRY. I NEED A MINUTE.
I'LL BE INSIDE.
WHAT DO YOU WANT?
MR. WING, YOUR PRESENCE IS REQUESTED IN DENVER TOMORROW NIGHT IN THE CAPITOL TOWER'S BALLROOM.
. . .
INDEPENDENCE DAY, HUH?
MR. WING? DID YOU HEAR ME?
THIS INVITATION IS AT THE BEHEST OF THE GLORIOUS ELECTOR . . . AND THE PRINCEPS-ELECT.

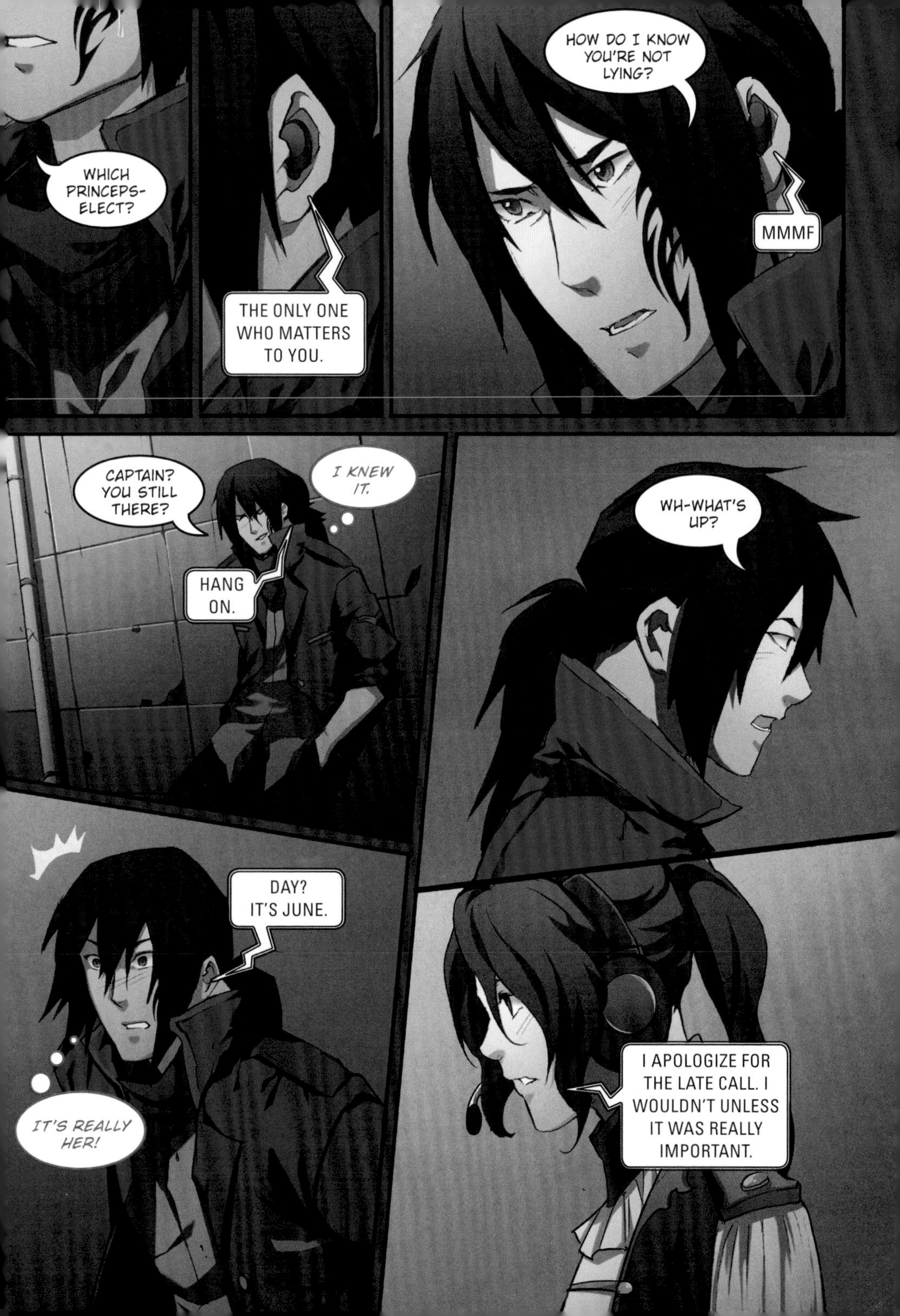
WHICH PRINCEPS-ELECT?
THE ONLY ONE WHO MATTERS TO YOU.
HOW DO I KNOW YOU'RE NOT LYING?
MMMF
CAPTAIN? YOU STILL THERE?
I KNEW IT.
HANG ON.
WH-WHAT'S UP?
DAY? IT'S JUNE.
IT'S REALLY HER!
I APOLOGIZE FOR THE LATE CALL. I WOULDN'T UNLESS IT WAS REALLY IMPORTANT.

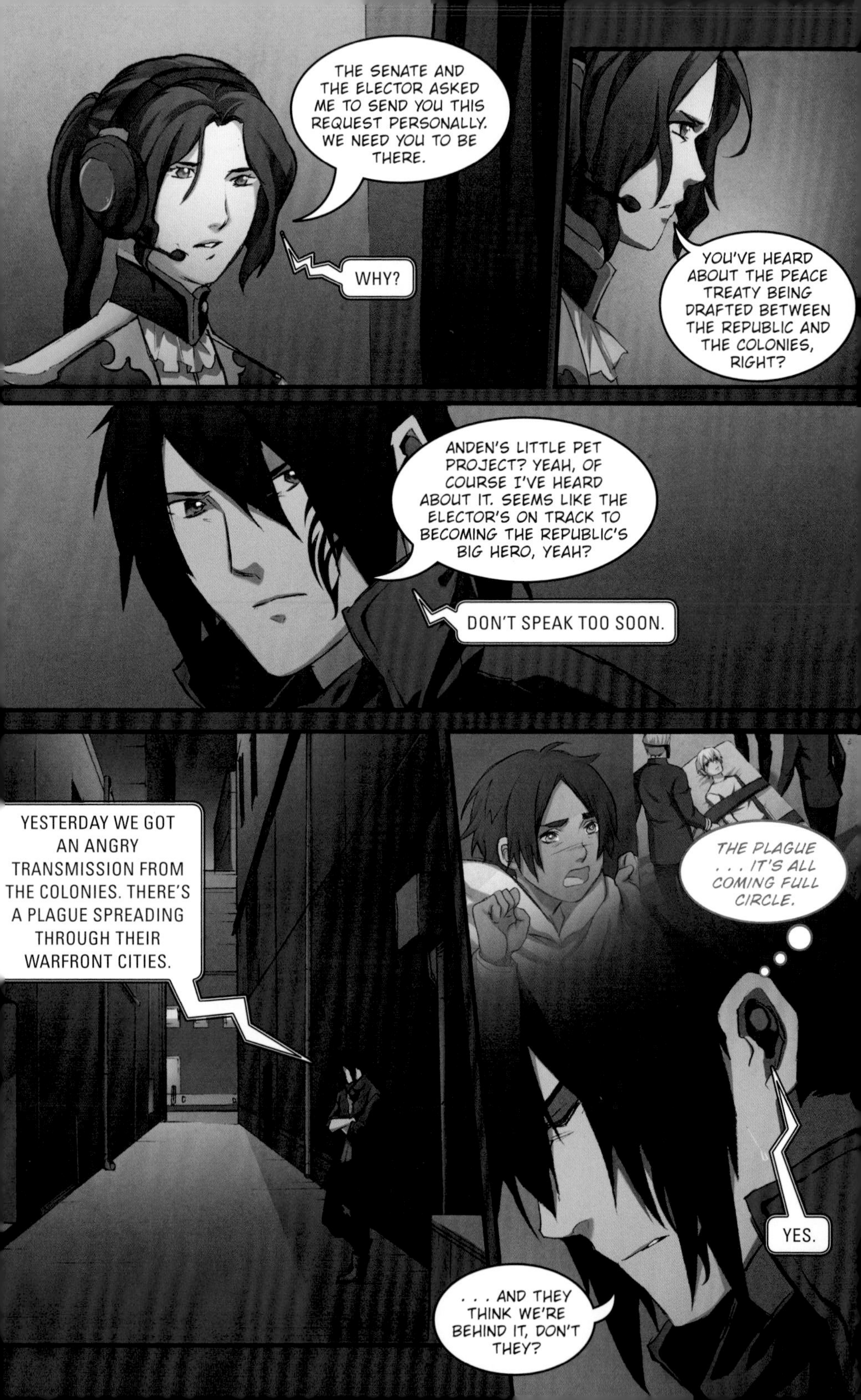
THE SENATE AND THE ELECTOR ASKED ME TO SEND YOU THIS REQUEST PERSONALLY. WE NEED YOU TO BE THERE.
WHY?
YOU'VE HEARD ABOUT THE PEACE TREATY BEING DRAFTED BETWEEN THE REPUBLIC AND THE COLONIES, RIGHT?
ANDEN'S LITTLE PET PROJECT? YEAH, OF COURSE I'VE HEARD ABOUT IT. SEEMS LIKE THE ELECTOR'S ON TRACK TO BECOMING THE REPUBLIC'S BIG HERO, YEAH?
DON'T SPEAK TOO SOON.
YESTERDAY WE GOT AN ANGRY TRANSMISSION FROM THE COLONIES. THERE'S A PLAGUE SPREADING THROUGH THEIR WARFRONT CITIES.
THE PLAGUE . . . IT'S ALL COMING FULL CIRCLE.
. . . AND THEY THINK WE'RE BEHIND IT, DON'T THEY?
YES.

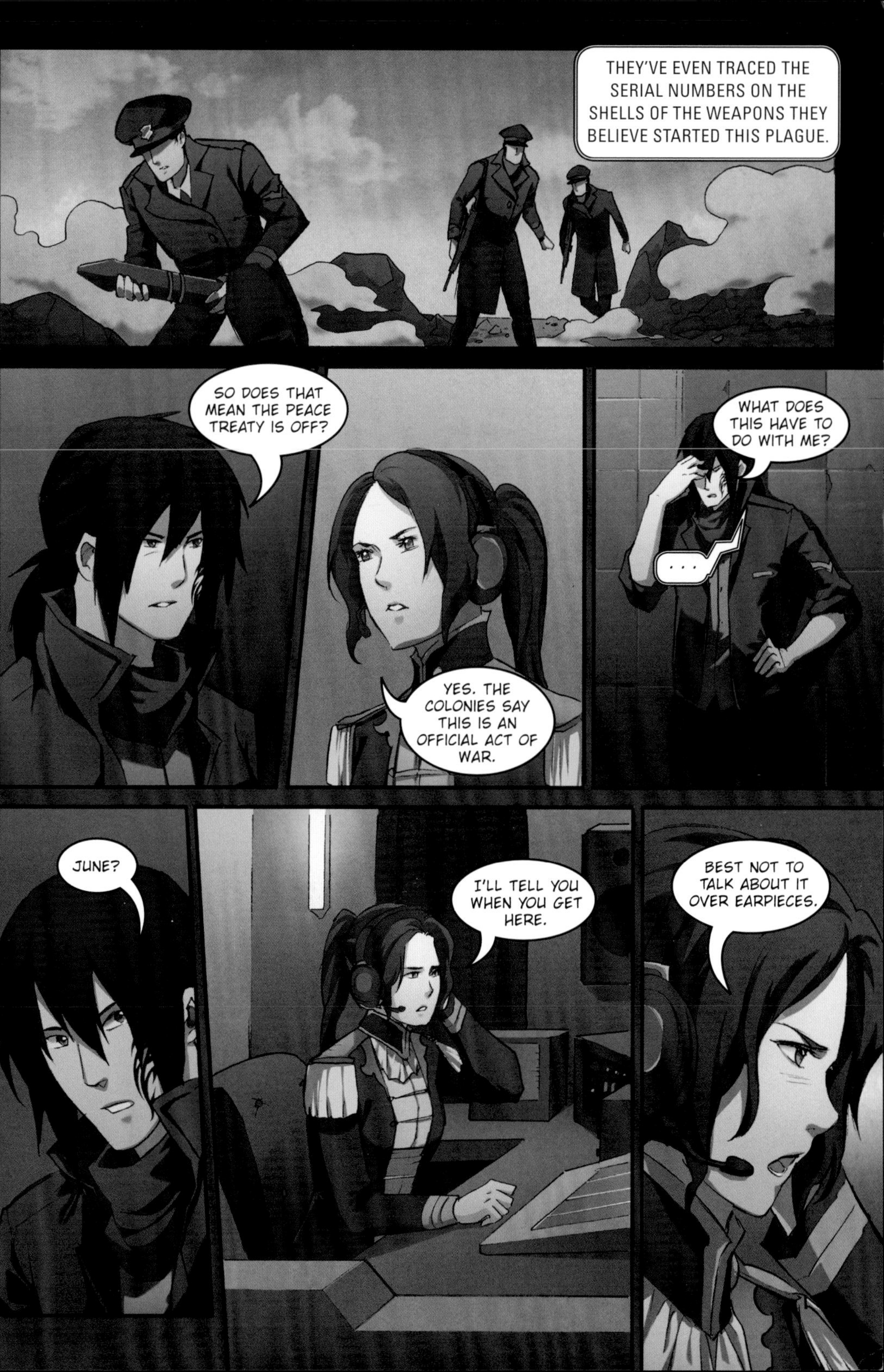
THEY'VE EVEN TRACED THE SERIAL NUMBERS ON THE SHELLS OF THE WEAPONS THEY BELIEVE STARTED THIS PLAGUE.
SO DOES THAT MEAN THE PEACE TREATY IS OFF?
YES. THE COLONIES SAY THIS IS AN OFFICIAL ACT OF WAR.
WHAT DOES THIS HAVE TO DO WITH ME?
. . .
JUNE?
I'LL TELL YOU WHEN YOU GET HERE.
BEST NOT TO TALK ABOUT IT OVER EARPIECES.

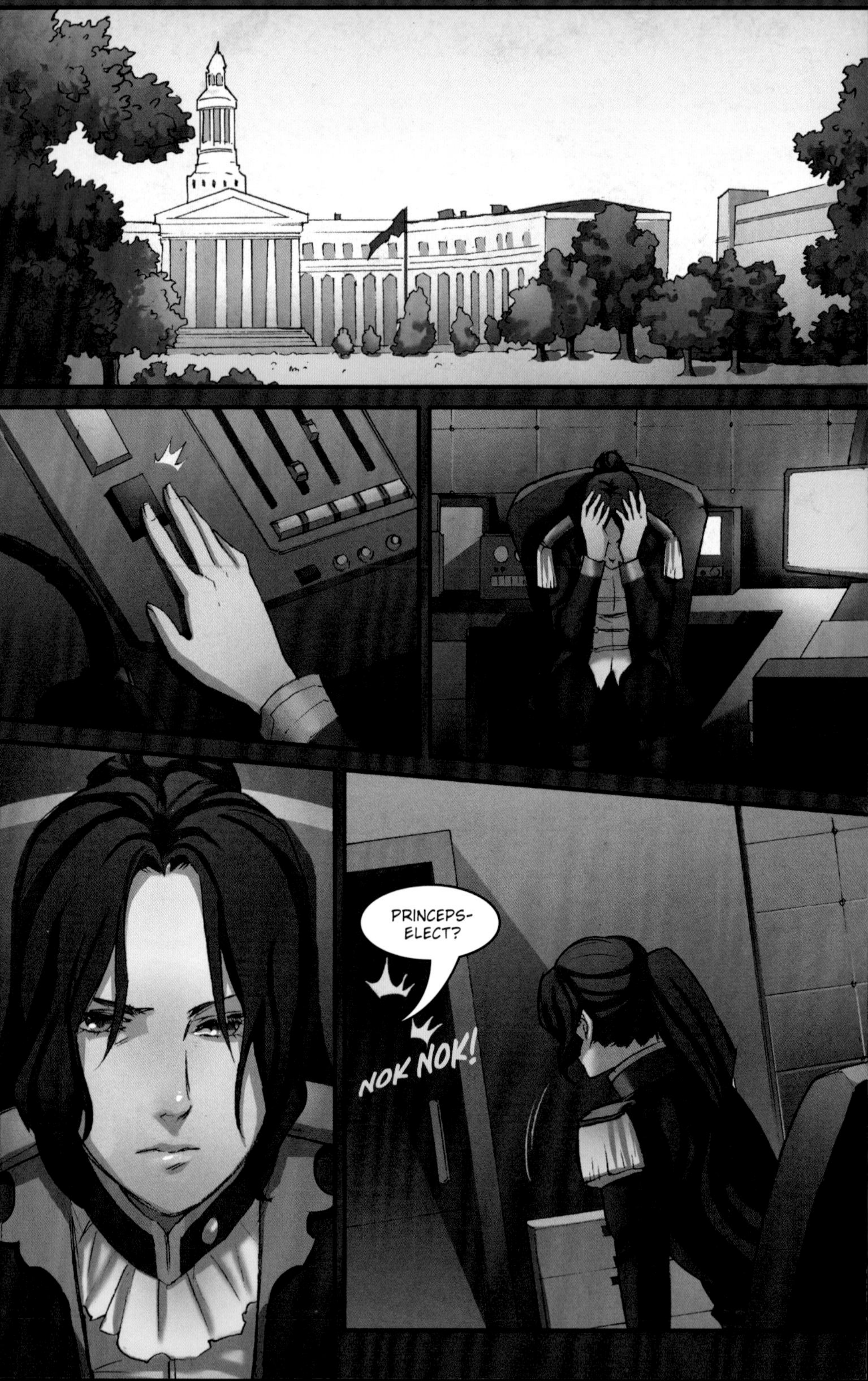
PRINCEPS-ELECT?
NOK NOK!

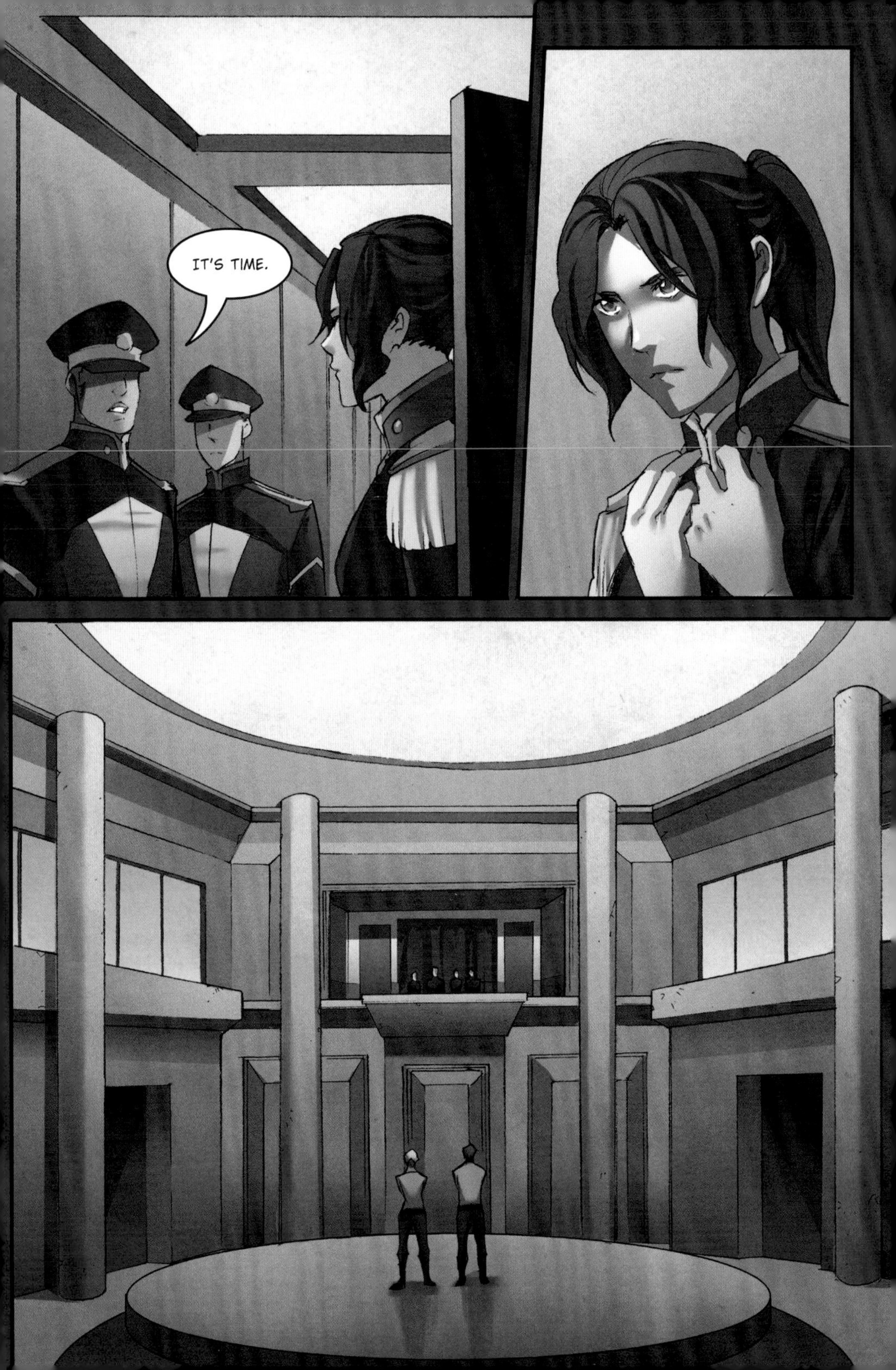
IT'S TIME.

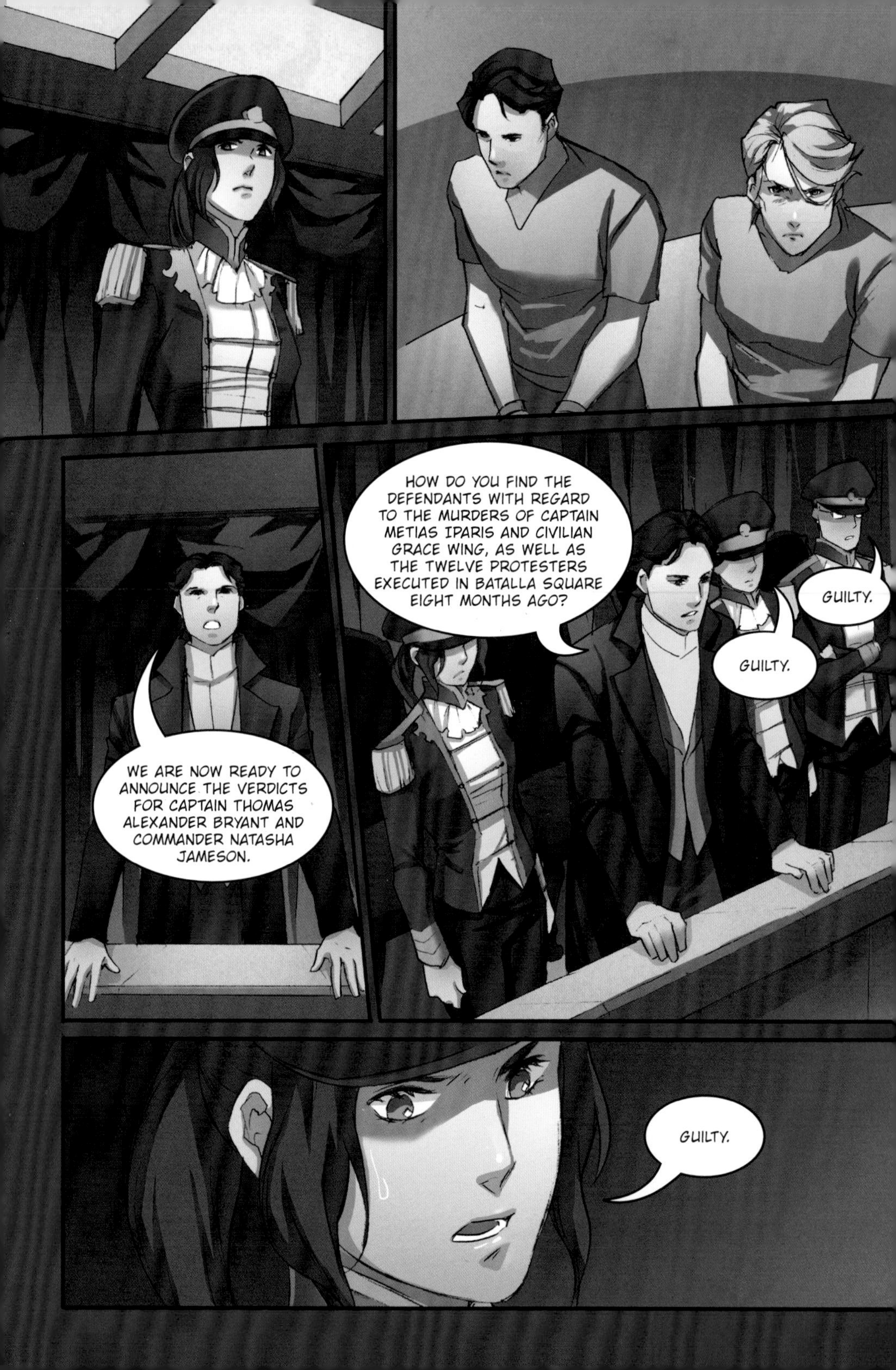
WE ARE NOW READY TO ANNOUNCE THE VERDICTS FOR CAPTAIN THOMAS ALEXANDER BRYANT AND COMMANDER NATASHA JAMESON.
HOW DO YOU FIND THE DEFENDANTS WITH REGARD TO THE MURDERS OF CAPTAIN METIAS IPARIS AND CIVILIAN GRACE WING, AS WELL AS THE TWELVE PROTESTERS EXECUTED IN BATALLA SQUARE EIGHT MONTHS AGO?
GUILTY.
GUILTY.
GUILTY.

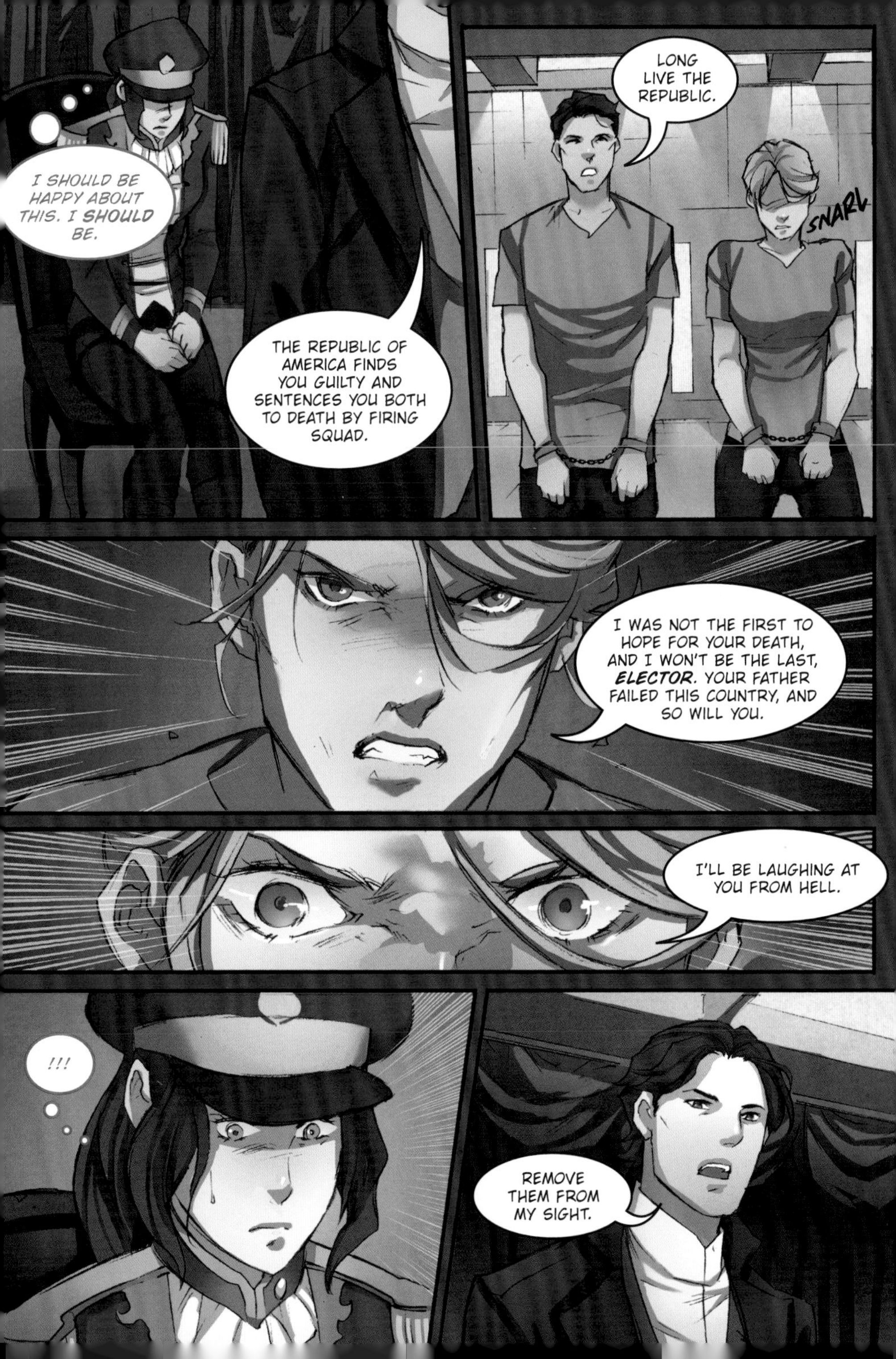
I SHOULD BE HAPPY ABOUT THIS. I SHOULD BE.
THE REPUBLIC OF AMERICA FINDS YOU GUILTY AND SENTENCES YOU BOTH TO DEATH BY FIRING SQUAD.
LONG LIVE THE REPUBLIC.
SNARL
I WAS NOT THE FIRST TO HOPE FOR YOUR DEATH, AND I WON'T BE THE LAST, ELECTOR. YOUR FATHER FAILED THIS COUNTRY, AND SO WILL YOU.
I'LL BE LAUGHING AT YOU FROM HELL.
!!!
REMOVE THEM FROM MY SIGHT.

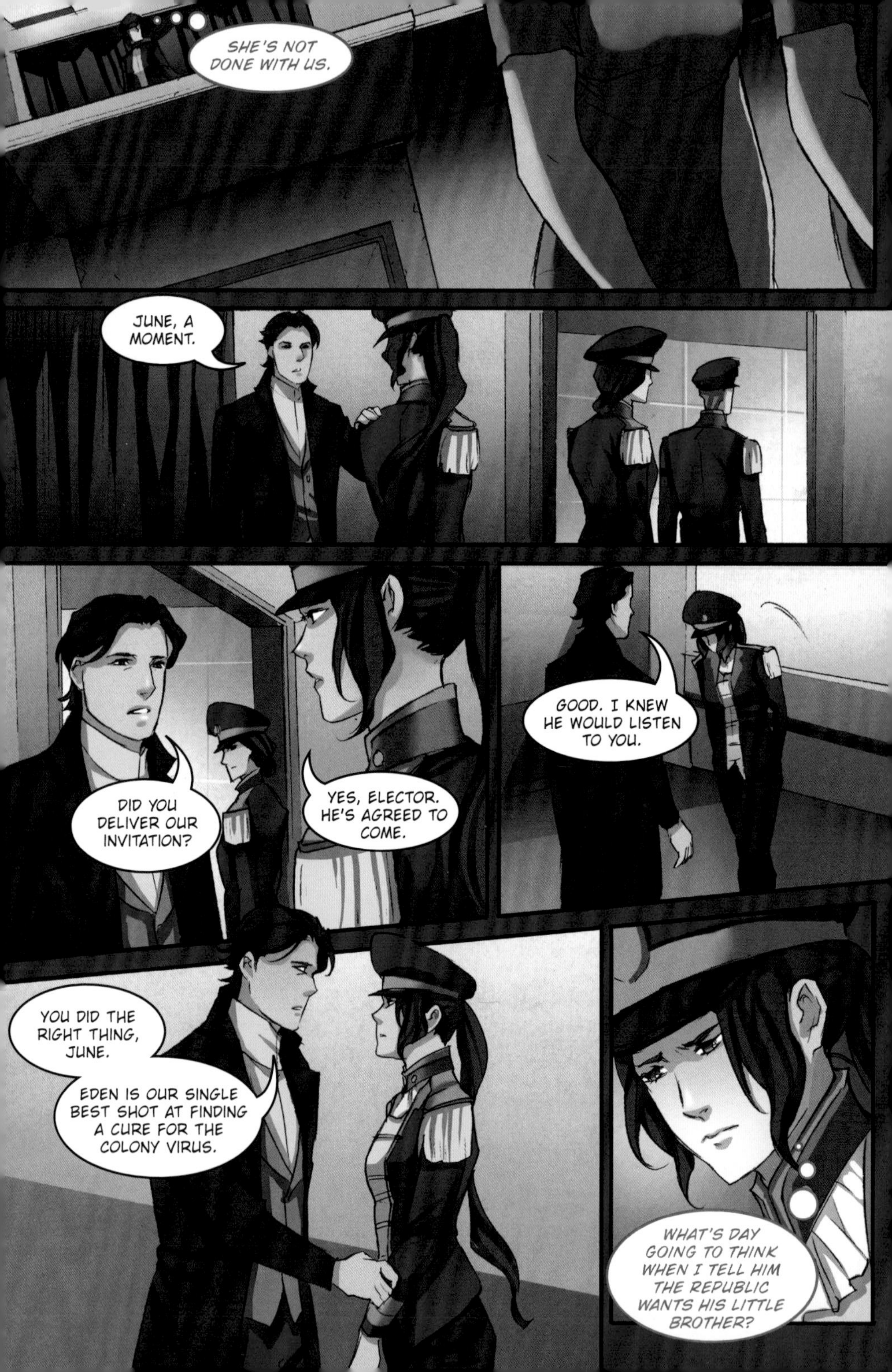
SHE'S NOT DONE WITH US.
JUNE, A MOMENT.
DID YOU DELIVER OUR INVITATION?
YES, ELECTOR. HE'S AGREED TO COME.
GOOD. I KNEW HE WOULD LISTEN TO YOU.
YOU DID THE RIGHT THING, JUNE.
EDEN IS OUR SINGLE BEST SHOT AT FINDING A CURE FOR THE COLONY VIRUS.
WHAT'S DAY GOING TO THINK WHEN I TELL HIM THE REPUBLIC WANTS HIS LITTLE BROTHER?

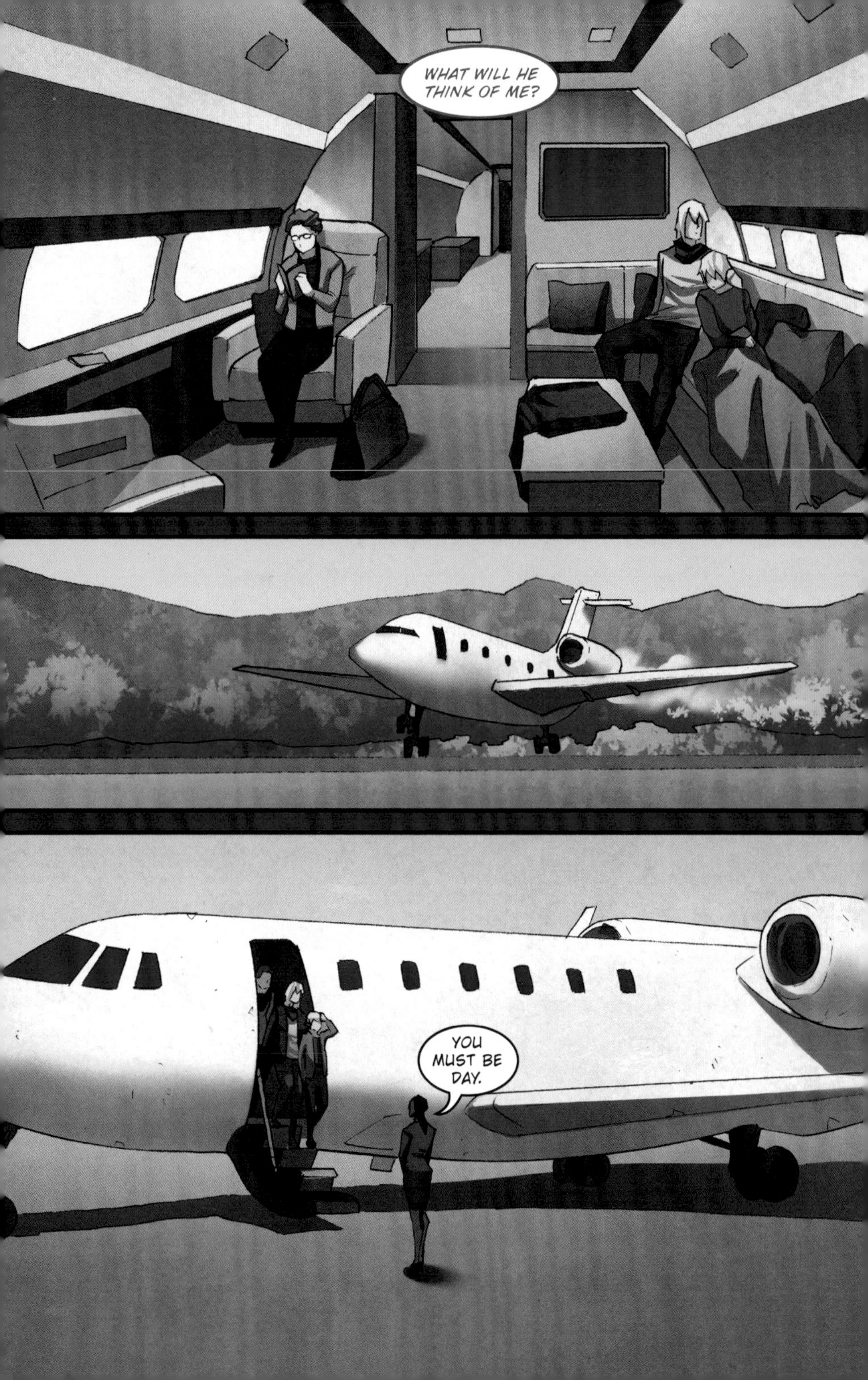
WHAT WILL HE THINK OF ME?
YOU MUST BE DAY.

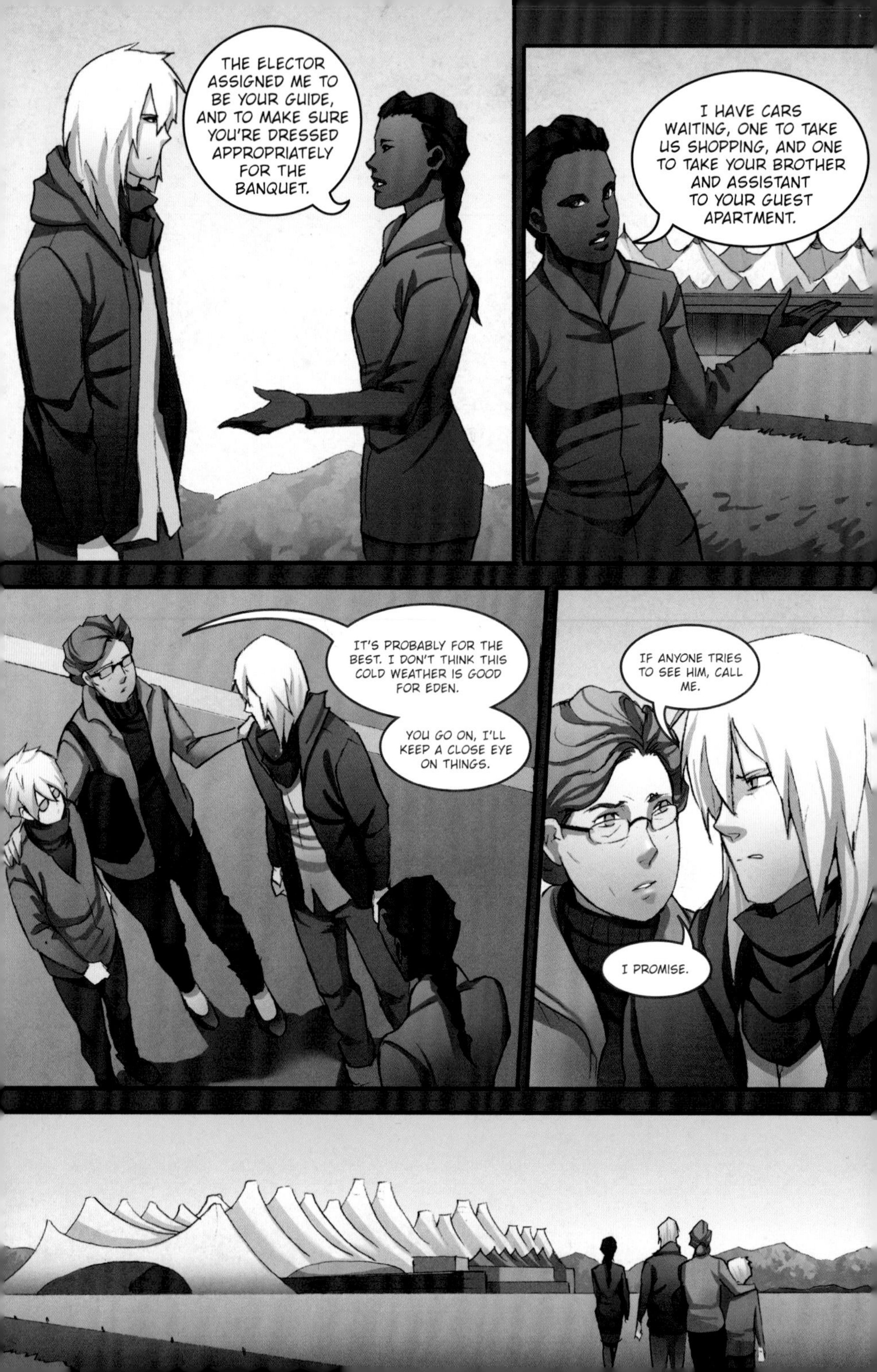
THE ELECTOR ASSIGNED ME TO BE YOUR GUIDE, AND TO MAKE SURE YOU'RE DRESSED APPROPRIATELY FOR THE BANQUET.
I HAVE CARS WAITING, ONE TO TAKE US SHOPPING, AND ONE TO TAKE YOUR BROTHER AND ASSISTANT TO YOUR GUEST APARTMENT.
IT'S PROBABLY FOR THE BEST. I DON'T THINK THIS COLD WEATHER IS GOOD FOR EDEN.
YOU GO ON, I'LL KEEP A CLOSE EYE ON THINGS.
IF ANYONE TRIES TO SEE HIM, CALL ME.
I PROMISE.

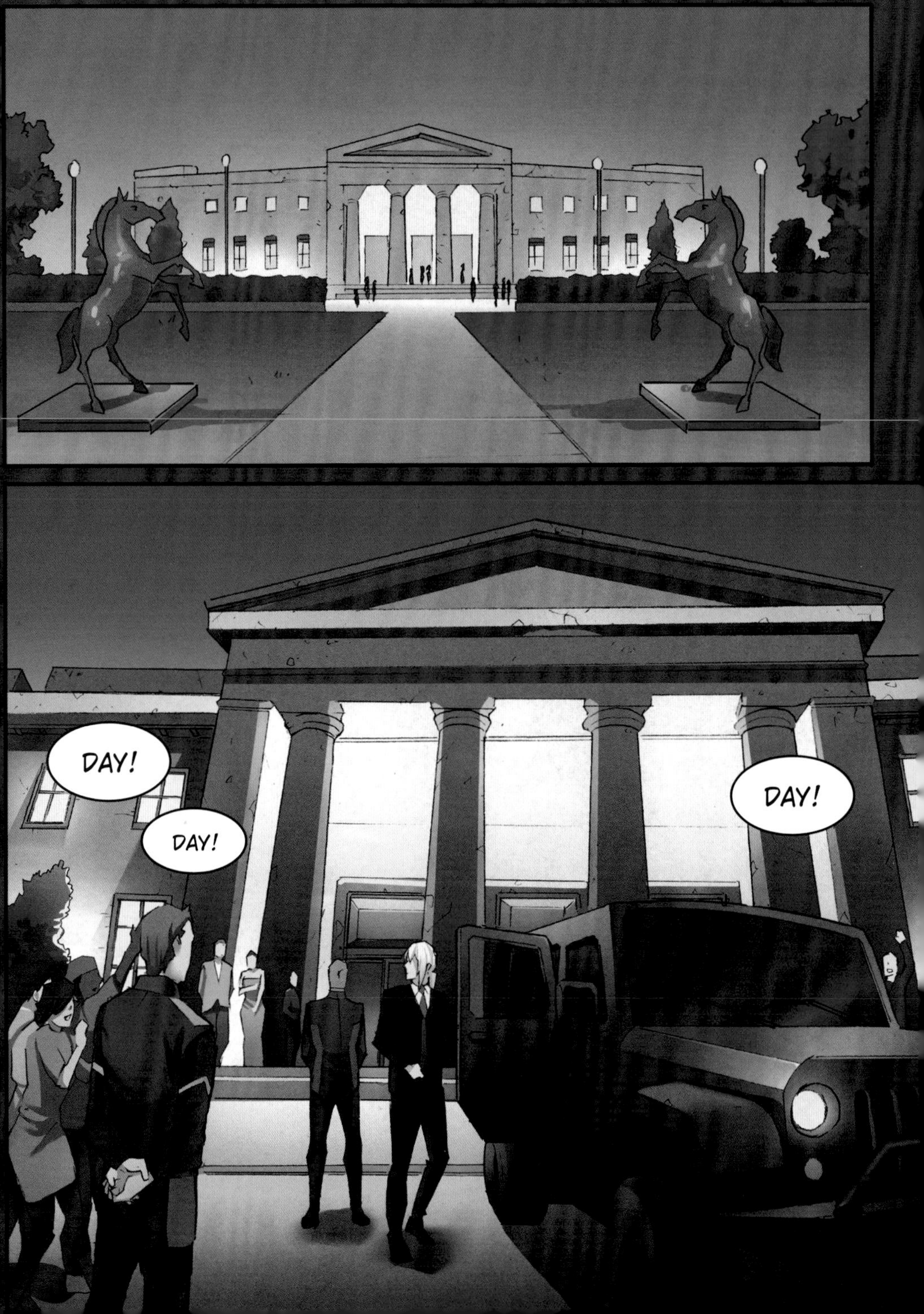
DAY!
DAY!
DAY!

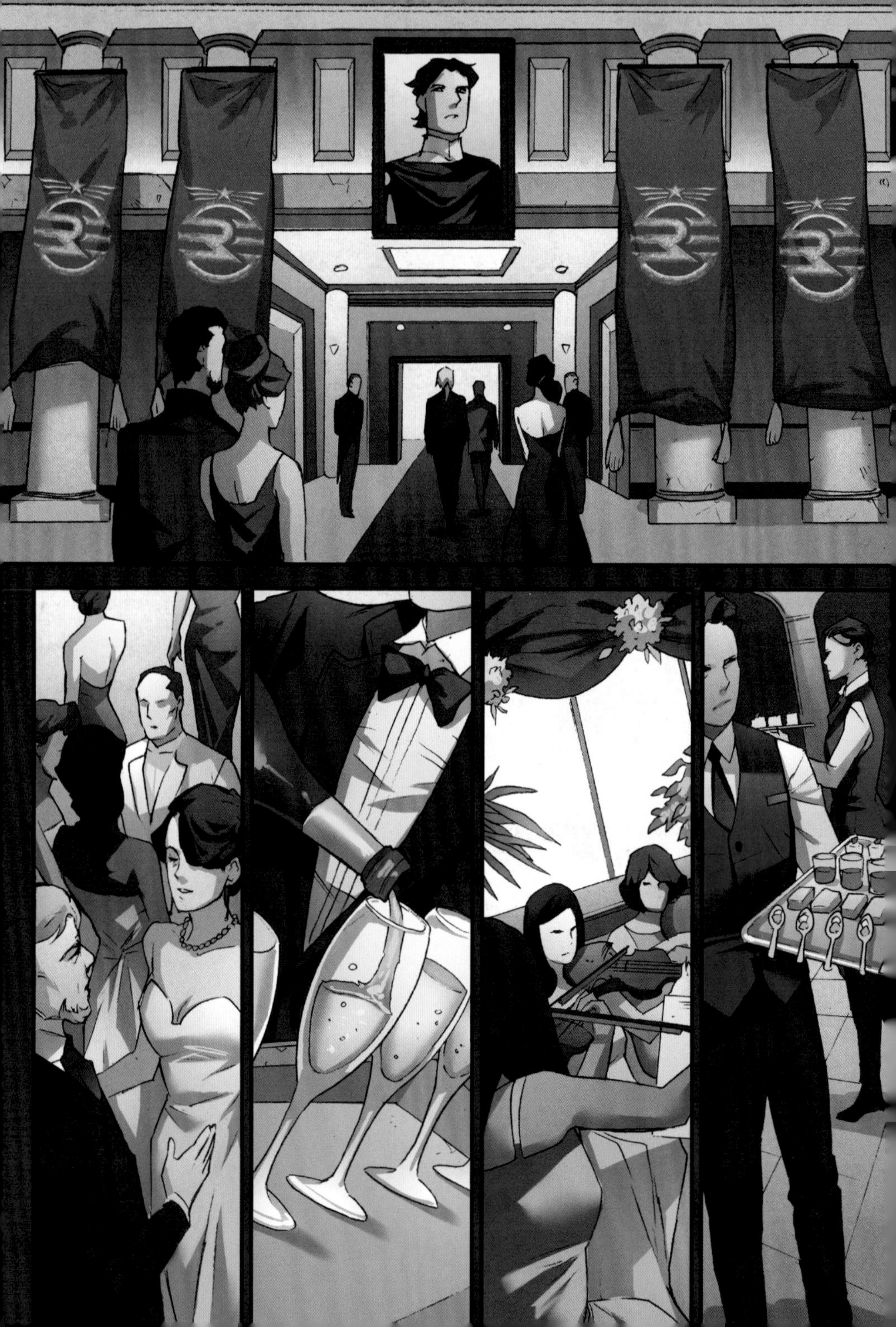

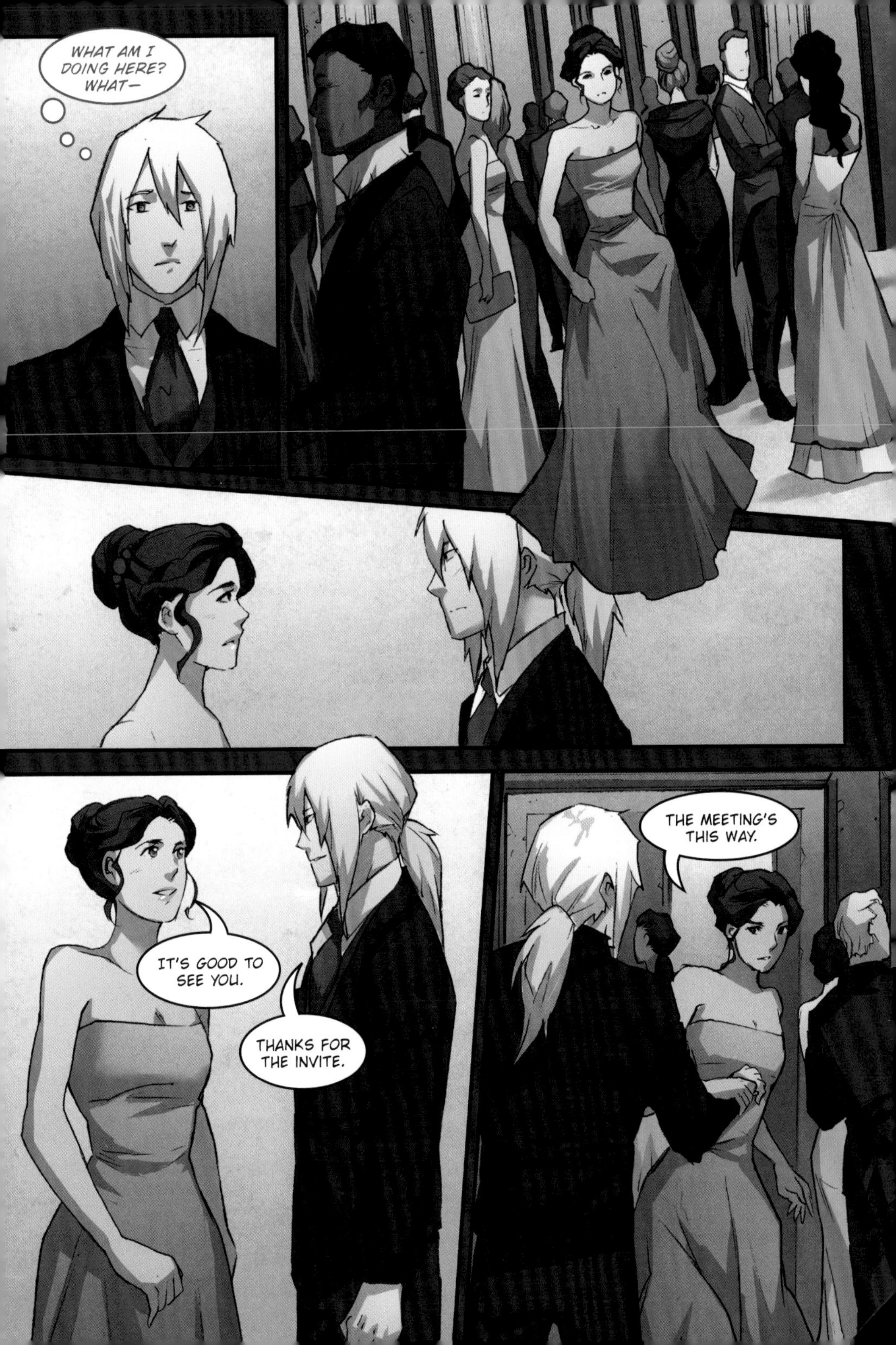
WHAT AM I DOING HERE? WHAT—
IT'S GOOD TO SEE YOU.
THANKS FOR THE INVITE.
THE MEETING'S THIS WAY.

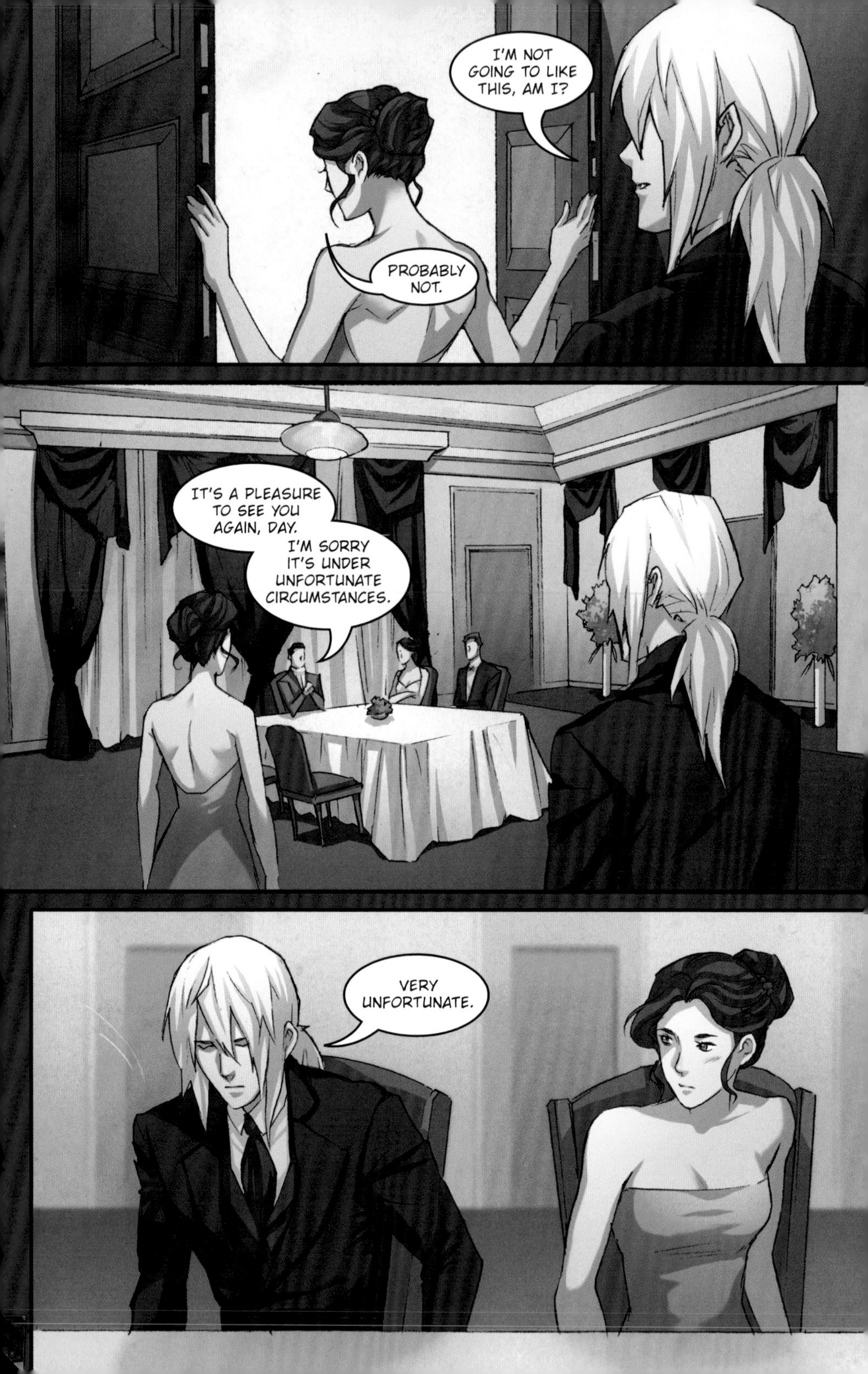
I'M NOT GOING TO LIKE THIS, AM I?
PROBABLY NOT.
IT'S A PLEASURE TO SEE YOU AGAIN, DAY.
I'M SORRY IT'S UNDER UNFORTUNATE CIRCUMSTANCES.
VERY UNFORTUNATE.

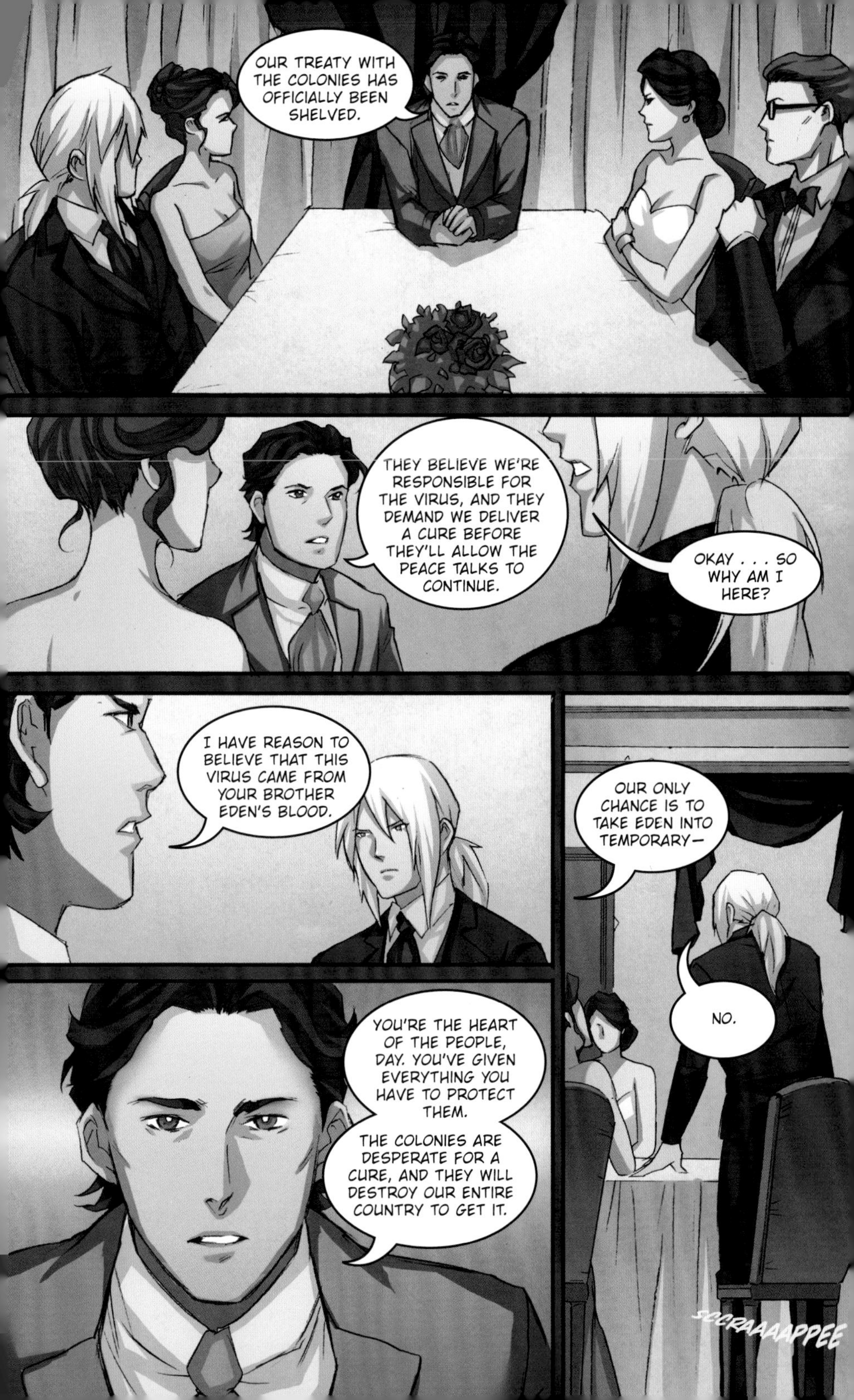
OUR TREATY WITH THE COLONIES HAS OFFICIALLY BEEN SHELVED.
THEY BELIEVE WE'RE RESPONSIBLE FOR THE VIRUS, AND THEY DEMAND WE DELIVER A CURE BEFORE THEY'LL ALLOW THE PEACE TALKS TO CONTINUE.
OKAY . . . SO WHY AM I HERE?
I HAVE REASON TO BELIEVE THAT THIS VIRUS CAME FROM YOUR BROTHER EDEN'S BLOOD.
YOU'RE THE HEART OF THE PEOPLE, DAY. YOU'VE GIVEN EVERYTHING YOU HAVE TO PROTECT THEM.
THE COLONIES ARE DESPERATE FOR A CURE, AND THEY WILL DESTROY OUR ENTIRE COUNTRY TO GET IT.
OUR ONLY CHANCE IS TO TAKE EDEN INTO TEMPORARY—
NO.
SCCRAAAAPPEE

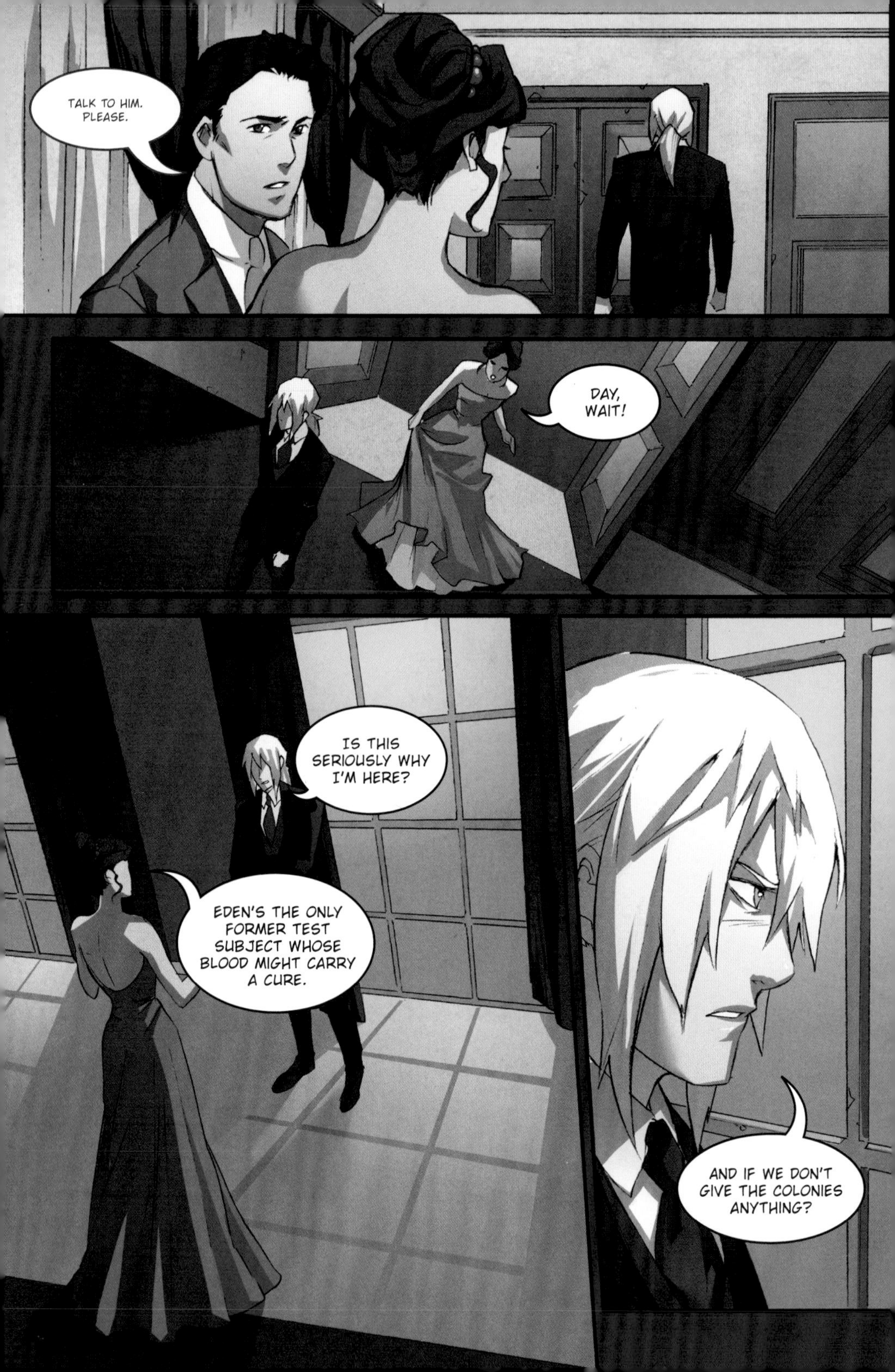
TALK TO HIM. PLEASE.
DAY, WAIT!
IS THIS SERIOUSLY WHY I'M HERE?
EDEN'S THE ONLY FORMER TEST SUBJECT WHOSE BLOOD MIGHT CARRY A CURE.
AND IF WE DON'T GIVE THE COLONIES ANYTHING?

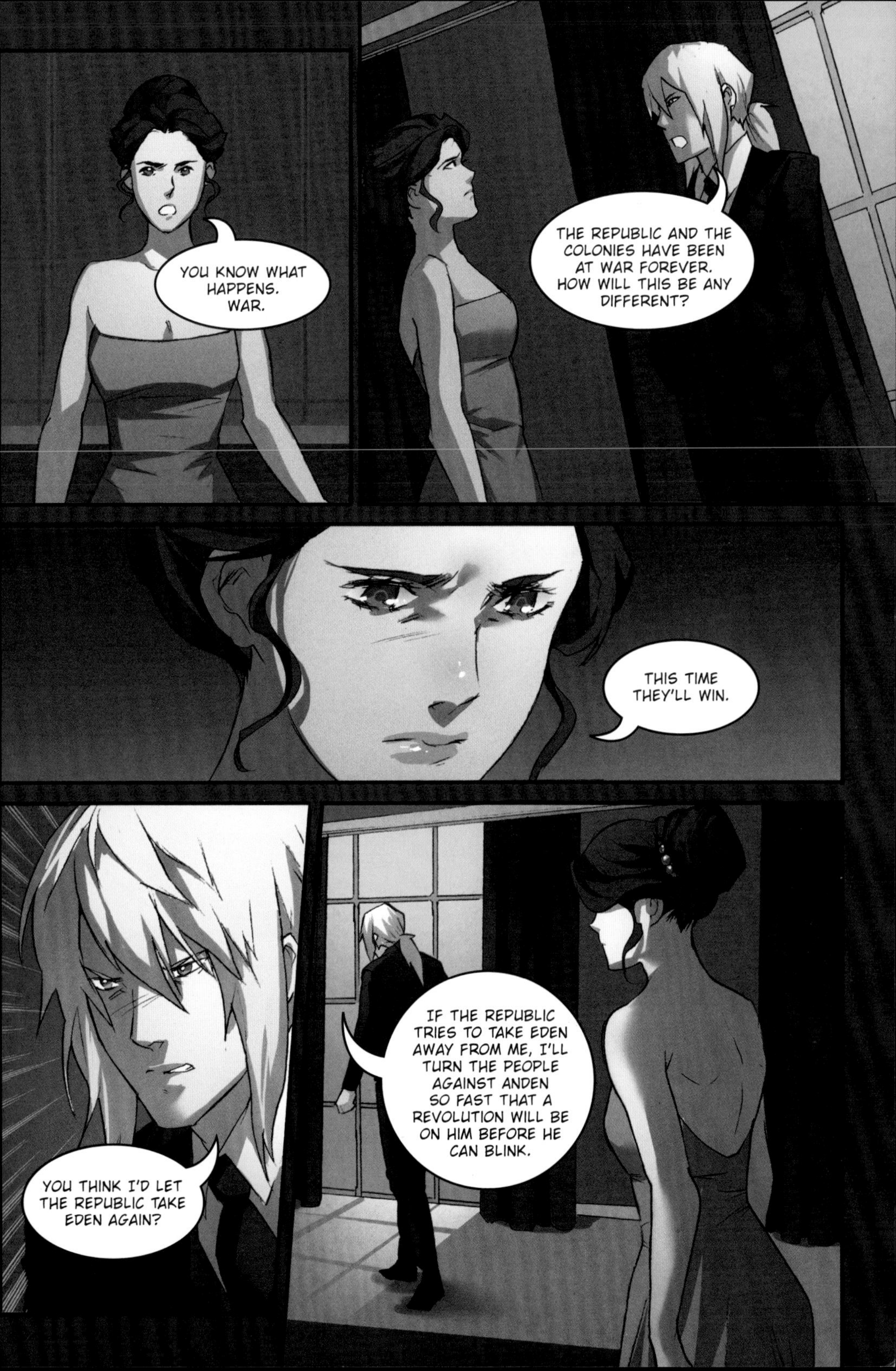
YOU KNOW WHAT HAPPENS. WAR.
THE REPUBLIC AND THE COLONIES HAVE BEEN AT WAR FOREVER. HOW WILL THIS BE ANY DIFFERENT?
THIS TIME THEY'LL WIN.
YOU THINK I'D LET THE REPUBLIC TAKE EDEN AGAIN?
IF THE REPUBLIC TRIES TO TAKE EDEN AWAY FROM ME, I'LL TURN THE PEOPLE AGAINST ANDEN SO FAST THAT A REVOLUTION WILL BE ON HIM BEFORE HE CAN BLINK.

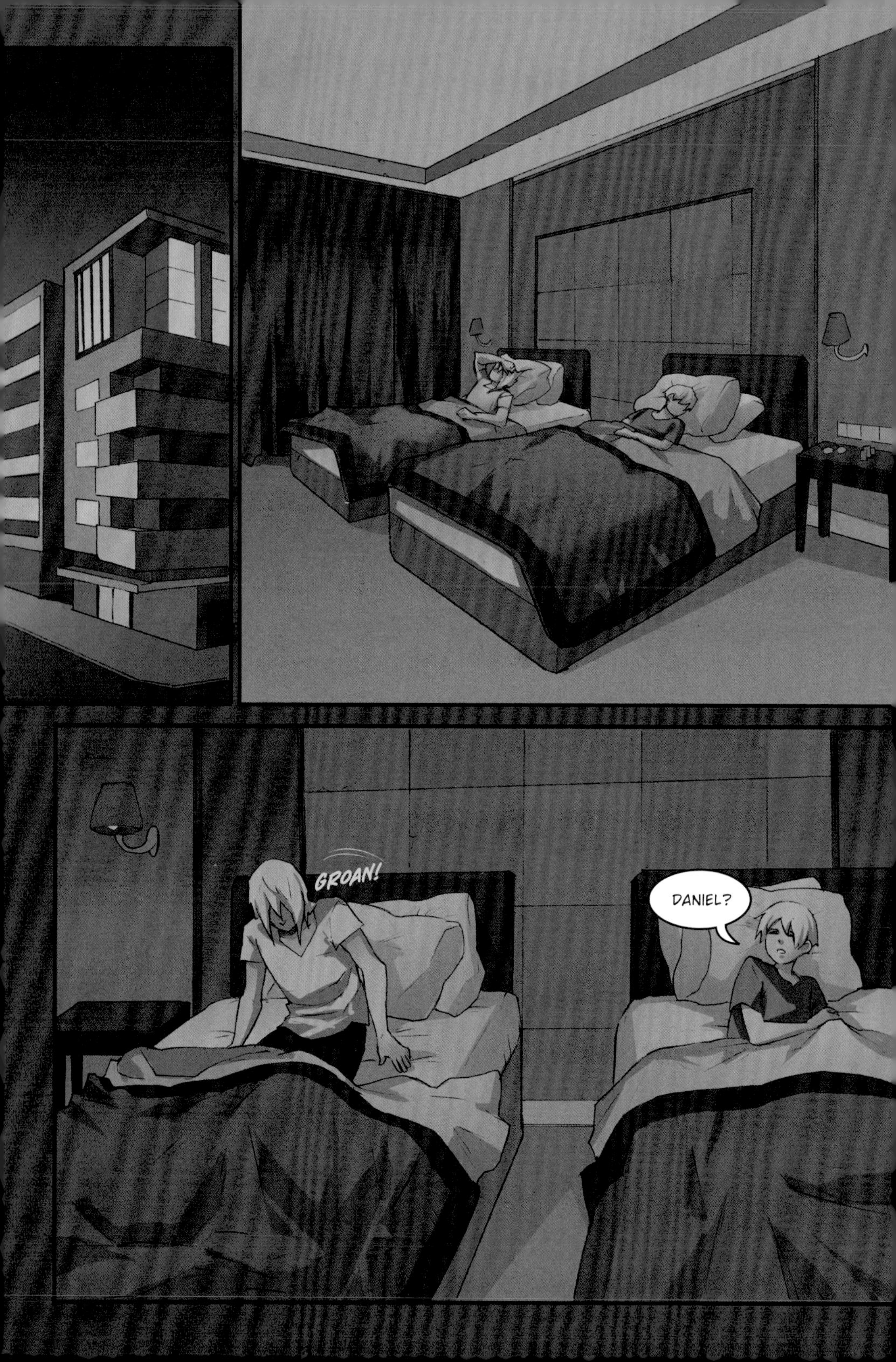
GROAN!
DANIEL?

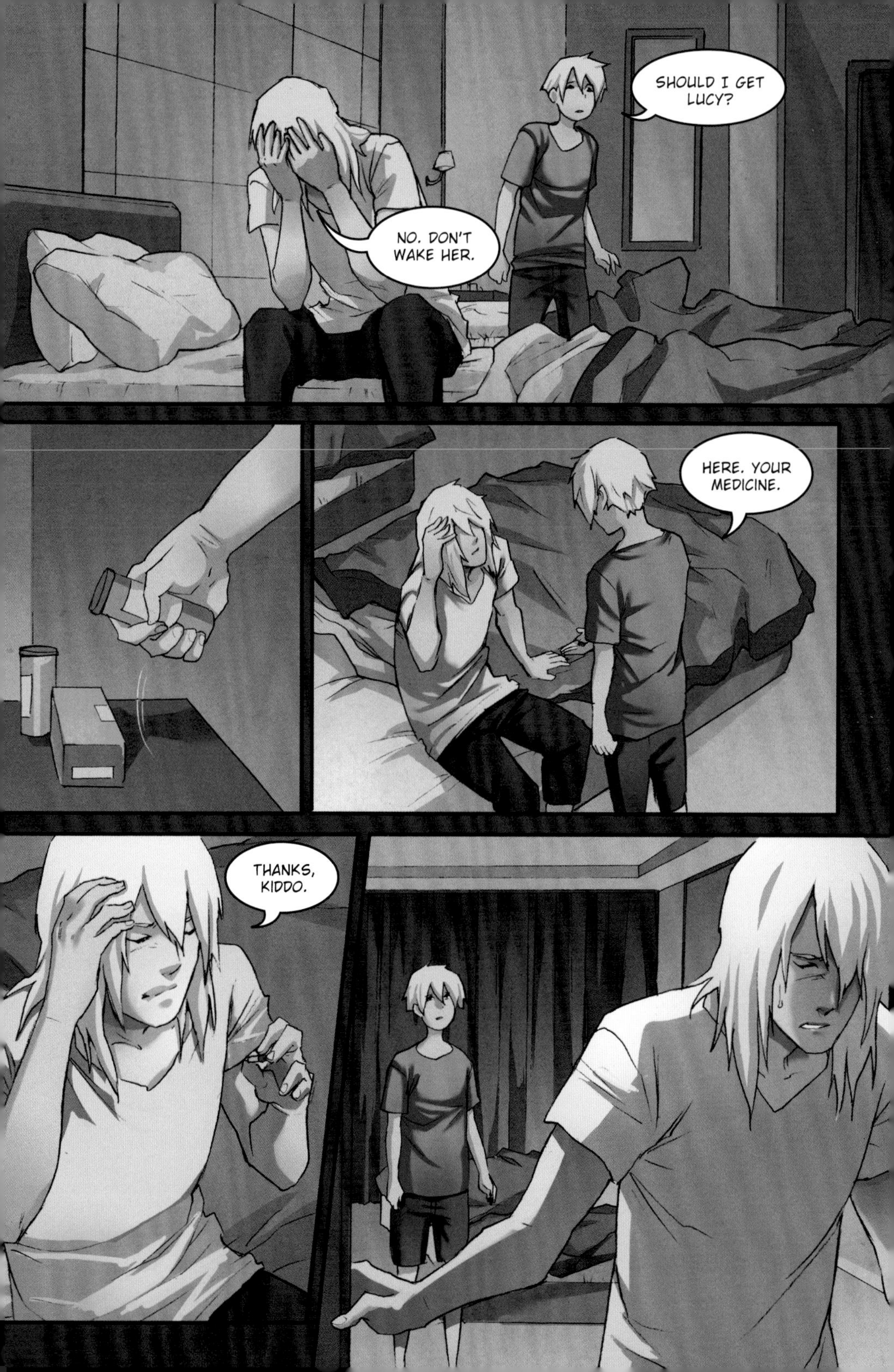
SHOULD I GET LUCY?
NO. DON'T WAKE HER.
HERE. YOUR MEDICINE.
THANKS, KIDDO.

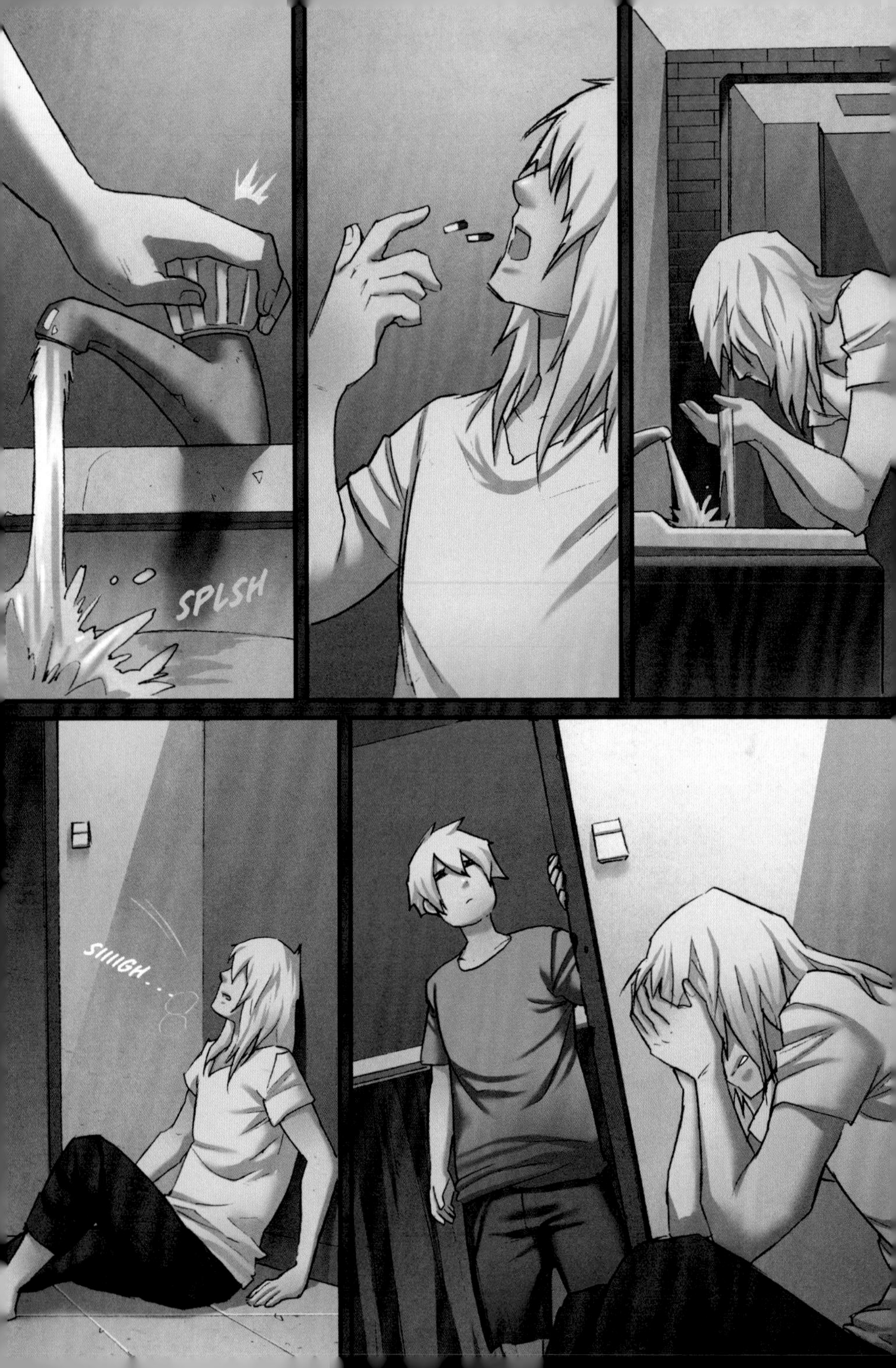
SPLSH
SIIIIGH...

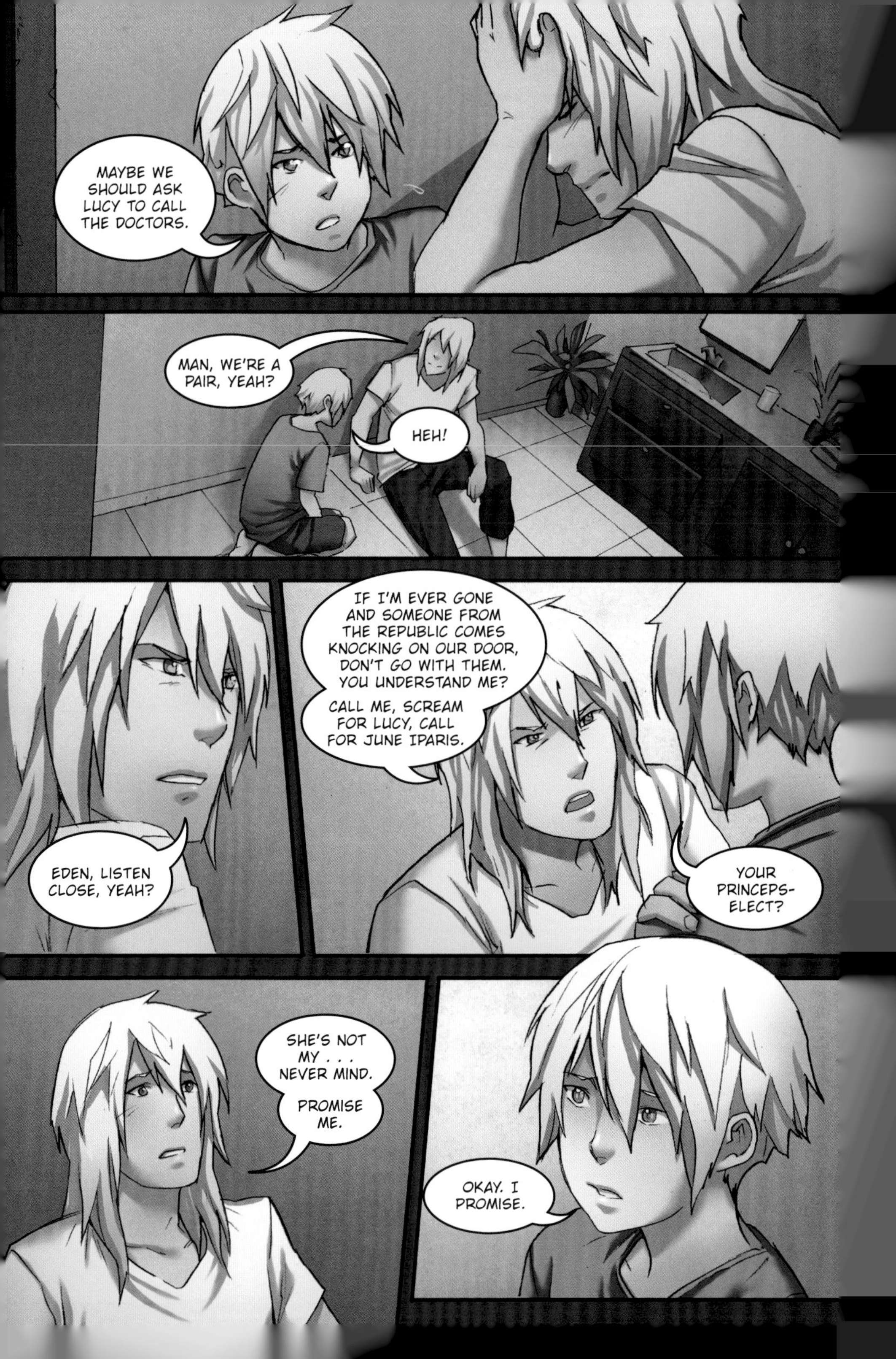
MAYBE WE SHOULD ASK LUCY TO CALL THE DOCTORS.
MAN, WE'RE A PAIR, YEAH?
HEH!
EDEN, LISTEN CLOSE, YEAH?
IF I'M EVER GONE AND SOMEONE FROM THE REPUBLIC COMES KNOCKING ON OUR DOOR, DON'T GO WITH THEM. YOU UNDERSTAND ME?
CALL ME, SCREAM FOR LUCY, CALL FOR JUNE IPARIS.
YOUR PRINCEPS-ELECT?
SHE'S NOT MY . . . NEVER MIND.
PROMISE ME.
OKAY. I PROMISE.

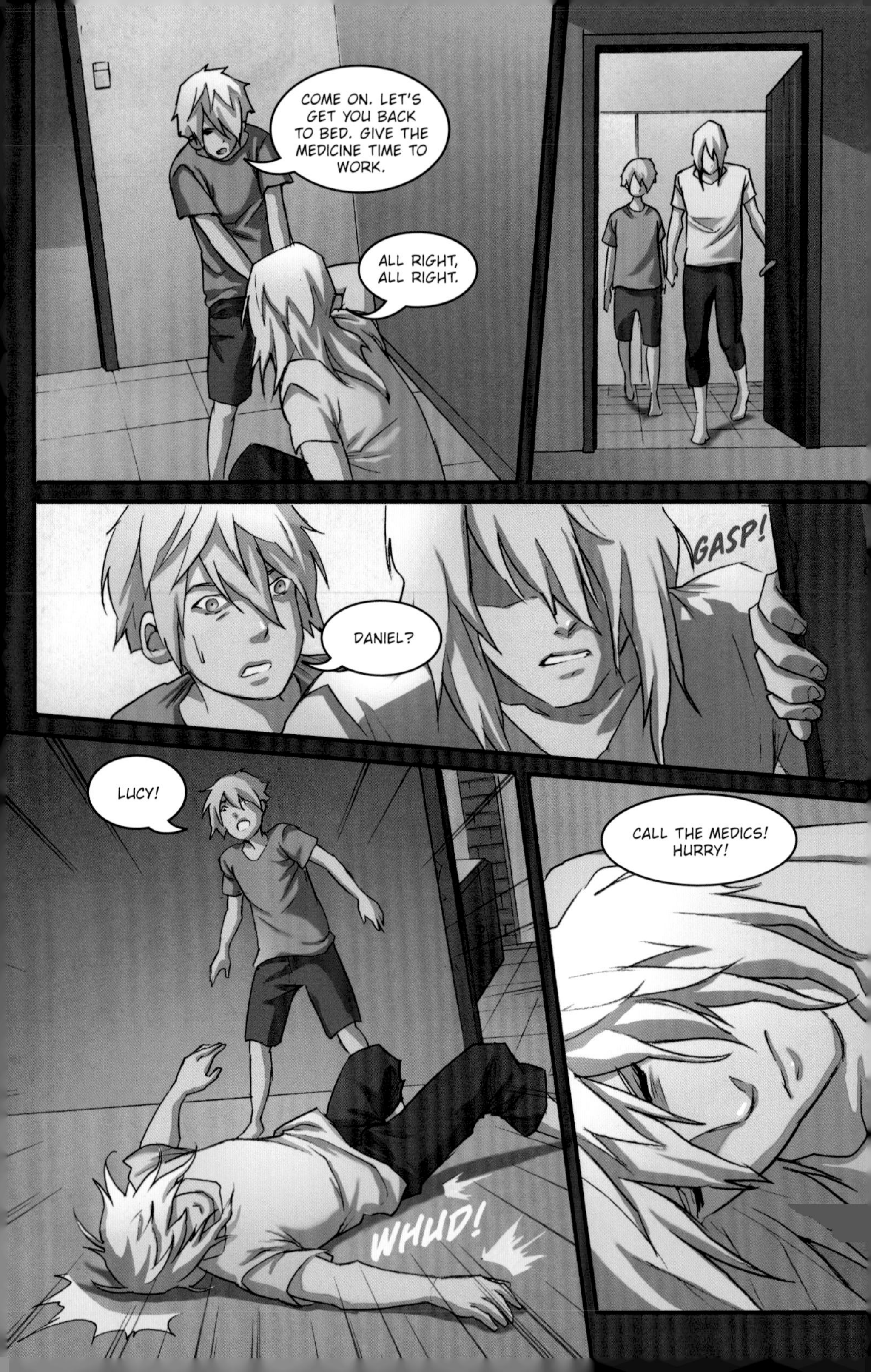
COME ON. LET'S GET YOU BACK TO BED. GIVE THE MEDICINE TIME TO WORK.
ALL RIGHT, ALL RIGHT.
GASP!
DANIEL?
LUCY!
WHUD!
CALL THE MEDICS! HURRY!

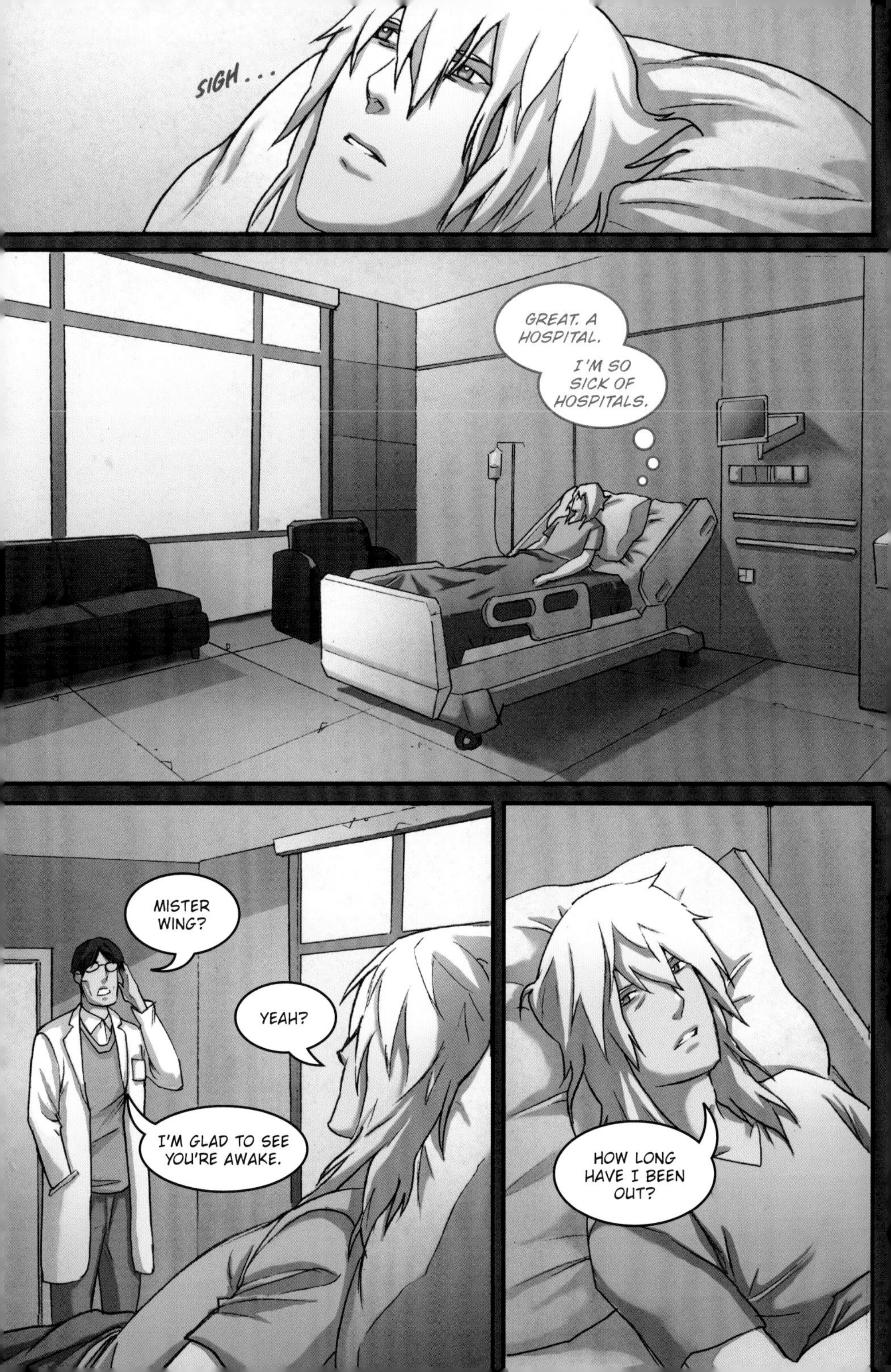
SIGH . . .
GREAT. A HOSPITAL.
I'M SO SICK OF HOSPITALS.
MISTER WING?
YEAH?
I'M GLAD TO SEE YOU'RE AWAKE.
HOW LONG HAVE I BEEN OUT?

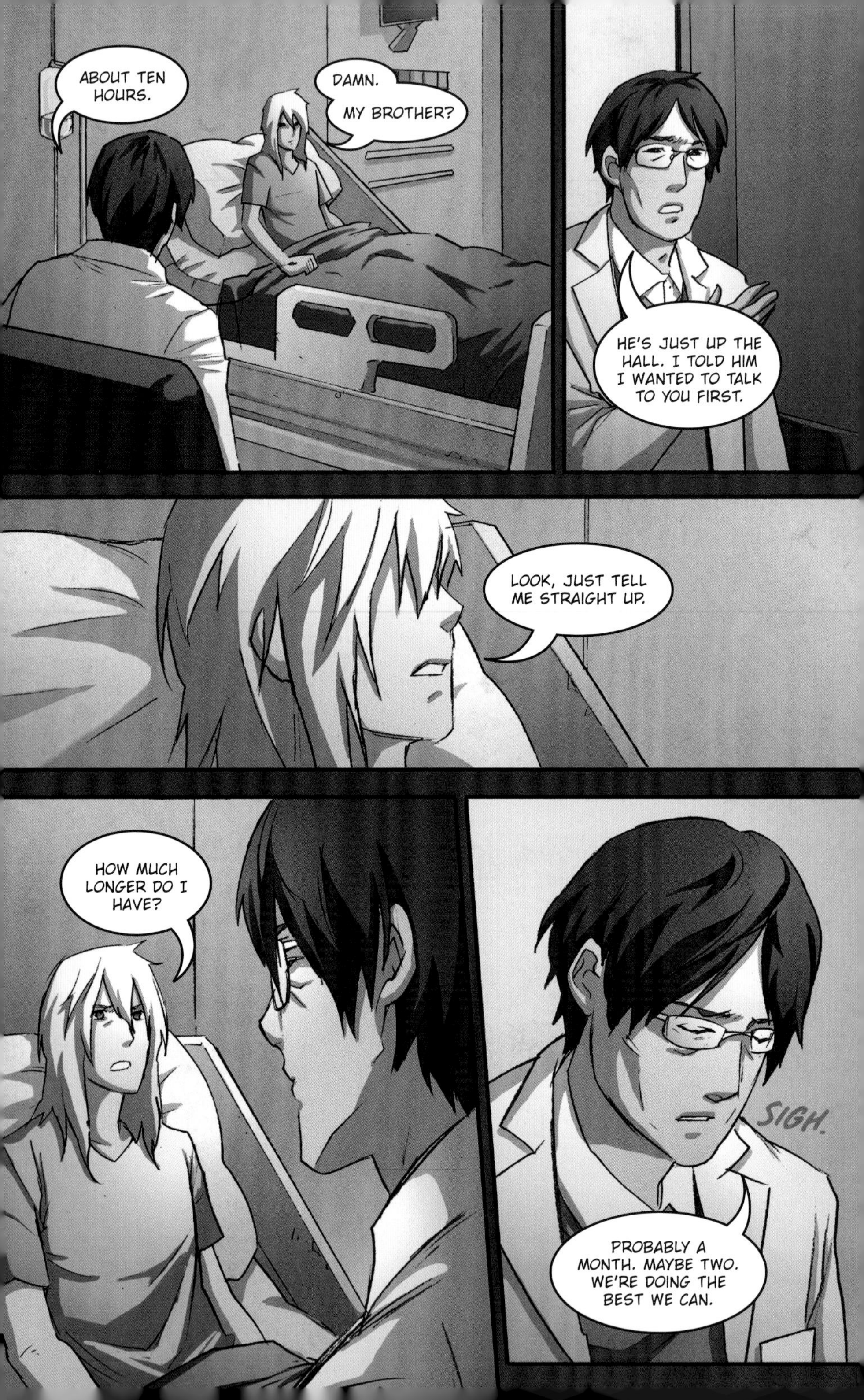

ABOUT TEN HOURS.
DAMN.
MY BROTHER?
HE'S JUST UP THE HALL. I TOLD HIM I WANTED TO TALK TO YOU FIRST.
LOOK, JUST TELL ME STRAIGHT UP.
HOW MUCH LONGER DO I HAVE?
SIGH.
PROBABLY A MONTH. MAYBE TWO. WE'RE DOING THE BEST WE CAN.

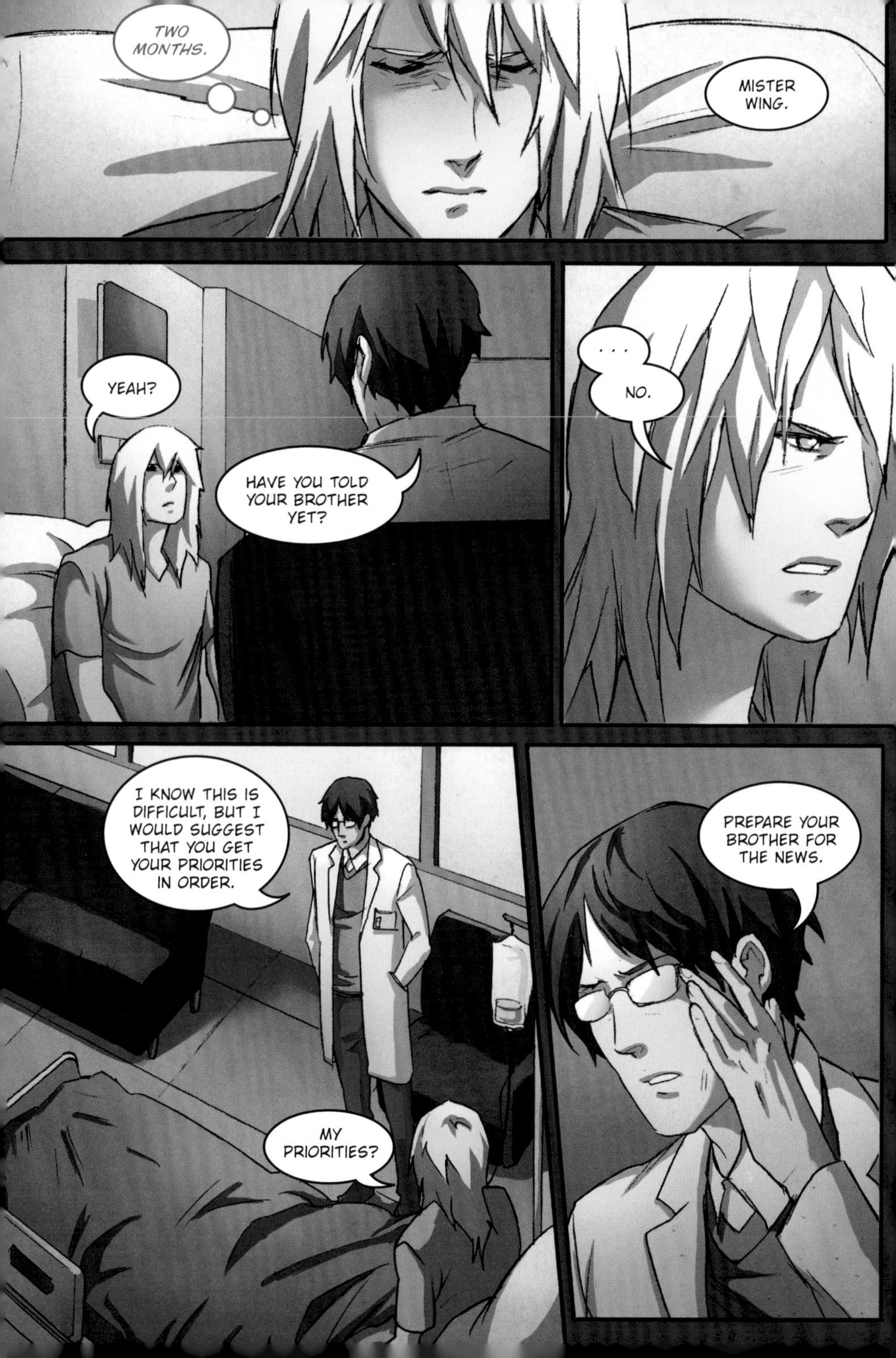
TWO MONTHS.
MISTER WING.
YEAH?
HAVE YOU TOLD YOUR BROTHER YET?
. . .
NO.
I KNOW THIS IS DIFFICULT, BUT I WOULD SUGGEST THAT YOU GET YOUR PRIORITIES IN ORDER.
MY PRIORITIES?
PREPARE YOUR BROTHER FOR THE NEWS.

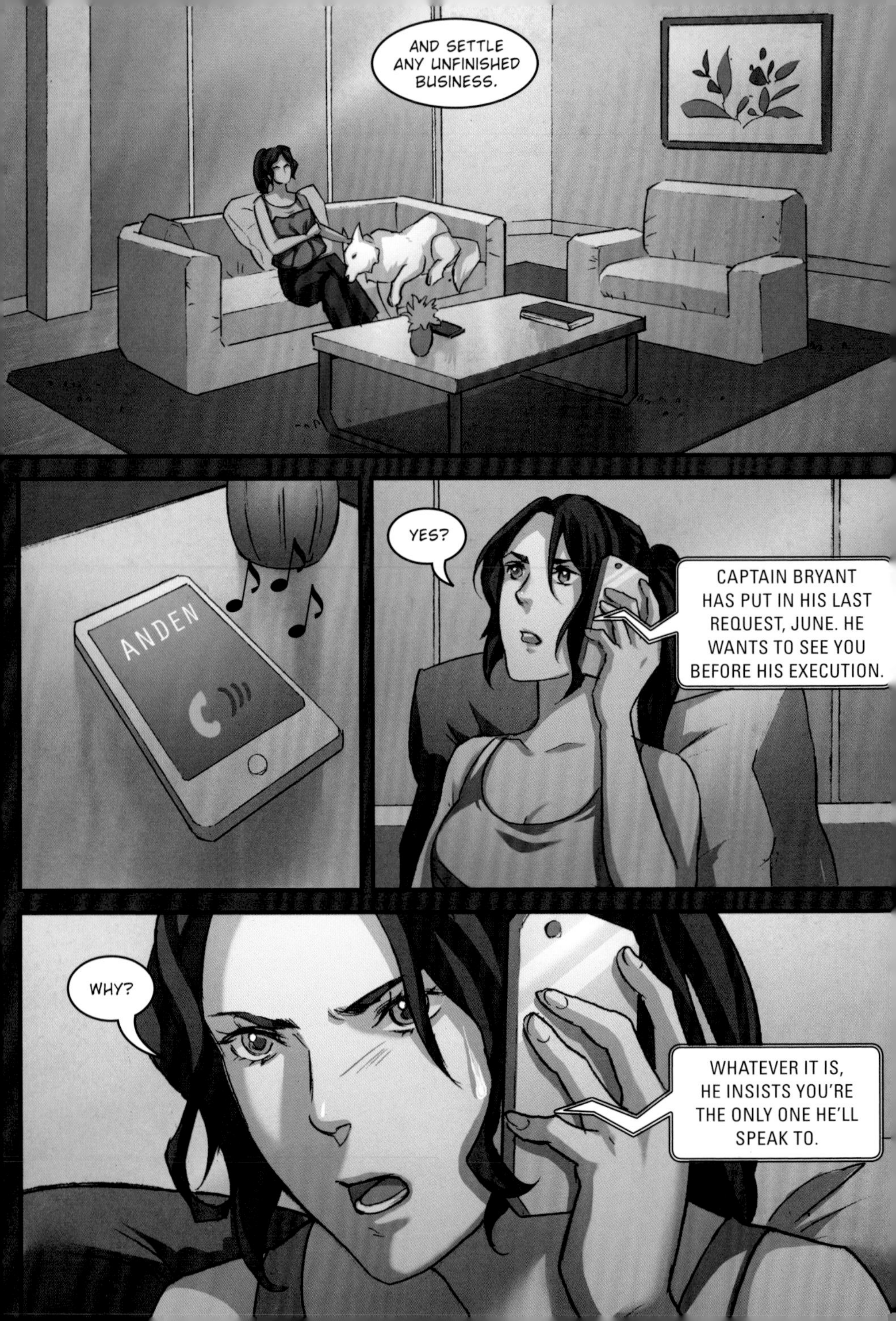
AND SETTLE ANY UNFINISHED BUSINESS.
ANDEN
YES?
CAPTAIN BRYANT HAS PUT IN HIS LAST REQUEST, JUNE. HE WANTS TO SEE YOU BEFORE HIS EXECUTION.
WHY?
WHATEVER IT IS, HE INSISTS YOU'RE THE ONLY ONE HE'LL SPEAK TO.

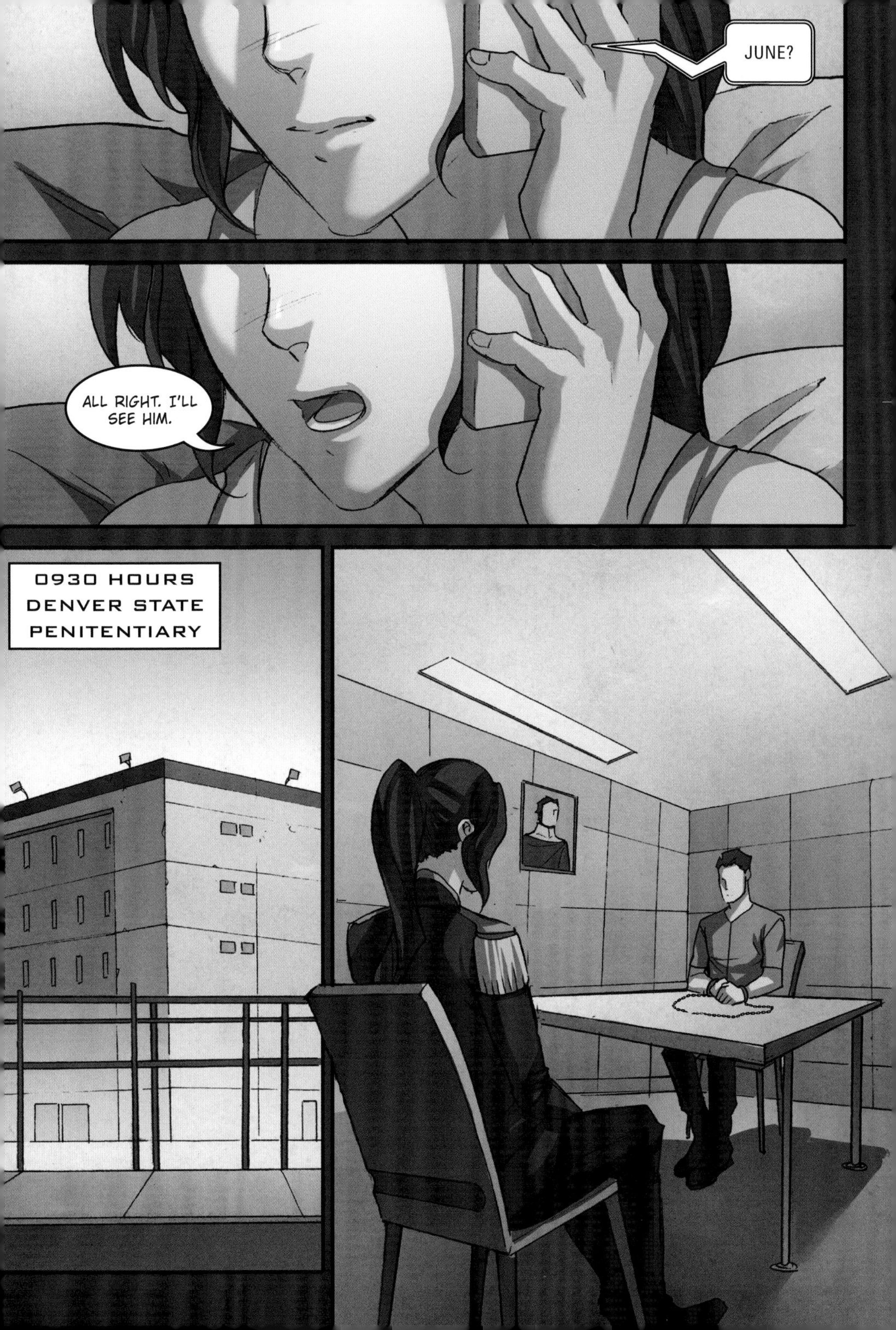
JUNE?
ALL RIGHT. I'LL SEE HIM.
0930 HOURS
DENVER STATE
PENITENTIARY

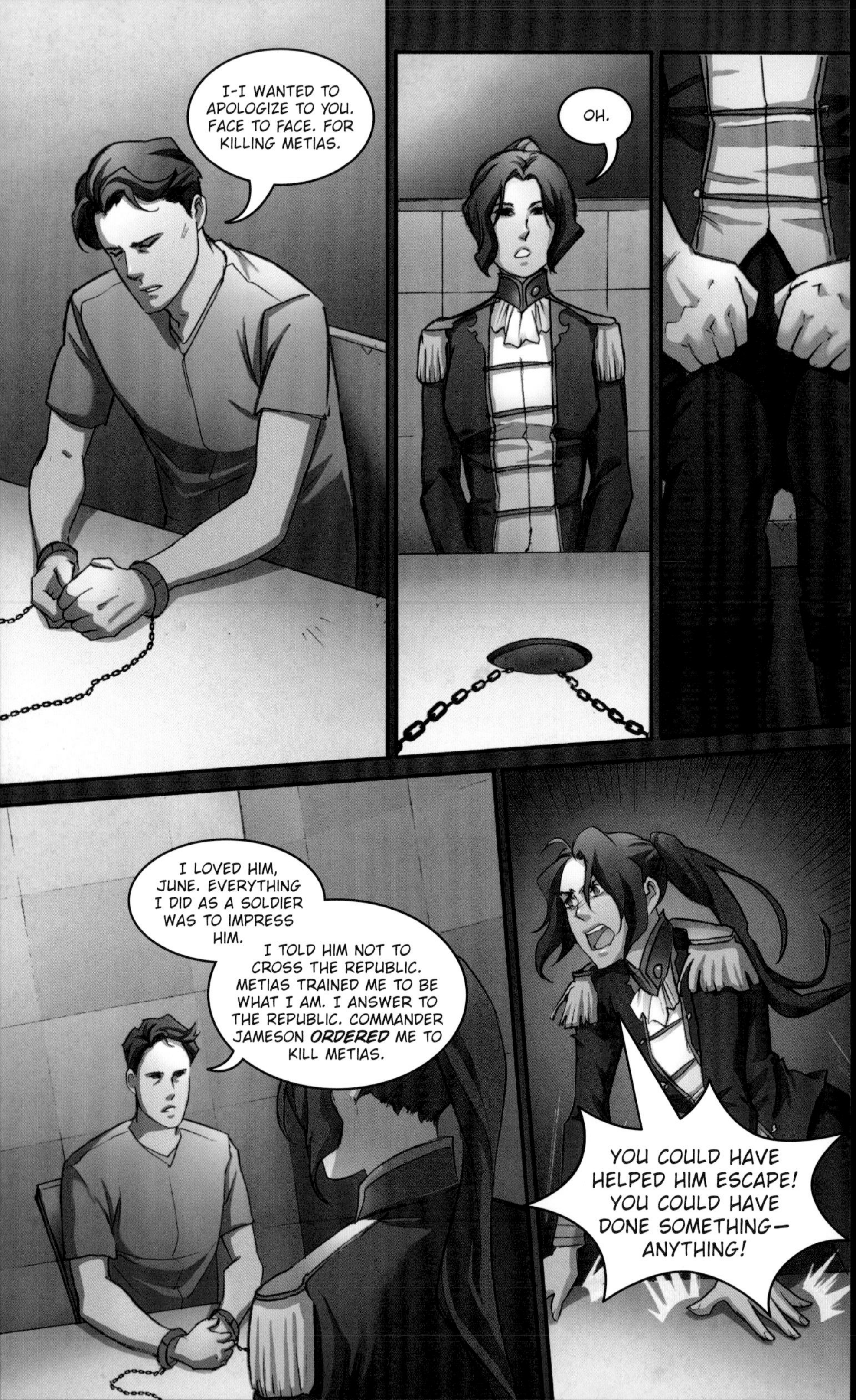
I-I WANTED TO APOLOGIZE TO YOU. FACE TO FACE. FOR KILLING METIAS.
OH.
I LOVED HIM, JUNE. EVERYTHING I DID AS A SOLDIER WAS TO IMPRESS HIM.
I TOLD HIM NOT TO CROSS THE REPUBLIC. METIAS TRAINED ME TO BE WHAT I AM. I ANSWER TO THE REPUBLIC. COMMANDER JAMESON ***ORDERED*** ME TO KILL METIAS.
YOU COULD HAVE HELPED HIM ESCAPE! YOU COULD HAVE DONE SOMETHING— ANYTHING!

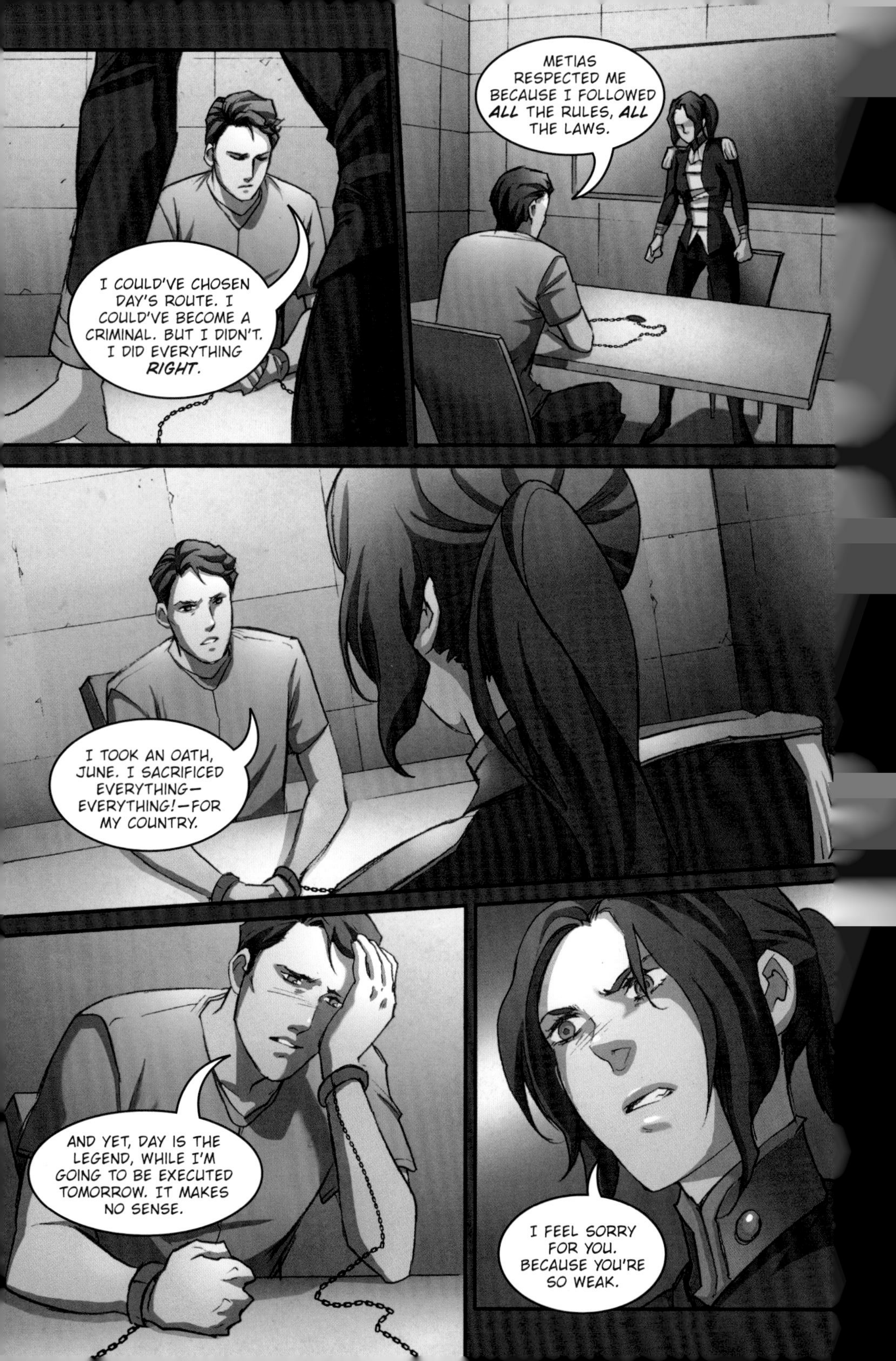
I COULD'VE CHOSEN DAY'S ROUTE. I COULD'VE BECOME A CRIMINAL. BUT I DIDN'T. I DID EVERYTHING ***RIGHT***.
METIAS RESPECTED ME BECAUSE I FOLLOWED ***ALL*** THE RULES, ***ALL*** THE LAWS.
I TOOK AN OATH, JUNE. I SACRIFICED EVERYTHING— EVERYTHING!—FOR MY COUNTRY.
AND YET, DAY IS THE LEGEND, WHILE I'M GOING TO BE EXECUTED TOMORROW. IT MAKES NO SENSE.
I FEEL SORRY FOR YOU. BECAUSE YOU'RE SO WEAK.

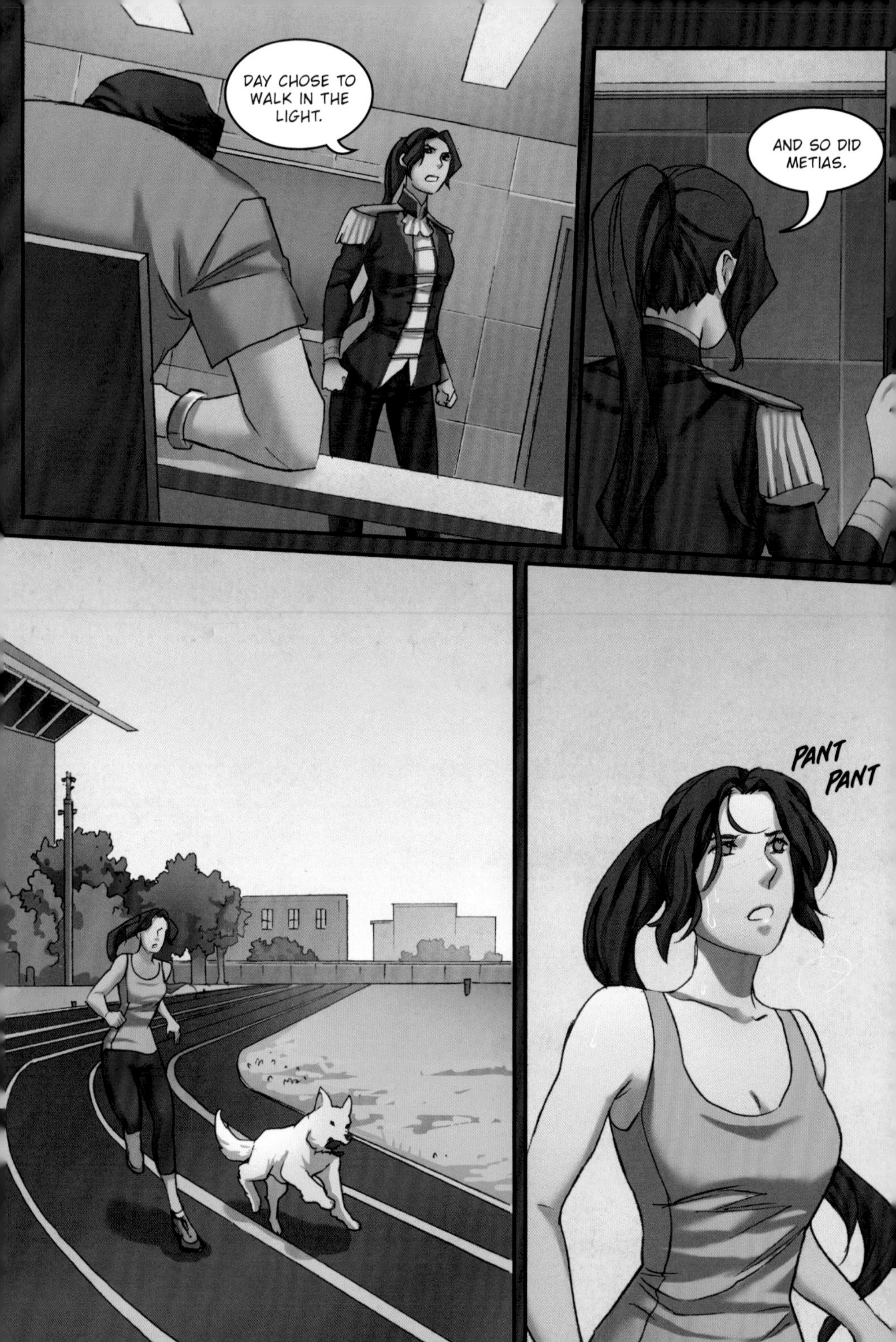
DAY CHOSE TO WALK IN THE LIGHT.
AND SO DID METIAS.
PANT
PANT

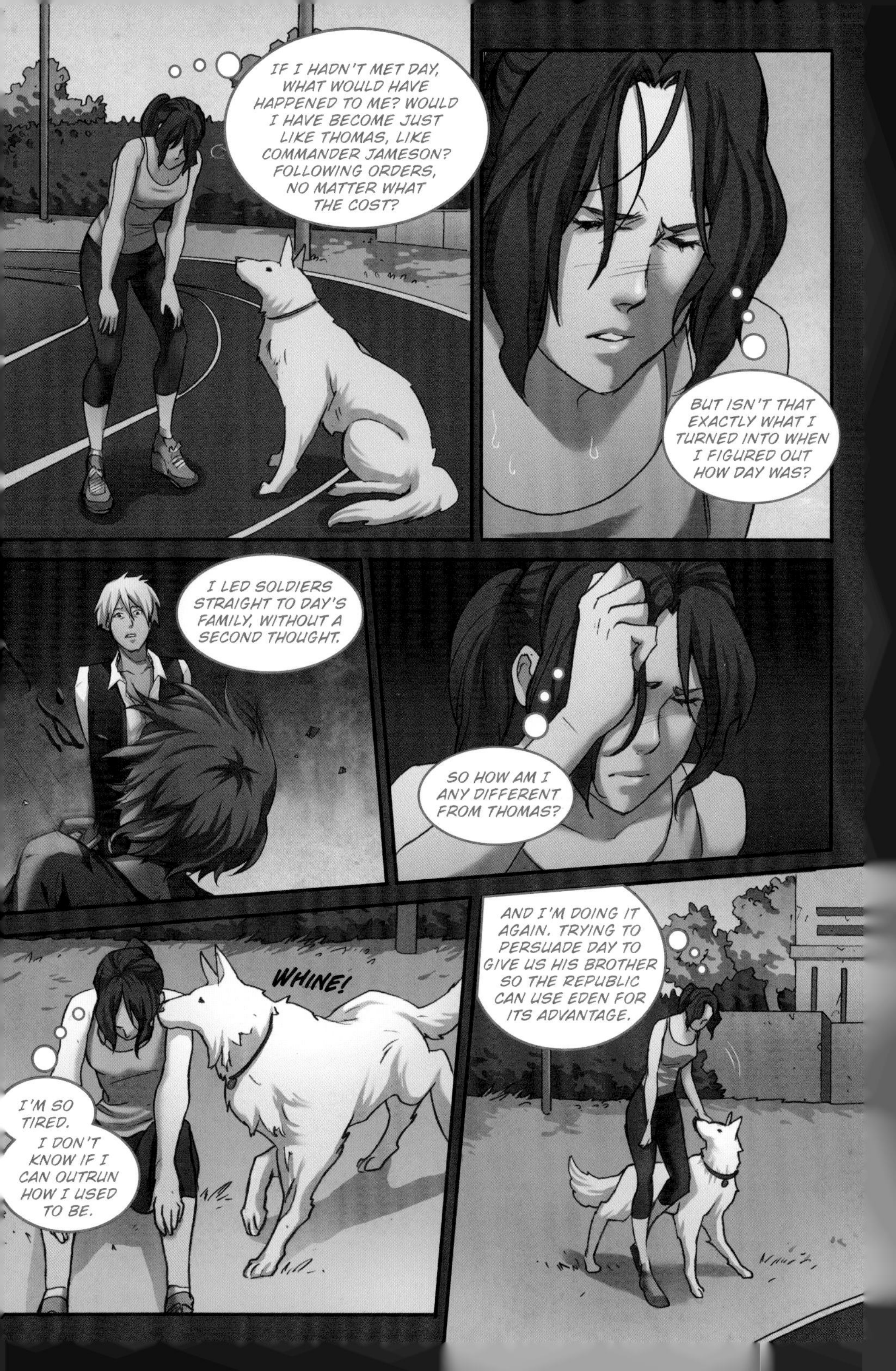
IF I HADN'T MET DAY, WHAT WOULD HAVE HAPPENED TO ME? WOULD I HAVE BECOME JUST LIKE THOMAS, LIKE COMMANDER JAMESON? FOLLOWING ORDERS, NO MATTER WHAT THE COST?
BUT ISN'T THAT EXACTLY WHAT I TURNED INTO WHEN I FIGURED OUT HOW DAY WAS?
I LED SOLDIERS STRAIGHT TO DAY'S FAMILY, WITHOUT A SECOND THOUGHT.
SO HOW AM I ANY DIFFERENT FROM THOMAS?
WHINE!
I'M SO TIRED.
I DON'T KNOW IF I CAN OUTRUN HOW I USED TO BE.
AND I'M DOING IT AGAIN. TRYING TO PERSUADE DAY TO GIVE US HIS BROTHER SO THE REPUBLIC CAN USE EDEN FOR ITS ADVANTAGE.

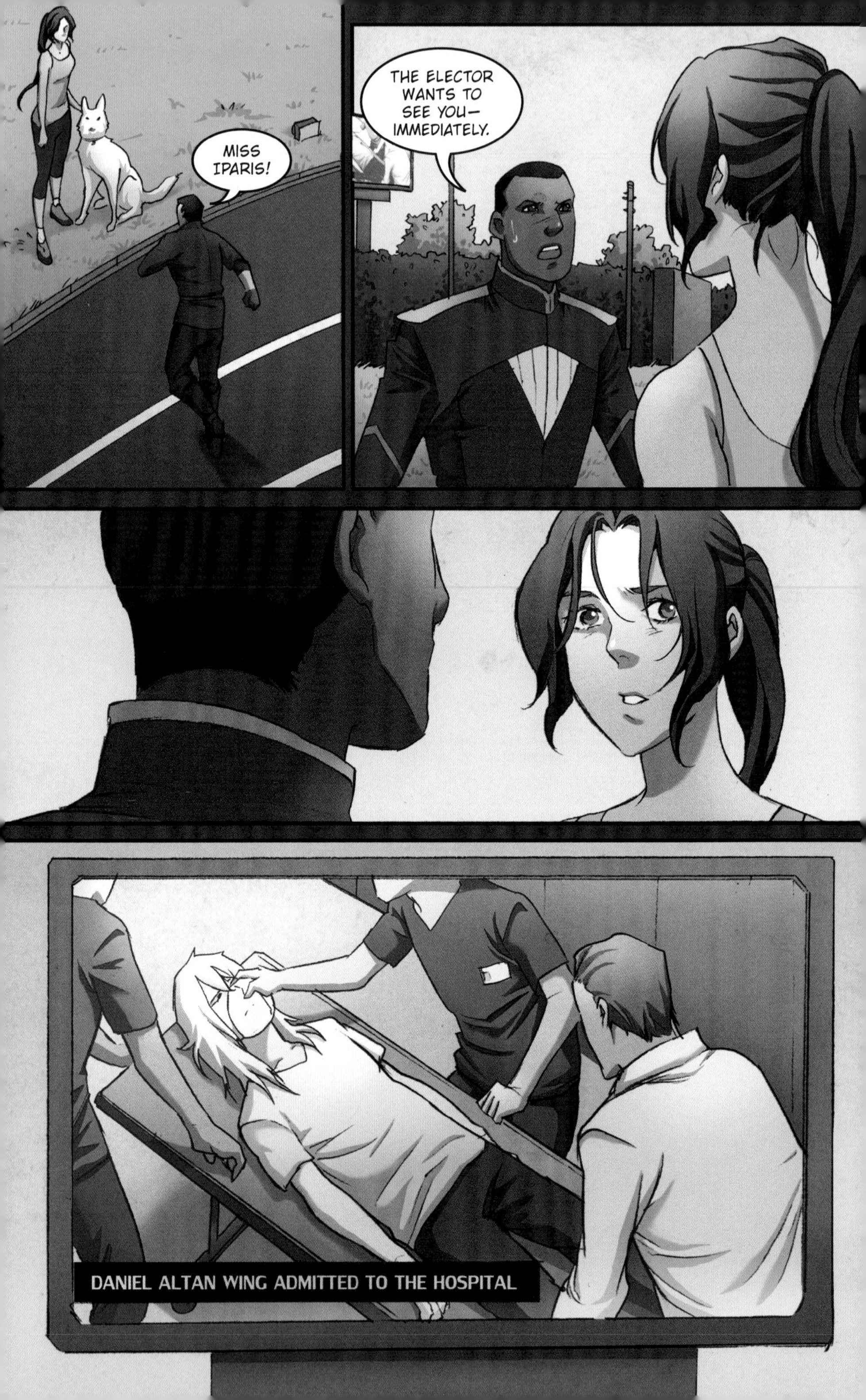
MISS IPARIS!
THE ELECTOR WANTS TO SEE YOU— IMMEDIATELY.
DANIEL ALTAN WING ADMITTED TO THE HOSPITAL

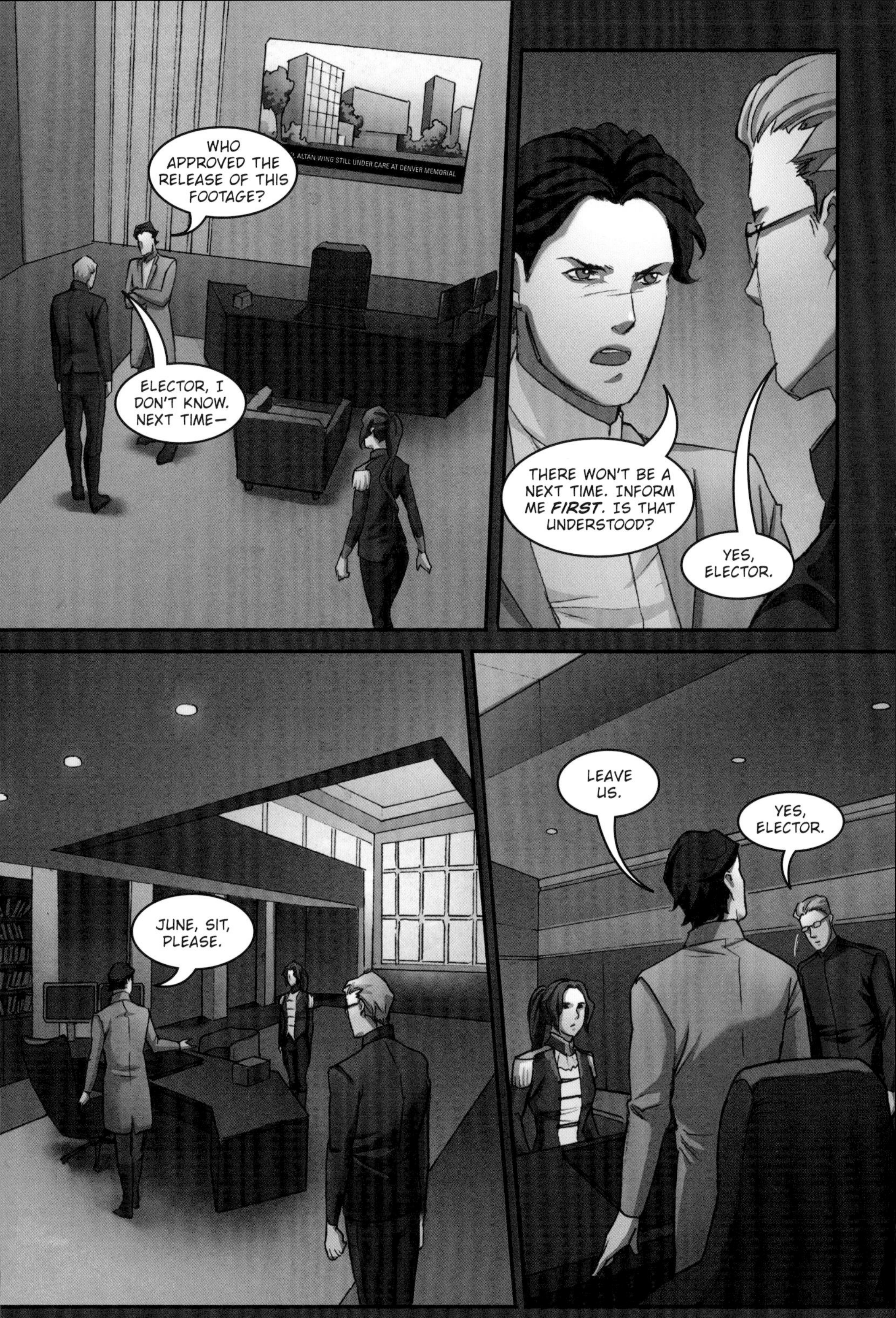
ALTAN WING STILL UNDER CARE AT DENVER MEMORIAL
WHO APPROVED THE RELEASE OF THIS FOOTAGE?
ELECTOR, I DON'T KNOW. NEXT TIME—
THERE WON'T BE A NEXT TIME. INFORM ME ***FIRST***. IS THAT UNDERSTOOD?
YES, ELECTOR.
JUNE, SIT, PLEASE.
LEAVE US.
YES, ELECTOR.

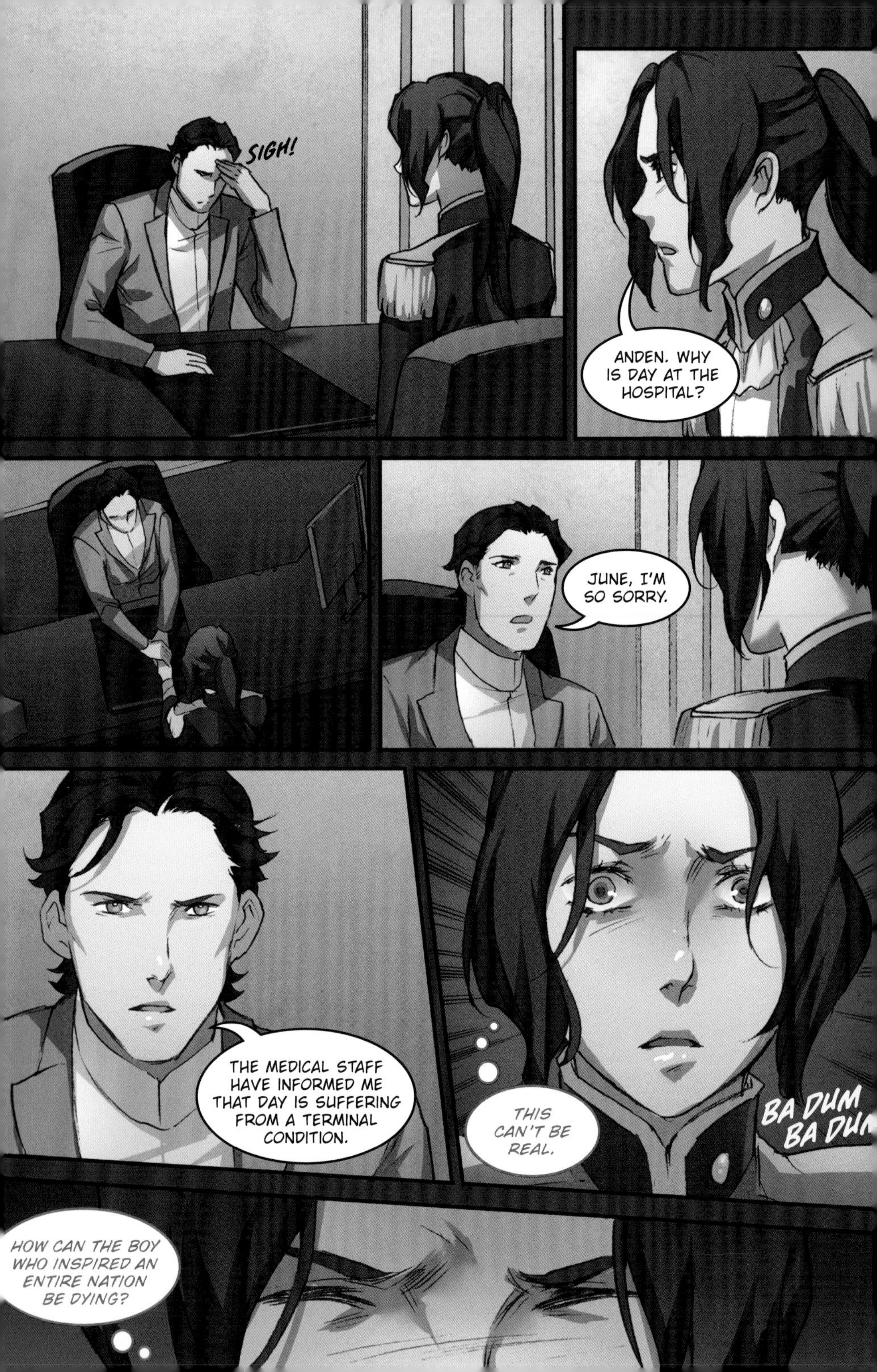
SIGH!
ANDEN. WHY IS DAY AT THE HOSPITAL?
JUNE, I'M SO SORRY.
THE MEDICAL STAFF HAVE INFORMED ME THAT DAY IS SUFFERING FROM A TERMINAL CONDITION.
THIS CAN'T BE REAL.
BA DUM BA DUM
HOW CAN THE BOY WHO INSPIRED AN ENTIRE NATION BE DYING?

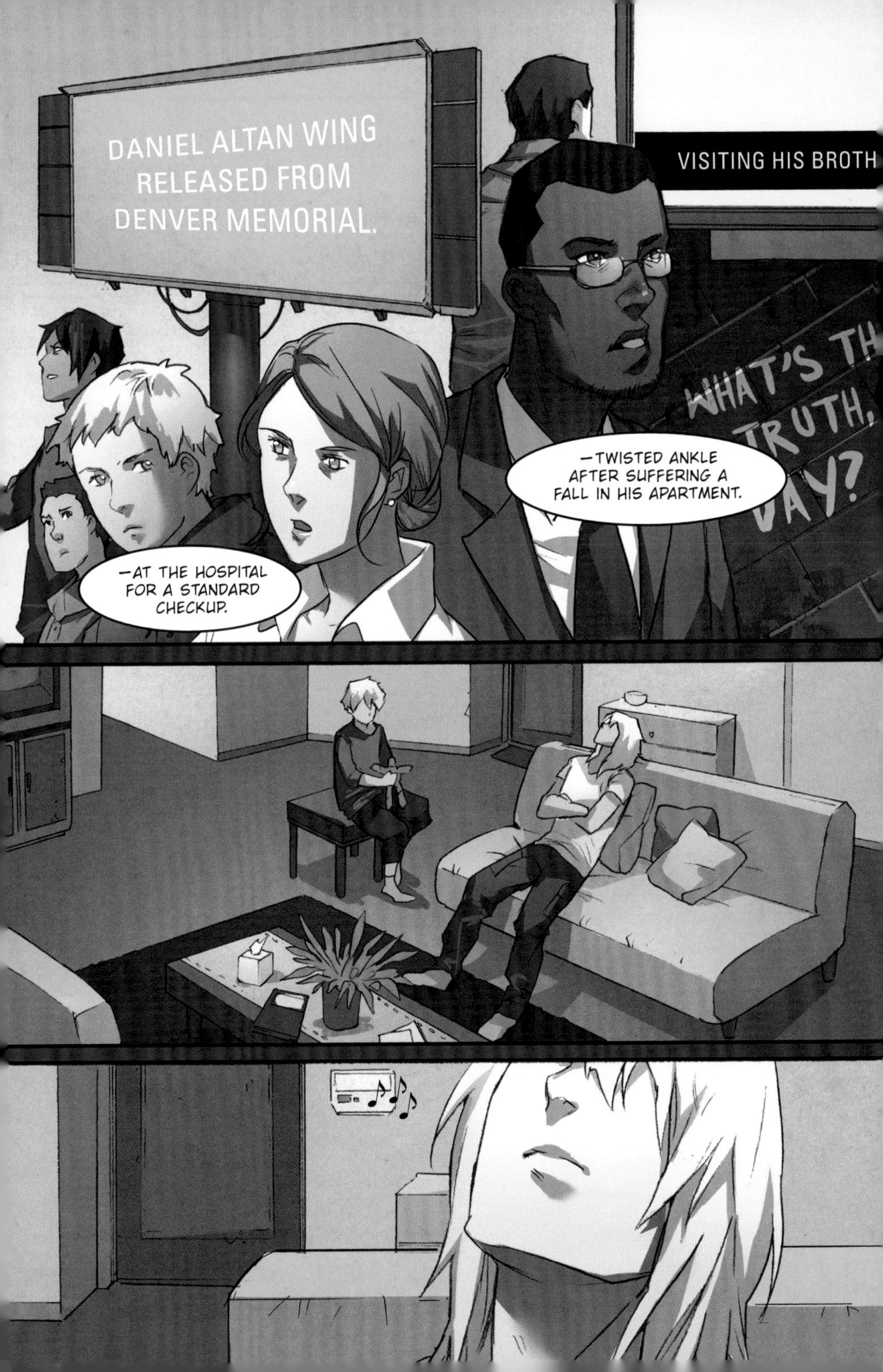
DANIEL ALTAN WING RELEASED FROM DENVER MEMORIAL.
VISITING HIS BROTH
WHAT'S TH TRUTH, DAY?
—TWISTED ANKLE AFTER SUFFERING A FALL IN HIS APARTMENT.
—AT THE HOSPITAL FOR A STANDARD CHECKUP.

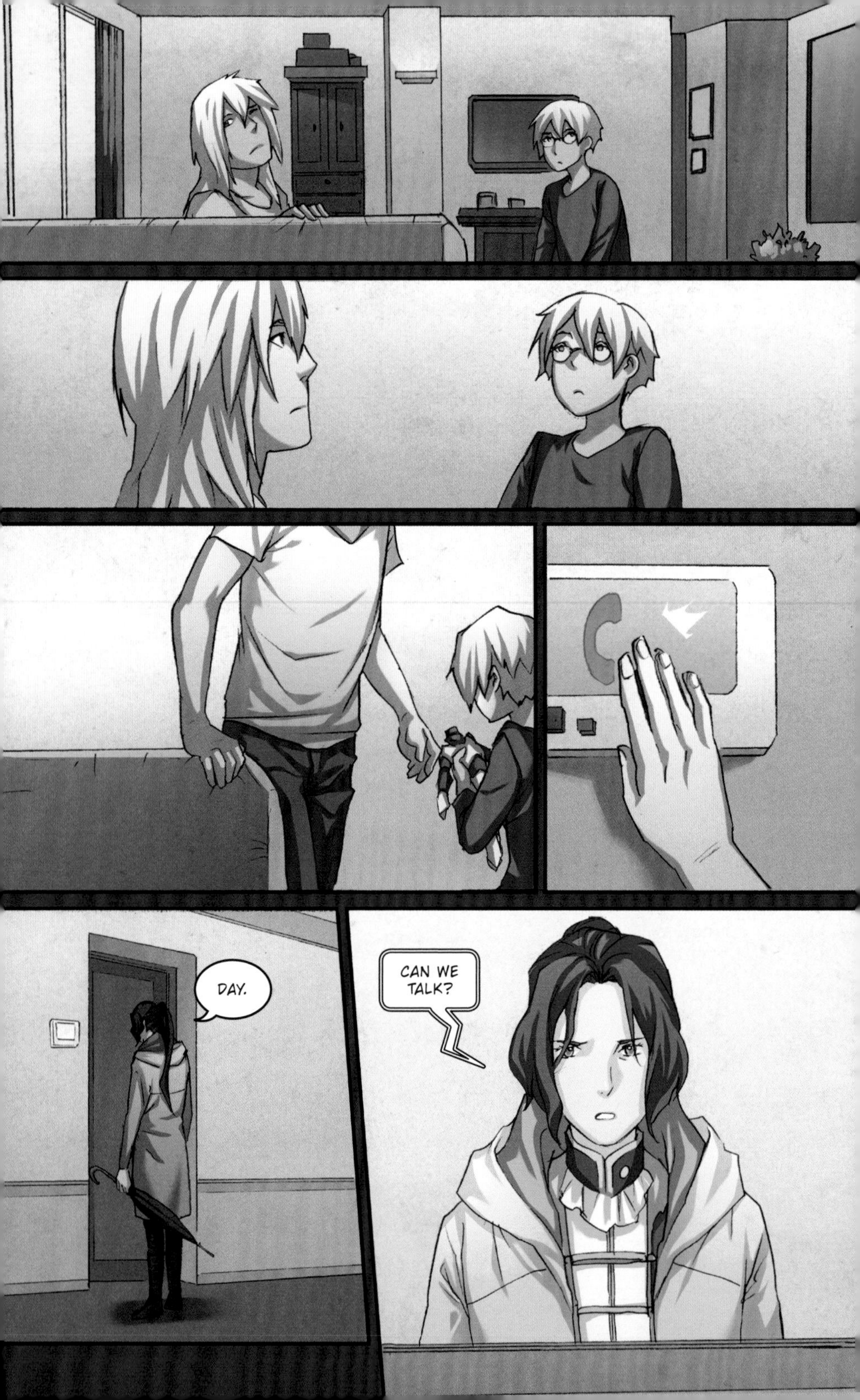
DAY.
CAN WE TALK?

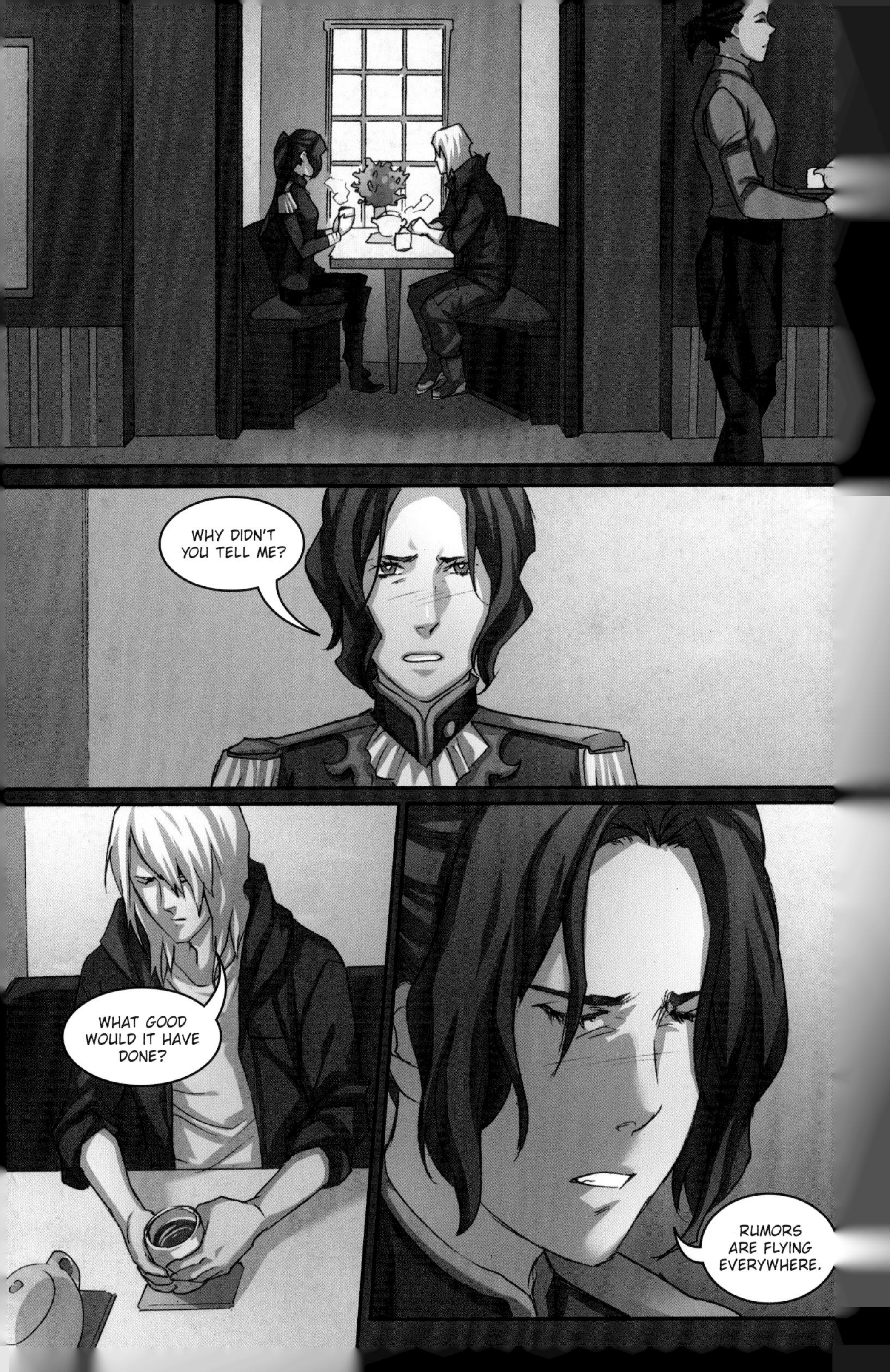
WHY DIDN'T YOU TELL ME?
WHAT GOOD WOULD IT HAVE DONE?
RUMORS ARE FLYING EVERYWHERE.

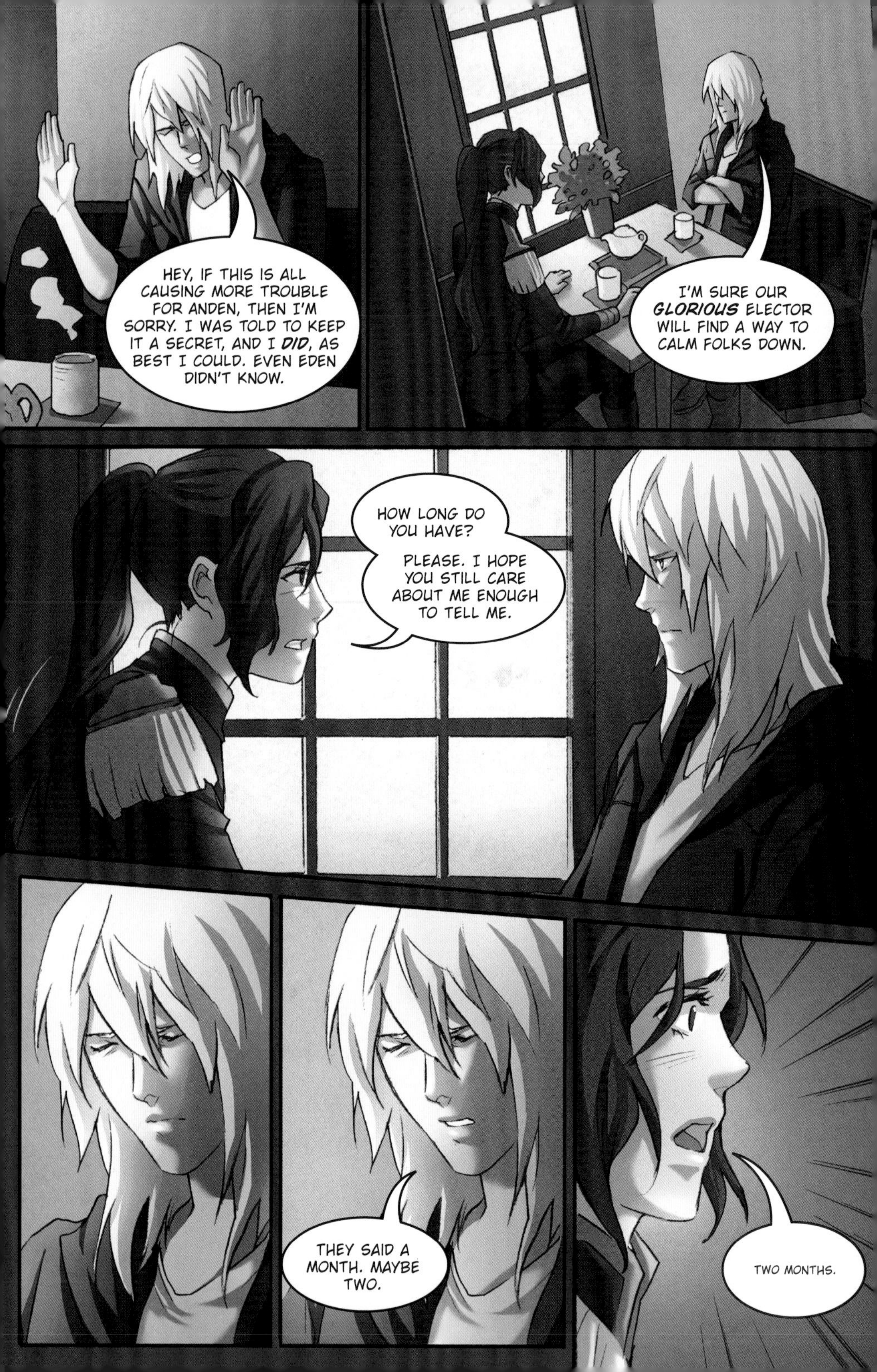
HEY, IF THIS IS ALL CAUSING MORE TROUBLE FOR ANDEN, THEN I'M SORRY. I WAS TOLD TO KEEP IT A SECRET, AND I *DID*, AS BEST I COULD. EVEN EDEN DIDN'T KNOW.
I'M SURE OUR *GLORIOUS* ELECTOR WILL FIND A WAY TO CALM FOLKS DOWN.
HOW LONG DO YOU HAVE?
PLEASE. I HOPE YOU STILL CARE ABOUT ME ENOUGH TO TELL ME.
THEY SAID A MONTH. MAYBE TWO.
TWO MONTHS.

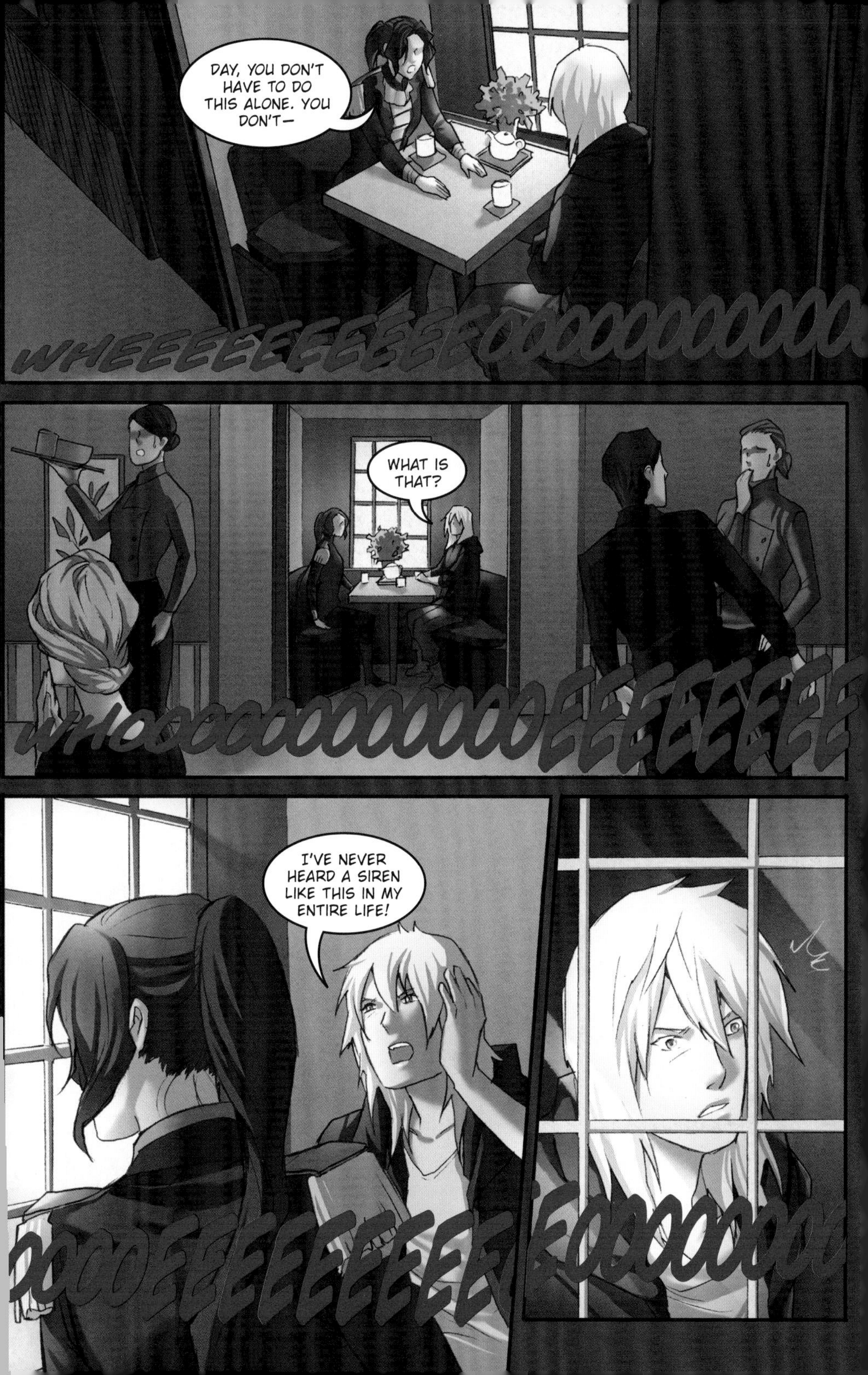
DAY, YOU DON'T HAVE TO DO THIS ALONE. YOU DON'T—
WHEEEEEEEEEEEEOOOOOOOOOOOO
WHAT IS THAT?
WHOOOOOOOOOOOOOEEEEEEEE
I'VE NEVER HEARD A SIREN LIKE THIS IN MY ENTIRE LIFE!
OOOOEEEEEEEEEEEE
EOOOOOOO

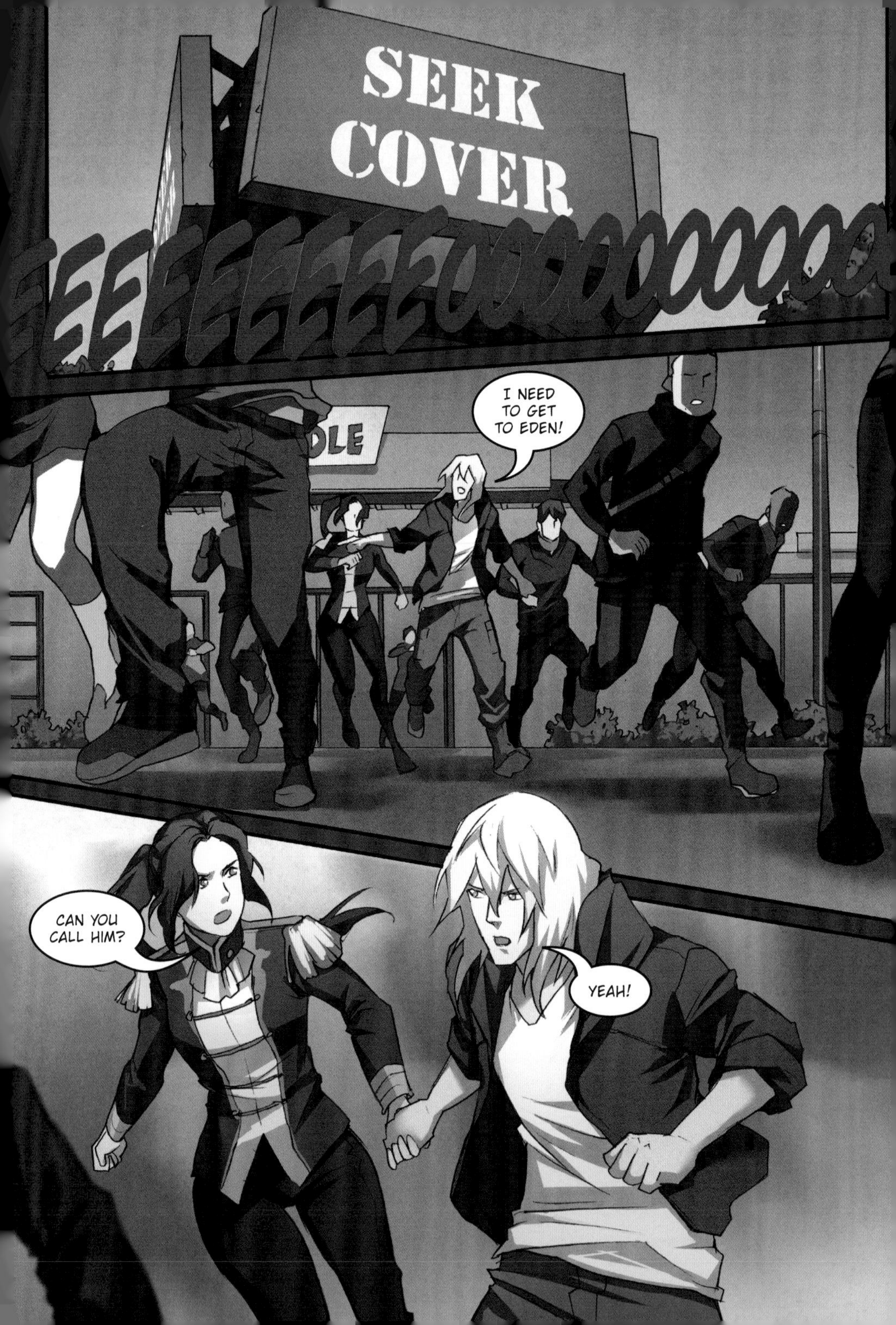
SEEK
COVER
EEEEEEEEOOOOOOOO
I NEED TO GET TO EDEN!
OLE
CAN YOU CALL HIM?
YEAH!

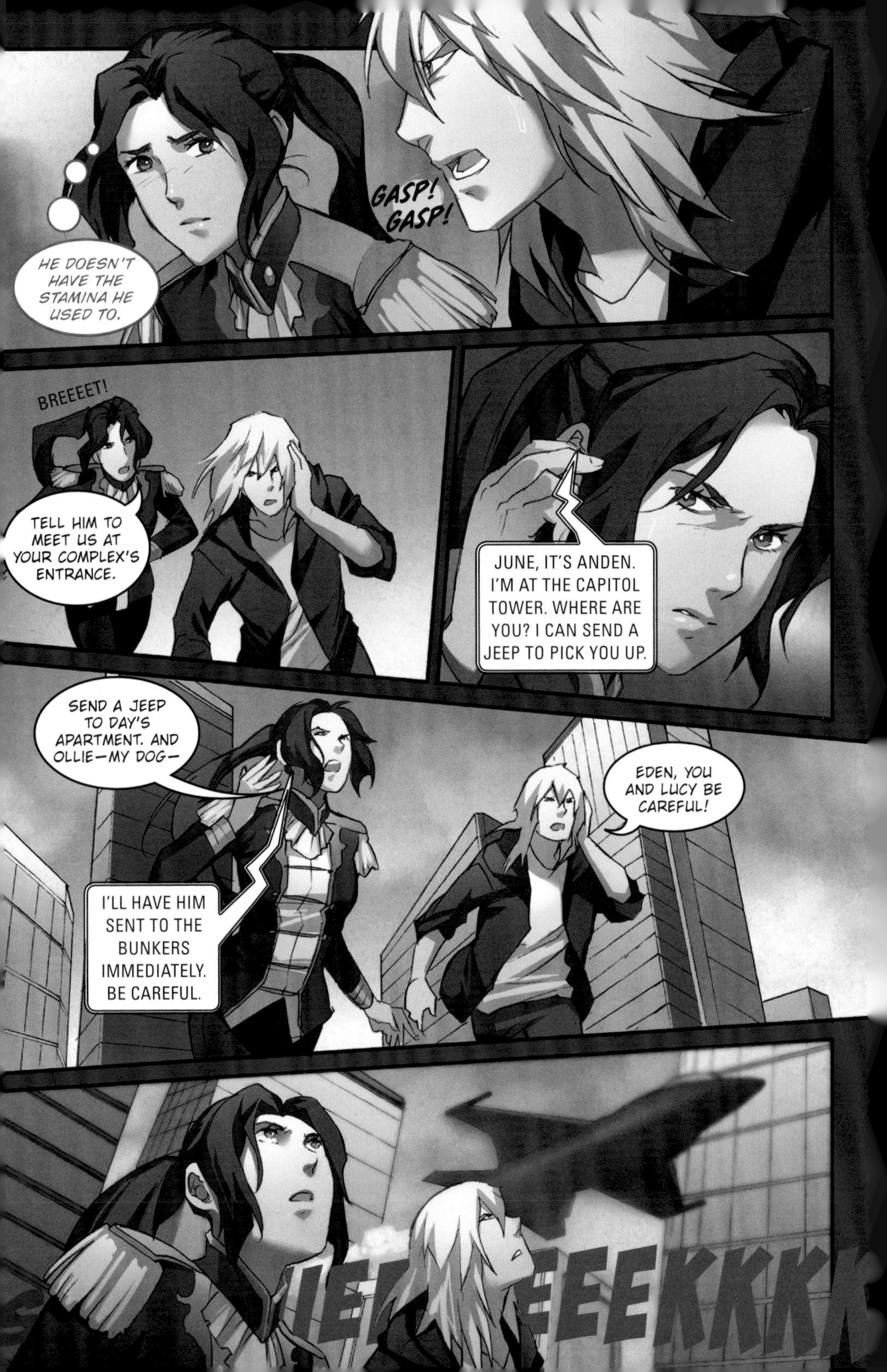
GASP! GASP!
HE DOESN'T HAVE THE STAMINA HE USED TO.
BREEEET!
TELL HIM TO MEET US AT YOUR COMPLEX'S ENTRANCE.
JUNE, IT'S ANDEN. I'M AT THE CAPITOL TOWER. WHERE ARE YOU? I CAN SEND A JEEP TO PICK YOU UP.
SEND A JEEP TO DAY'S APARTMENT. AND OLLIE—MY DOG—
EDEN, YOU AND LUCY BE CAREFUL!
I'LL HAVE HIM SENT TO THE BUNKERS IMMEDIATELY. BE CAREFUL.

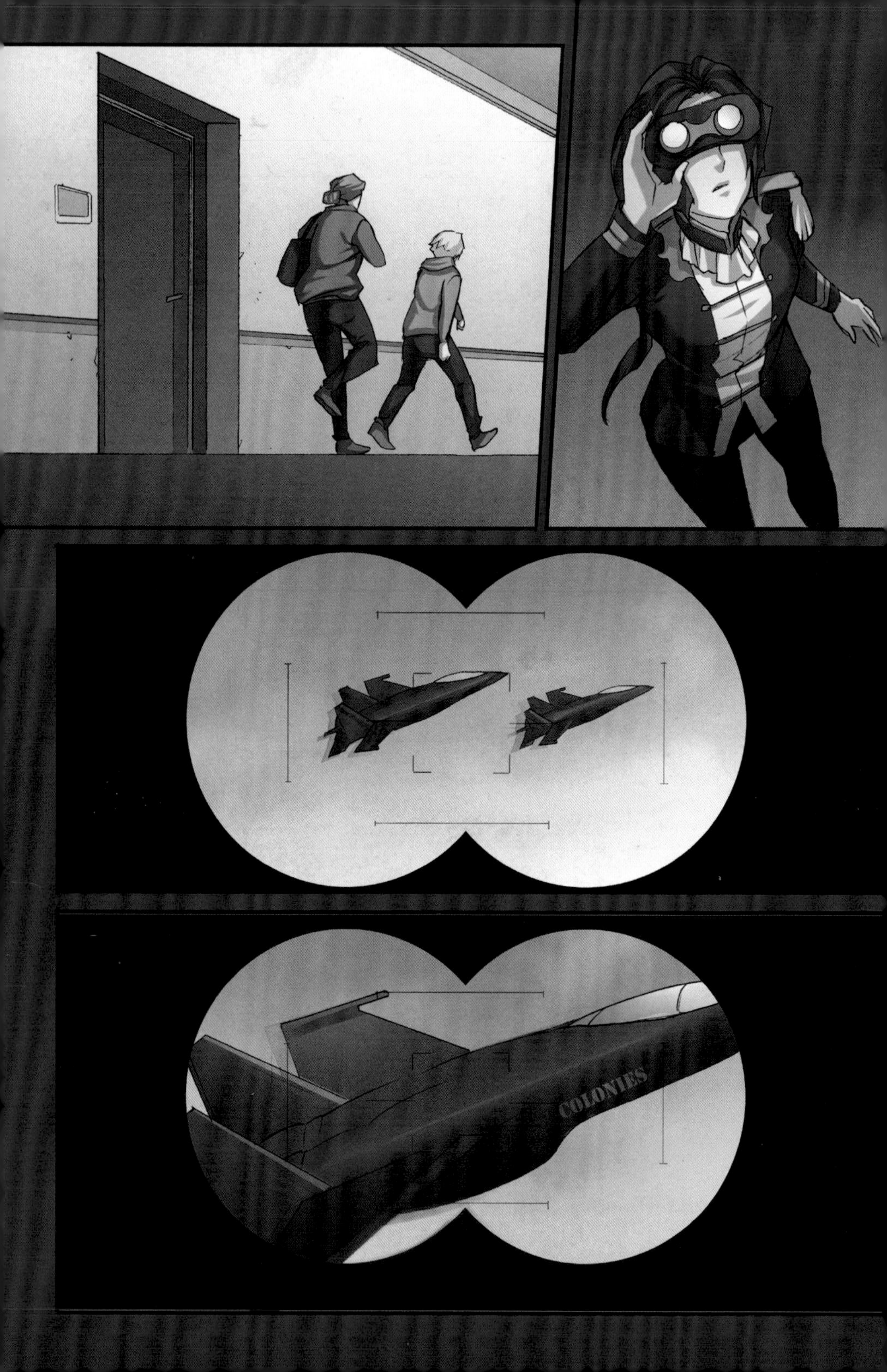
COLONIES

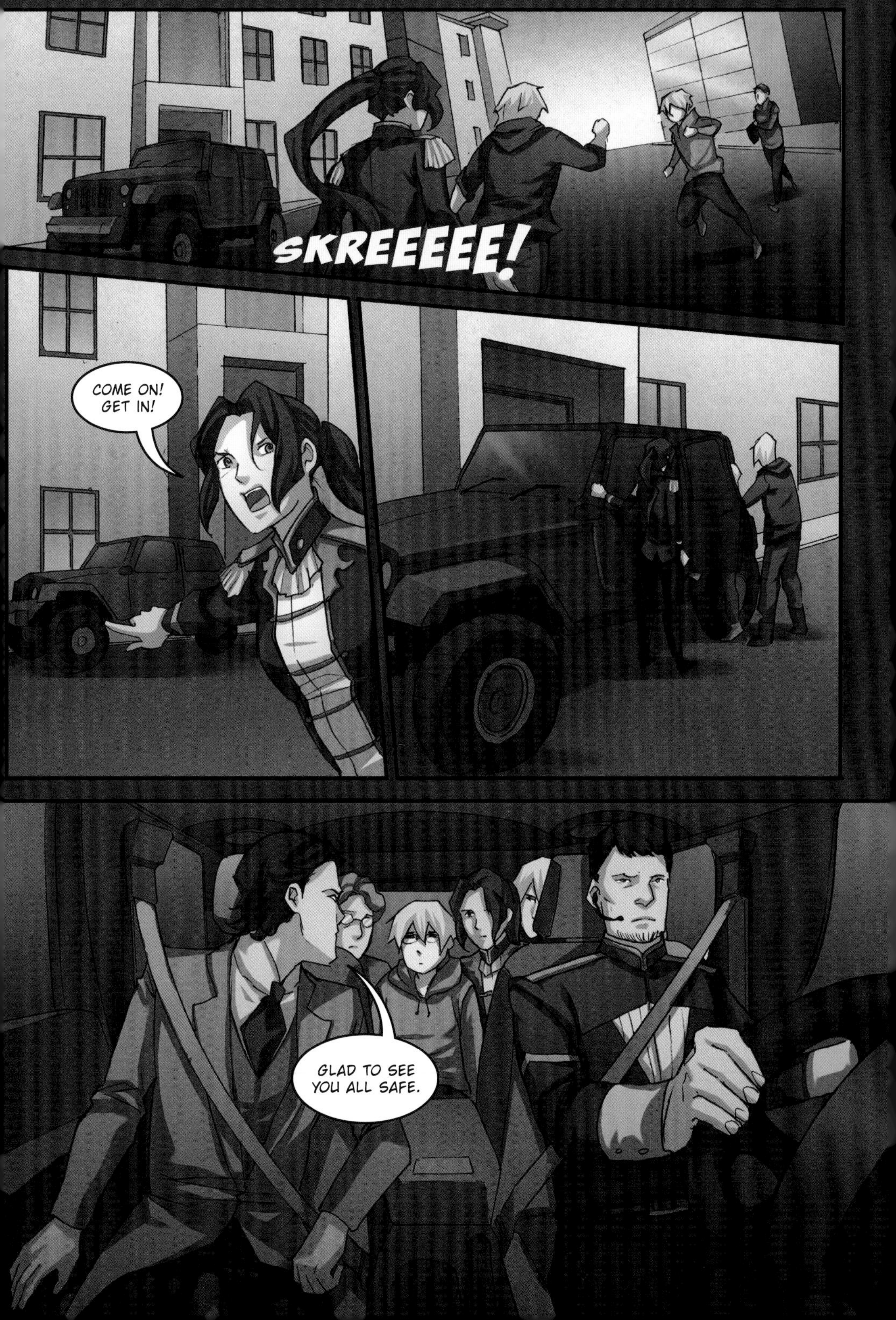
SKREEEEEE!
COME ON!
GET IN!
GLAD TO SEE
YOU ALL SAFE.

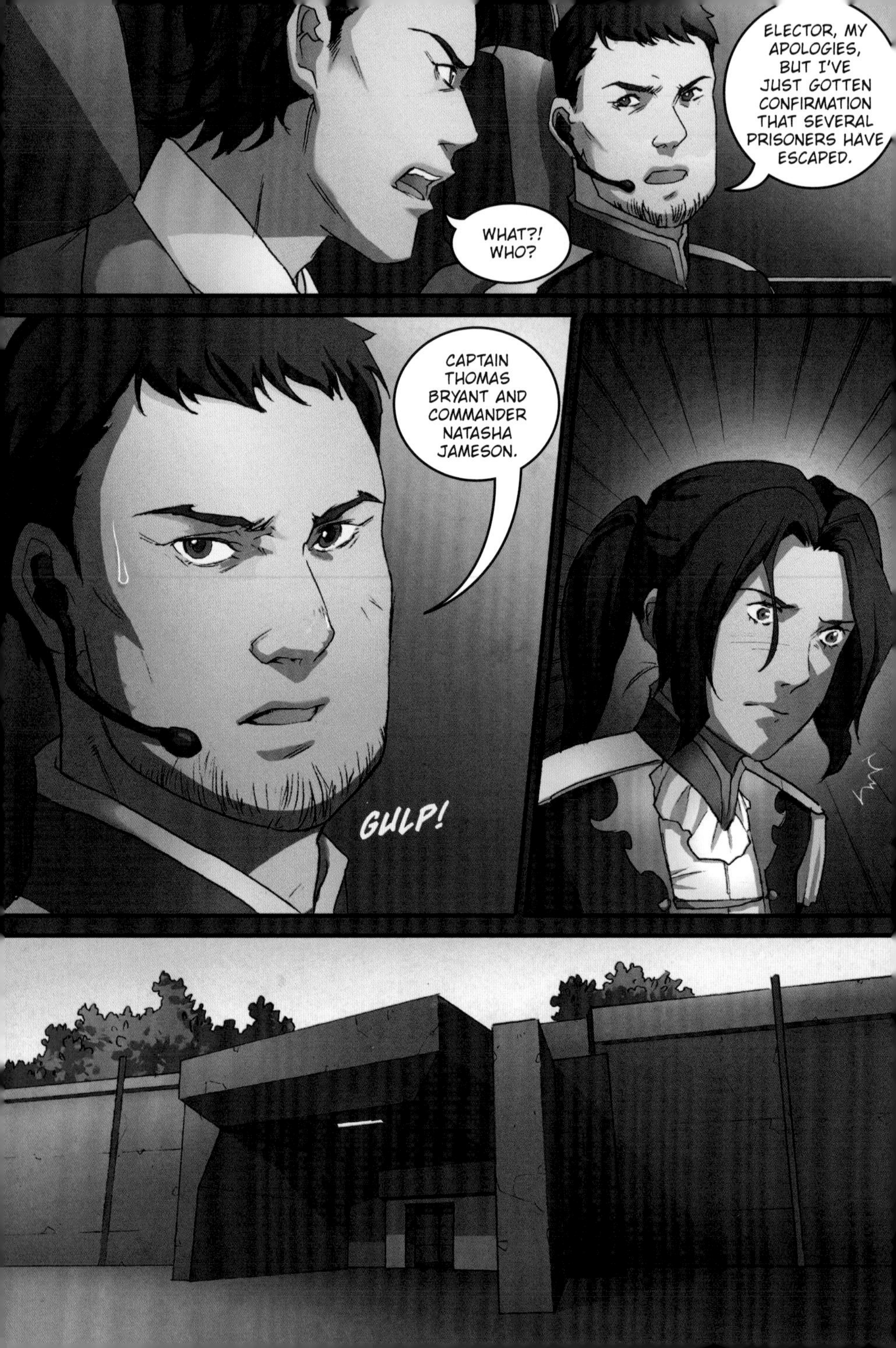
ELECTOR, MY APOLOGIES, BUT I'VE JUST GOTTEN CONFIRMATION THAT SEVERAL PRISONERS HAVE ESCAPED.
WHAT?! WHO?
CAPTAIN THOMAS BRYANT AND COMMANDER NATASHA JAMESON.
GULP!

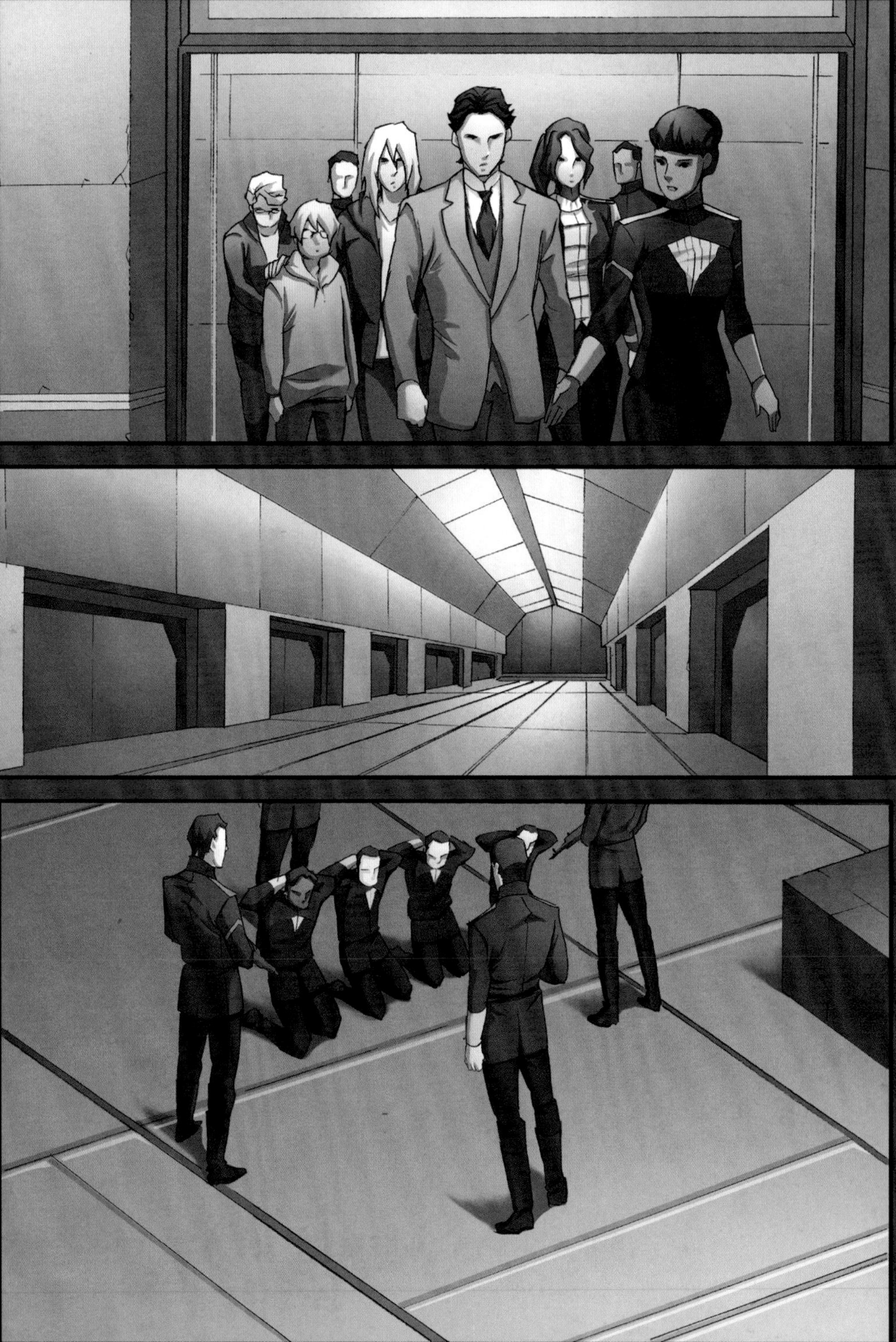

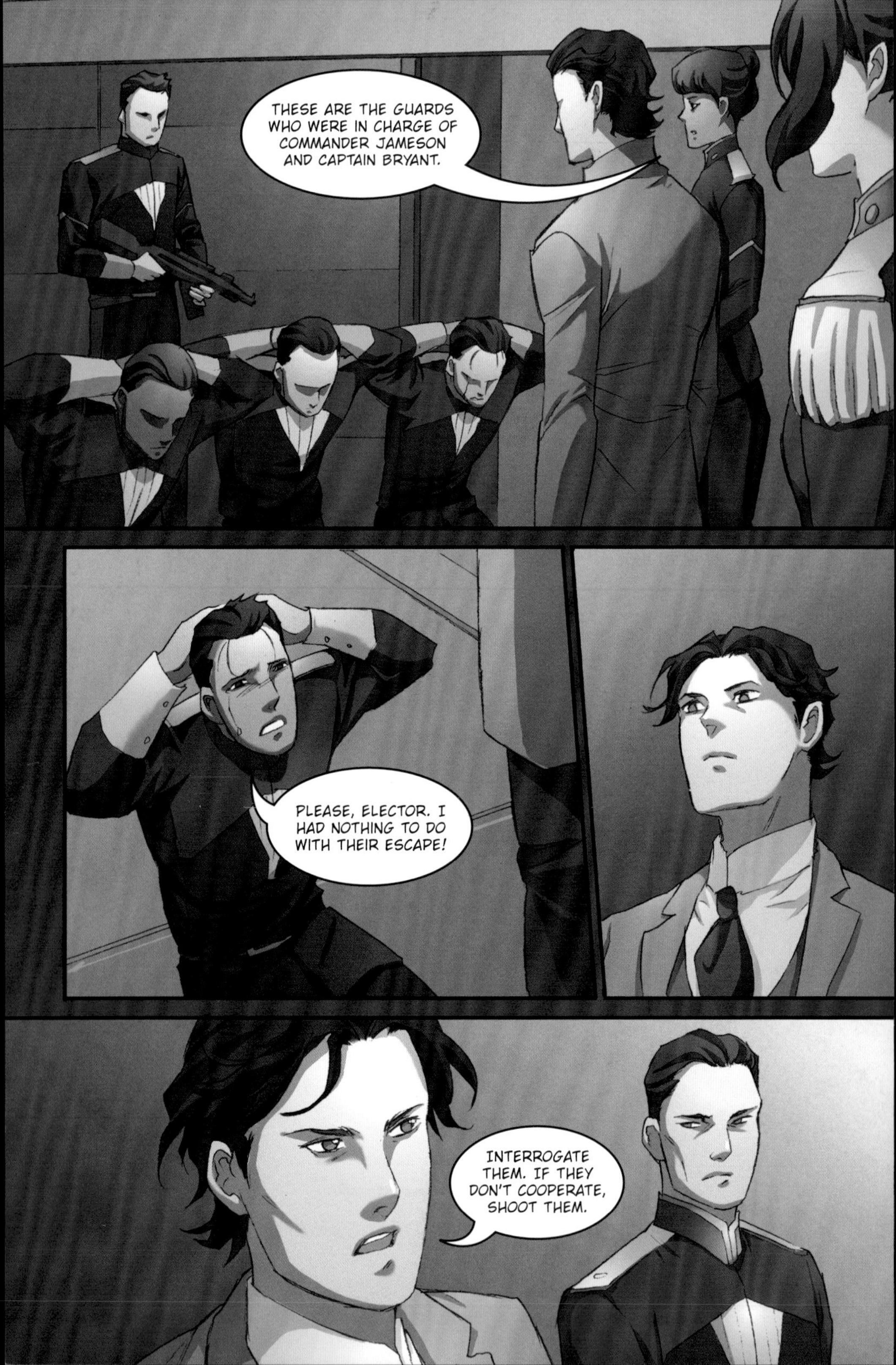
THESE ARE THE GUARDS WHO WERE IN CHARGE OF COMMANDER JAMESON AND CAPTAIN BRYANT.
PLEASE, ELECTOR. I HAD NOTHING TO DO WITH THEIR ESCAPE!
INTERROGATE THEM. IF THEY DON'T COOPERATE, SHOOT THEM.

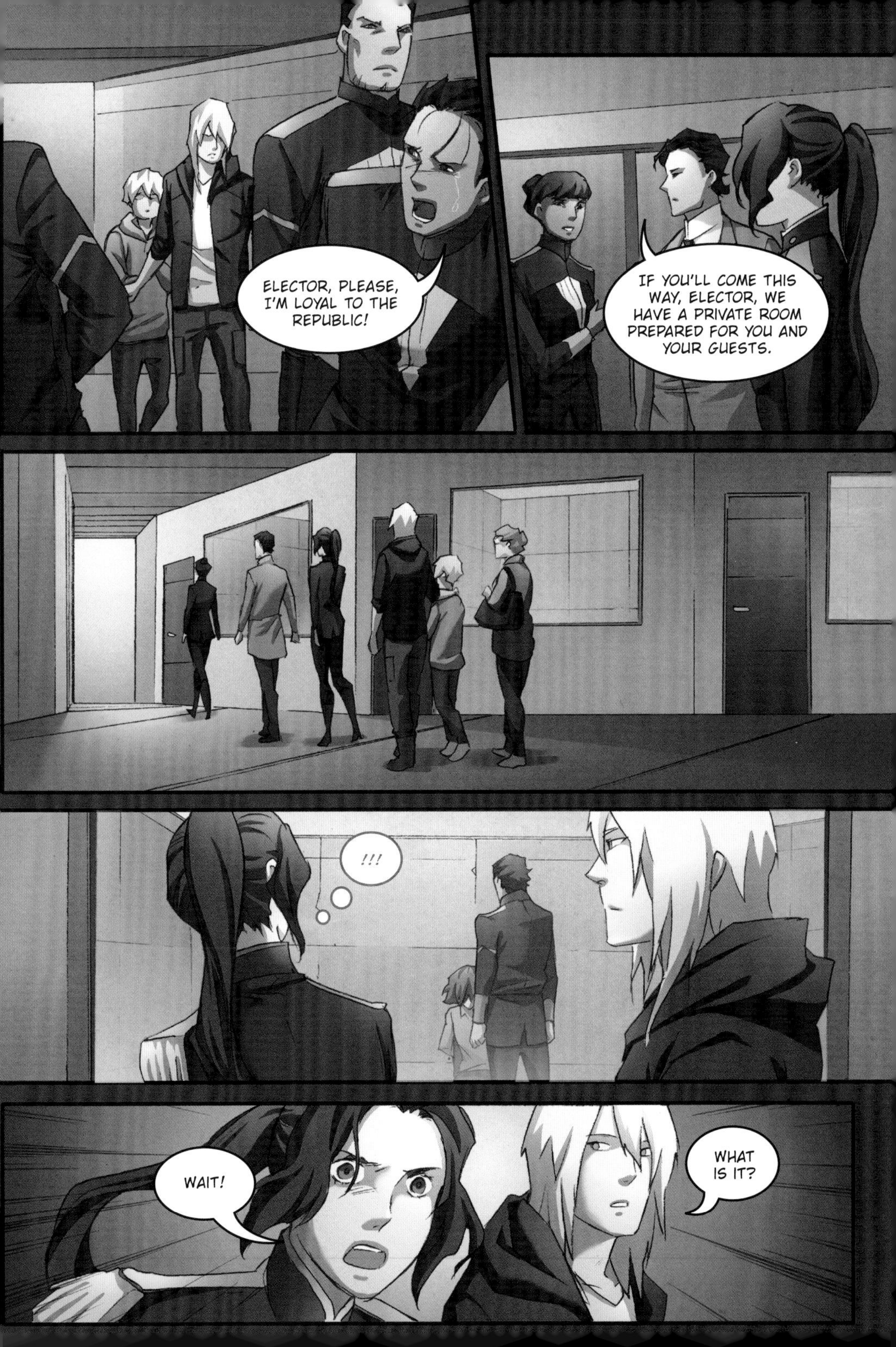
ELECTOR, PLEASE, I'M LOYAL TO THE REPUBLIC!
IF YOU'LL COME THIS WAY, ELECTOR, WE HAVE A PRIVATE ROOM PREPARED FOR YOU AND YOUR GUESTS.
!!!
WAIT!
WHAT IS IT?

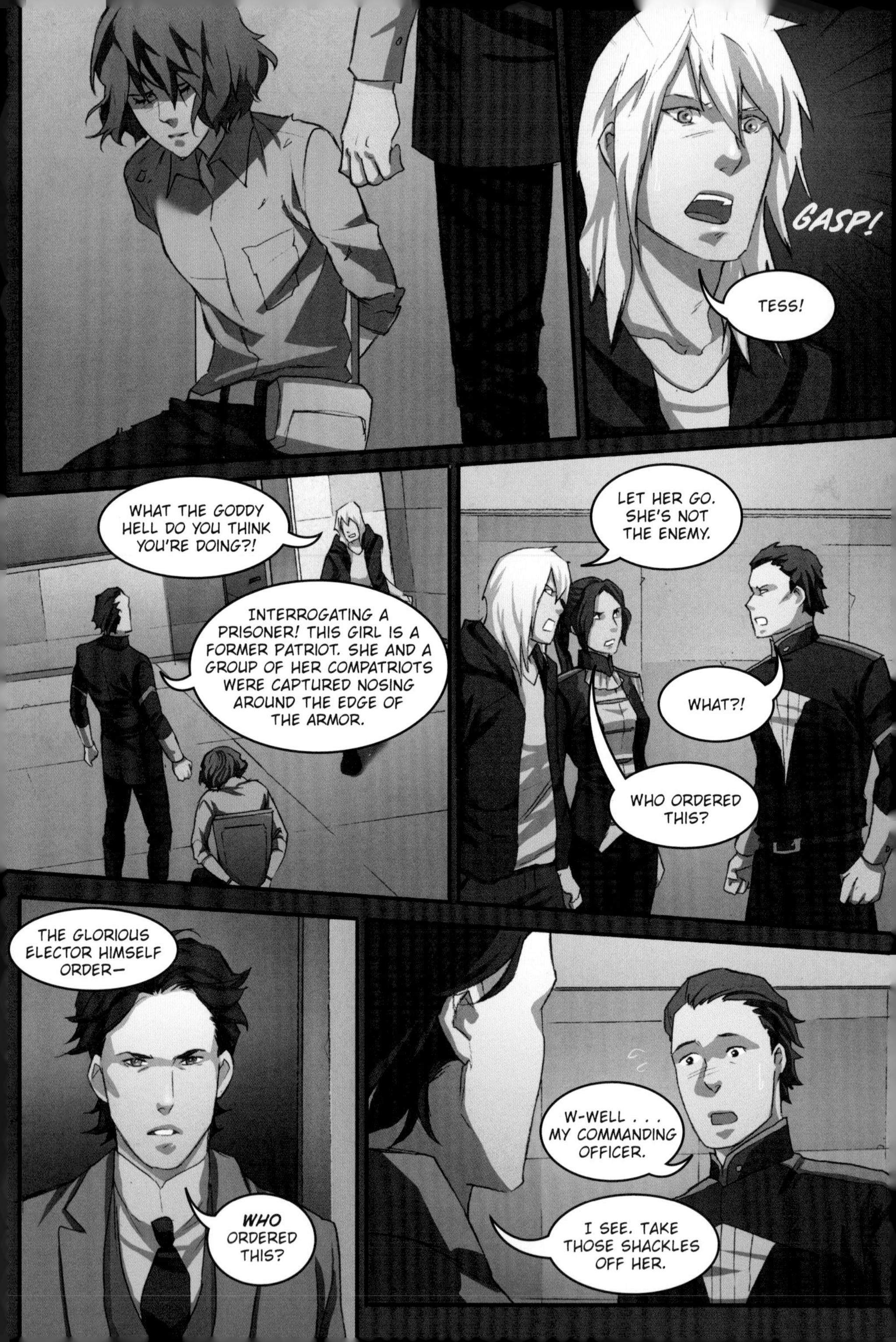
GASP!
TESS!
WHAT THE GODDY HELL DO YOU THINK YOU'RE DOING?!
INTERROGATING A PRISONER! THIS GIRL IS A FORMER PATRIOT. SHE AND A GROUP OF HER COMPATRIOTS WERE CAPTURED NOSING AROUND THE EDGE OF THE ARMOR.
LET HER GO. SHE'S NOT THE ENEMY.
WHAT?!
WHO ORDERED THIS?
THE GLORIOUS ELECTOR HIMSELF ORDER—
WHO ORDERED THIS?
W-WELL . . . MY COMMANDING OFFICER.
I SEE. TAKE THOSE SHACKLES OFF HER.

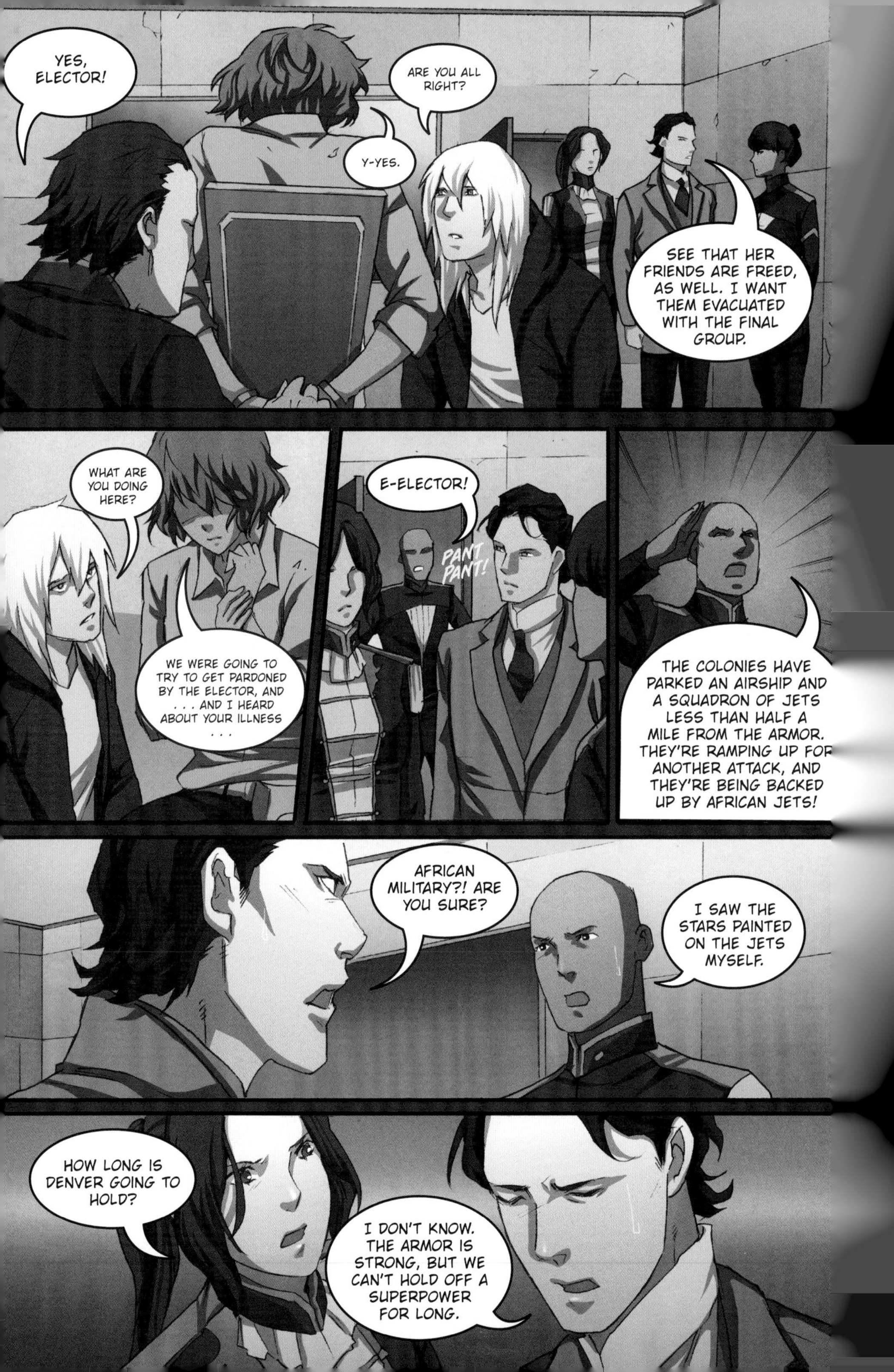
YES, ELECTOR!
ARE YOU ALL RIGHT?
Y-YES.
SEE THAT HER FRIENDS ARE FREED, AS WELL. I WANT THEM EVACUATED WITH THE FINAL GROUP.
WHAT ARE YOU DOING HERE?
WE WERE GOING TO TRY TO GET PARDONED BY THE ELECTOR, AND . . . AND I HEARD ABOUT YOUR ILLNESS . . .
E-ELECTOR!
PANT PANT!
THE COLONIES HAVE PARKED AN AIRSHIP AND A SQUADRON OF JETS LESS THAN HALF A MILE FROM THE ARMOR. THEY'RE RAMPING UP FOR ANOTHER ATTACK, AND THEY'RE BEING BACKED UP BY AFRICAN JETS!
AFRICAN MILITARY?! ARE YOU SURE?
I SAW THE STARS PAINTED ON THE JETS MYSELF.
HOW LONG IS DENVER GOING TO HOLD?
I DON'T KNOW. THE ARMOR IS STRONG, BUT WE CAN'T HOLD OFF A SUPERPOWER FOR LONG.

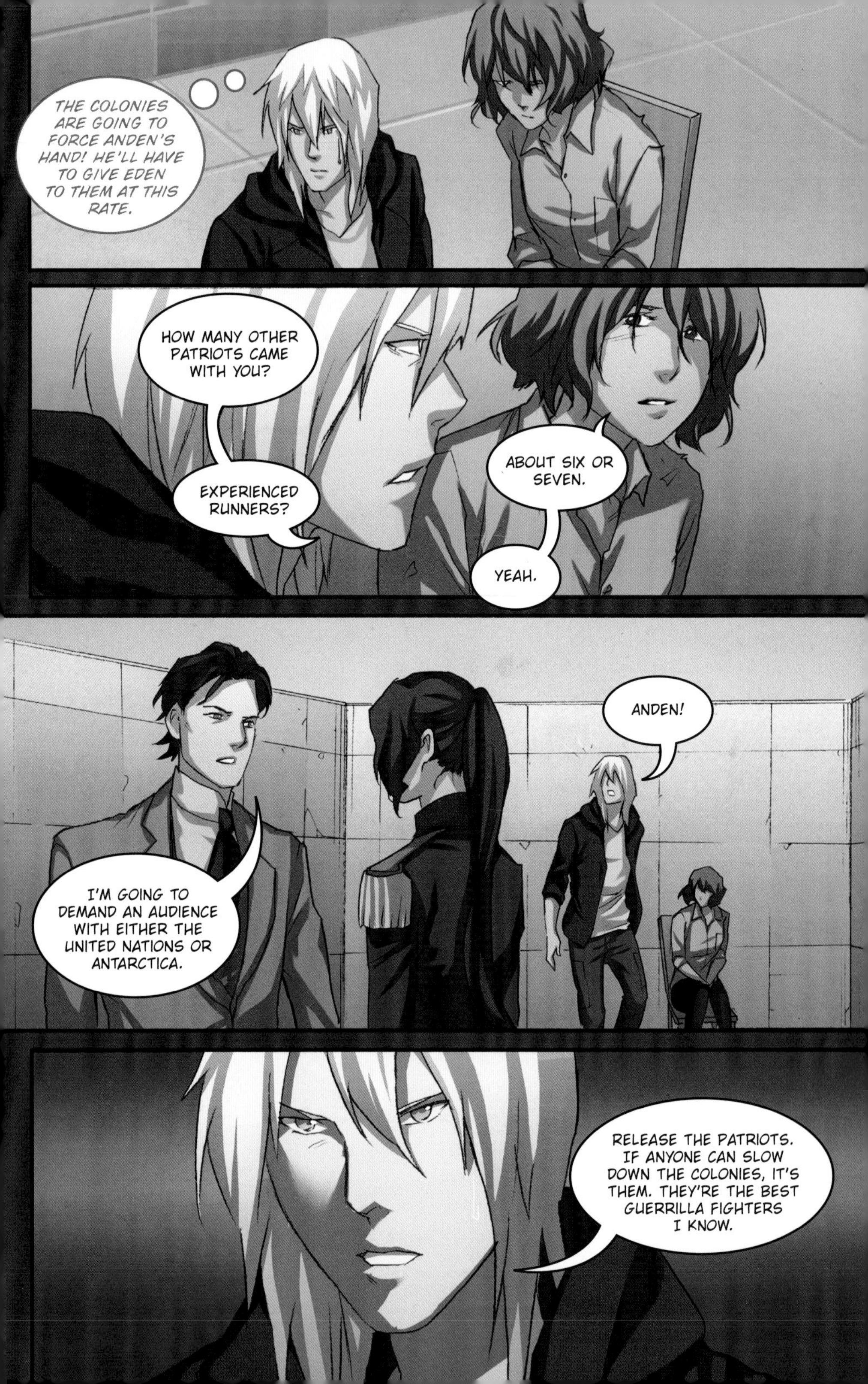
THE COLONIES ARE GOING TO FORCE ANDEN'S HAND! HE'LL HAVE TO GIVE EDEN TO THEM AT THIS RATE.
HOW MANY OTHER PATRIOTS CAME WITH YOU?
EXPERIENCED RUNNERS?
ABOUT SIX OR SEVEN.
YEAH.
ANDEN!
I'M GOING TO DEMAND AN AUDIENCE WITH EITHER THE UNITED NATIONS OR ANTARCTICA.
RELEASE THE PATRIOTS. IF ANYONE CAN SLOW DOWN THE COLONIES, IT'S THEM. THEY'RE THE BEST GUERRILLA FIGHTERS I KNOW.

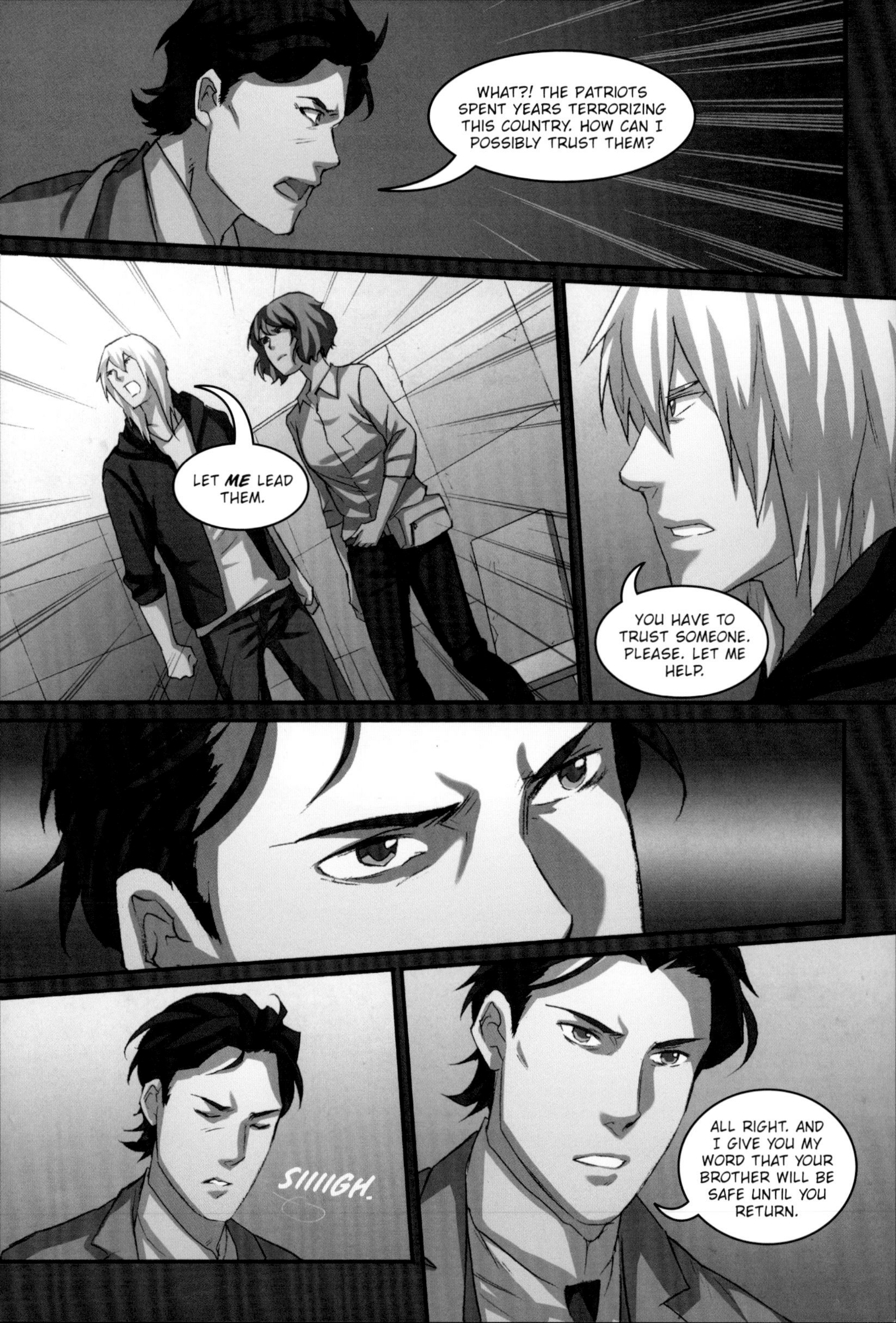
WHAT?! THE PATRIOTS SPENT YEARS TERRORIZING THIS COUNTRY. HOW CAN I POSSIBLY TRUST THEM?
LET *ME* LEAD THEM.
YOU HAVE TO TRUST SOMEONE. PLEASE. LET ME HELP.
SIIIIGH.
ALL RIGHT. AND I GIVE YOU MY WORD THAT YOUR BROTHER WILL BE SAFE UNTIL YOU RETURN.

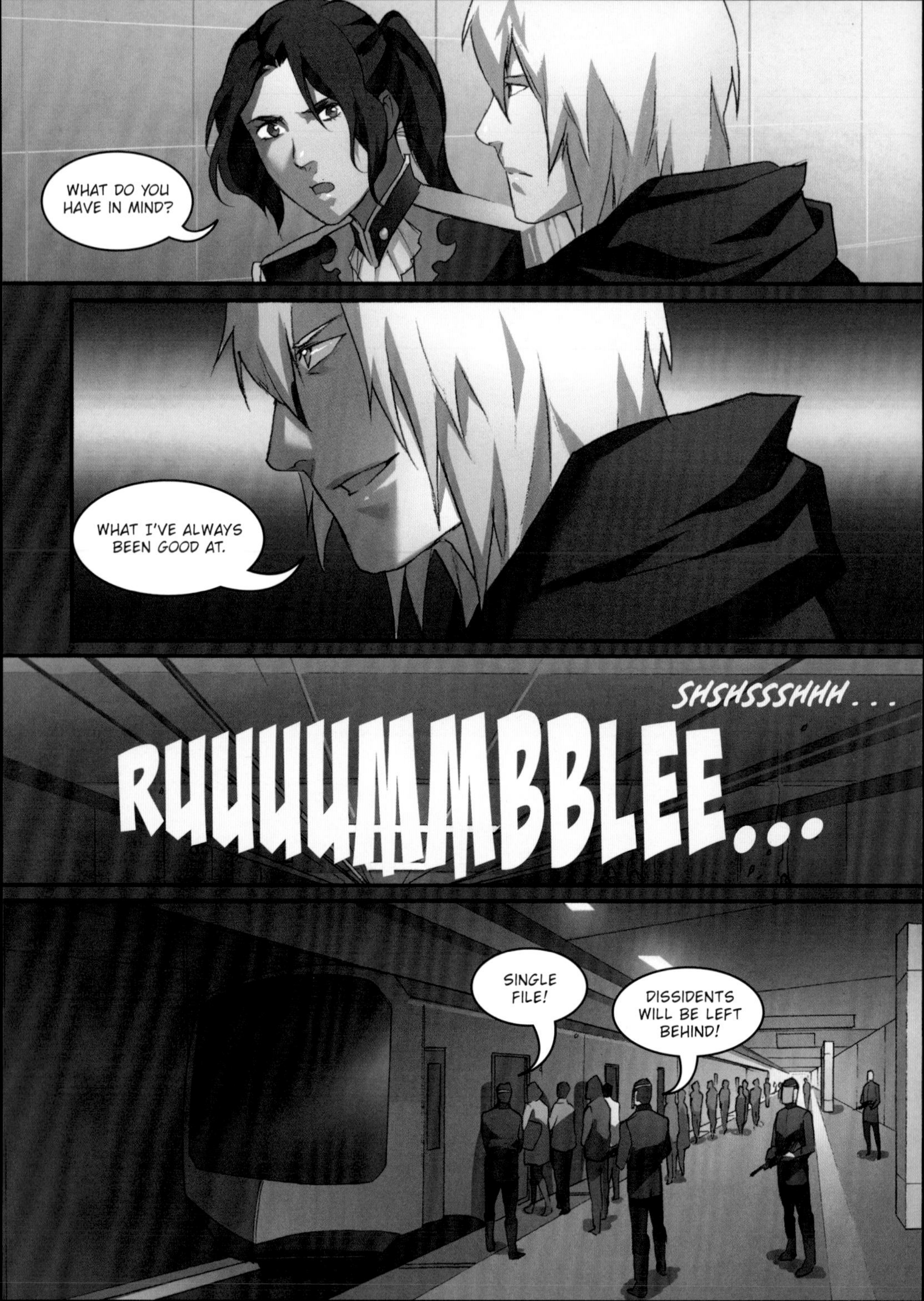
WHAT DO YOU HAVE IN MIND?
WHAT I'VE ALWAYS BEEN GOOD AT.
SHSHSSSHHH . . .
RUUUUMMMBBLEE...
SINGLE FILE!
DISSIDENTS WILL BE LEFT BEHIND!

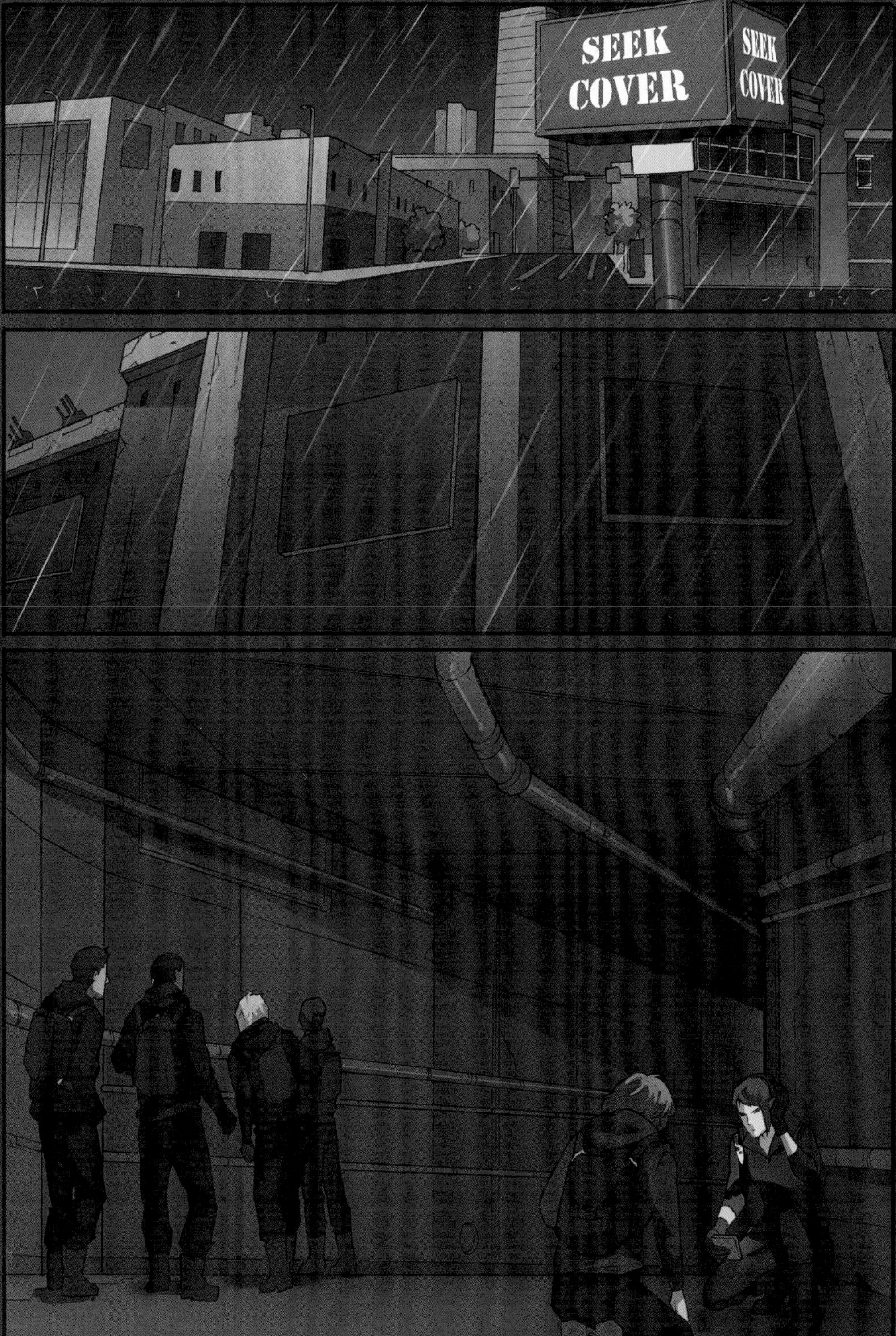
SEEK COVER
SEEK COVER

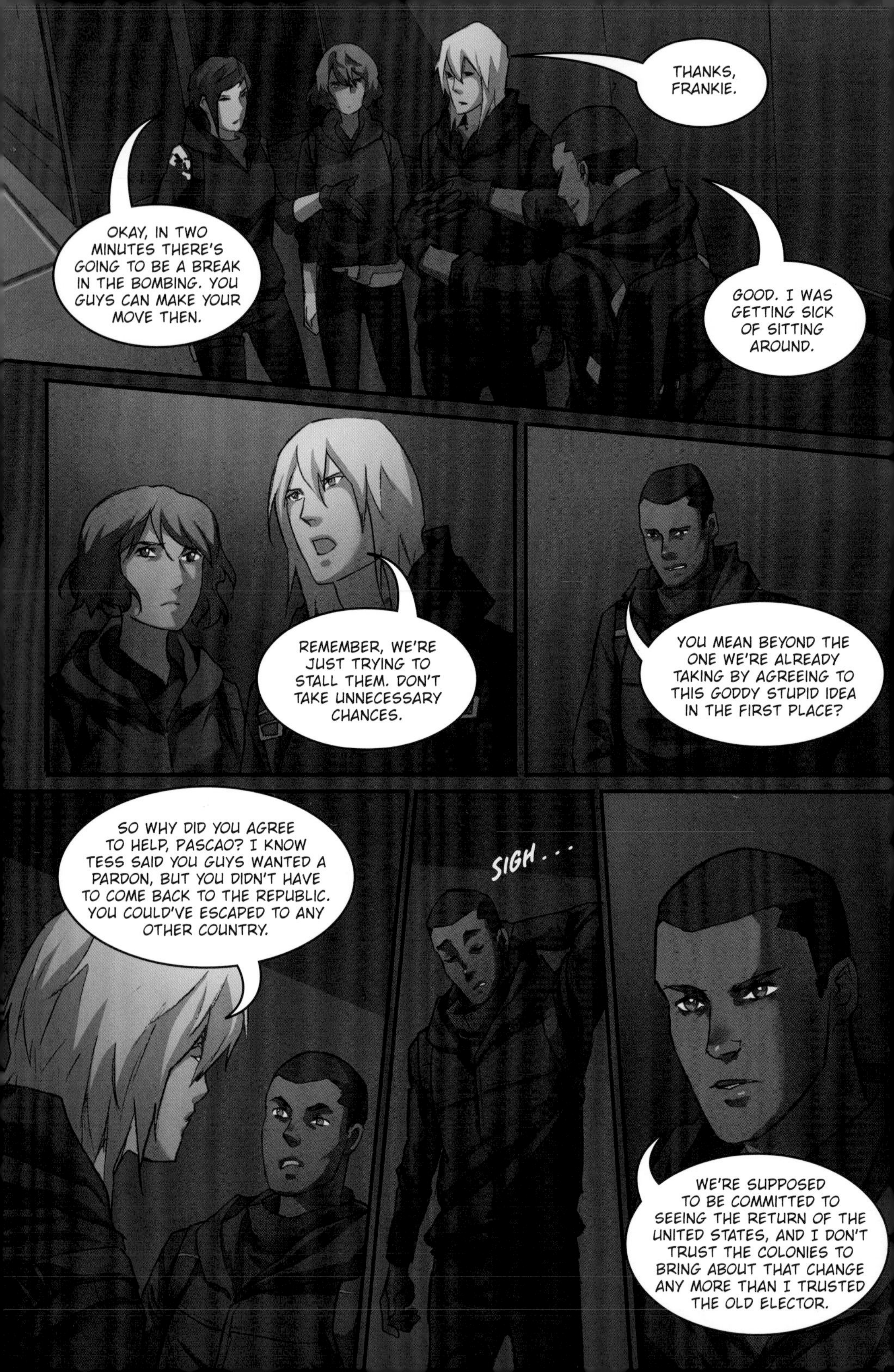
THANKS, FRANKIE.
OKAY, IN TWO MINUTES THERE'S GOING TO BE A BREAK IN THE BOMBING. YOU GUYS CAN MAKE YOUR MOVE THEN.
GOOD. I WAS GETTING SICK OF SITTING AROUND.
REMEMBER, WE'RE JUST TRYING TO STALL THEM. DON'T TAKE UNNECESSARY CHANCES.
YOU MEAN BEYOND THE ONE WE'RE ALREADY TAKING BY AGREEING TO THIS GODDY STUPID IDEA IN THE FIRST PLACE?
SO WHY DID YOU AGREE TO HELP, PASCAO? I KNOW TESS SAID YOU GUYS WANTED A PARDON, BUT YOU DIDN'T HAVE TO COME BACK TO THE REPUBLIC. YOU COULD'VE ESCAPED TO ANY OTHER COUNTRY.
SIGH...
WE'RE SUPPOSED TO BE COMMITTED TO SEEING THE RETURN OF THE UNITED STATES, AND I DON'T TRUST THE COLONIES TO BRING ABOUT THAT CHANGE ANY MORE THAN I TRUSTED THE OLD ELECTOR.

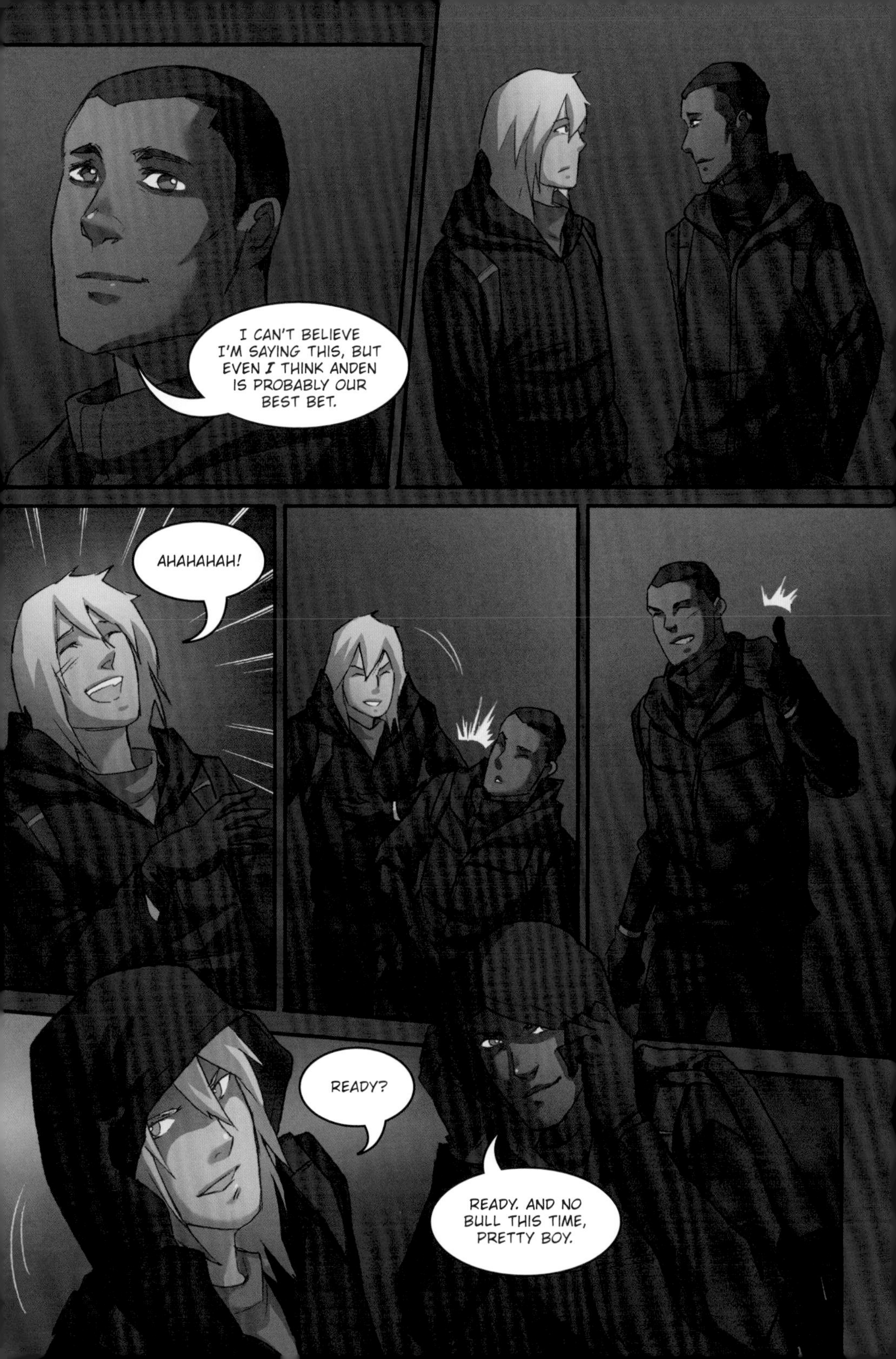
I CAN'T BELIEVE I'M SAYING THIS, BUT EVEN *I* THINK ANDEN IS PROBABLY OUR BEST BET.
AHAHAHAH!
READY?
READY. AND NO BULL THIS TIME, PRETTY BOY.

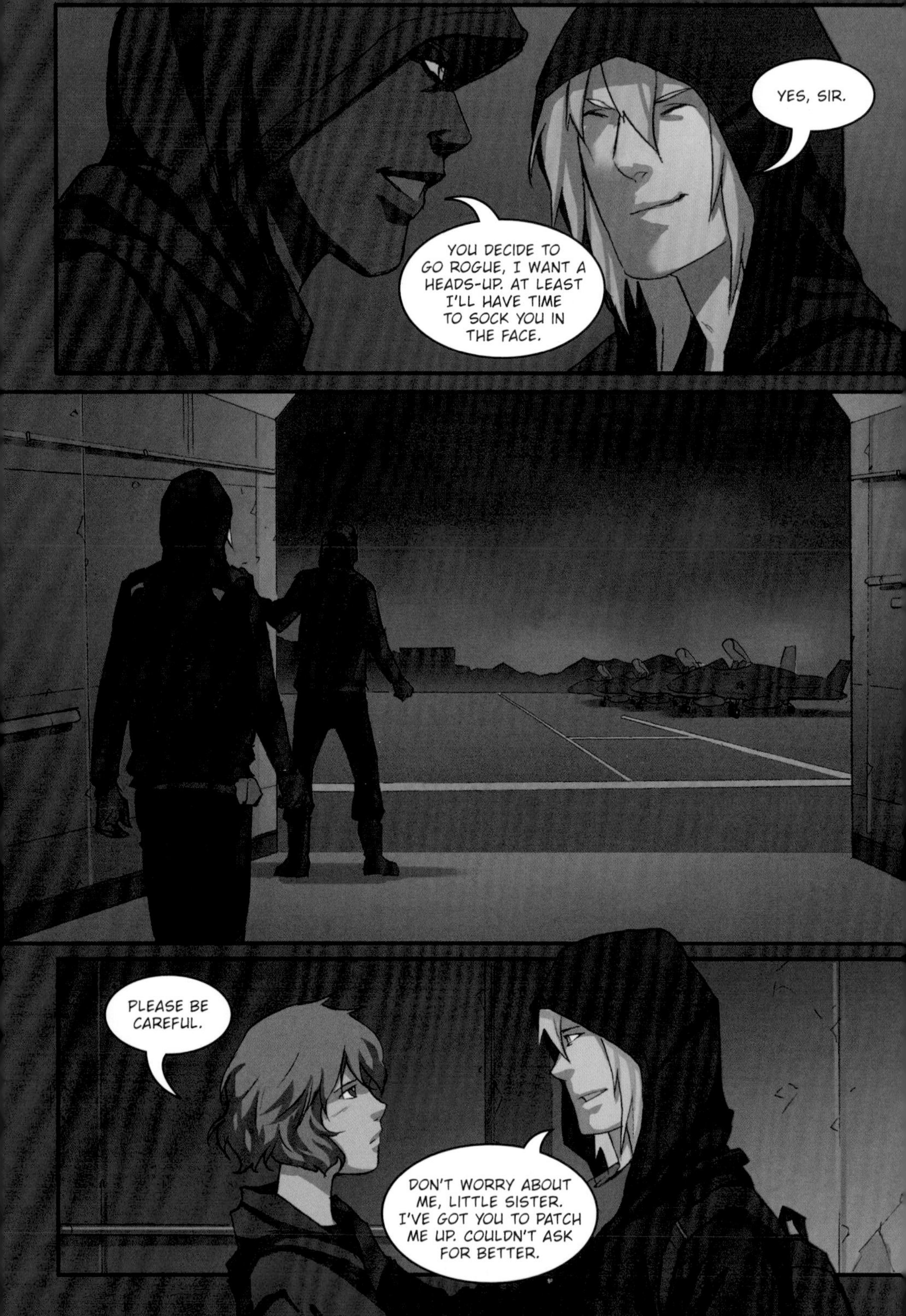
YES, SIR.
YOU DECIDE TO GO ROGUE, I WANT A HEADS-UP. AT LEAST I'LL HAVE TIME TO SOCK YOU IN THE FACE.
PLEASE BE CAREFUL.
DON'T WORRY ABOUT ME, LITTLE SISTER. I'VE GOT YOU TO PATCH ME UP. COULDN'T ASK FOR BETTER.

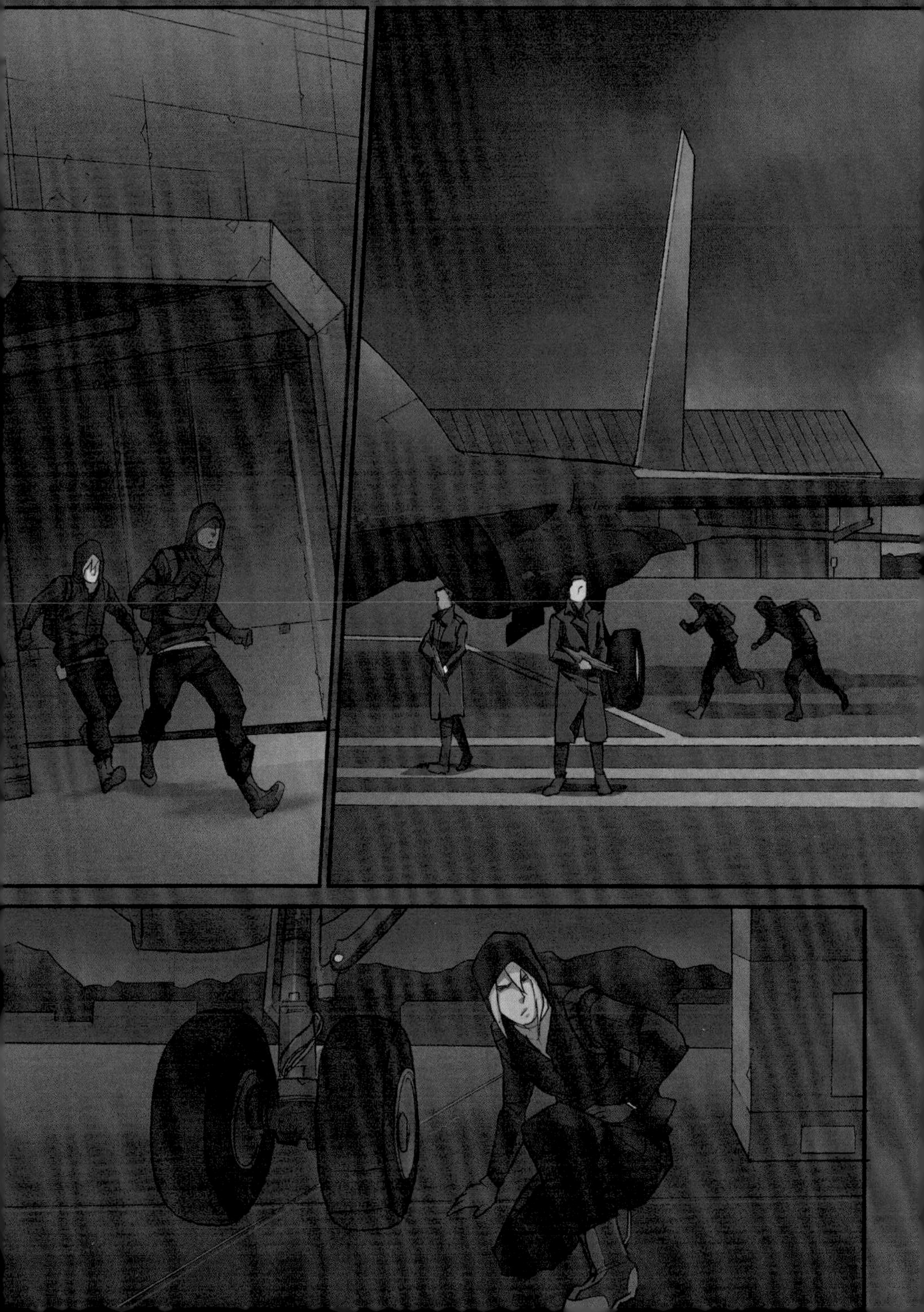

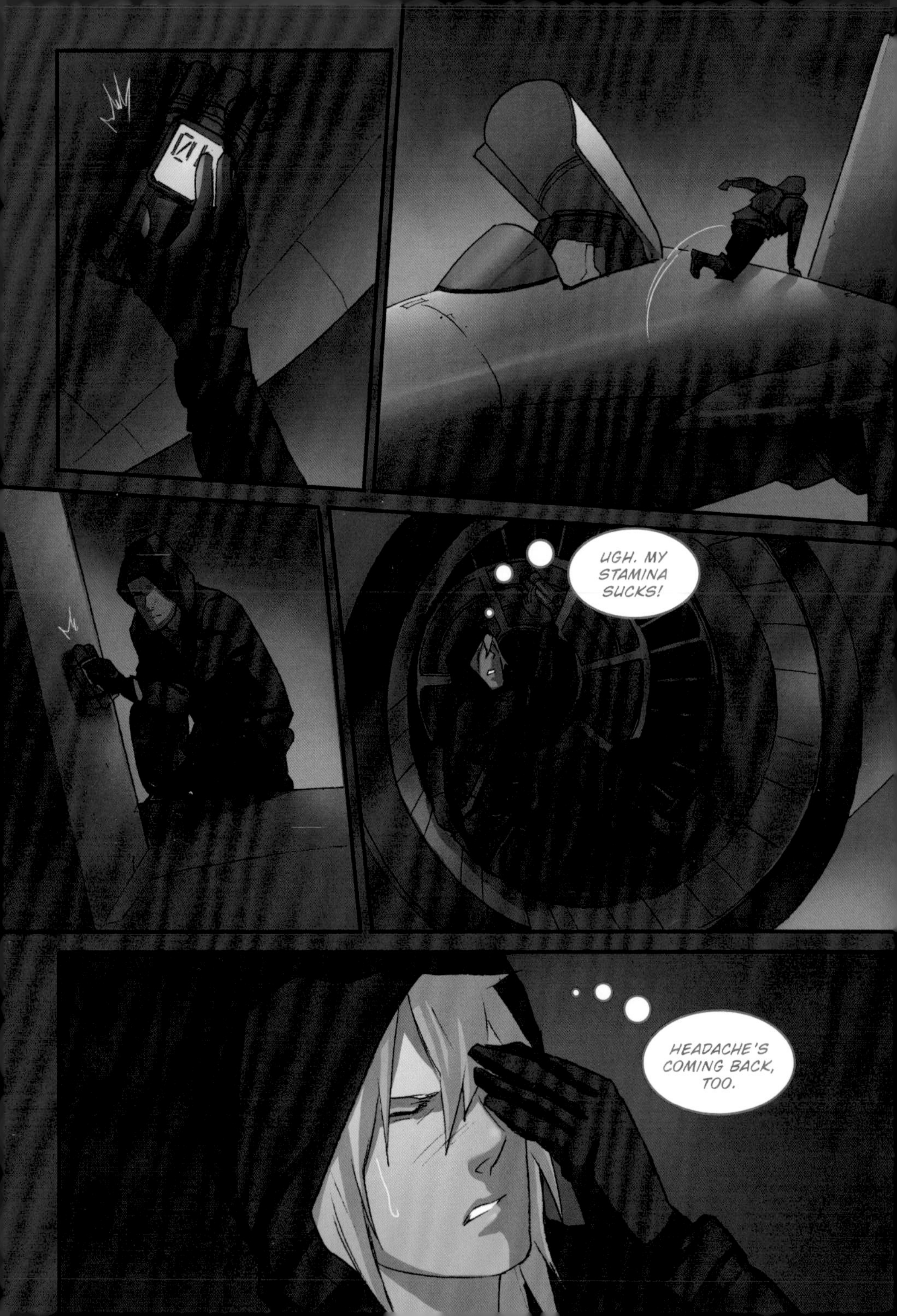
UGH. MY STAMINA SUCKS!
HEADACHE'S COMING BACK, TOO.

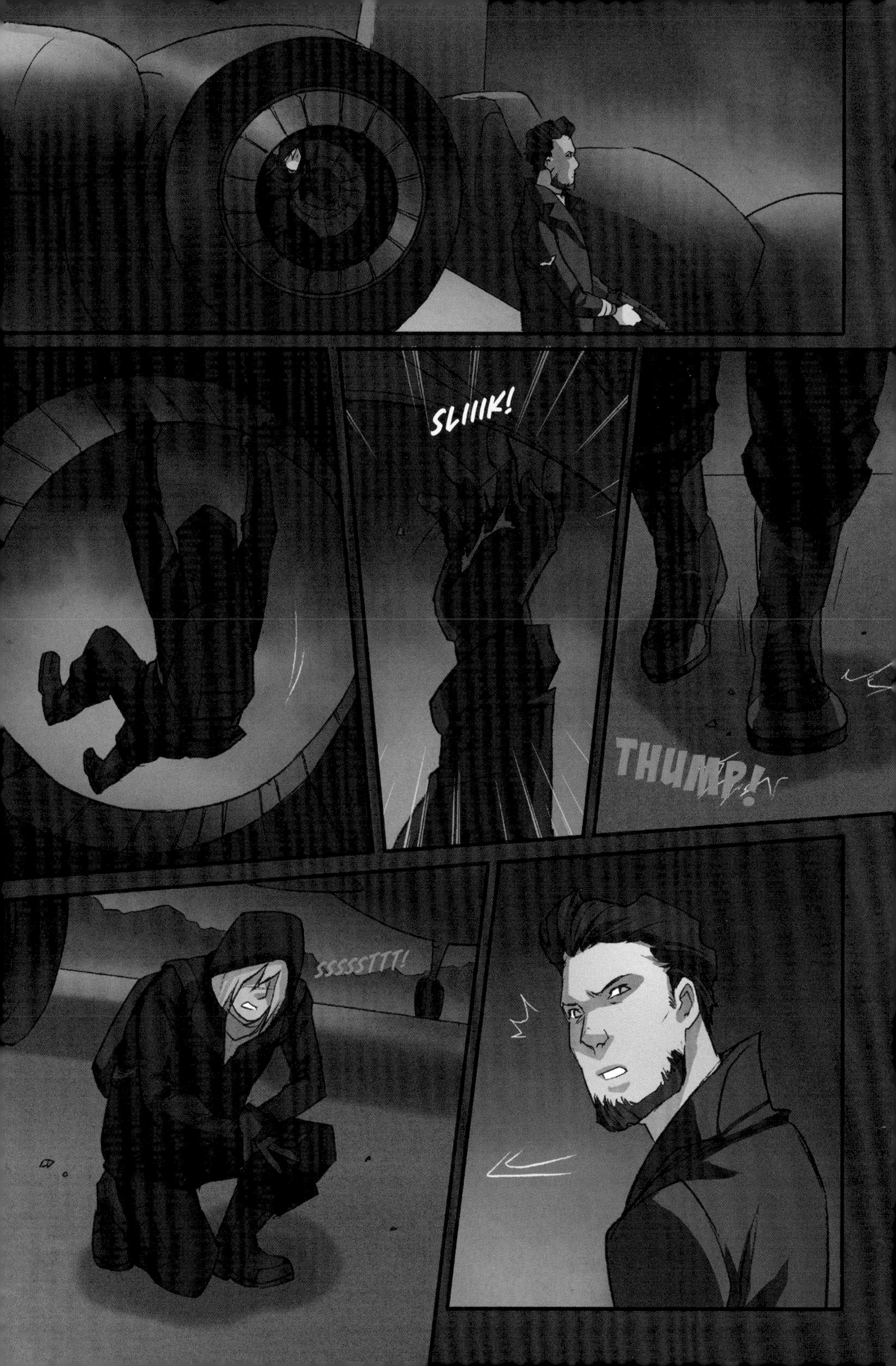
SLIIIK!
THUMP!
SSSSSTTT!

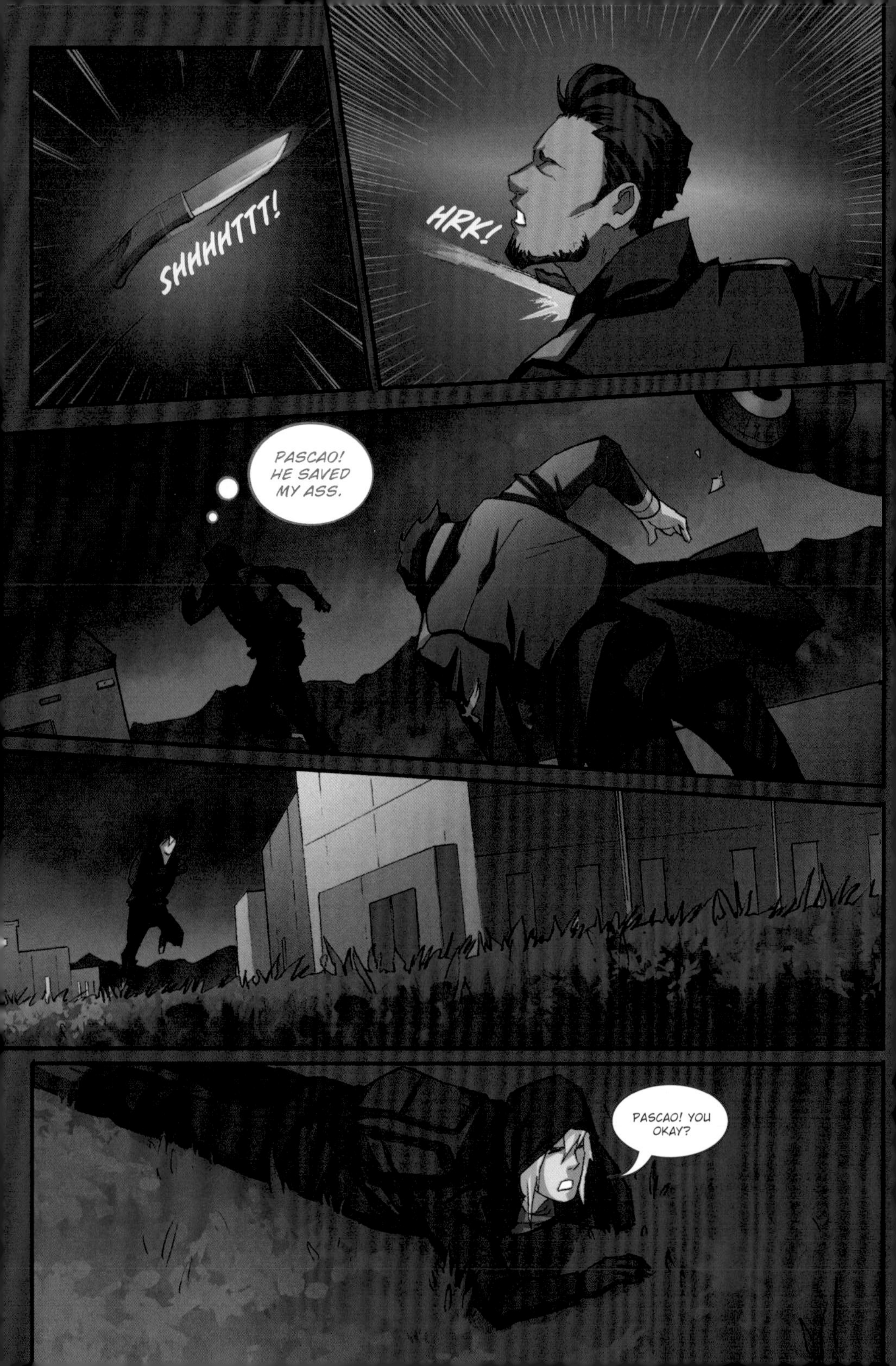
SHHHHTTT!
HRK!
PASCAO! HE SAVED MY ASS.
PASCAO! YOU OKAY?

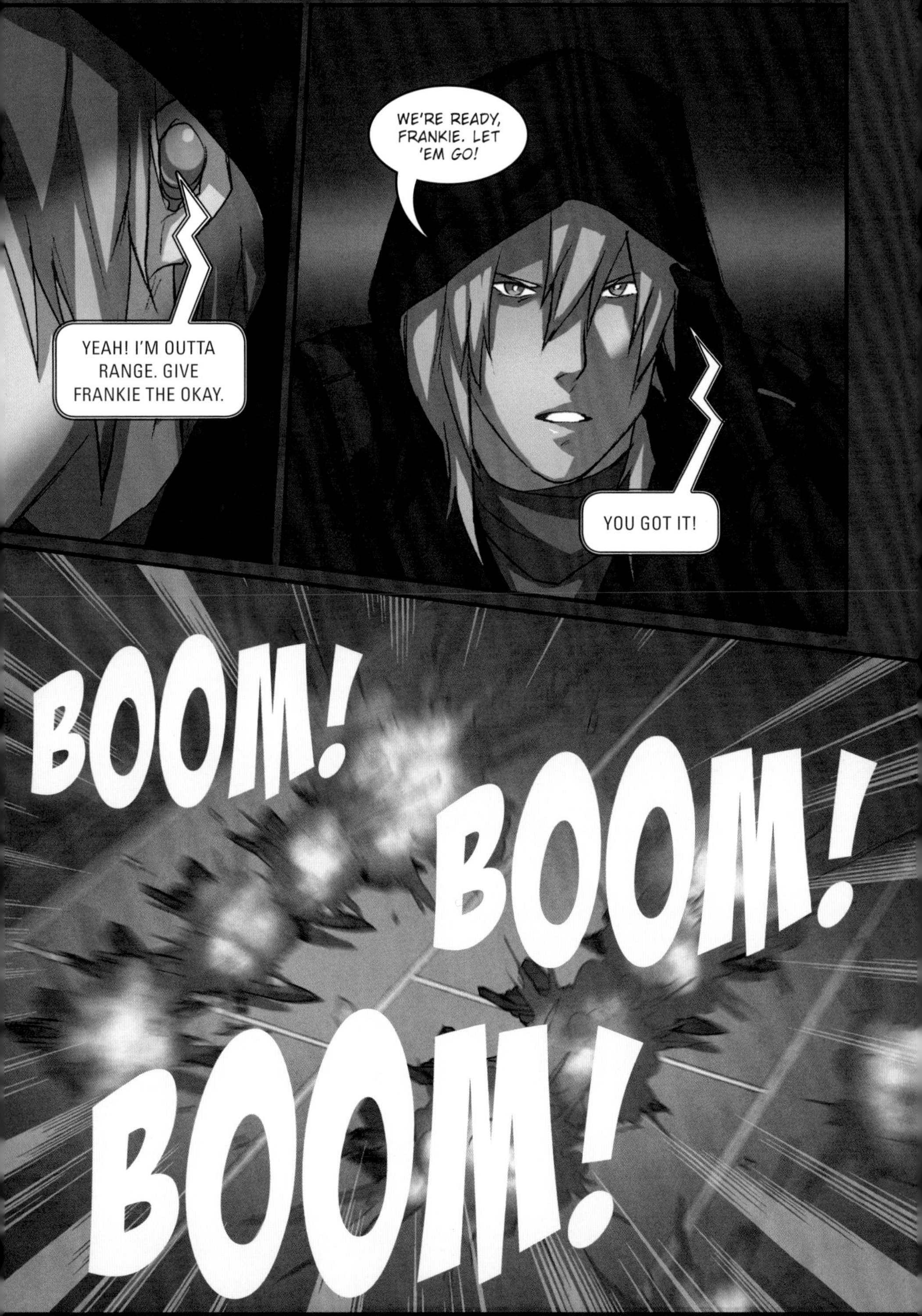
WE'RE READY, FRANKIE. LET 'EM GO!
YEAH! I'M OUTTA RANGE. GIVE FRANKIE THE OKAY.
YOU GOT IT!
BOOM!
BOOM!
BOOM!

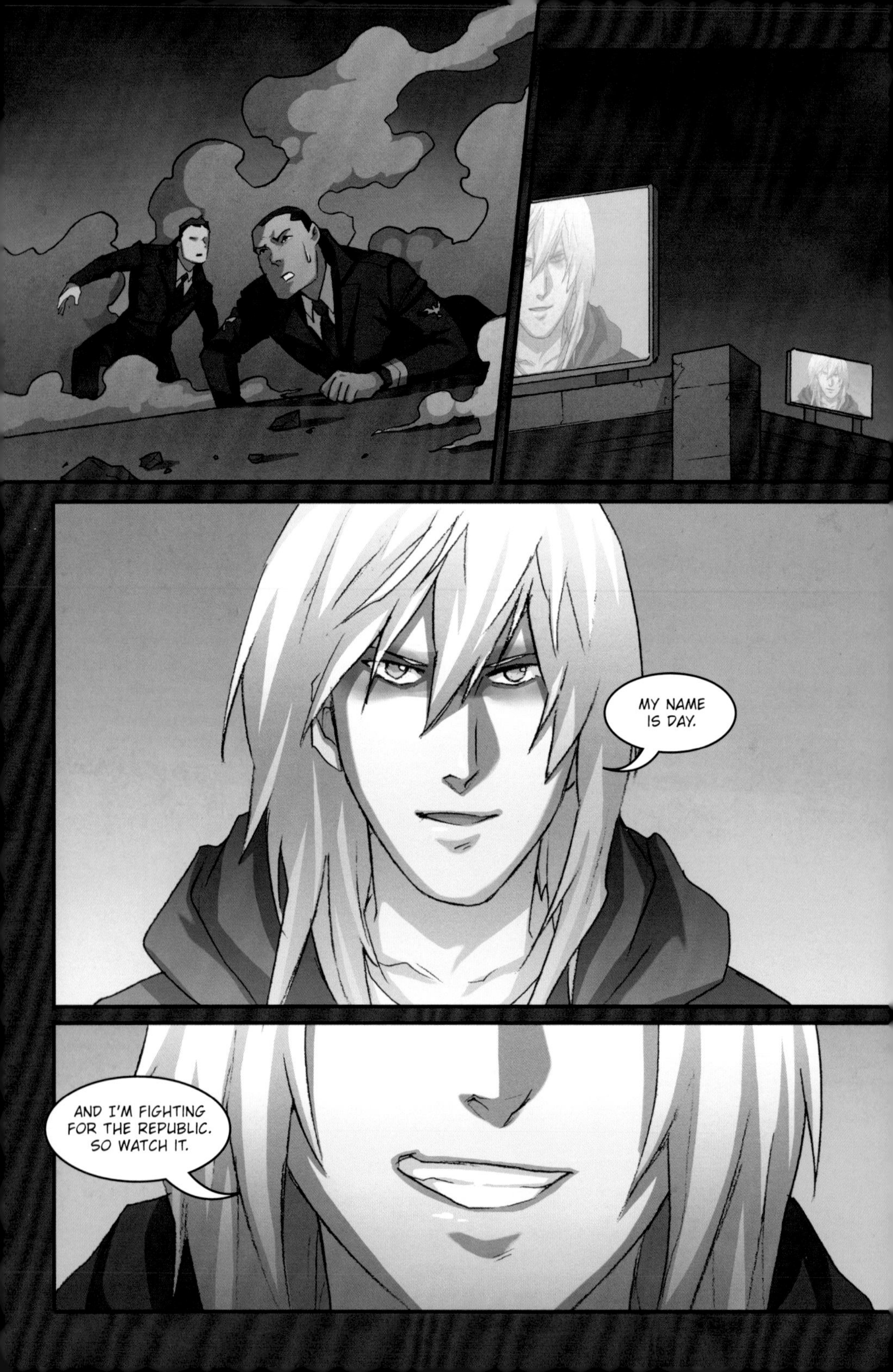
MY NAME IS DAY.
AND I'M FIGHTING FOR THE REPUBLIC. SO WATCH IT.

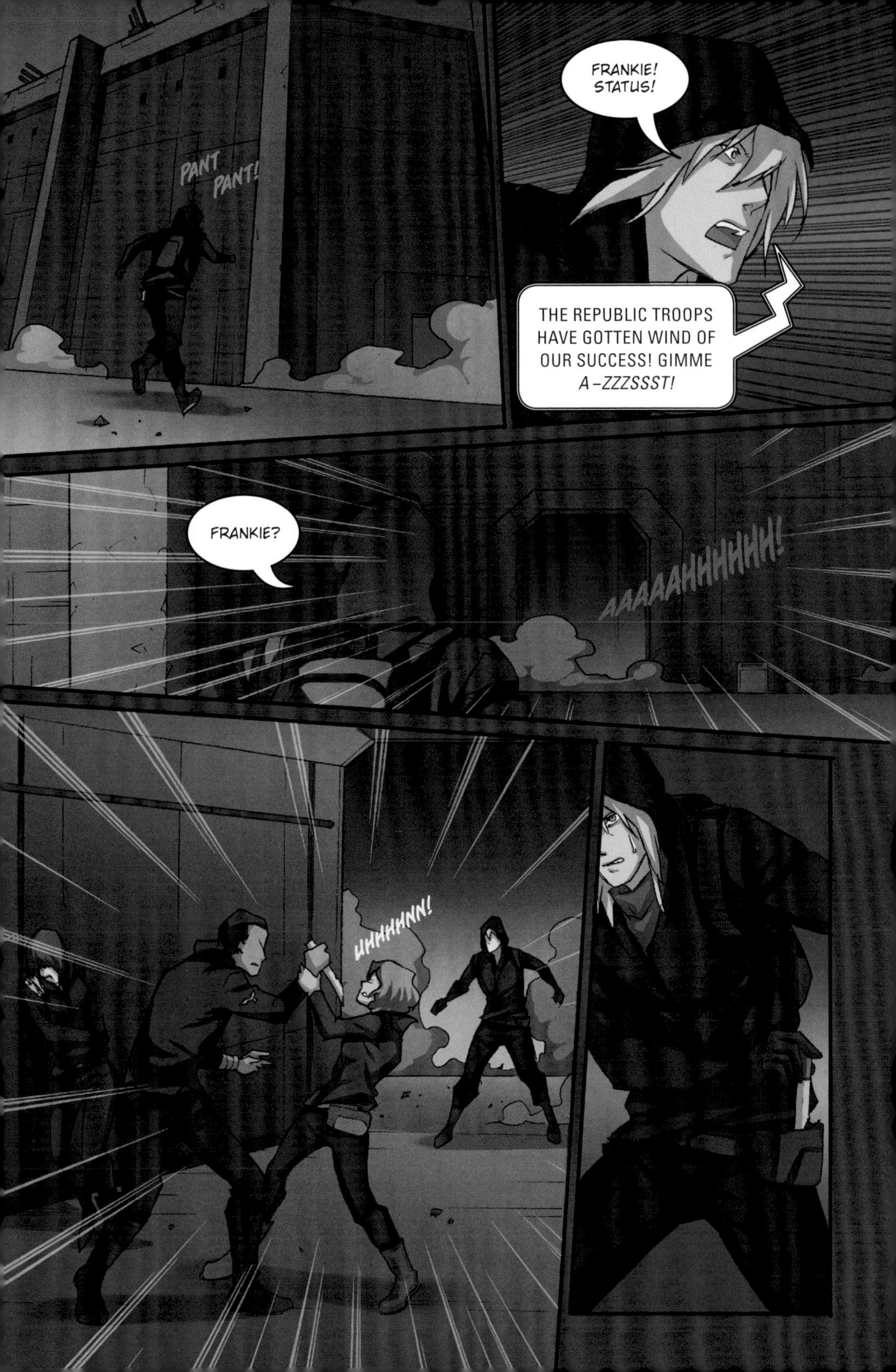
PANT PANT!
FRANKIE! STATUS!
THE REPUBLIC TROOPS HAVE GOTTEN WIND OF OUR SUCCESS! GIMME A–ZZZSSST!
FRANKIE?
AAAAAHHHHHHH!
UHHHHNN!

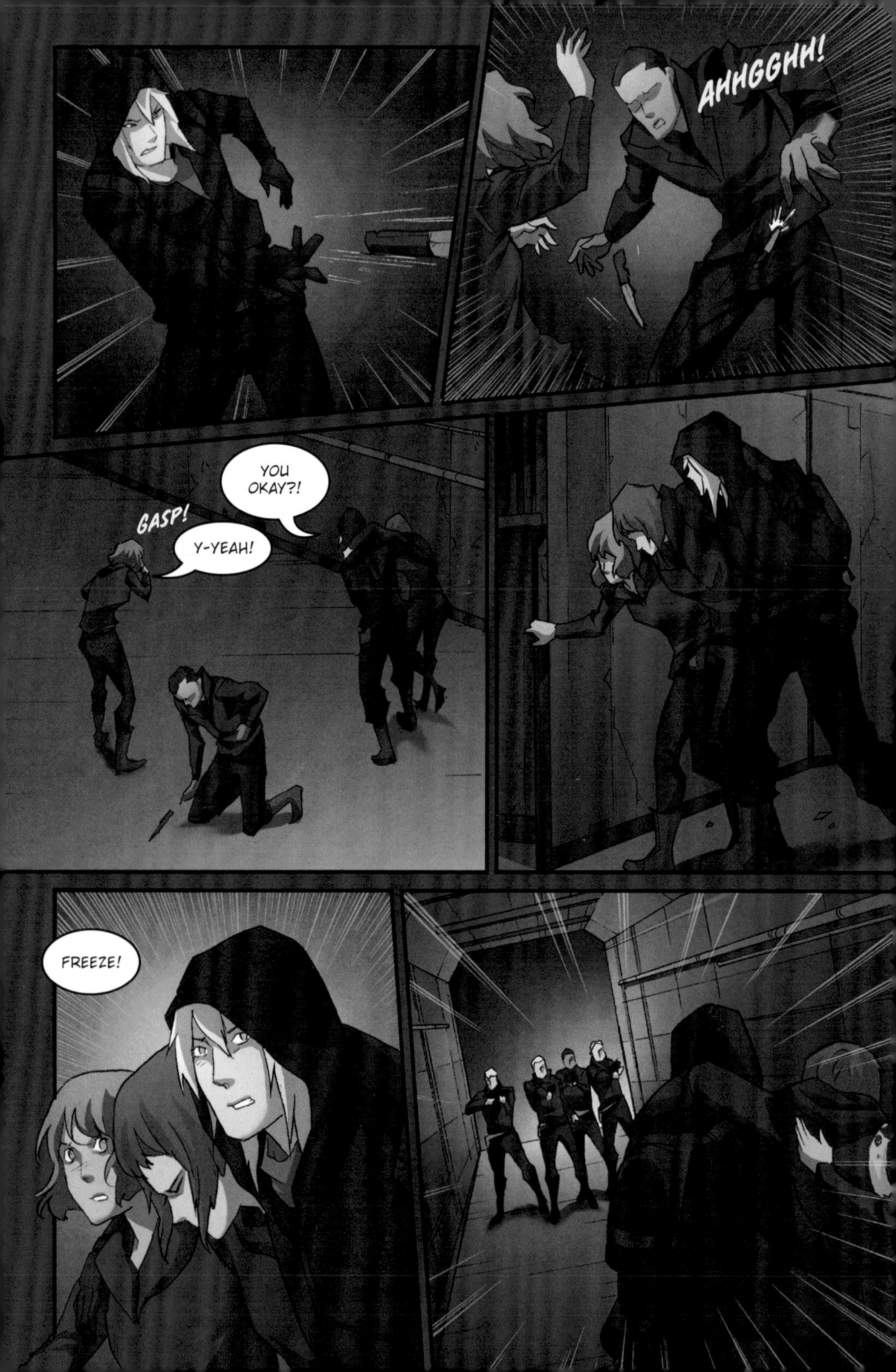
AHHGGHH!
GASP!
YOU OKAY?!
Y-YEAH!
FREEZE!

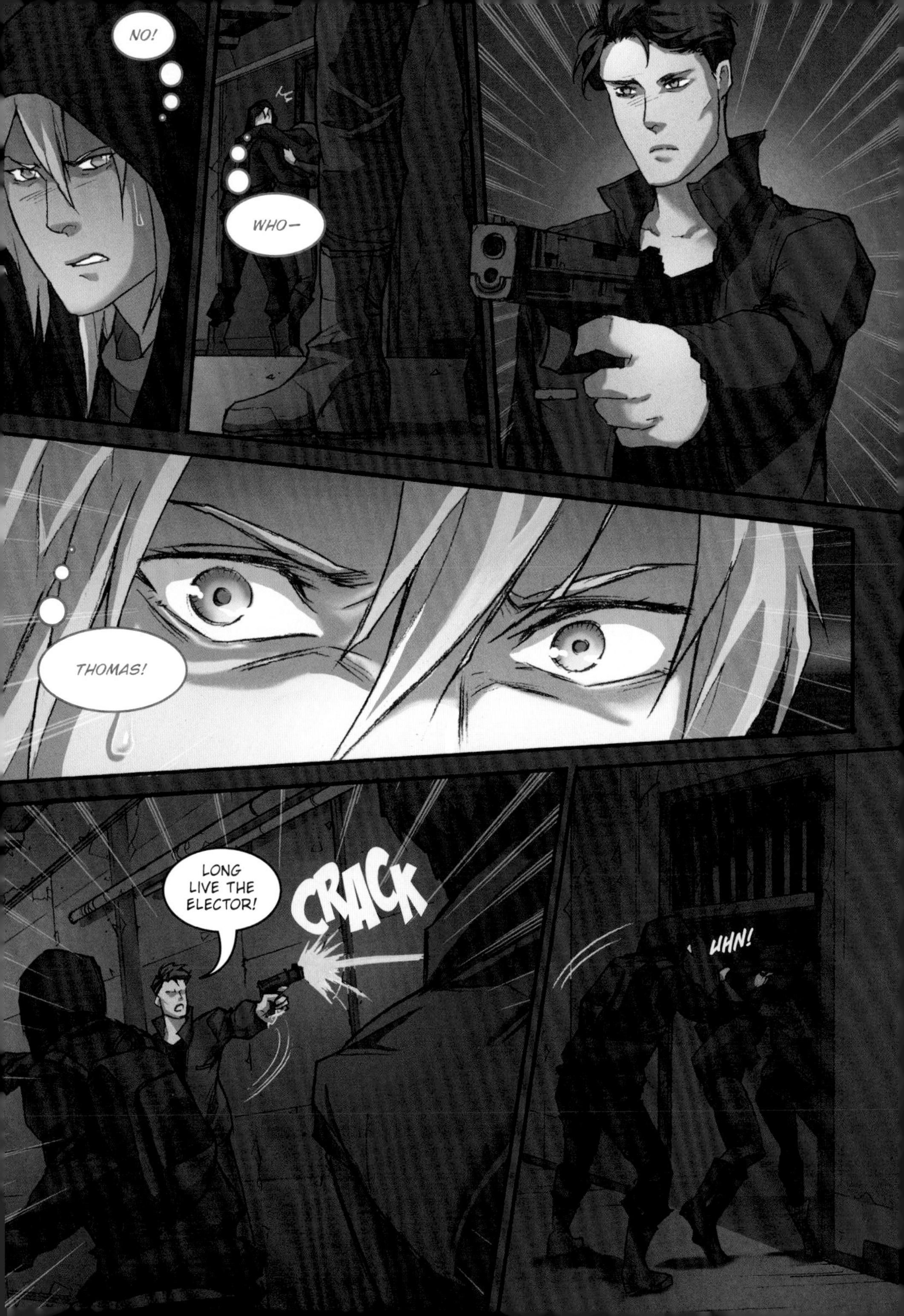
NO!
WHO—
THOMAS!
LONG LIVE THE ELECTOR!
CRACK
UHN!

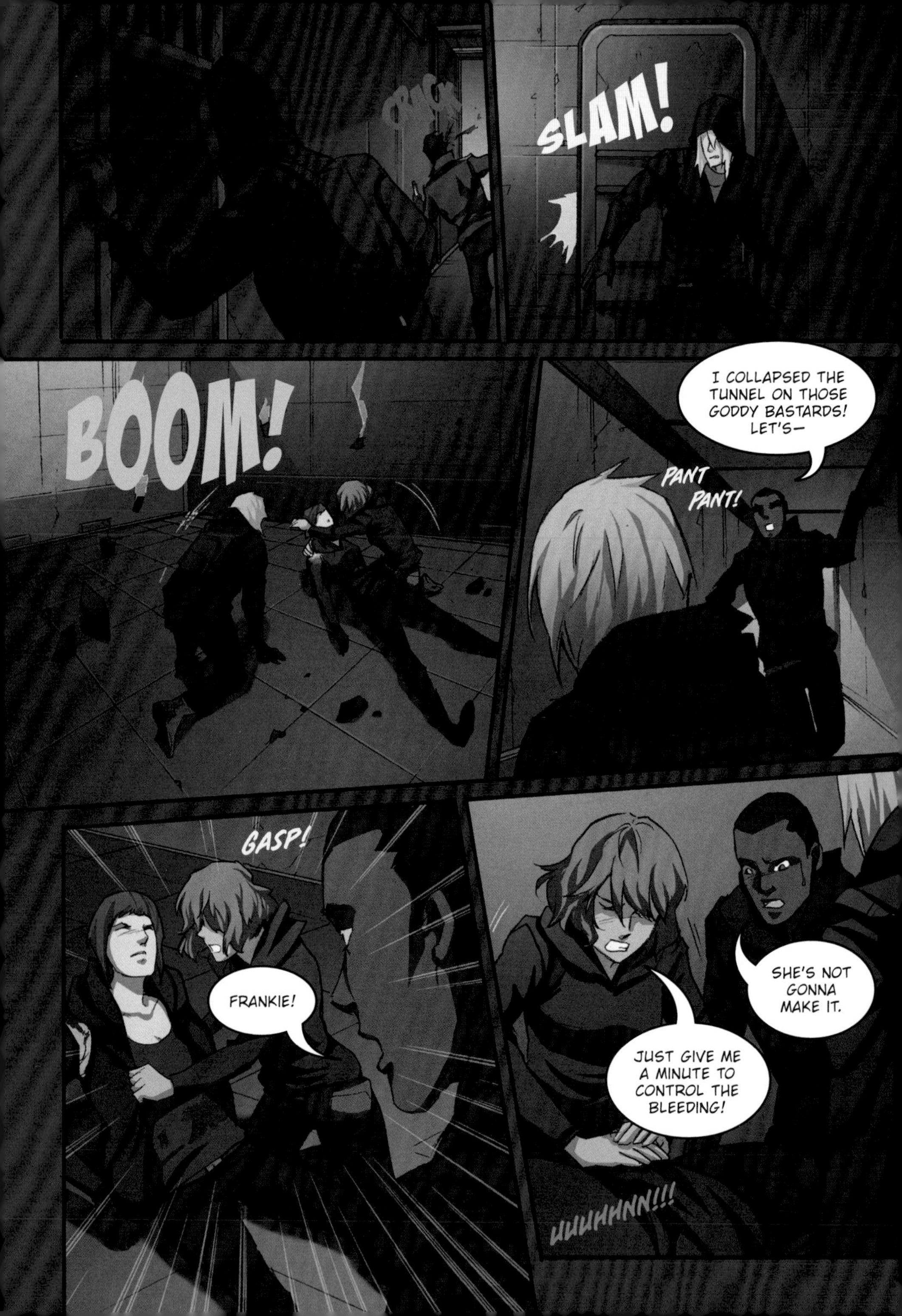
CRACK
SLAM!
BOOM!
PANT PANT!
I COLLAPSED THE TUNNEL ON THOSE GODDY BASTARDS! LET'S—
GASP!
FRANKIE!
SHE'S NOT GONNA MAKE IT.
JUST GIVE ME A MINUTE TO CONTROL THE BLEEDING!
UUUHHNN!!!

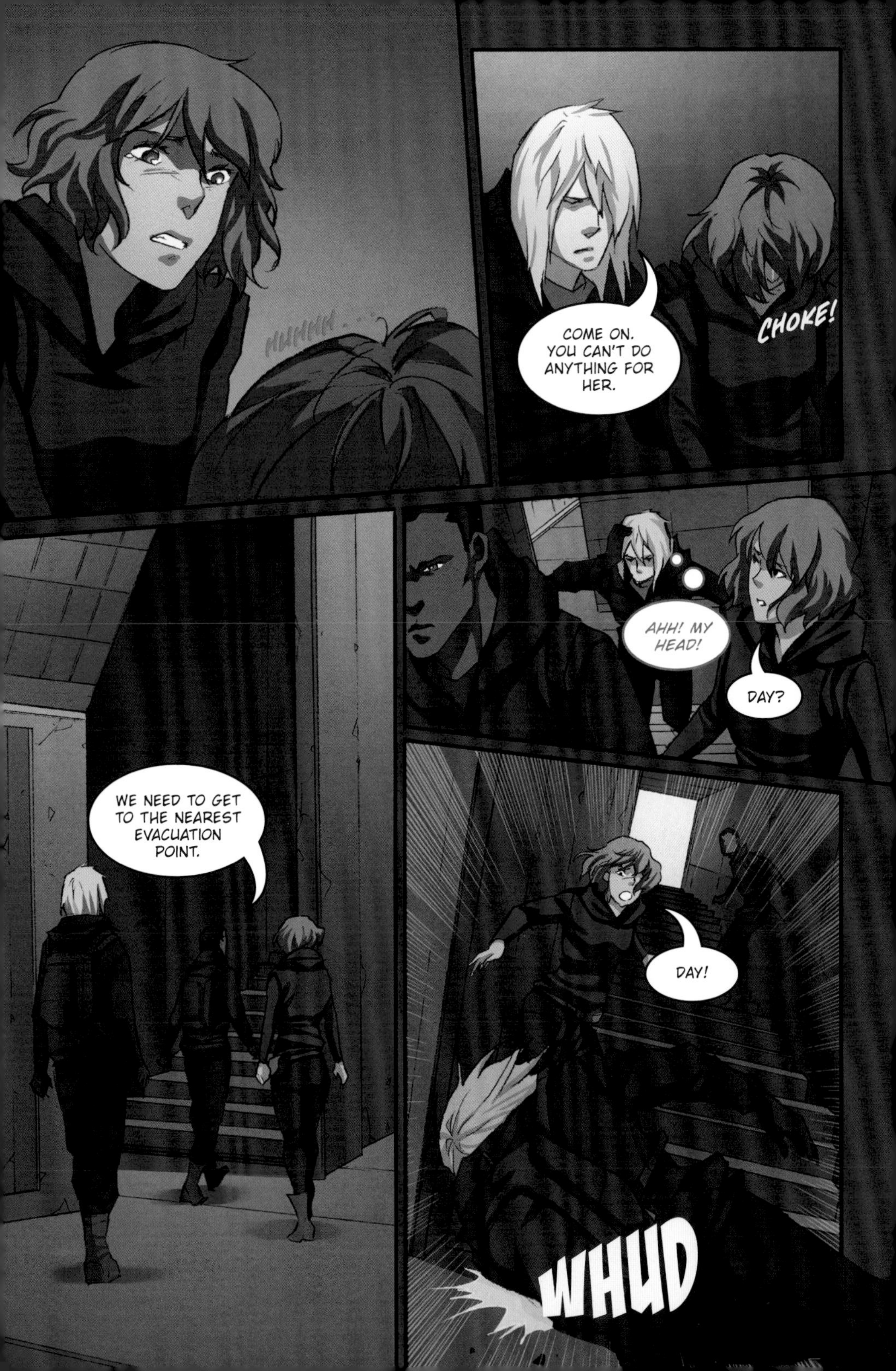
MMMMM...
COME ON. YOU CAN'T DO ANYTHING FOR HER.
CHOKE!
WE NEED TO GET TO THE NEAREST EVACUATION POINT.
AHH! MY HEAD!
DAY?
DAY!
WHUD

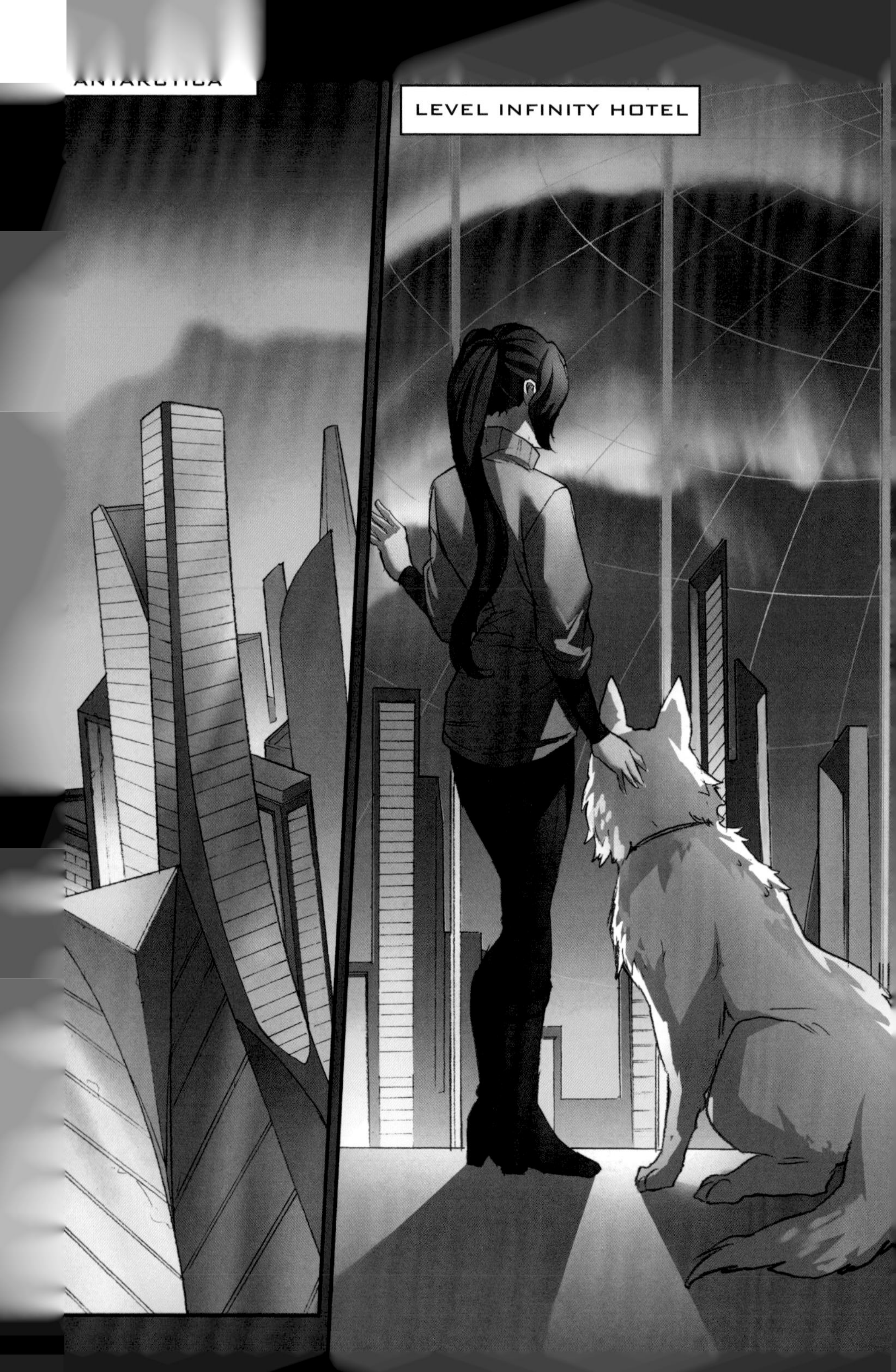
LEVEL INFINITY HOTEL

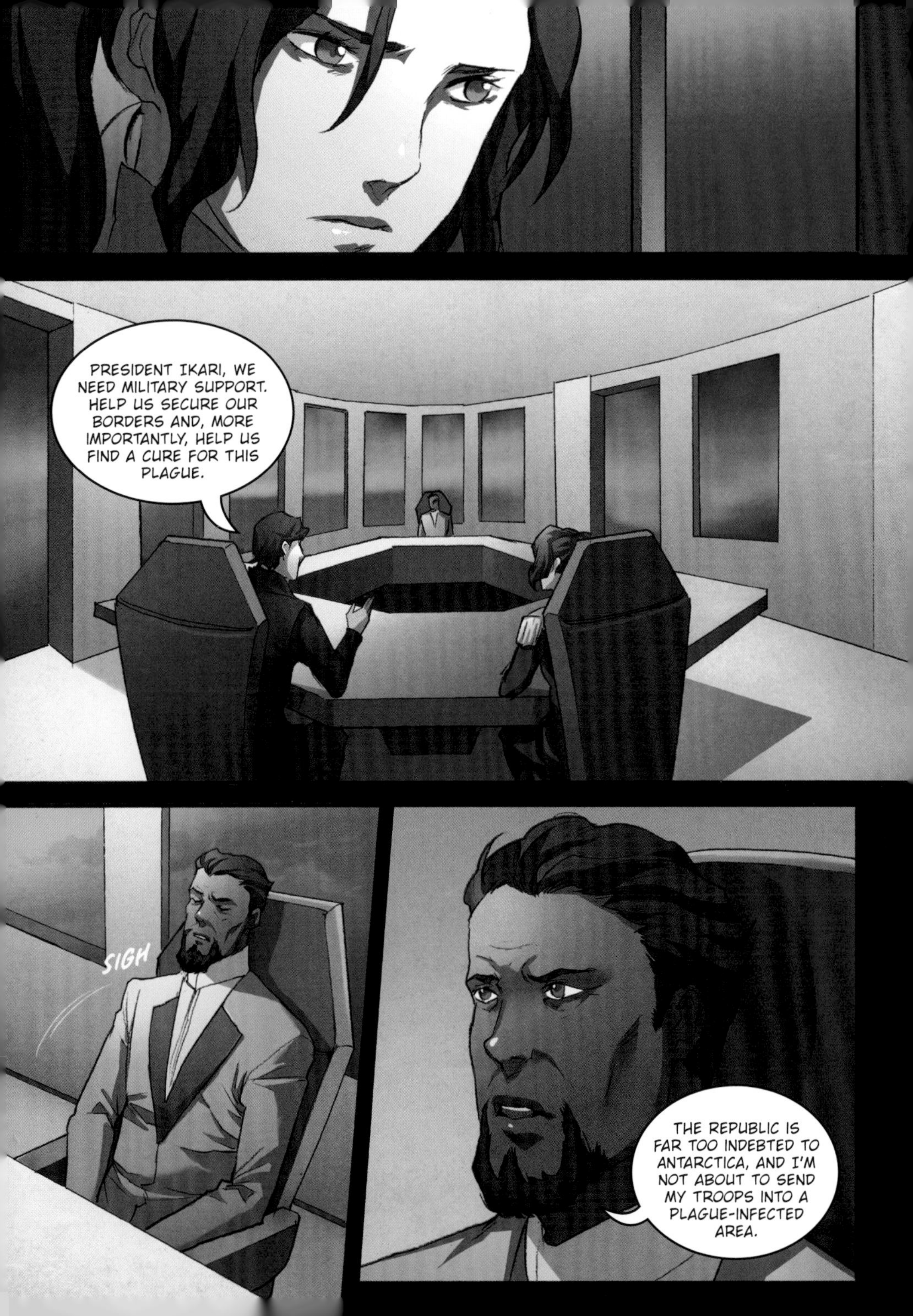
PRESIDENT IKARI, WE NEED MILITARY SUPPORT. HELP US SECURE OUR BORDERS AND, MORE IMPORTANTLY, HELP US FIND A CURE FOR THIS PLAGUE.
SIGH
THE REPUBLIC IS FAR TOO INDEBTED TO ANTARCTICA, AND I'M NOT ABOUT TO SEND MY TROOPS INTO A PLAGUE-INFECTED AREA.

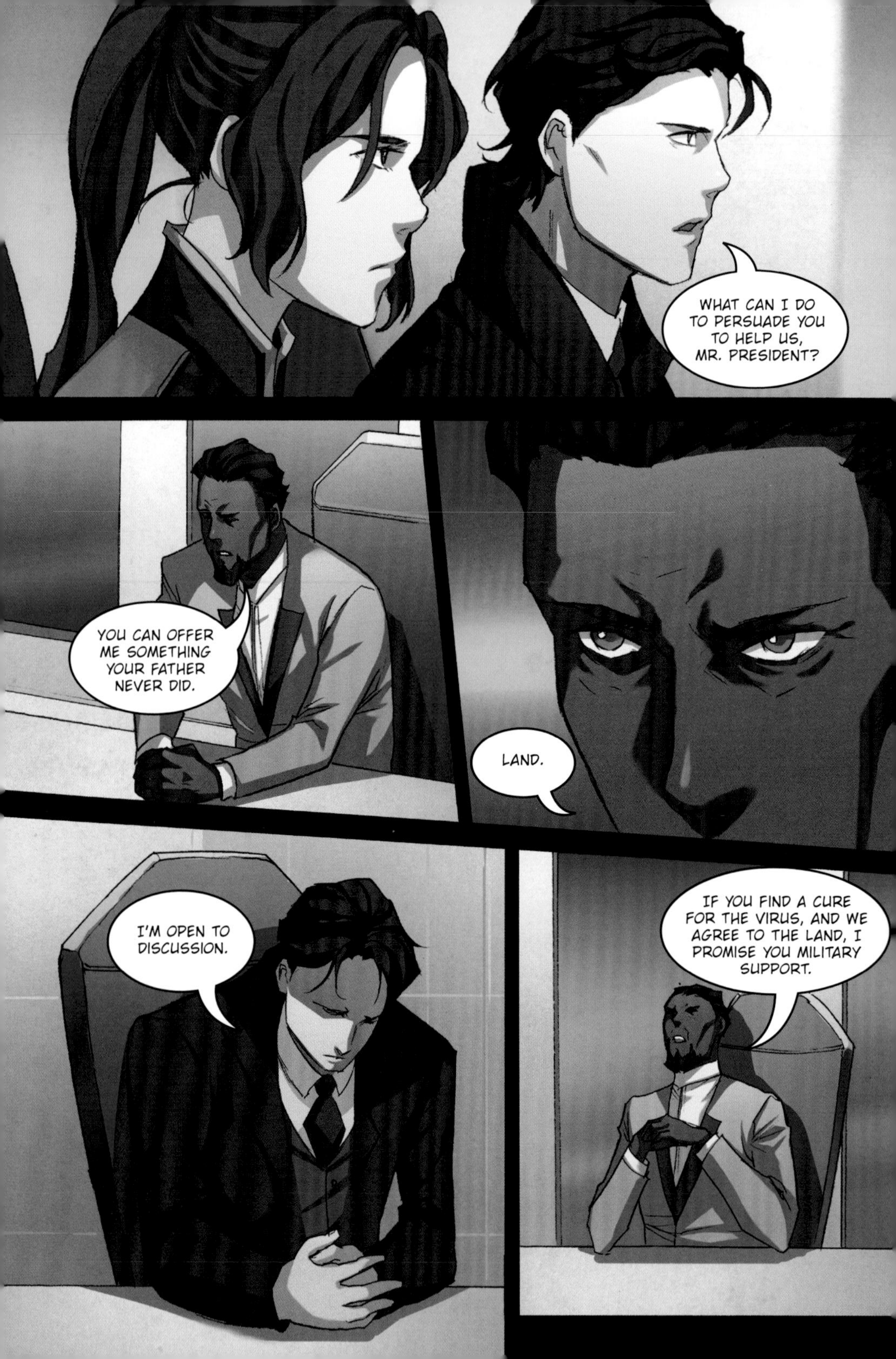
WHAT CAN I DO TO PERSUADE YOU TO HELP US, MR. PRESIDENT?
YOU CAN OFFER ME SOMETHING YOUR FATHER NEVER DID.
LAND.
I'M OPEN TO DISCUSSION.
IF YOU FIND A CURE FOR THE VIRUS, AND WE AGREE TO THE LAND, I PROMISE YOU MILITARY SUPPORT.

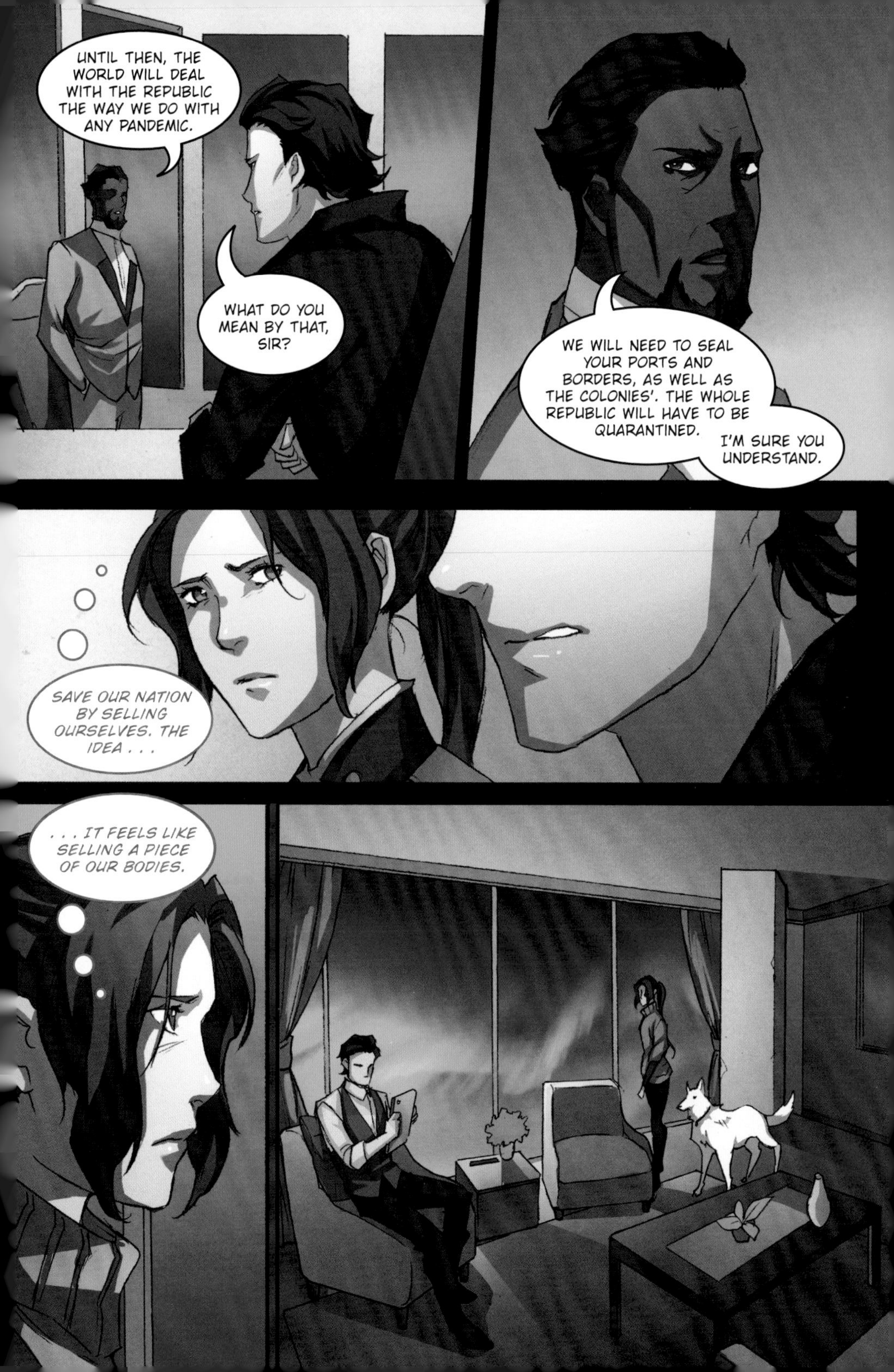
UNTIL THEN, THE WORLD WILL DEAL WITH THE REPUBLIC THE WAY WE DO WITH ANY PANDEMIC.
WHAT DO YOU MEAN BY THAT, SIR?
WE WILL NEED TO SEAL YOUR PORTS AND BORDERS, AS WELL AS THE COLONIES'. THE WHOLE REPUBLIC WILL HAVE TO BE QUARANTINED.
I'M SURE YOU UNDERSTAND.
SAVE OUR NATION BY SELLING OURSELVES. THE IDEA . . .
. . . IT FEELS LIKE SELLING A PIECE OF OUR BODIES.

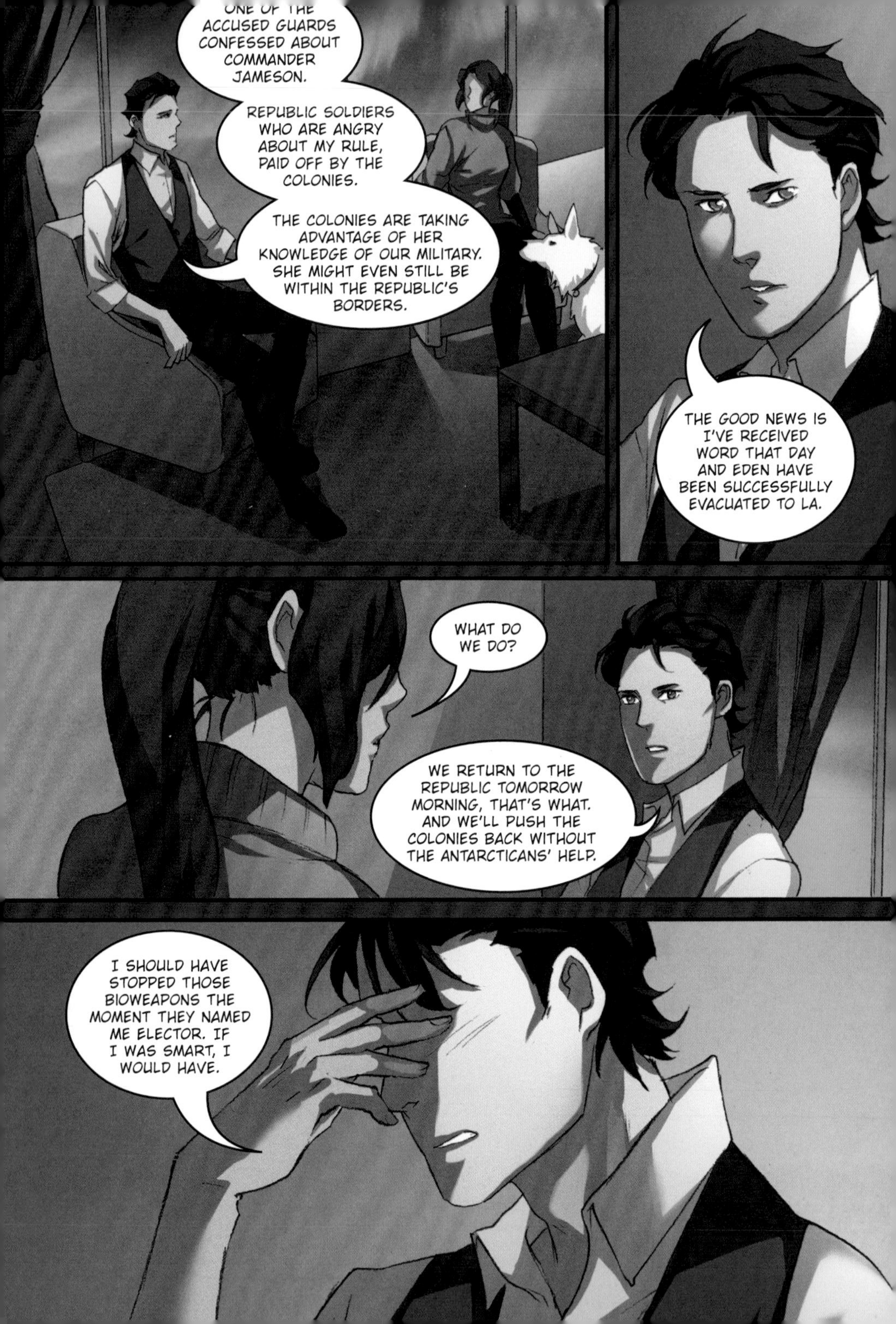
ONE OF THE ACCUSED GUARDS CONFESSED ABOUT COMMANDER JAMESON.
REPUBLIC SOLDIERS WHO ARE ANGRY ABOUT MY RULE, PAID OFF BY THE COLONIES.
THE COLONIES ARE TAKING ADVANTAGE OF HER KNOWLEDGE OF OUR MILITARY. SHE MIGHT EVEN STILL BE WITHIN THE REPUBLIC'S BORDERS.
THE GOOD NEWS IS I'VE RECEIVED WORD THAT DAY AND EDEN HAVE BEEN SUCCESSFULLY EVACUATED TO LA.
WHAT DO WE DO?
WE RETURN TO THE REPUBLIC TOMORROW MORNING, THAT'S WHAT. AND WE'LL PUSH THE COLONIES BACK WITHOUT THE ANTARCTICANS' HELP.
I SHOULD HAVE STOPPED THOSE BIOWEAPONS THE MOMENT THEY NAMED ME ELECTOR. IF I WAS SMART, I WOULD HAVE.

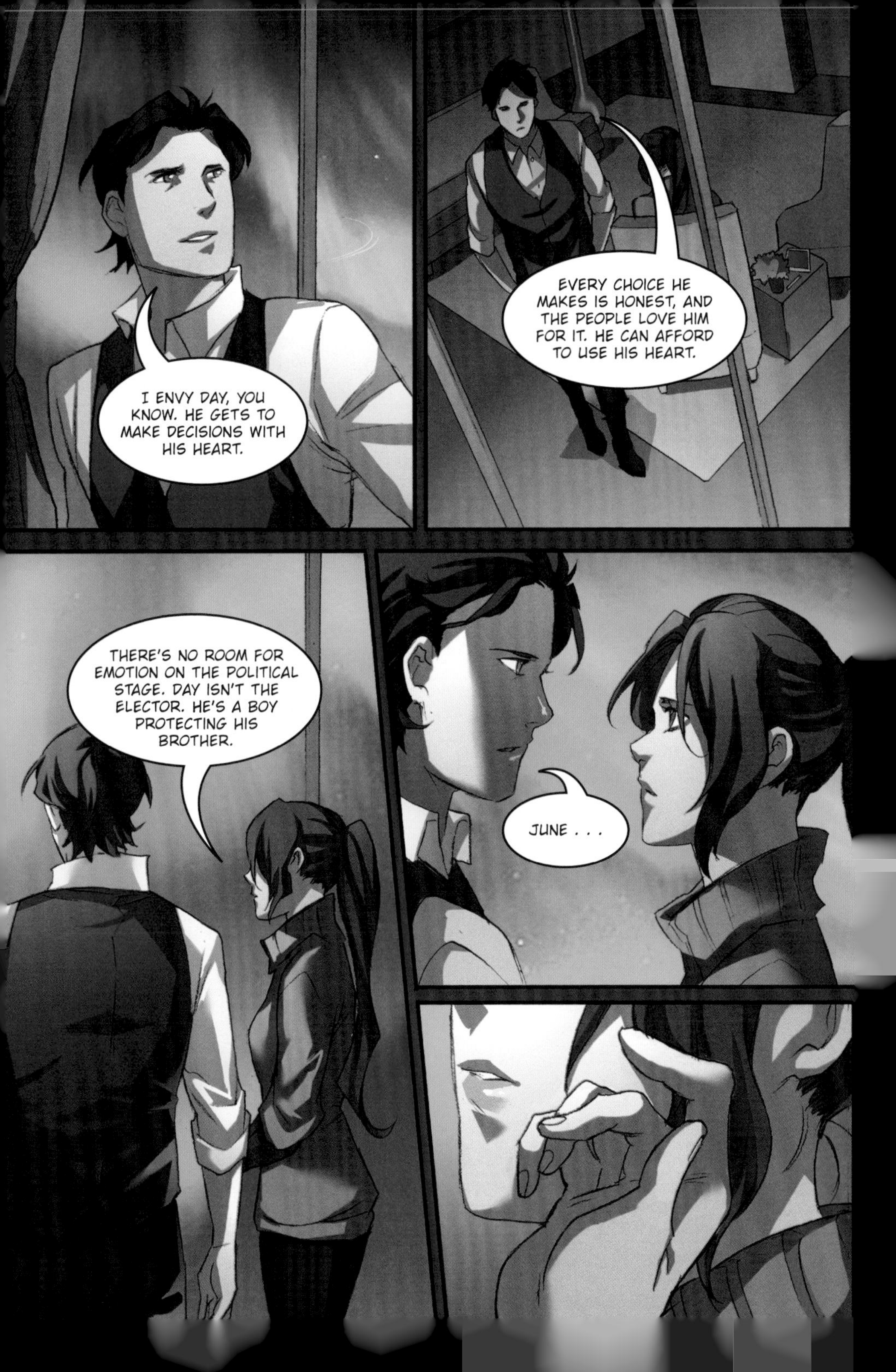
I ENVY DAY, YOU KNOW. HE GETS TO MAKE DECISIONS WITH HIS HEART.
EVERY CHOICE HE MAKES IS HONEST, AND THE PEOPLE LOVE HIM FOR IT. HE CAN AFFORD TO USE HIS HEART.
THERE'S NO ROOM FOR EMOTION ON THE POLITICAL STAGE. DAY ISN'T THE ELECTOR. HE'S A BOY PROTECTING HIS BROTHER.
JUNE . . .

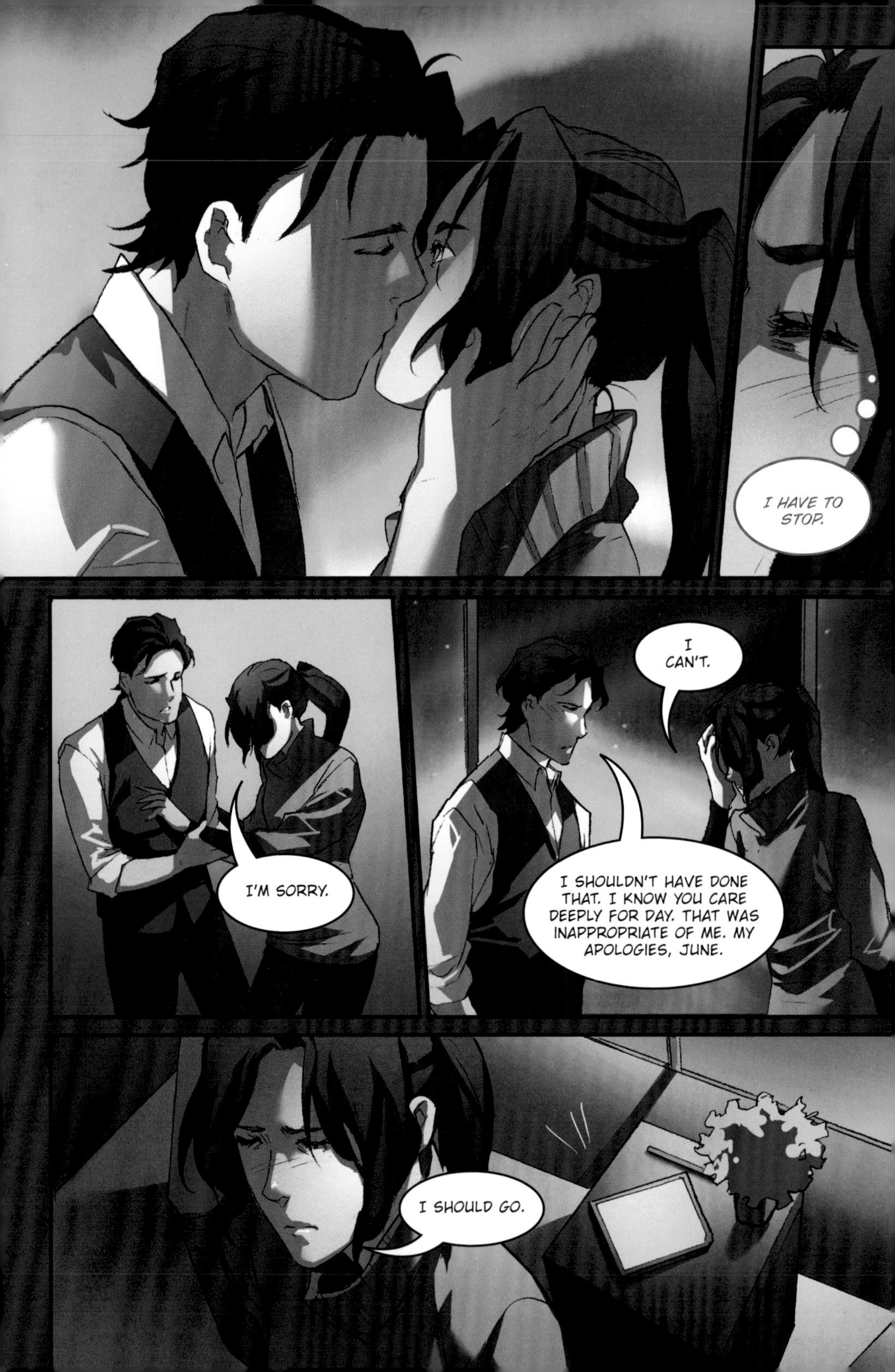
I HAVE TO STOP.
I'M SORRY.
I CAN'T.
I SHOULDN'T HAVE DONE THAT. I KNOW YOU CARE DEEPLY FOR DAY. THAT WAS INAPPROPRIATE OF ME. MY APOLOGIES, JUNE.
I SHOULD GO.

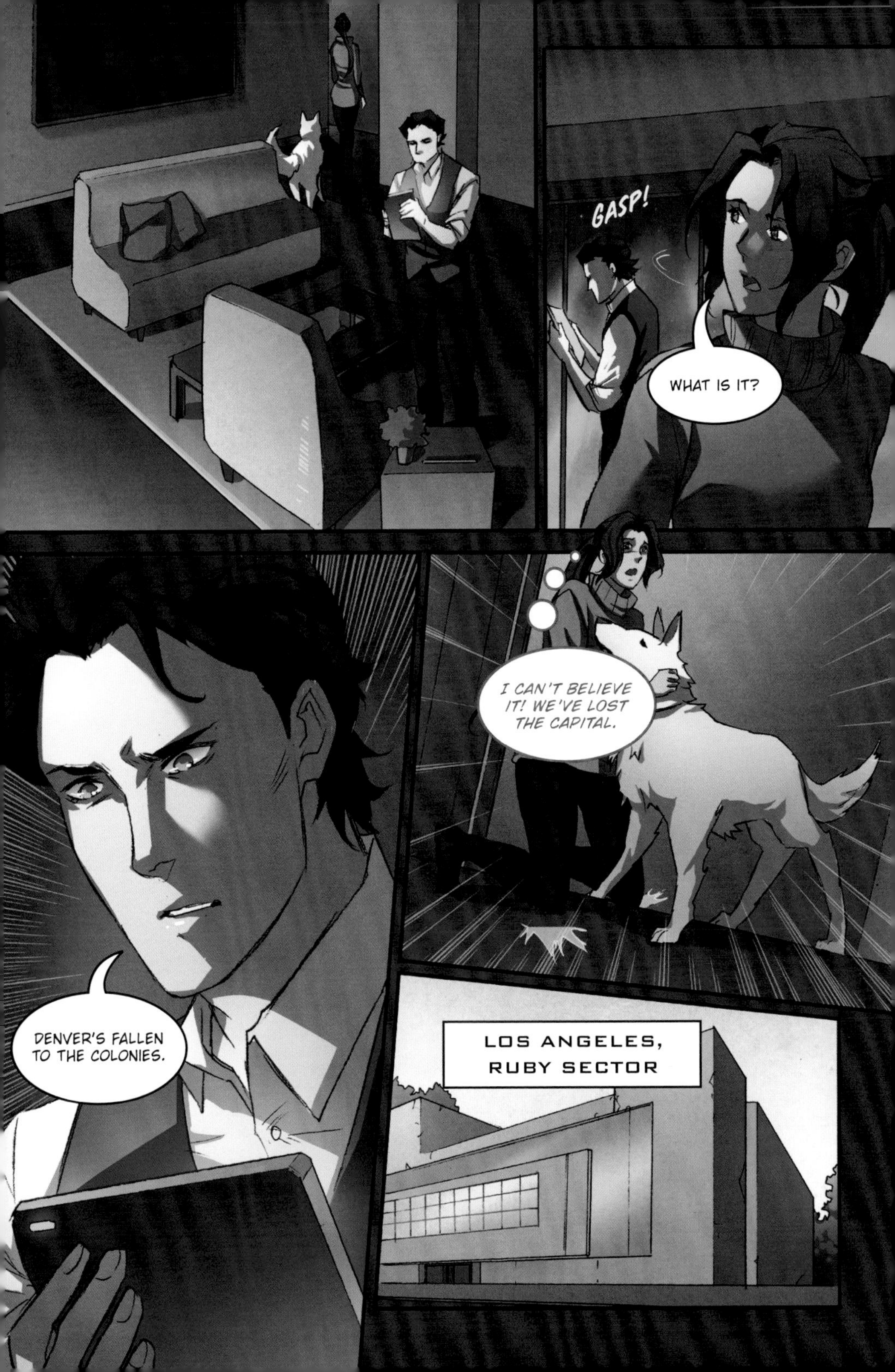
GASP!
WHAT IS IT?
DENVER'S FALLEN TO THE COLONIES.
I CAN'T BELIEVE IT! WE'VE LOST THE CAPITAL.
LOS ANGELES, RUBY SECTOR

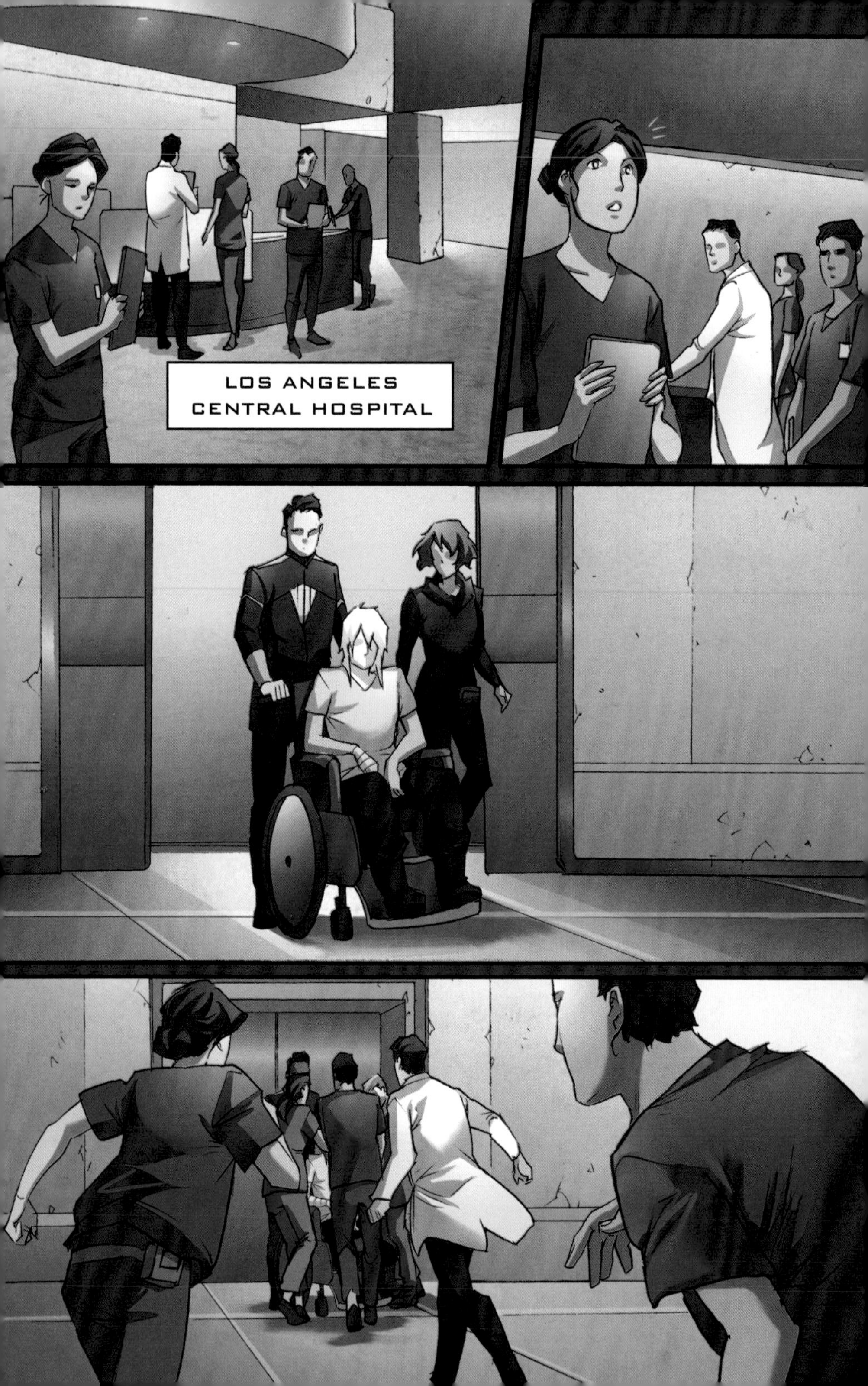
LOS ANGELES
CENTRAL HOSPITAL

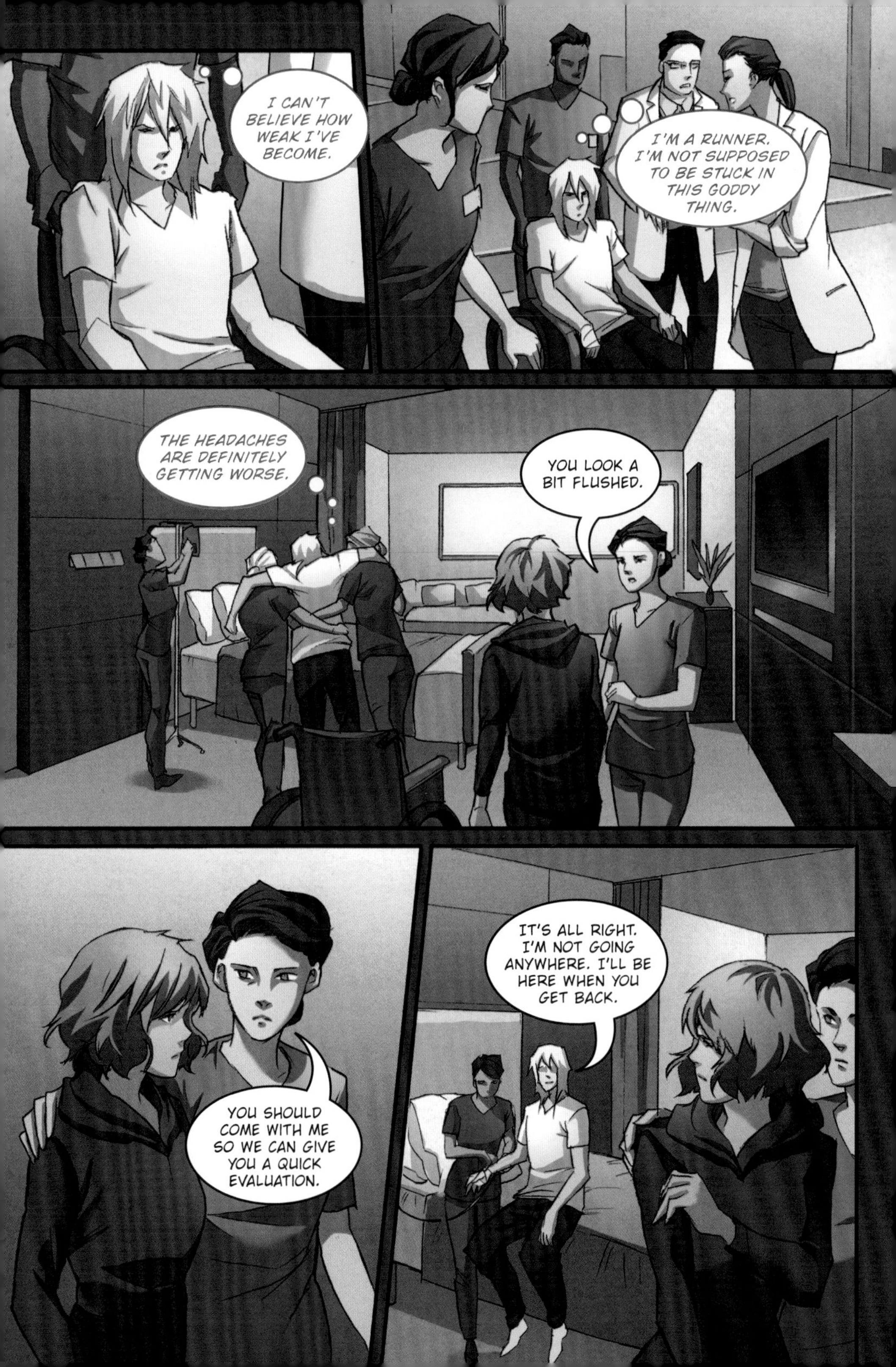
I CAN'T BELIEVE HOW WEAK I'VE BECOME.
I'M A RUNNER. I'M NOT SUPPOSED TO BE STUCK IN THIS GODDY THING.
THE HEADACHES ARE DEFINITELY GETTING WORSE.
YOU LOOK A BIT FLUSHED.
YOU SHOULD COME WITH ME SO WE CAN GIVE YOU A QUICK EVALUATION.
IT'S ALL RIGHT. I'M NOT GOING ANYWHERE. I'LL BE HERE WHEN YOU GET BACK.

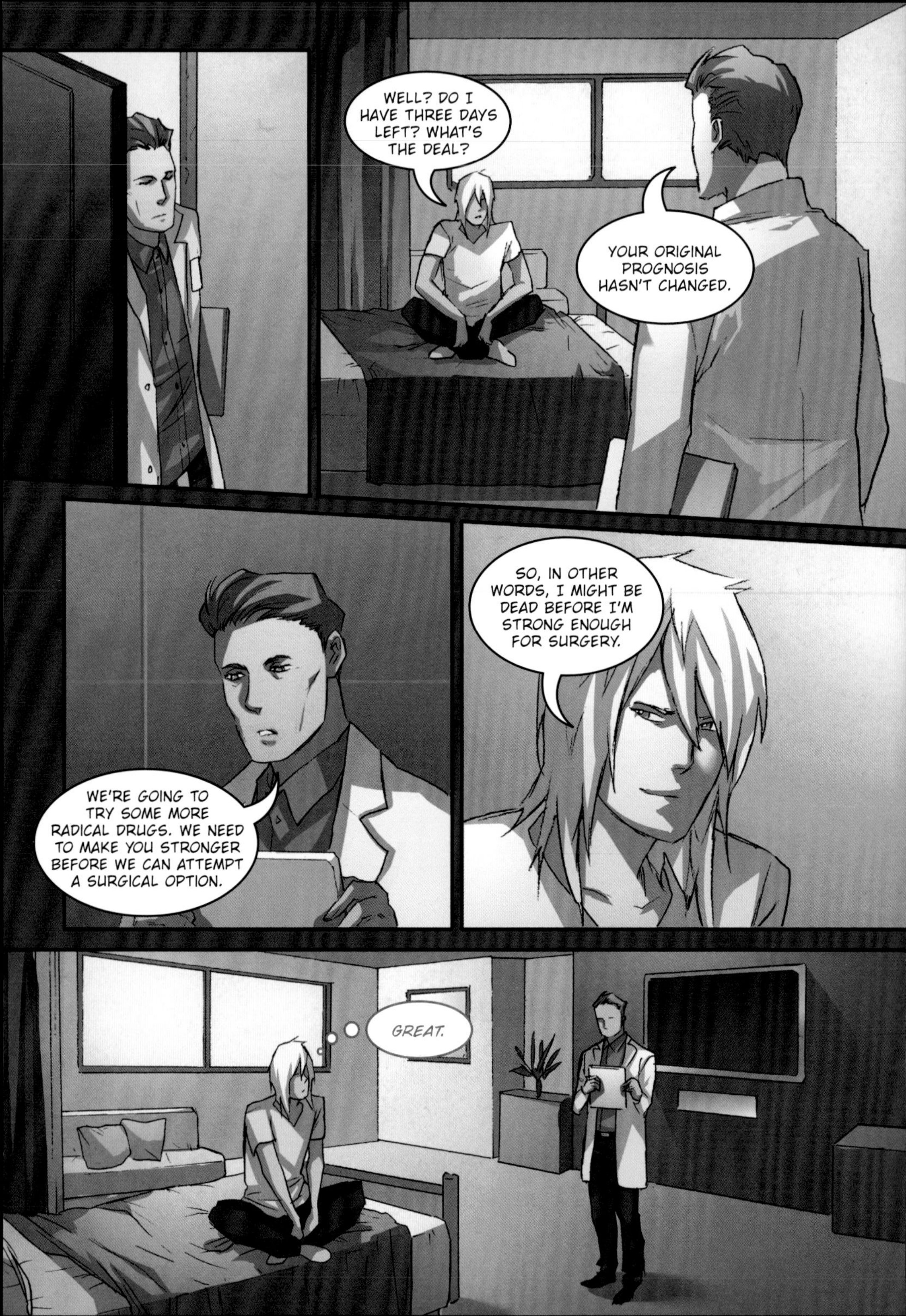
WELL? DO I HAVE THREE DAYS LEFT? WHAT'S THE DEAL?
YOUR ORIGINAL PROGNOSIS HASN'T CHANGED.
WE'RE GOING TO TRY SOME MORE RADICAL DRUGS. WE NEED TO MAKE YOU STRONGER BEFORE WE CAN ATTEMPT A SURGICAL OPTION.
SO, IN OTHER WORDS, I MIGHT BE DEAD BEFORE I'M STRONG ENOUGH FOR SURGERY.
GREAT.

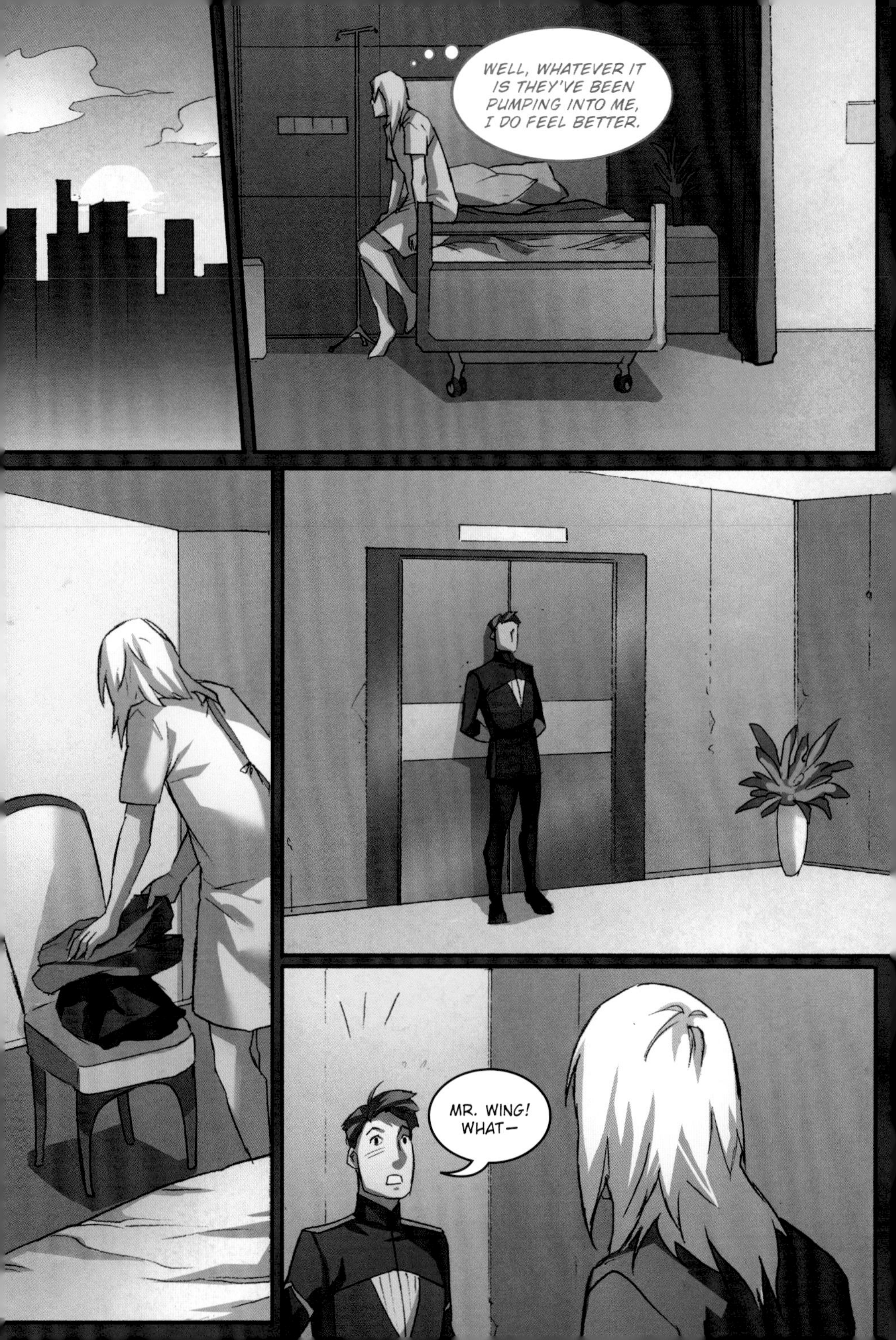
WELL, WHATEVER IT IS THEY'VE BEEN PUMPING INTO ME, I DO FEEL BETTER.
MR. WING! WHAT—

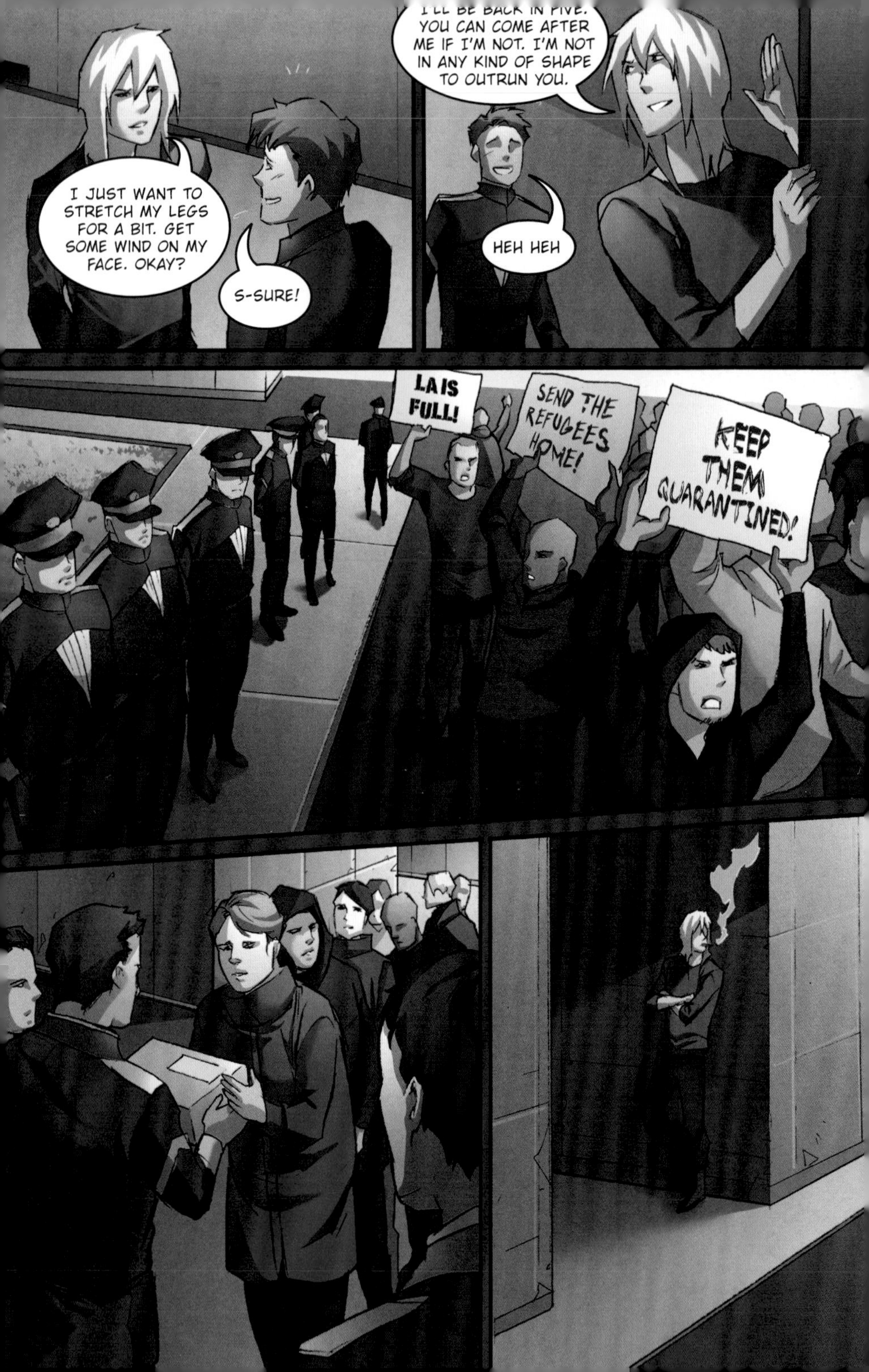
I JUST WANT TO STRETCH MY LEGS FOR A BIT. GET SOME WIND ON MY FACE. OKAY?
S-SURE!
I'LL BE BACK IN FIVE. YOU CAN COME AFTER ME IF I'M NOT. I'M NOT IN ANY KIND OF SHAPE TO OUTRUN YOU.
HEH HEH
LA IS FULL!
SEND THE REFUGEES HOME!
KEEP THEM QUARANTINED!

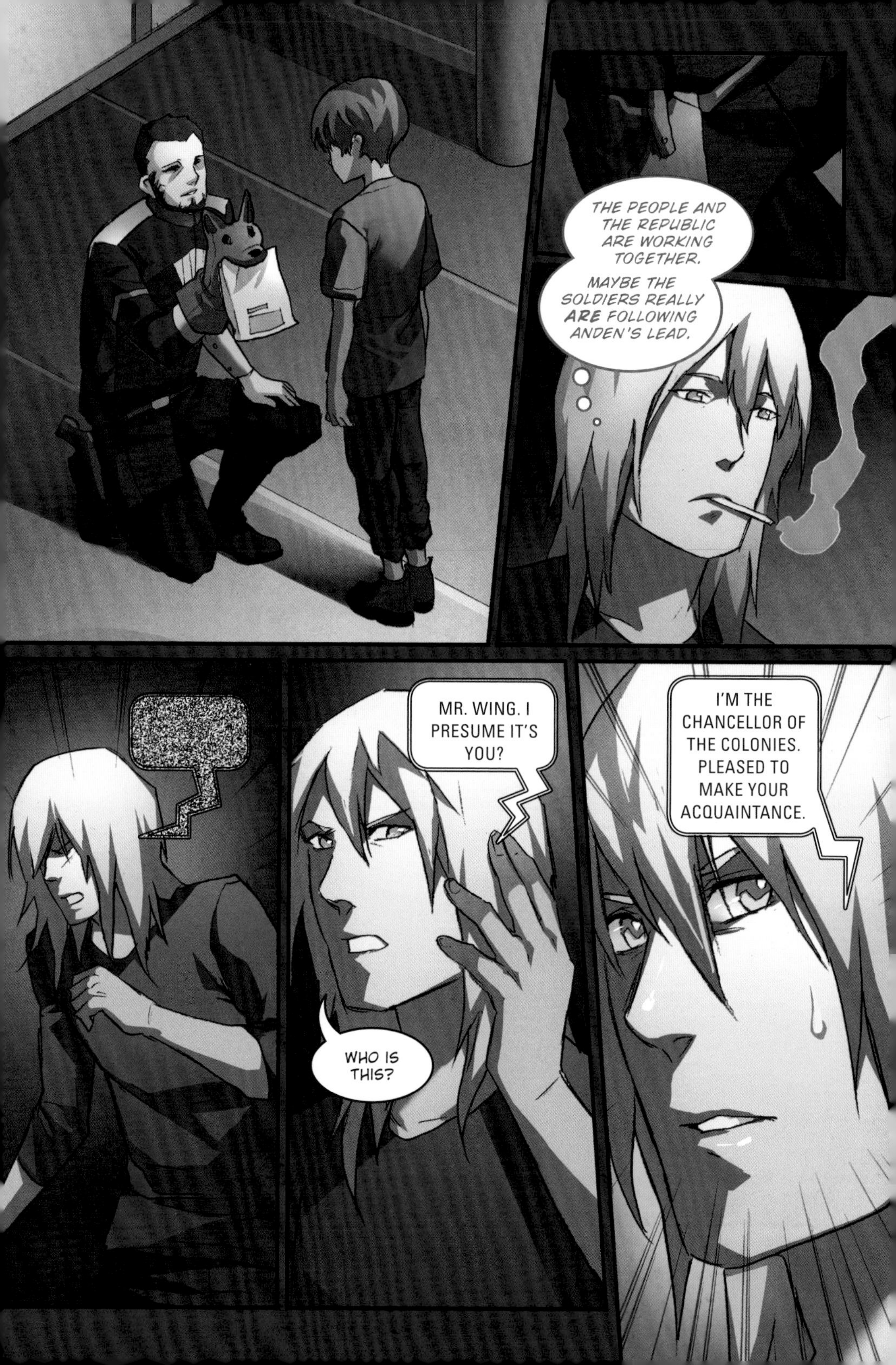
THE PEOPLE AND THE REPUBLIC ARE WORKING TOGETHER.
MAYBE THE SOLDIERS REALLY **ARE** FOLLOWING ANDEN'S LEAD.
MR. WING. I PRESUME IT'S YOU?
WHO IS THIS?
I'M THE CHANCELLOR OF THE COLONIES. PLEASED TO MAKE YOUR ACQUAINTANCE.

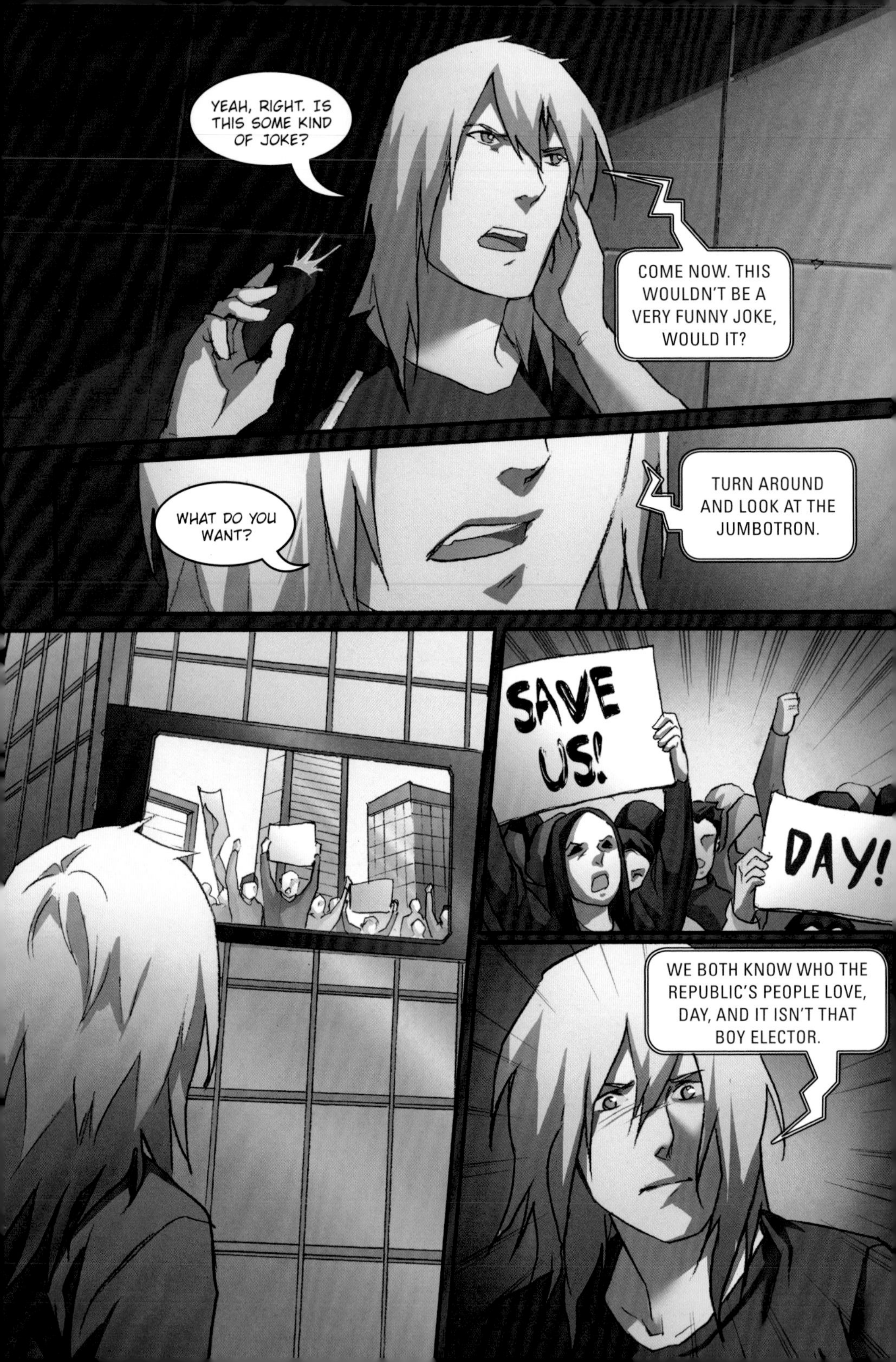
YEAH, RIGHT. IS THIS SOME KIND OF JOKE?
COME NOW. THIS WOULDN'T BE A VERY FUNNY JOKE, WOULD IT?
WHAT DO YOU WANT?
TURN AROUND AND LOOK AT THE JUMBOTRON.
SAVE US!
DAY!
WE BOTH KNOW WHO THE REPUBLIC'S PEOPLE LOVE, DAY, AND IT ISN'T THAT BOY ELECTOR.

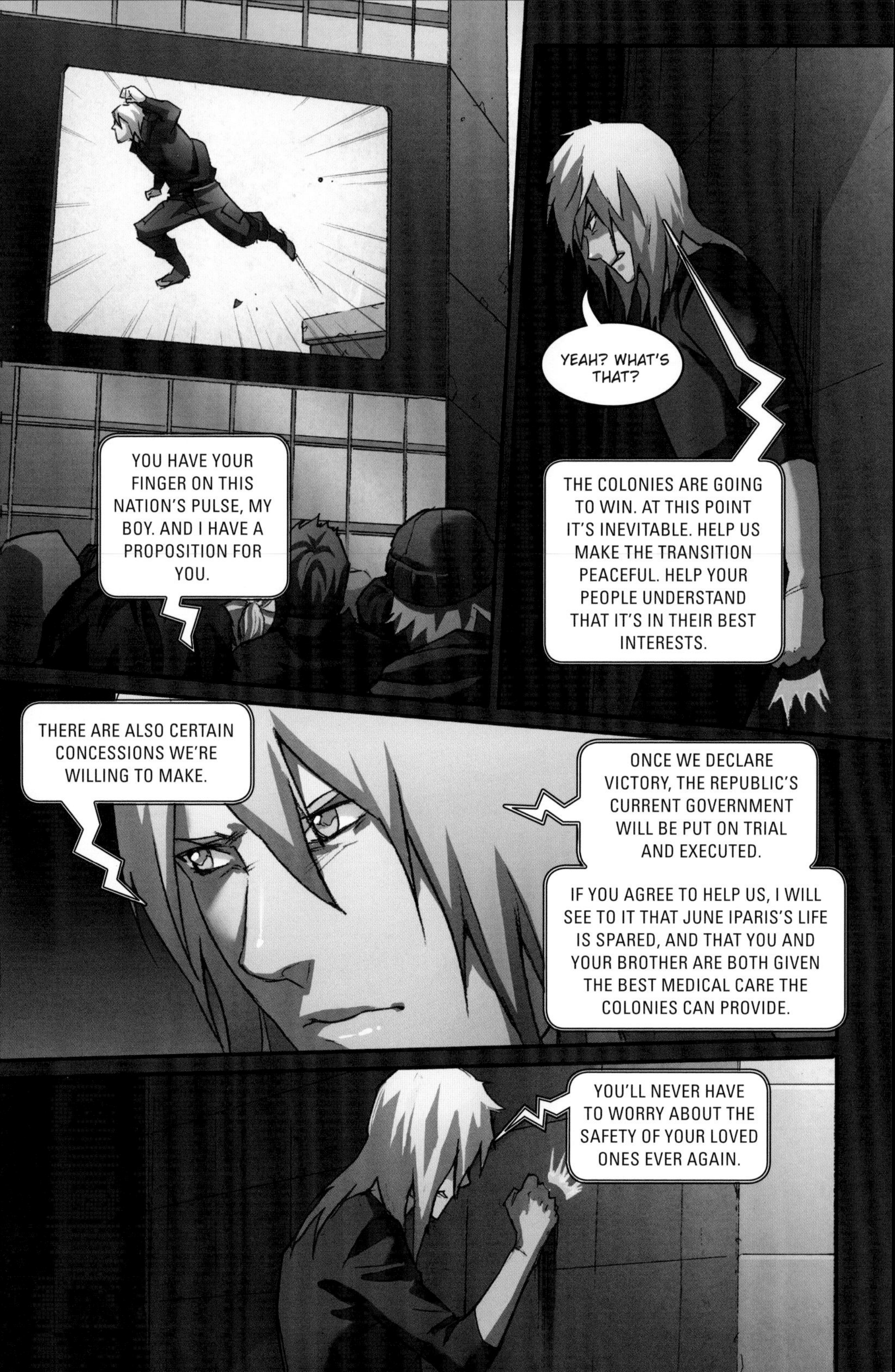
YEAH? WHAT'S THAT?
YOU HAVE YOUR FINGER ON THIS NATION'S PULSE, MY BOY. AND I HAVE A PROPOSITION FOR YOU.
THE COLONIES ARE GOING TO WIN. AT THIS POINT IT'S INEVITABLE. HELP US MAKE THE TRANSITION PEACEFUL. HELP YOUR PEOPLE UNDERSTAND THAT IT'S IN THEIR BEST INTERESTS.
THERE ARE ALSO CERTAIN CONCESSIONS WE'RE WILLING TO MAKE.
ONCE WE DECLARE VICTORY, THE REPUBLIC'S CURRENT GOVERNMENT WILL BE PUT ON TRIAL AND EXECUTED.
IF YOU AGREE TO HELP US, I WILL SEE TO IT THAT JUNE IPARIS'S LIFE IS SPARED, AND THAT YOU AND YOUR BROTHER ARE BOTH GIVEN THE BEST MEDICAL CARE THE COLONIES CAN PROVIDE.
YOU'LL NEVER HAVE TO WORRY ABOUT THE SAFETY OF YOUR LOVED ONES EVER AGAIN.

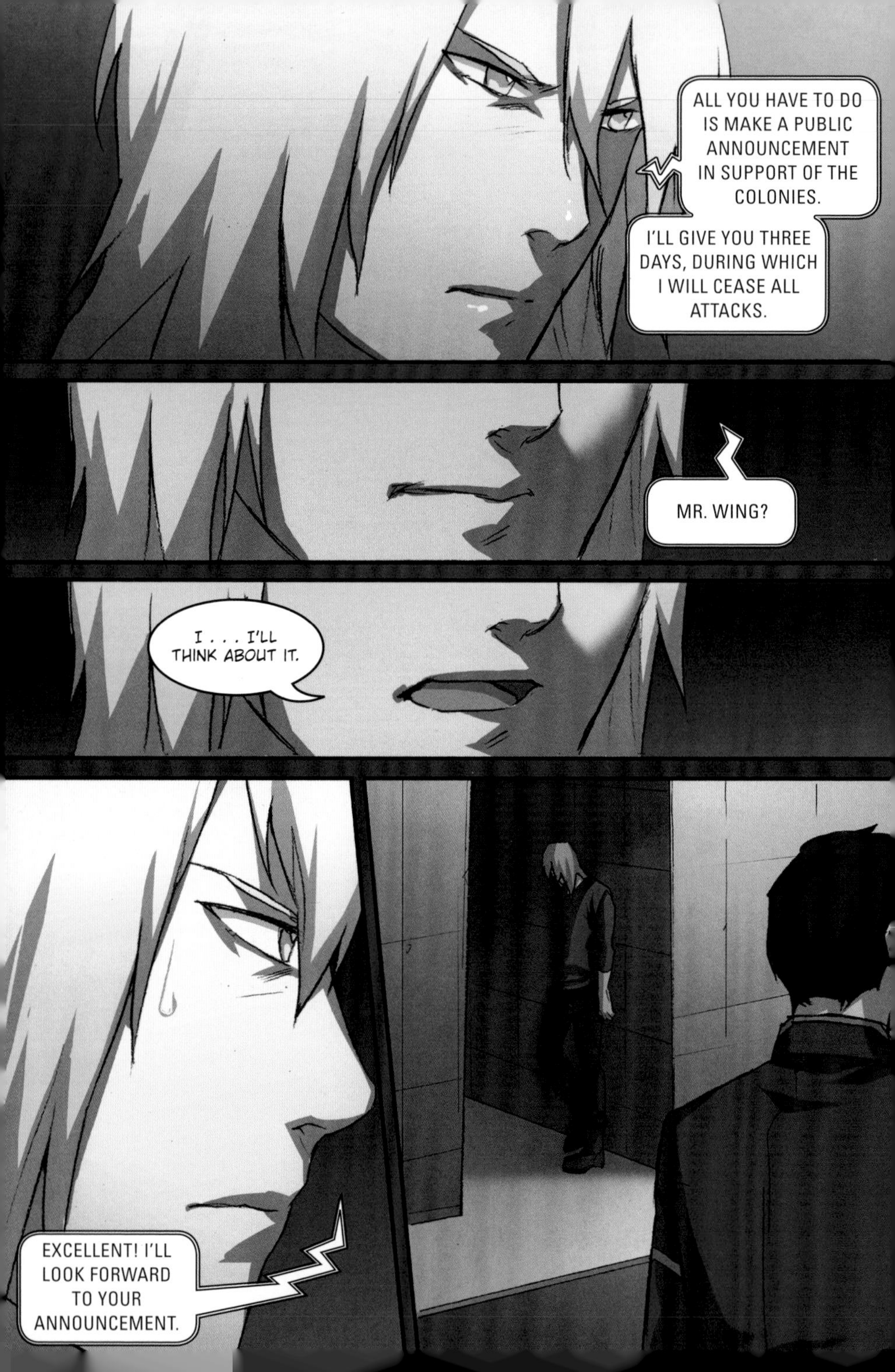
ALL YOU HAVE TO DO IS MAKE A PUBLIC ANNOUNCEMENT IN SUPPORT OF THE COLONIES.
I'LL GIVE YOU THREE DAYS, DURING WHICH I WILL CEASE ALL ATTACKS.
MR. WING?
I . . . I'LL THINK ABOUT IT.
EXCELLENT! I'LL LOOK FORWARD TO YOUR ANNOUNCEMENT.

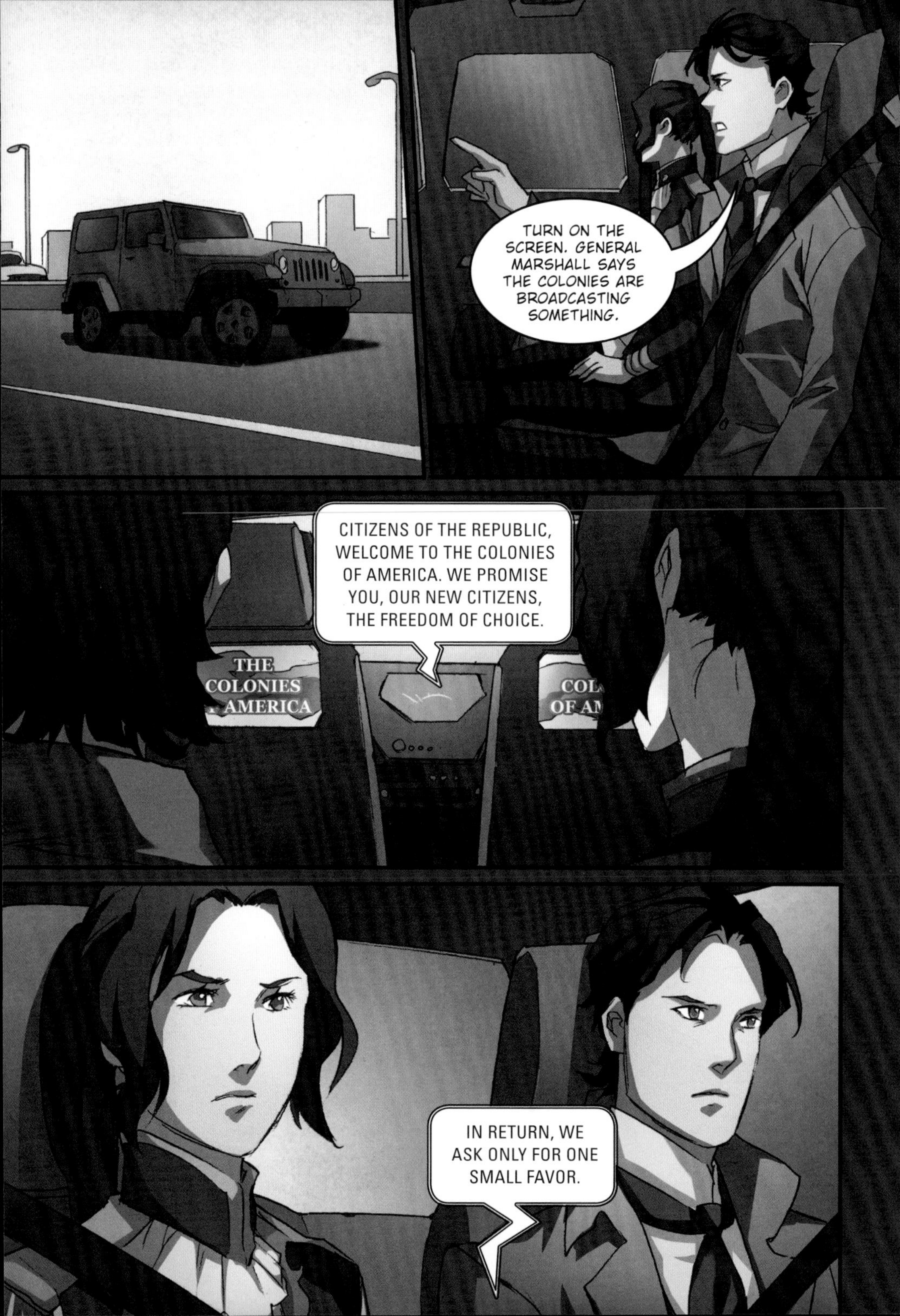
TURN ON THE SCREEN. GENERAL MARSHALL SAYS THE COLONIES ARE BROADCASTING SOMETHING.
CITIZENS OF THE REPUBLIC, WELCOME TO THE COLONIES OF AMERICA. WE PROMISE YOU, OUR NEW CITIZENS, THE FREEDOM OF CHOICE.
THE COLONIES
AMERICA
COL
OF AM
IN RETURN, WE ASK ONLY FOR ONE SMALL FAVOR.

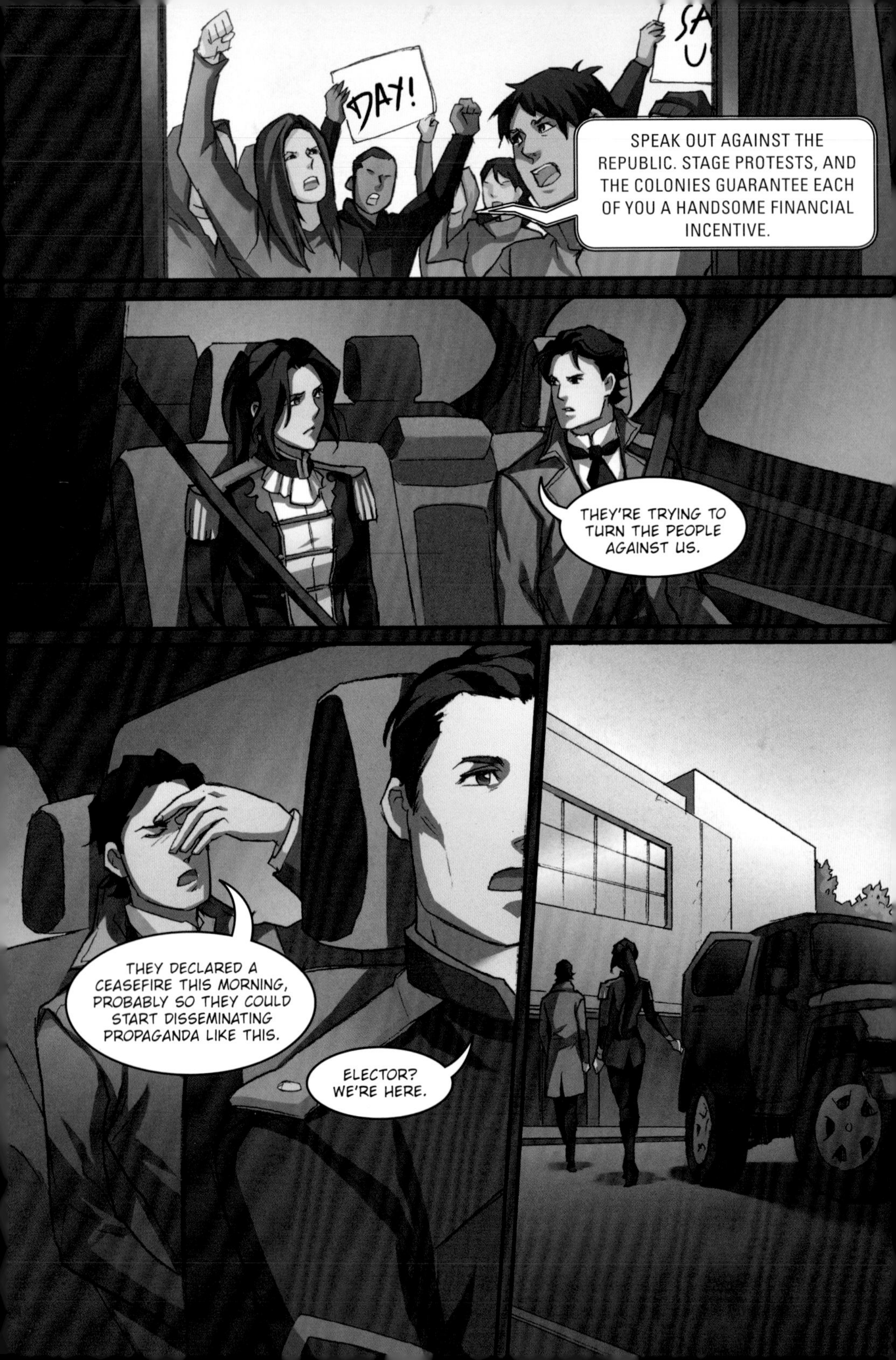
DAY!
SPEAK OUT AGAINST THE REPUBLIC. STAGE PROTESTS, AND THE COLONIES GUARANTEE EACH OF YOU A HANDSOME FINANCIAL INCENTIVE.
THEY'RE TRYING TO TURN THE PEOPLE AGAINST US.
THEY DECLARED A CEASEFIRE THIS MORNING, PROBABLY SO THEY COULD START DISSEMINATING PROPAGANDA LIKE THIS.
ELECTOR? WE'RE HERE.

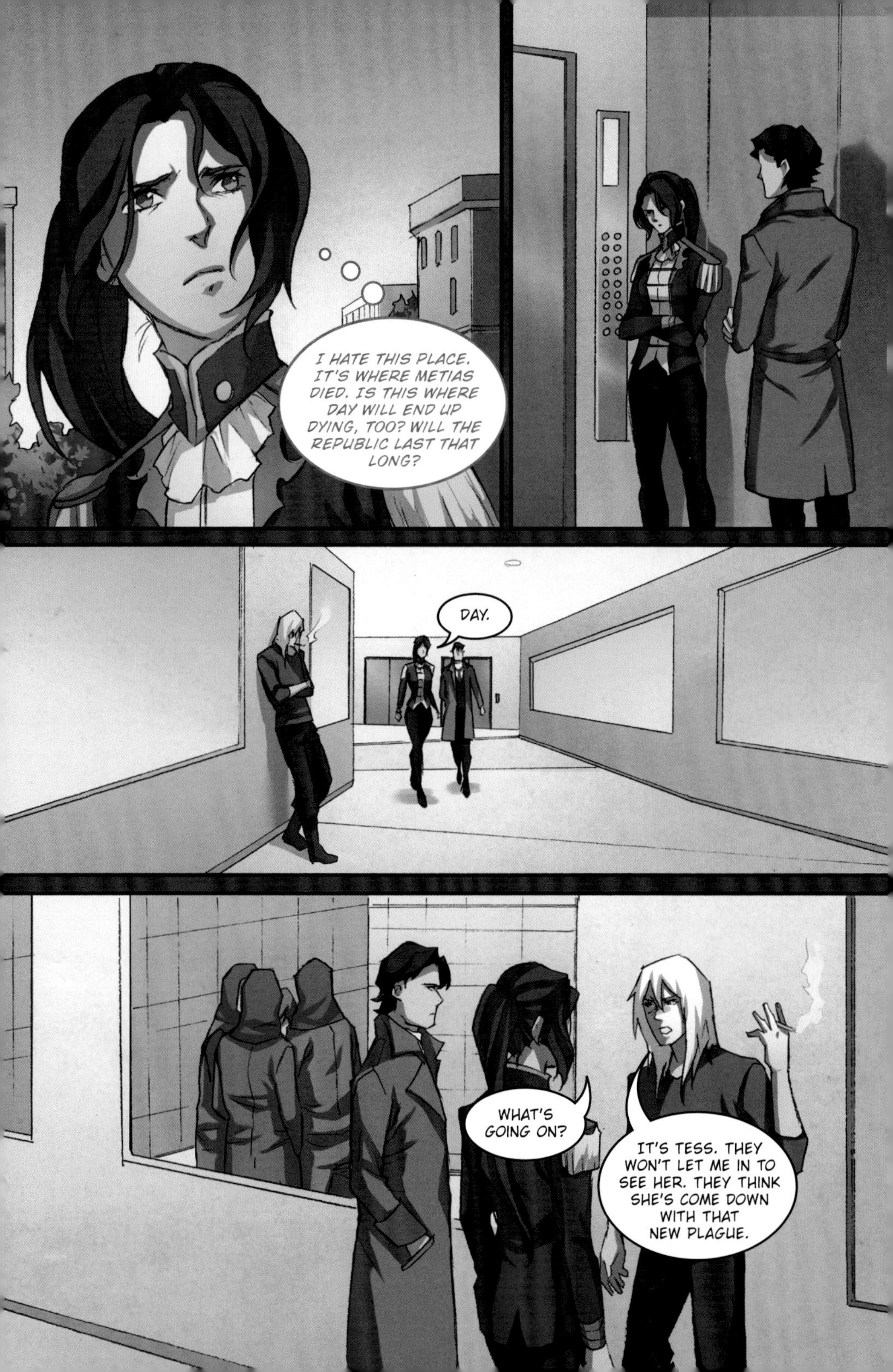
I HATE THIS PLACE. IT'S WHERE METIAS DIED. IS THIS WHERE DAY WILL END UP DYING, TOO? WILL THE REPUBLIC LAST THAT LONG?
DAY.
WHAT'S GOING ON?
IT'S TESS. THEY WON'T LET ME IN TO SEE HER. THEY THINK SHE'S COME DOWN WITH THAT NEW PLAGUE.

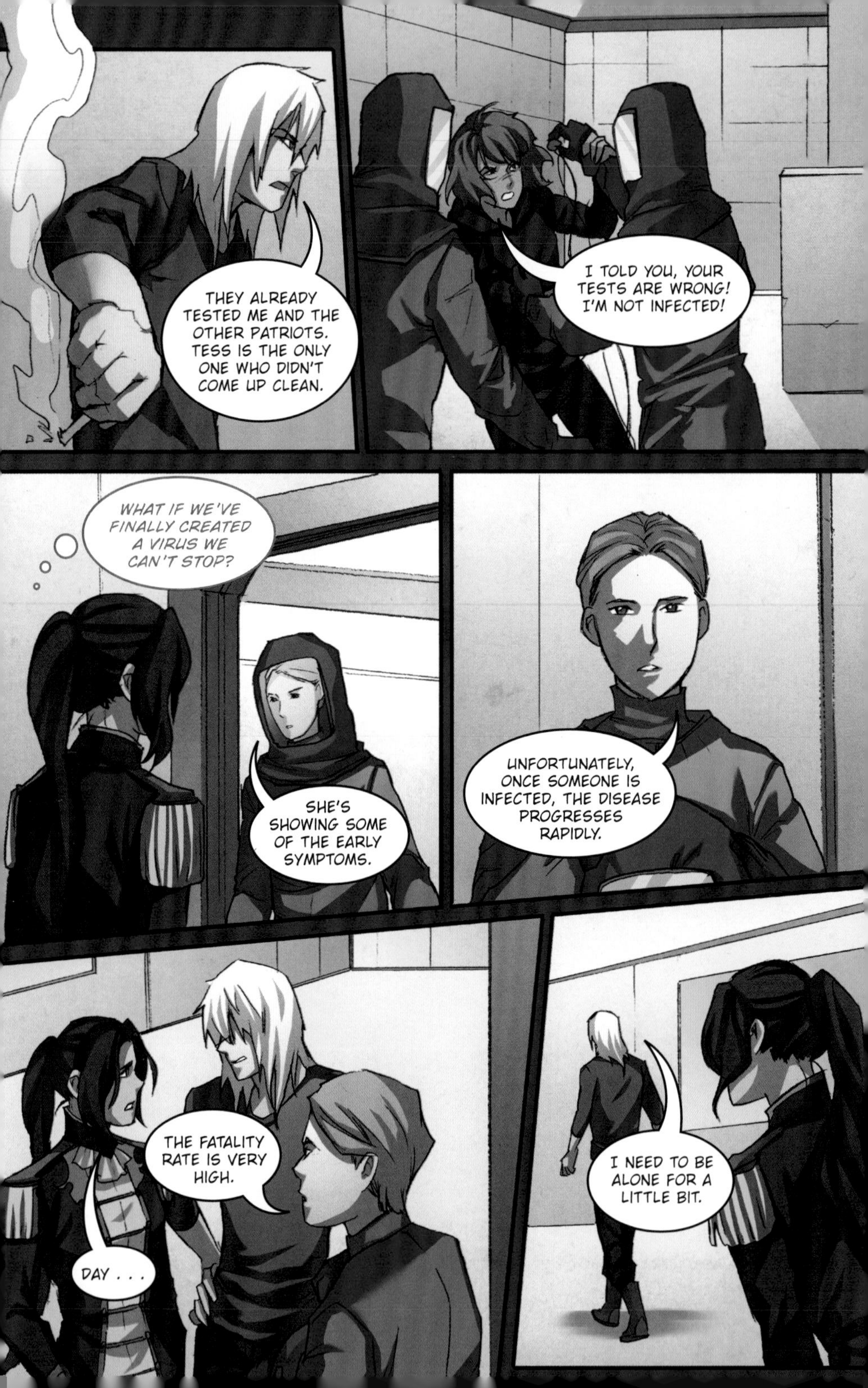
THEY ALREADY TESTED ME AND THE OTHER PATRIOTS. TESS IS THE ONLY ONE WHO DIDN'T COME UP CLEAN.
I TOLD YOU, YOUR TESTS ARE WRONG! I'M NOT INFECTED!
WHAT IF WE'VE FINALLY CREATED A VIRUS WE CAN'T STOP?
SHE'S SHOWING SOME OF THE EARLY SYMPTOMS.
UNFORTUNATELY, ONCE SOMEONE IS INFECTED, THE DISEASE PROGRESSES RAPIDLY.
THE FATALITY RATE IS VERY HIGH.
DAY . . .
I NEED TO BE ALONE FOR A LITTLE BIT.

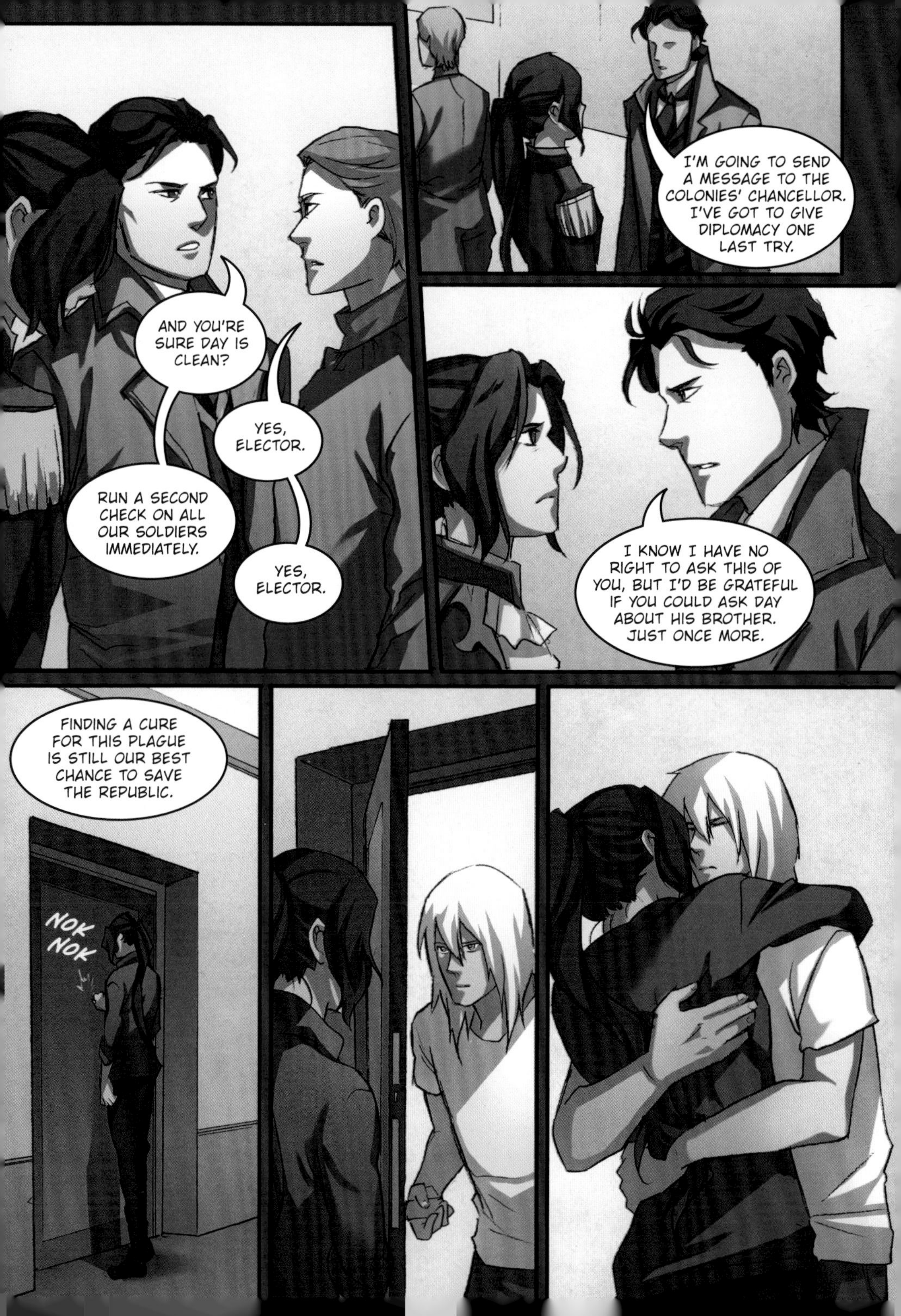
AND YOU'RE SURE DAY IS CLEAN?
YES, ELECTOR.
RUN A SECOND CHECK ON ALL OUR SOLDIERS IMMEDIATELY.
YES, ELECTOR.
I'M GOING TO SEND A MESSAGE TO THE COLONIES' CHANCELLOR. I'VE GOT TO GIVE DIPLOMACY ONE LAST TRY.
I KNOW I HAVE NO RIGHT TO ASK THIS OF YOU, BUT I'D BE GRATEFUL IF YOU COULD ASK DAY ABOUT HIS BROTHER. JUST ONCE MORE.
FINDING A CURE FOR THIS PLAGUE IS STILL OUR BEST CHANCE TO SAVE THE REPUBLIC.
NOK NOK

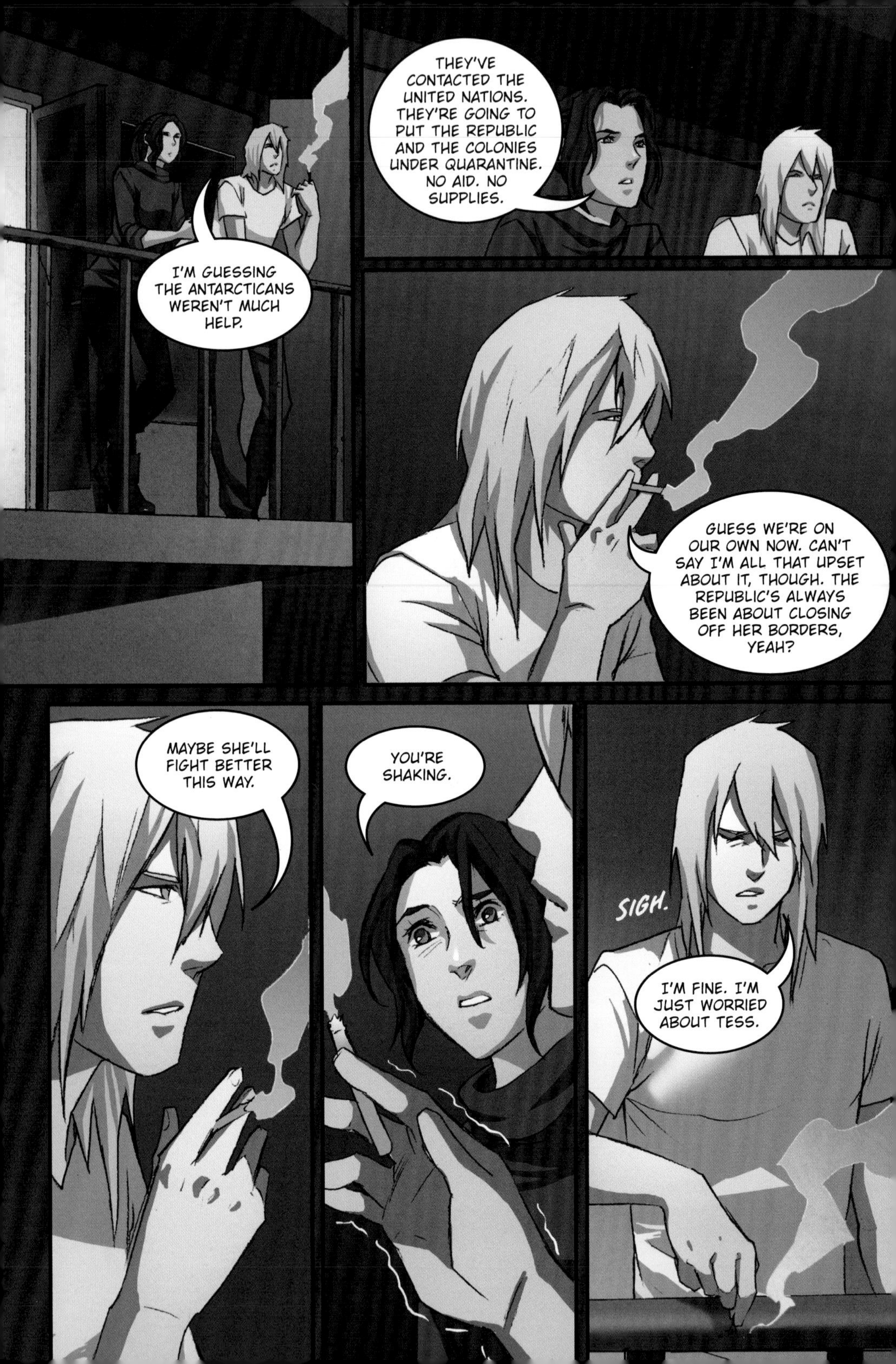
I'M GUESSING THE ANTARCTICANS WEREN'T MUCH HELP.
THEY'VE CONTACTED THE UNITED NATIONS. THEY'RE GOING TO PUT THE REPUBLIC AND THE COLONIES UNDER QUARANTINE. NO AID. NO SUPPLIES.
GUESS WE'RE ON OUR OWN NOW. CAN'T SAY I'M ALL THAT UPSET ABOUT IT, THOUGH. THE REPUBLIC'S ALWAYS BEEN ABOUT CLOSING OFF HER BORDERS, YEAH?
MAYBE SHE'LL FIGHT BETTER THIS WAY.
YOU'RE SHAKING.
SIGH.
I'M FINE. I'M JUST WORRIED ABOUT TESS.

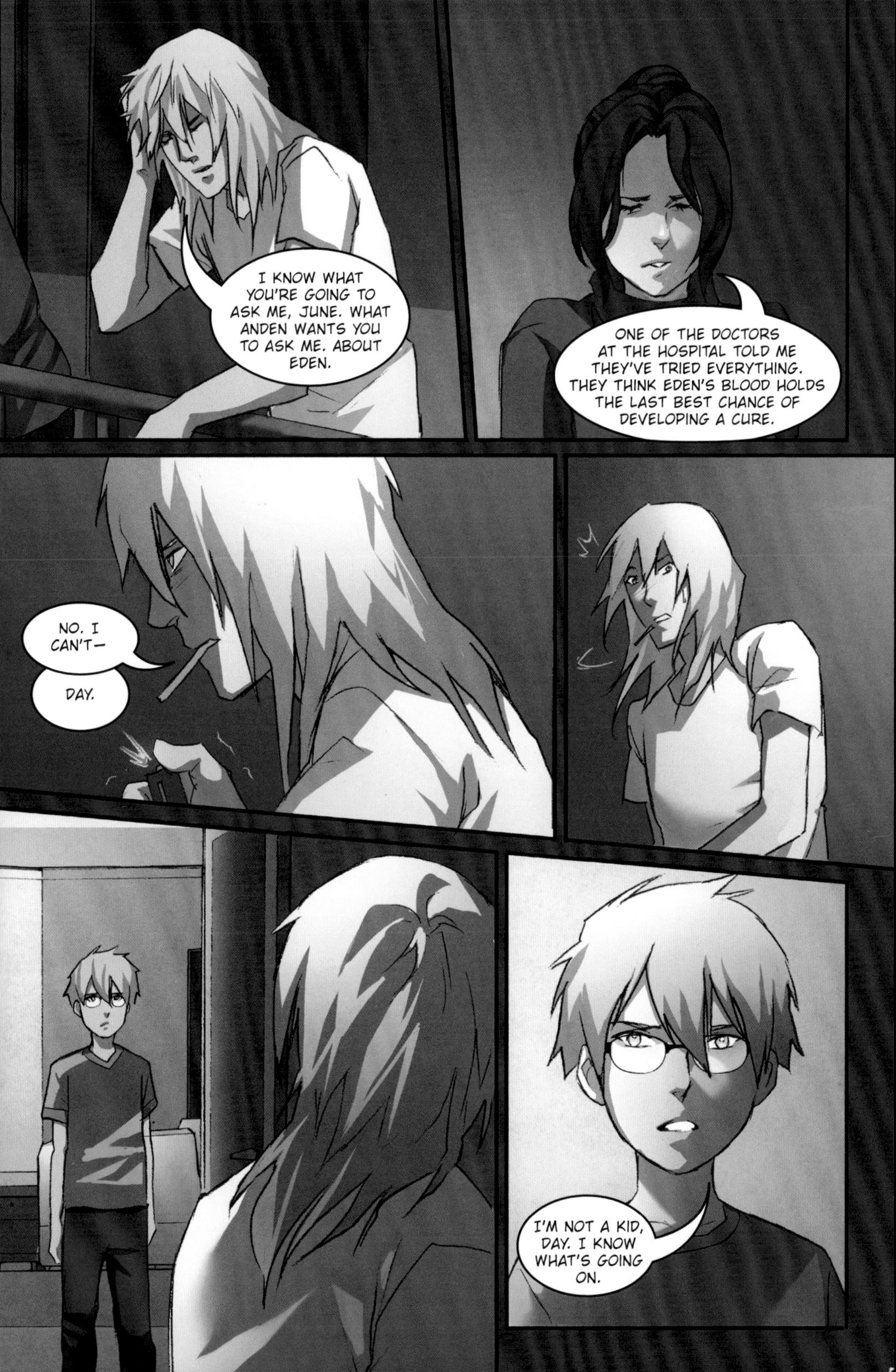
I KNOW WHAT YOU'RE GOING TO ASK ME, JUNE. WHAT ANDEN WANTS YOU TO ASK ME. ABOUT EDEN.
ONE OF THE DOCTORS AT THE HOSPITAL TOLD ME THEY'VE TRIED EVERYTHING. THEY THINK EDEN'S BLOOD HOLDS THE LAST BEST CHANCE OF DEVELOPING A CURE.
NO. I CAN'T—
DAY.
I'M NOT A KID, DAY. I KNOW WHAT'S GOING ON.

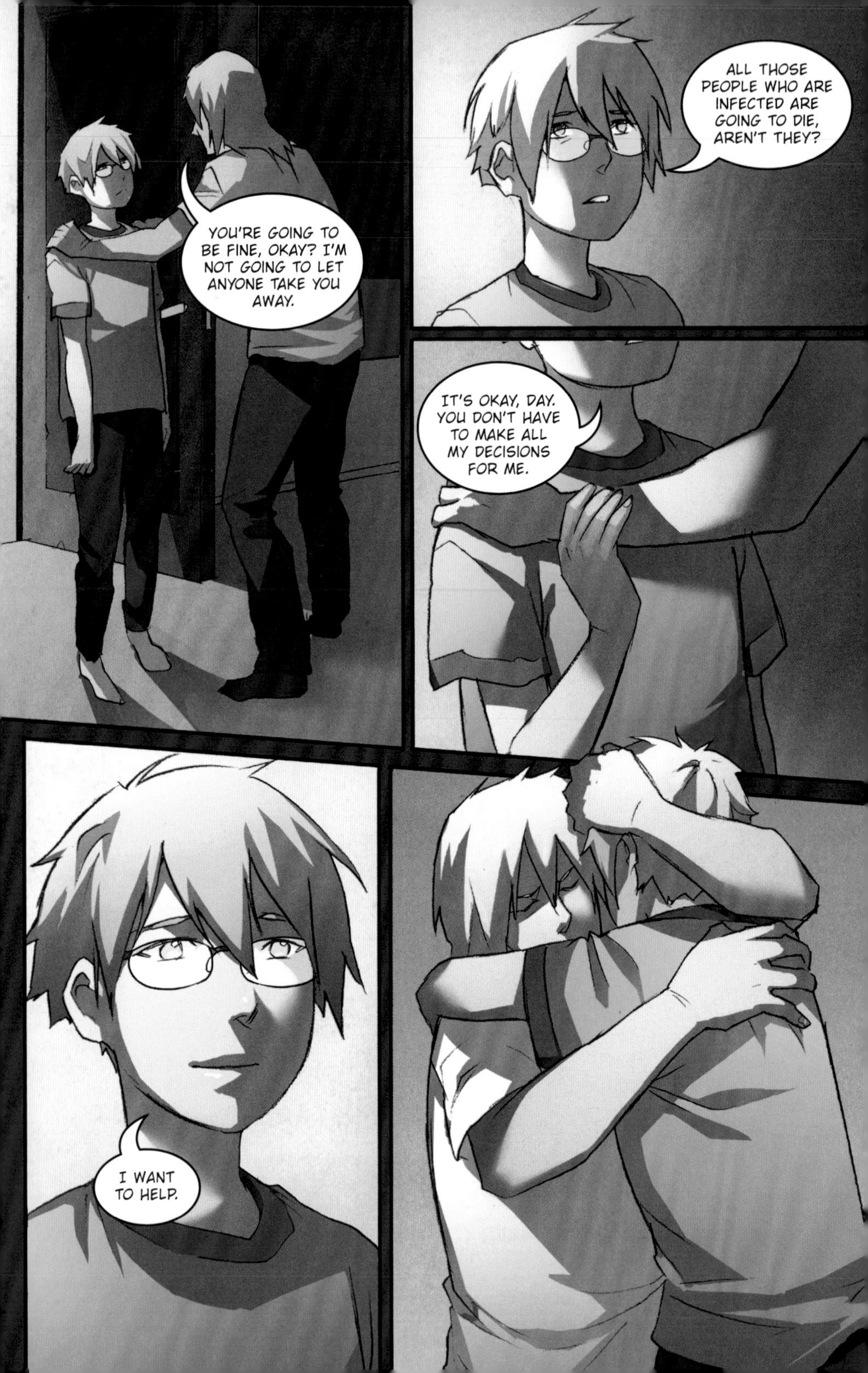
YOU'RE GOING TO BE FINE, OKAY? I'M NOT GOING TO LET ANYONE TAKE YOU AWAY.
ALL THOSE PEOPLE WHO ARE INFECTED ARE GOING TO DIE, AREN'T THEY?
IT'S OKAY, DAY. YOU DON'T HAVE TO MAKE ALL MY DECISIONS FOR ME.
I WANT TO HELP.

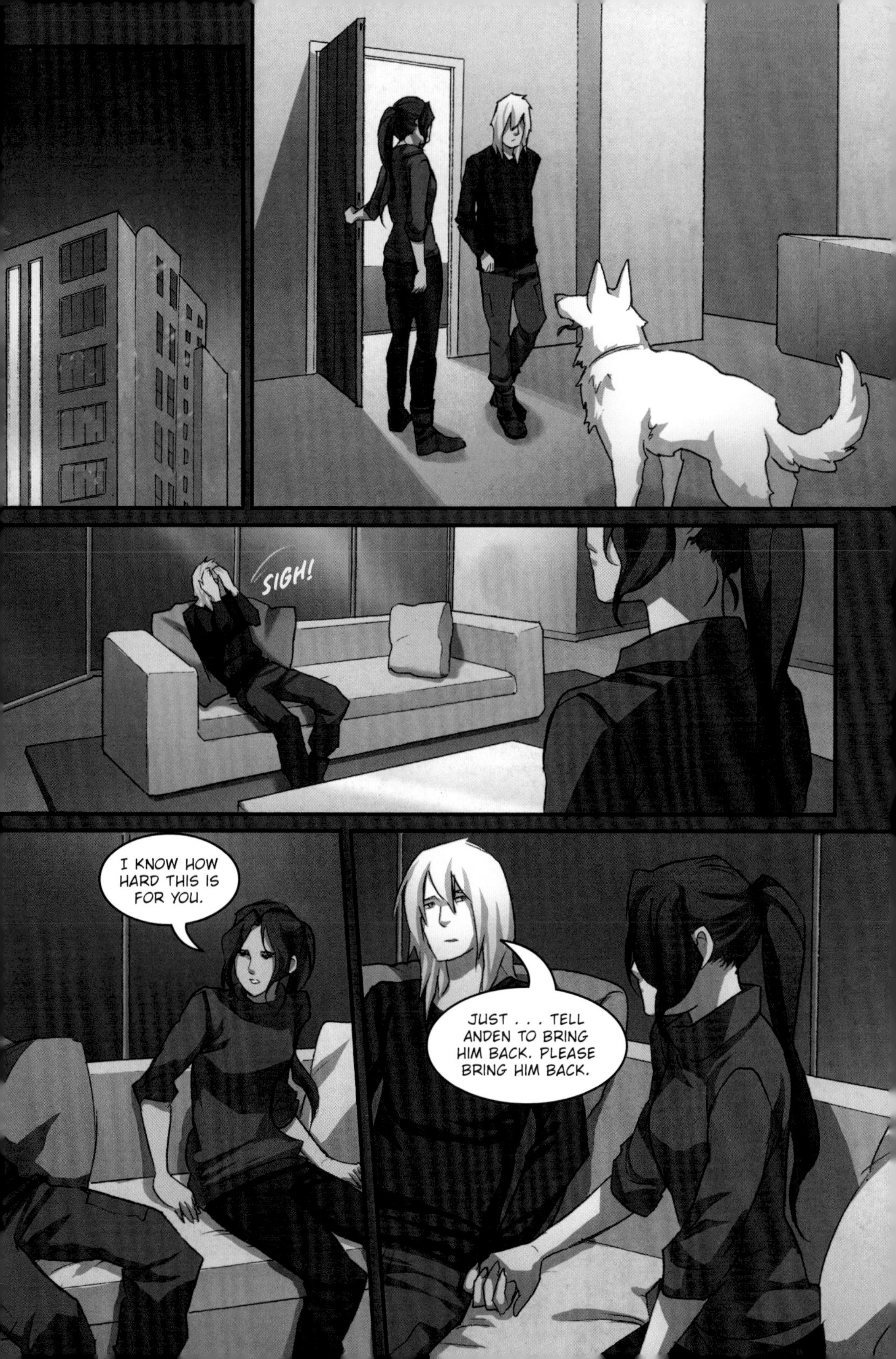
SIGH!
I KNOW HOW HARD THIS IS FOR YOU.
JUST . . . TELL ANDEN TO BRING HIM BACK. PLEASE BRING HIM BACK.

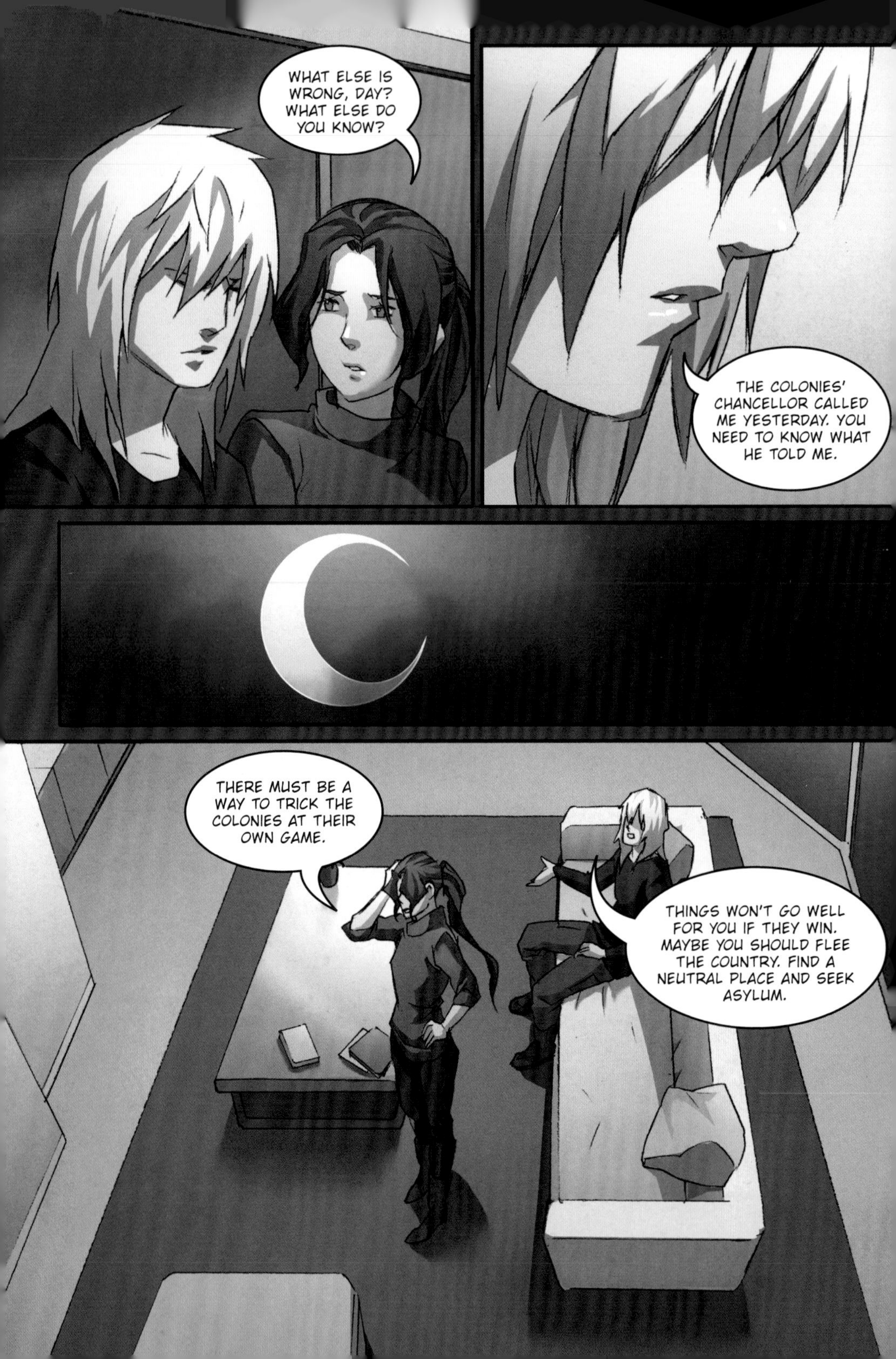
WHAT ELSE IS WRONG, DAY? WHAT ELSE DO YOU KNOW?
THE COLONIES' CHANCELLOR CALLED ME YESTERDAY. YOU NEED TO KNOW WHAT HE TOLD ME.
THERE MUST BE A WAY TO TRICK THE COLONIES AT THEIR OWN GAME.
THINGS WON'T GO WELL FOR YOU IF THEY WIN. MAYBE YOU SHOULD FLEE THE COUNTRY. FIND A NEUTRAL PLACE AND SEEK ASYLUM.

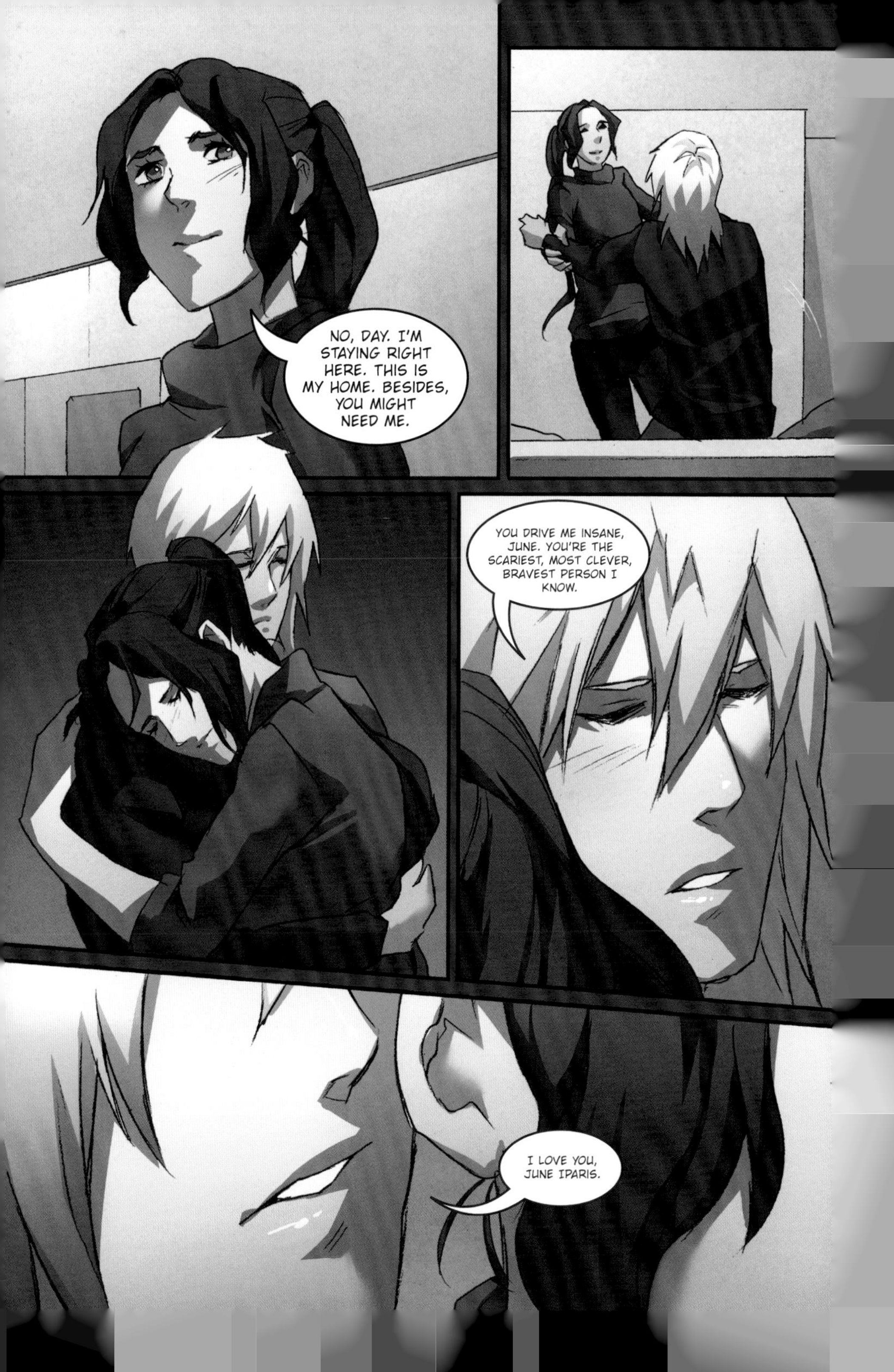
NO, DAY. I'M STAYING RIGHT HERE. THIS IS MY HOME. BESIDES, YOU MIGHT NEED ME.
YOU DRIVE ME INSANE, JUNE. YOU'RE THE SCARIEST, MOST CLEVER, BRAVEST PERSON I KNOW.
I LOVE YOU, JUNE IPARIS.

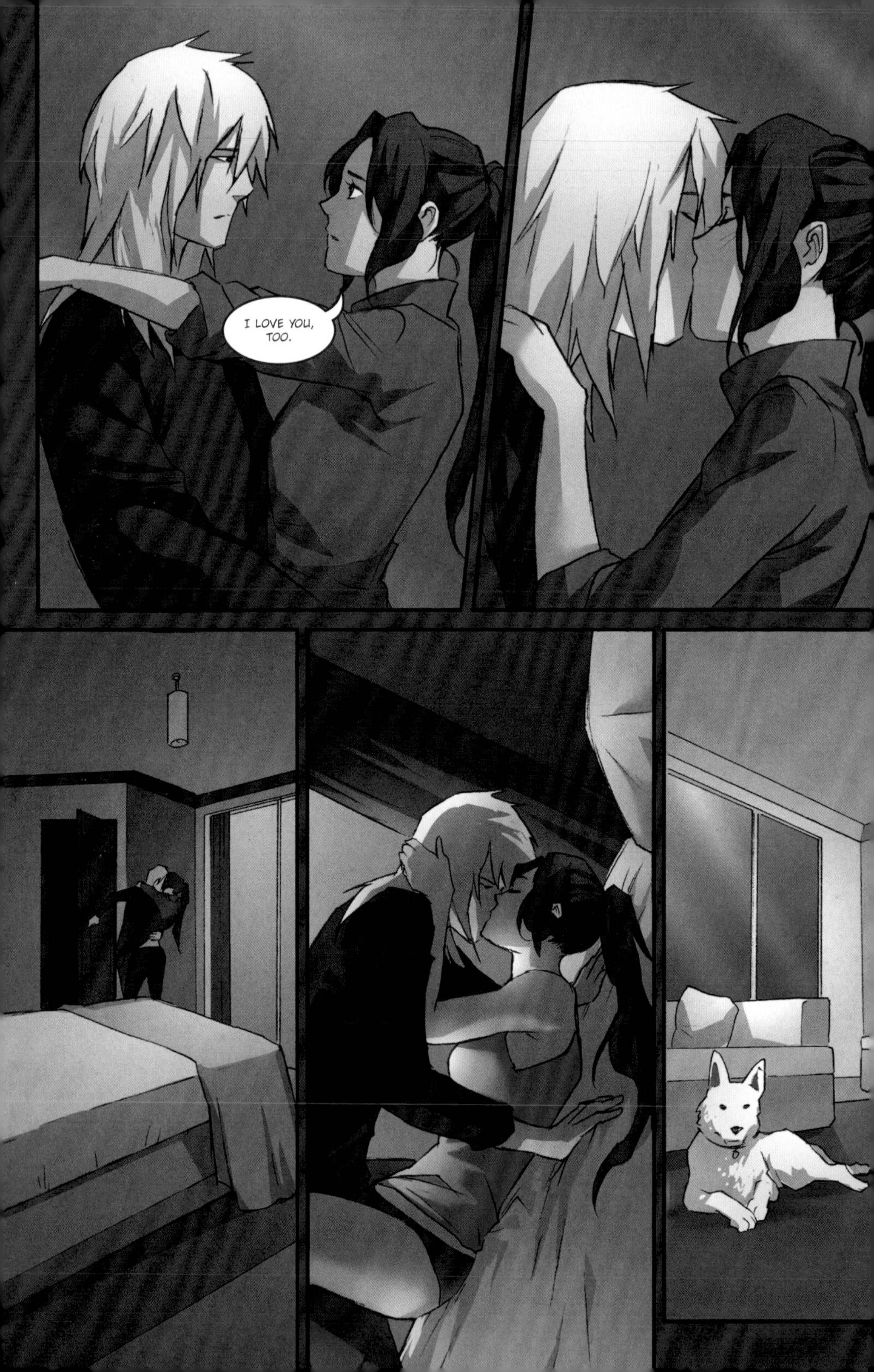
I LOVE YOU, TOO.

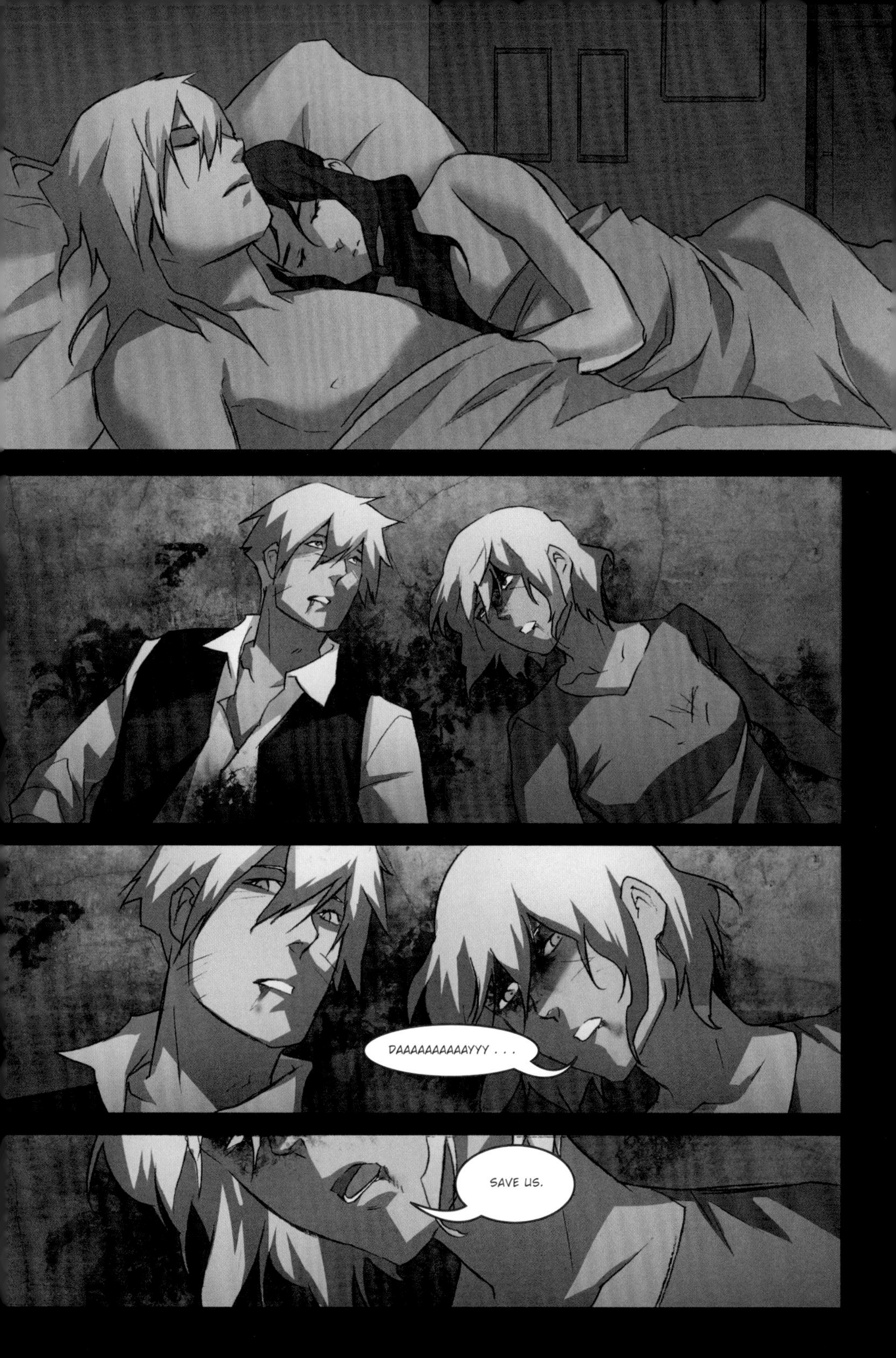
DAAAAAAAAAAYYY . . .
SAVE US.

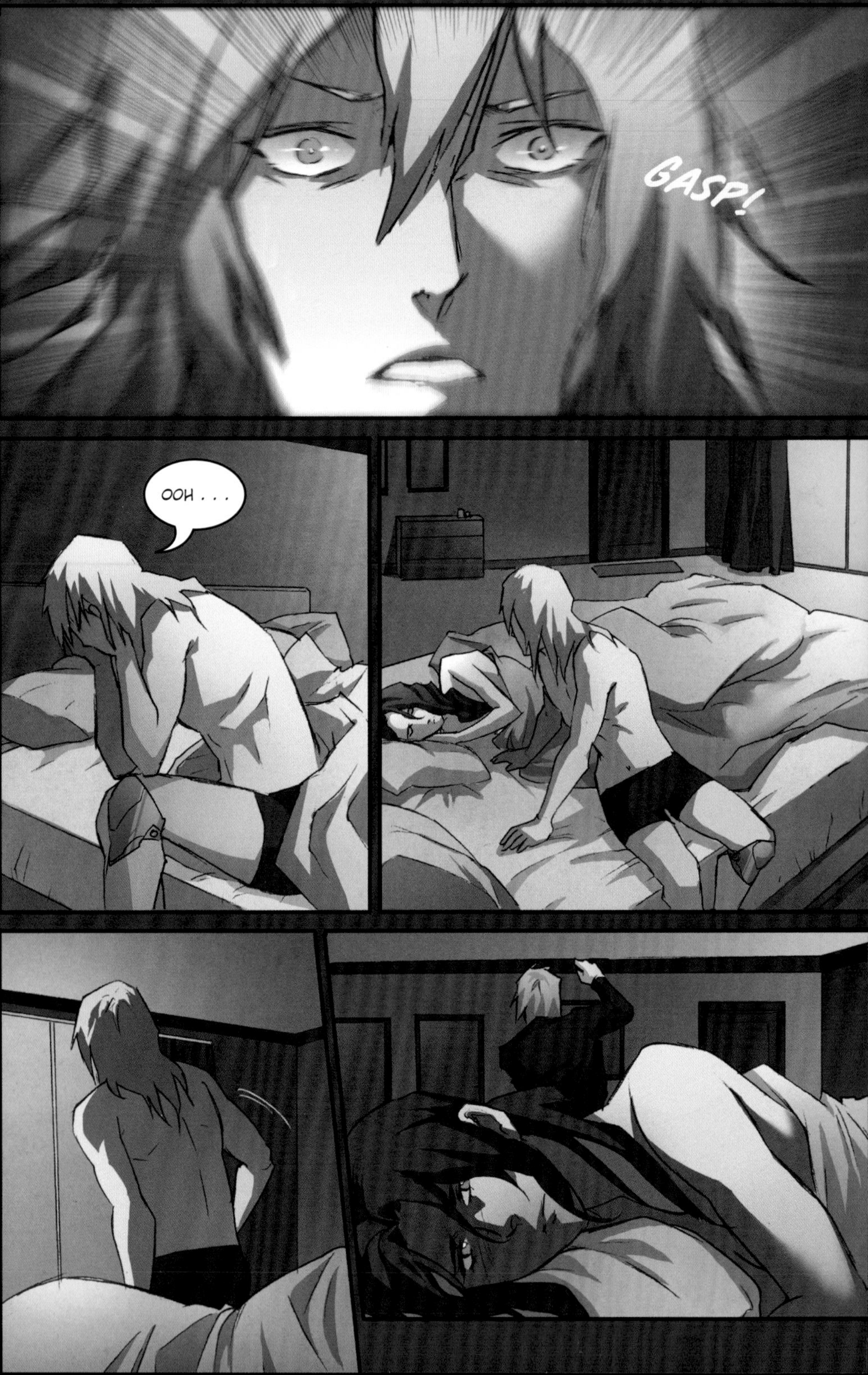
GASP!
OOH . . .

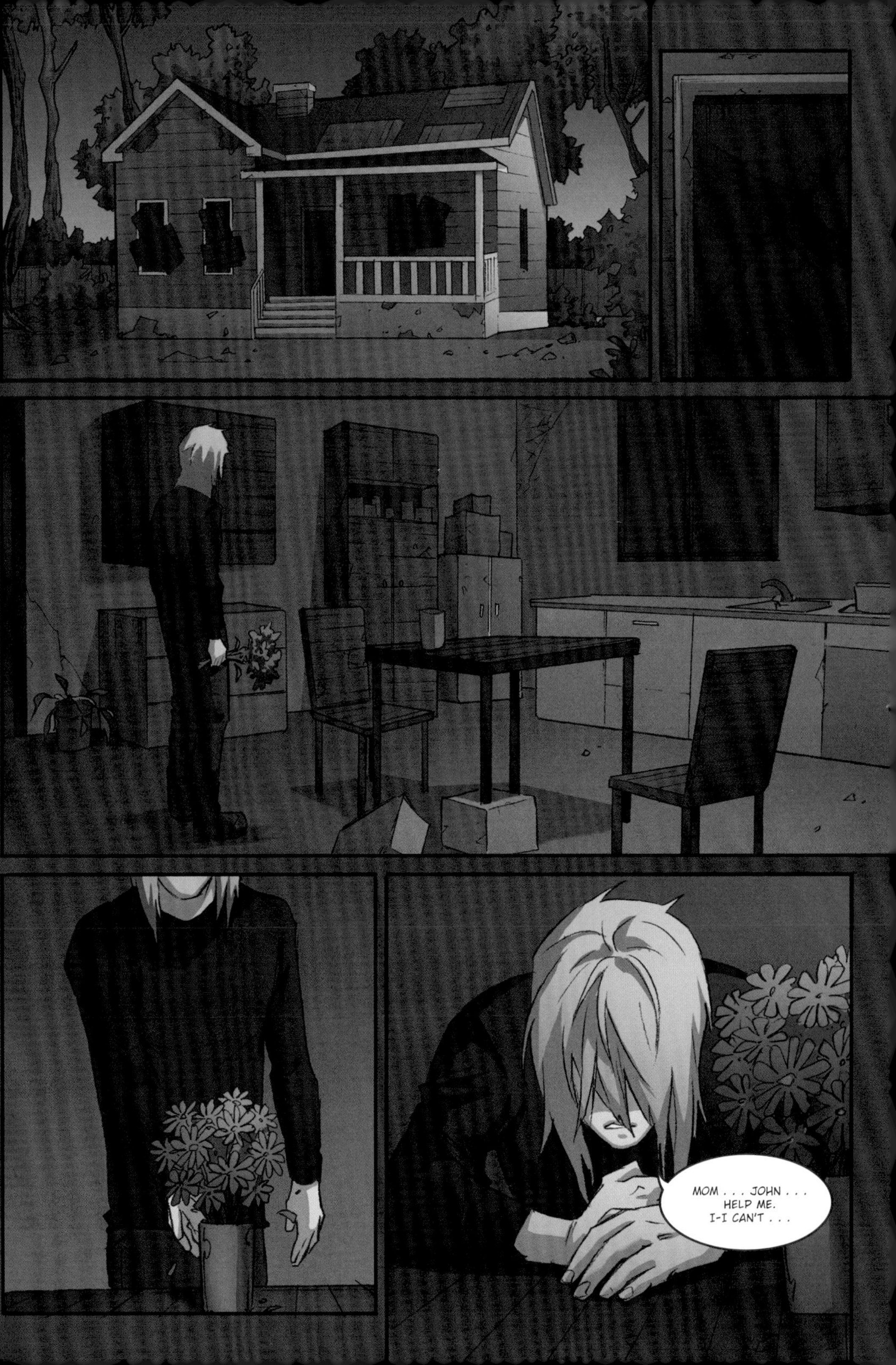
MOM . . . JOHN . . .
HELP ME.
I-I CAN'T . . .

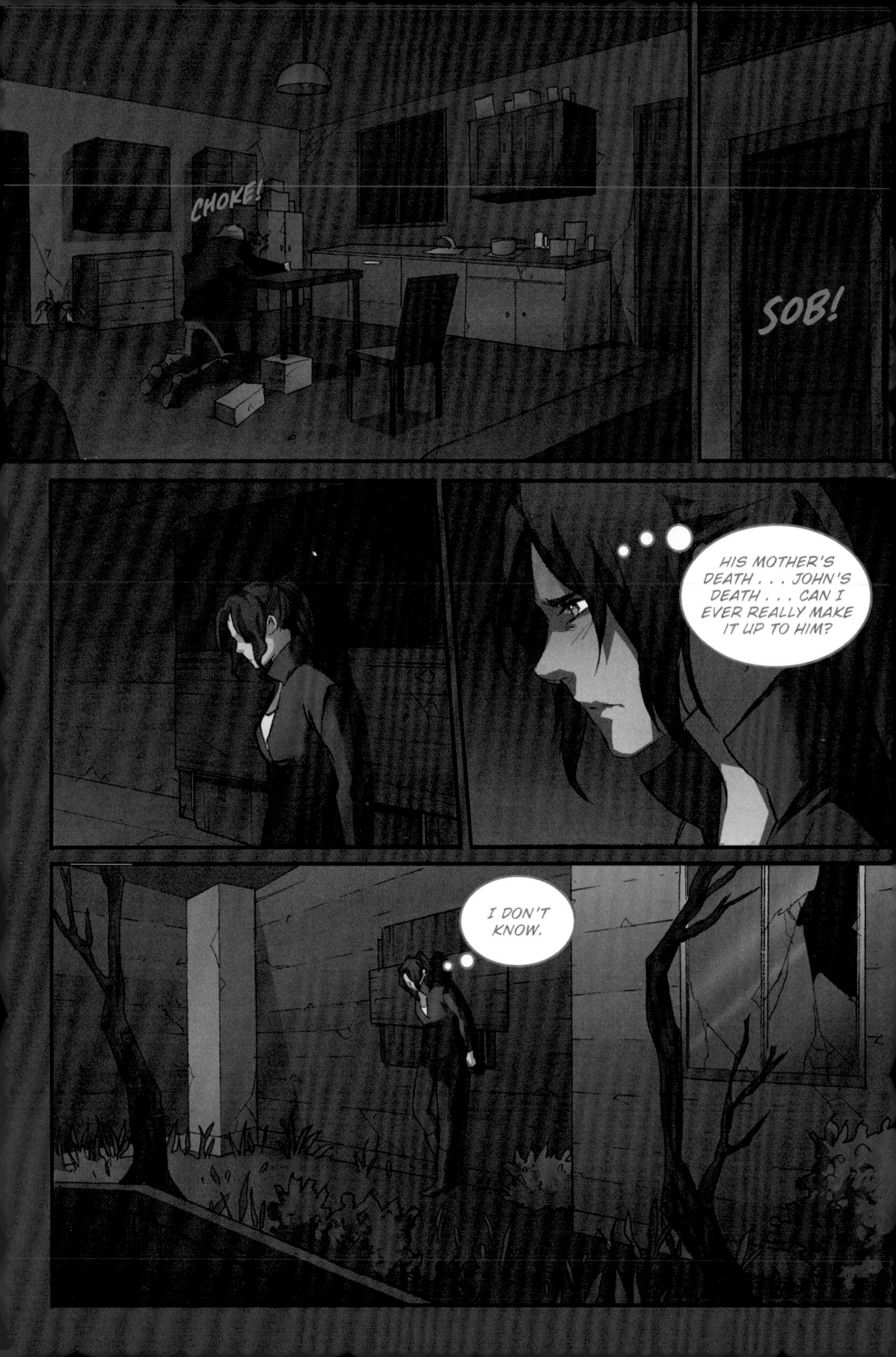
CHOKE!
SOB!
HIS MOTHER'S DEATH . . . JOHN'S DEATH . . . CAN I EVER REALLY MAKE IT UP TO HIM?
I DON'T KNOW.

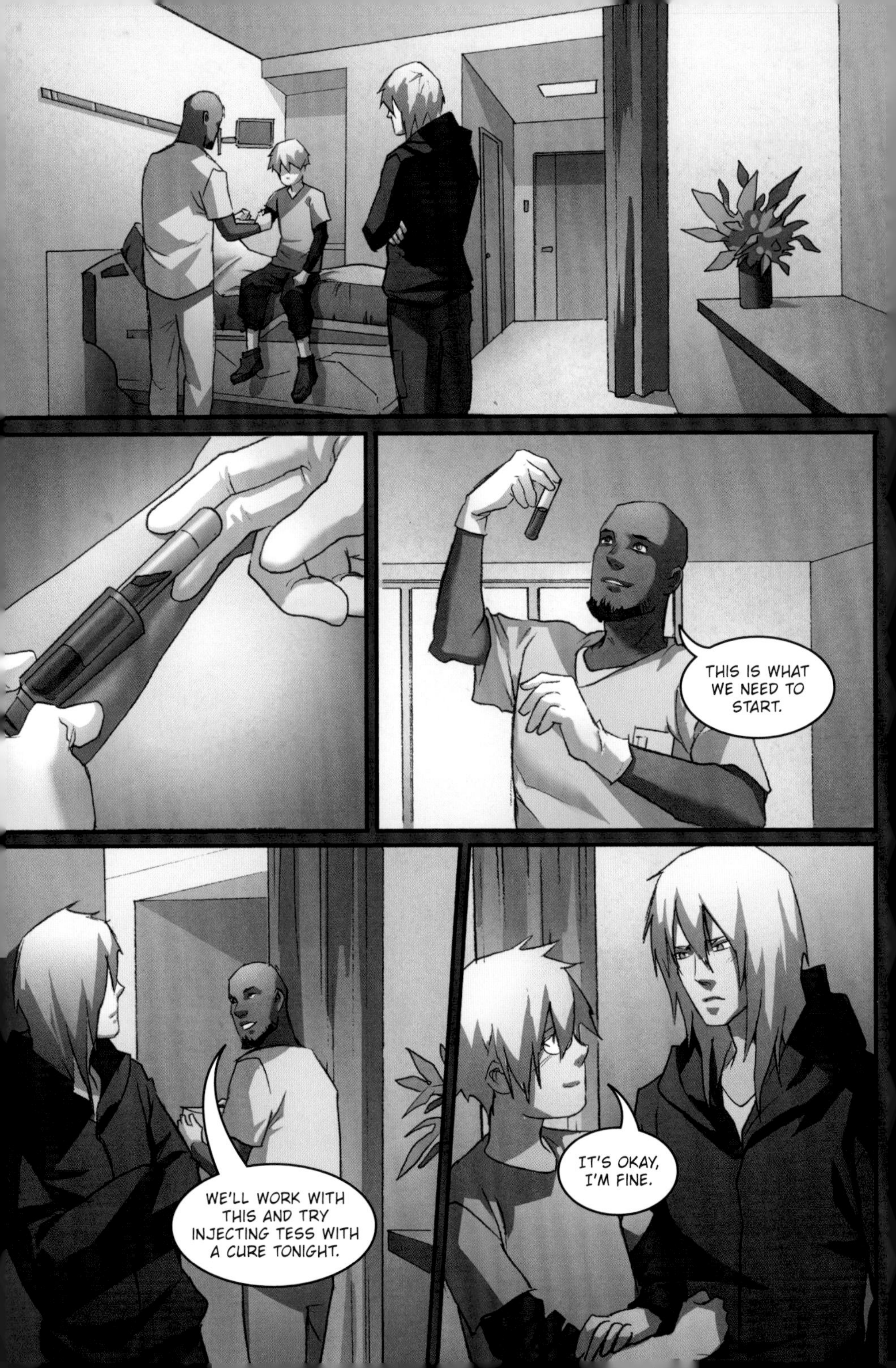
THIS IS WHAT WE NEED TO START.
WE'LL WORK WITH THIS AND TRY INJECTING TESS WITH A CURE TONIGHT.
IT'S OKAY, I'M FINE.

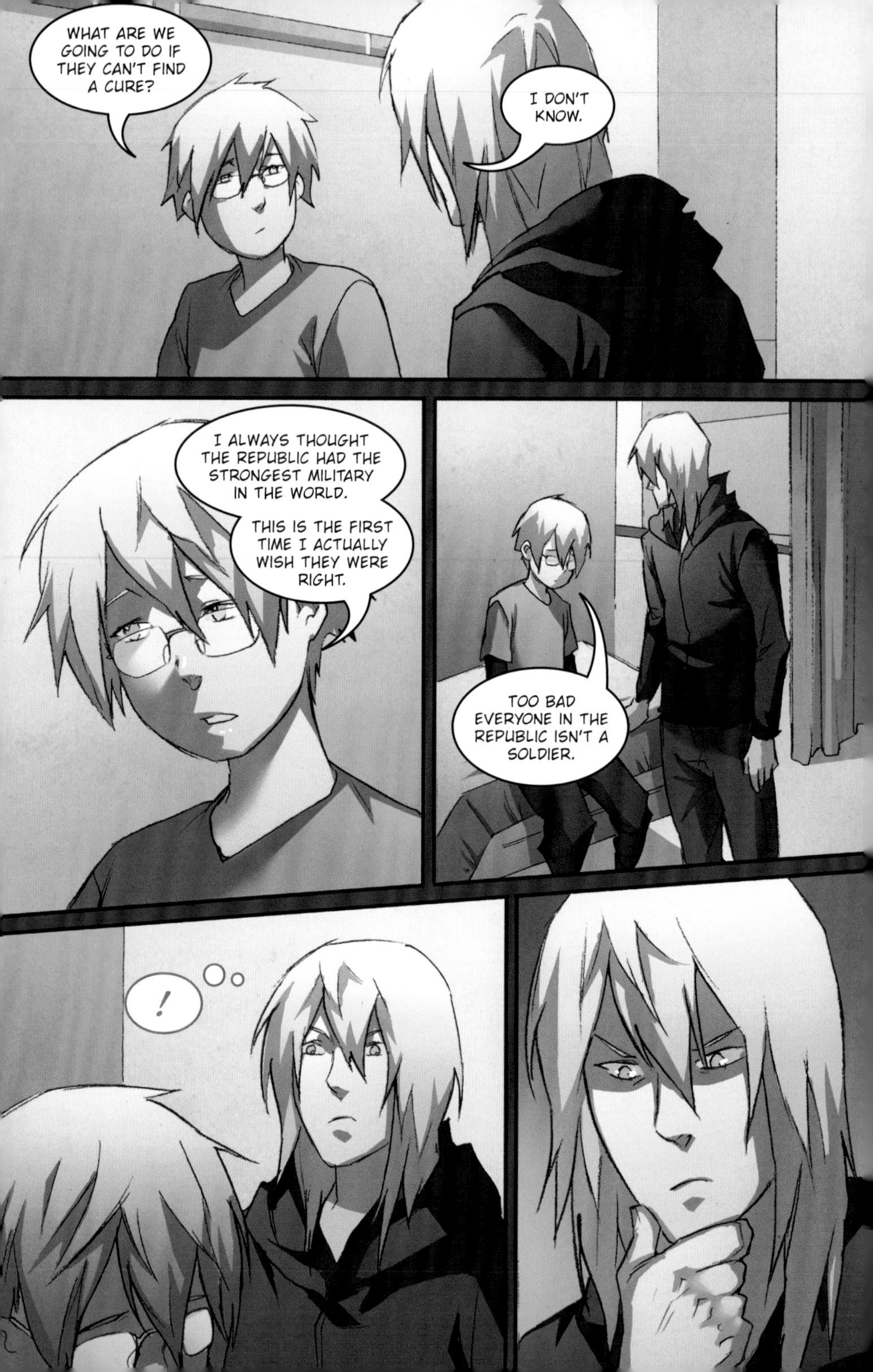
WHAT ARE WE GOING TO DO IF THEY CAN'T FIND A CURE?
I DON'T KNOW.
I ALWAYS THOUGHT THE REPUBLIC HAD THE STRONGEST MILITARY IN THE WORLD.
THIS IS THE FIRST TIME I ACTUALLY WISH THEY WERE RIGHT.
TOO BAD EVERYONE IN THE REPUBLIC ISN'T A SOLDIER.
!

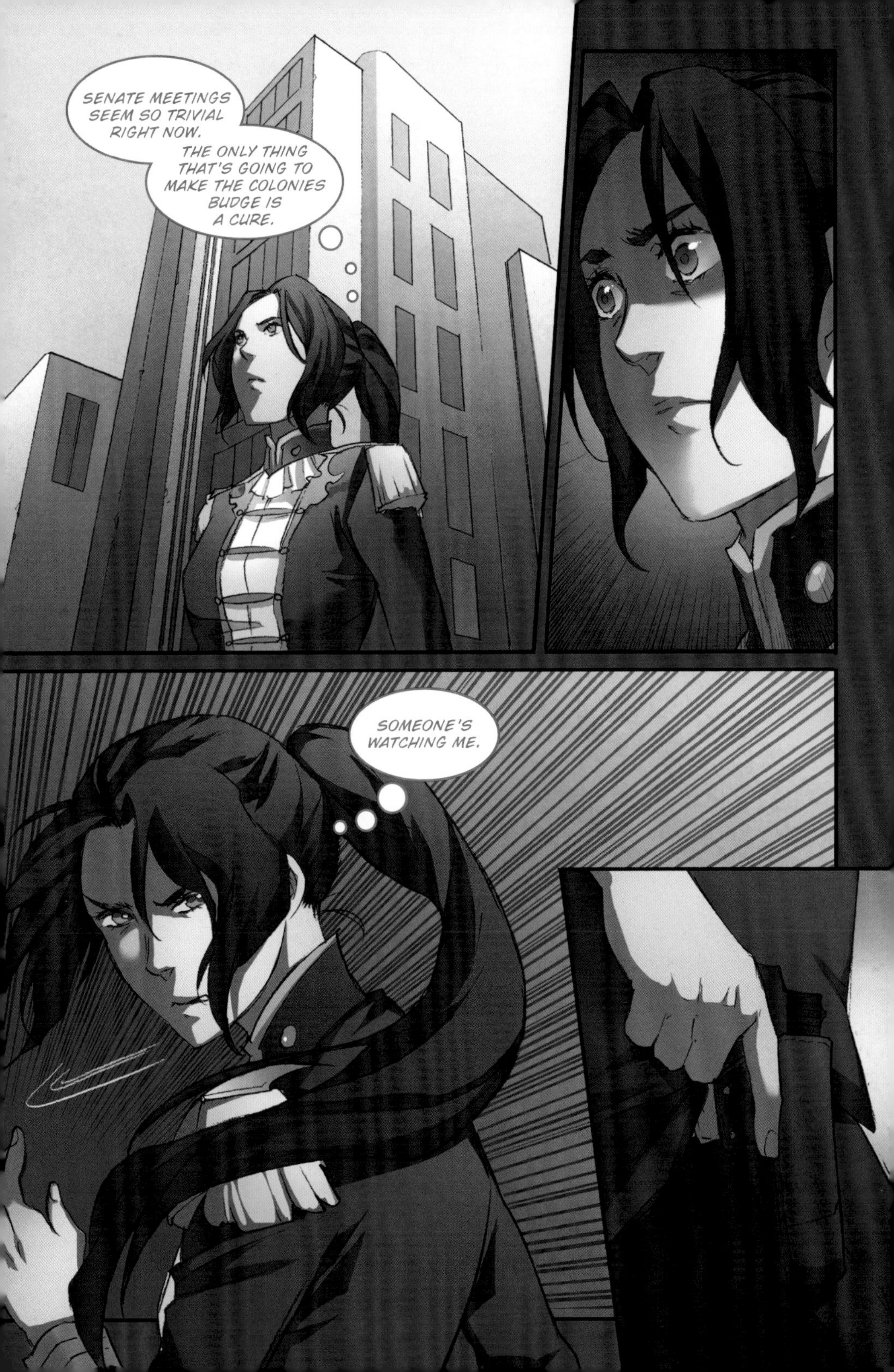
SENATE MEETINGS SEEM SO TRIVIAL RIGHT NOW.
THE ONLY THING THAT'S GOING TO MAKE THE COLONIES BUDGE IS A CURE.
SOMEONE'S WATCHING ME.

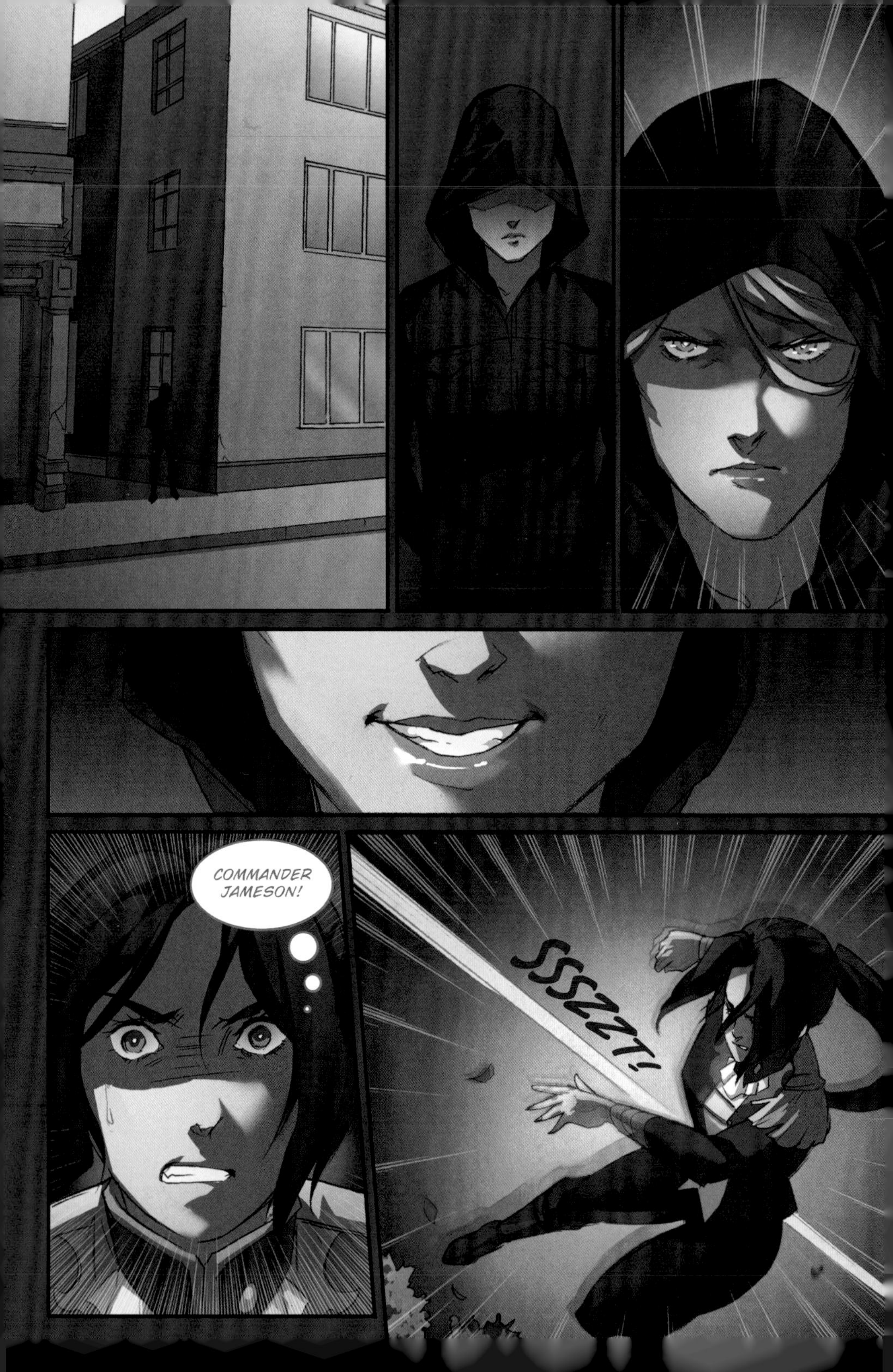
COMMANDER JAMESON!
SSSZZT!

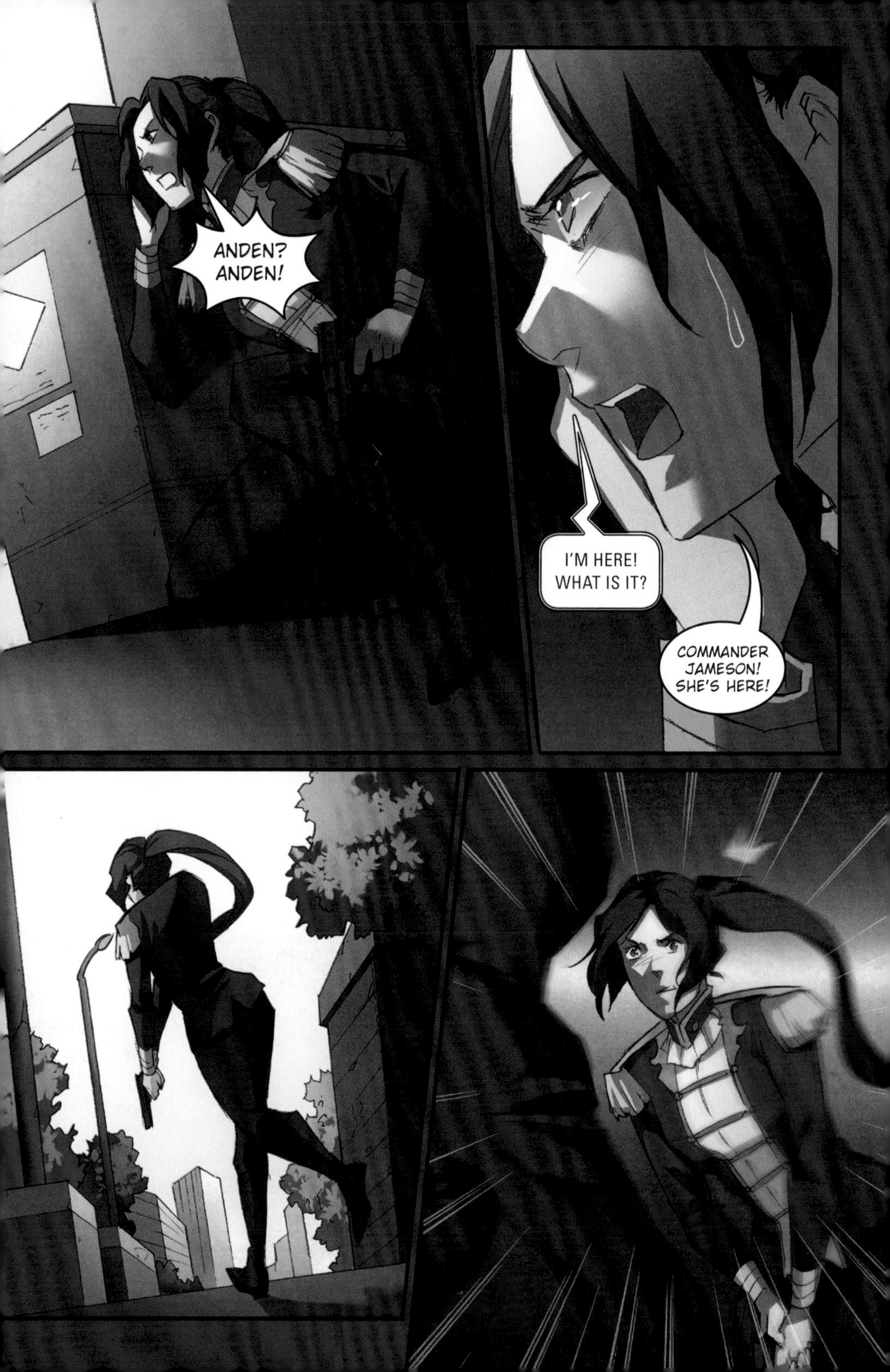
ANDEN? ANDEN!
I'M HERE! WHAT IS IT?
COMMANDER JAMESON! SHE'S HERE!

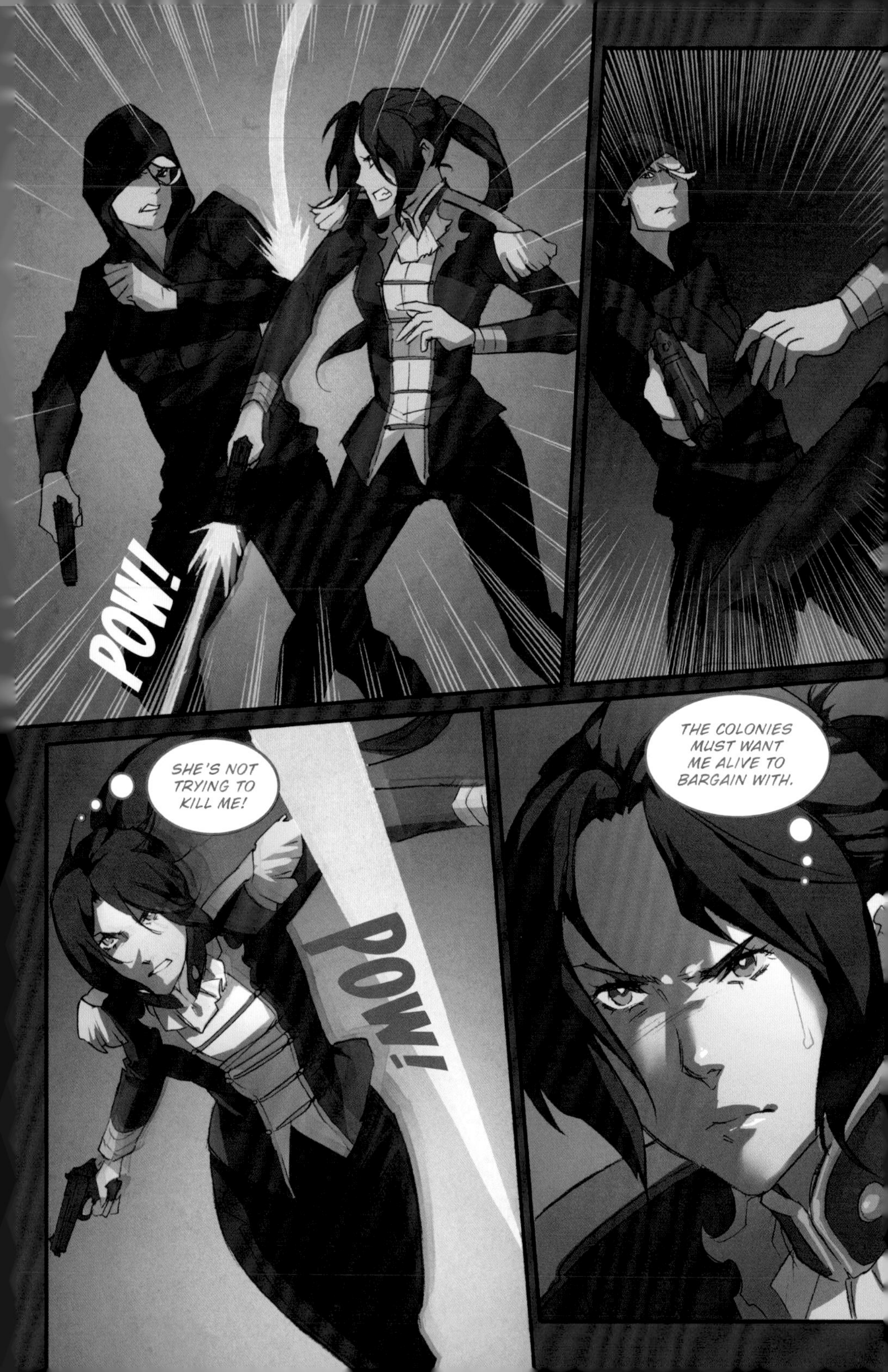
POW!
SHE'S NOT TRYING TO KILL ME!
POW!
THE COLONIES MUST WANT ME ALIVE TO BARGAIN WITH.

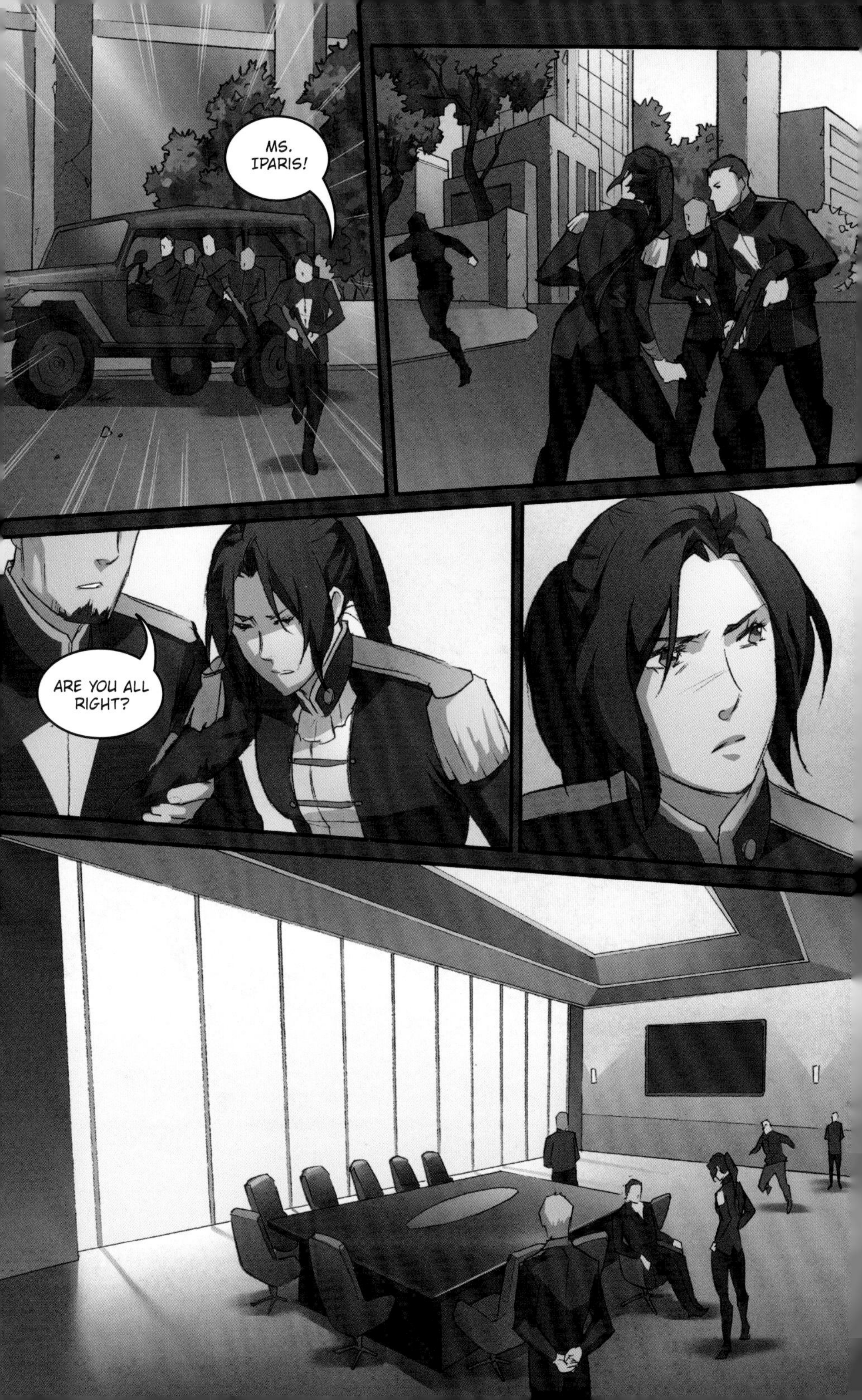
MS. IPARIS!
ARE YOU ALL RIGHT?

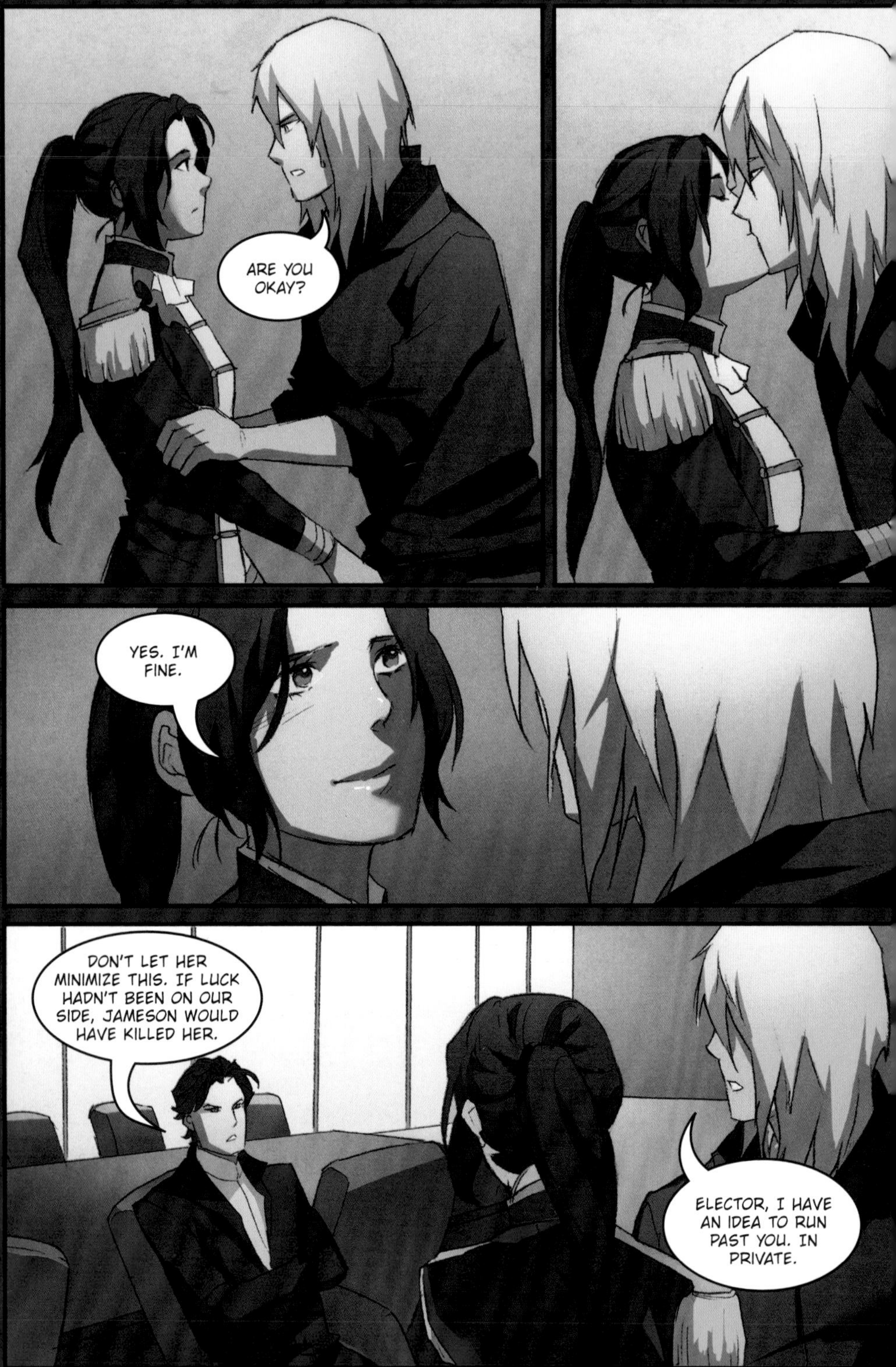
ARE YOU OKAY?
YES. I'M FINE.
DON'T LET HER MINIMIZE THIS. IF LUCK HADN'T BEEN ON OUR SIDE, JAMESON WOULD HAVE KILLED HER.
ELECTOR, I HAVE AN IDEA TO RUN PAST YOU. IN PRIVATE.

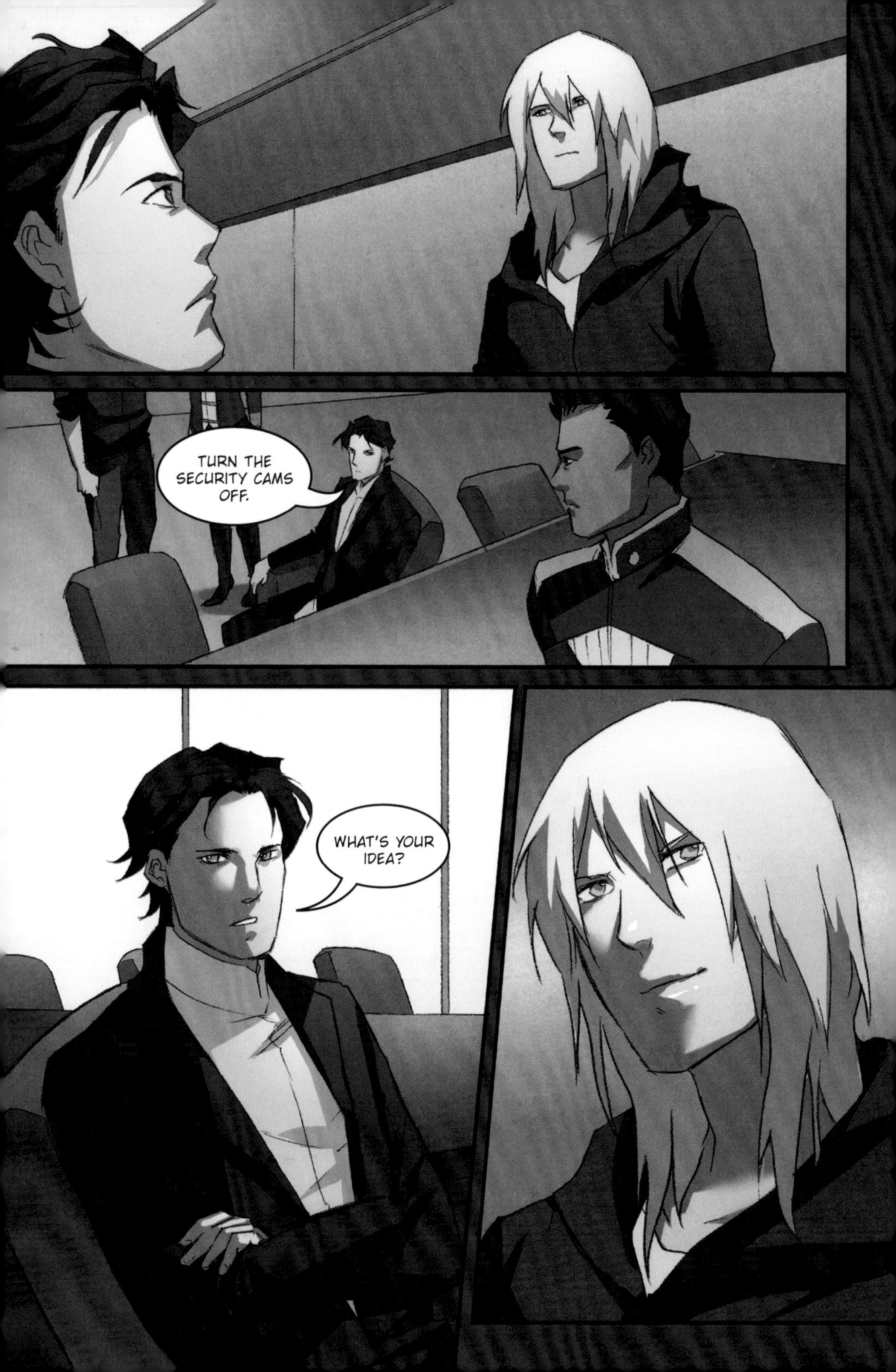
TURN THE SECURITY CAMS OFF.
WHAT'S YOUR IDEA?

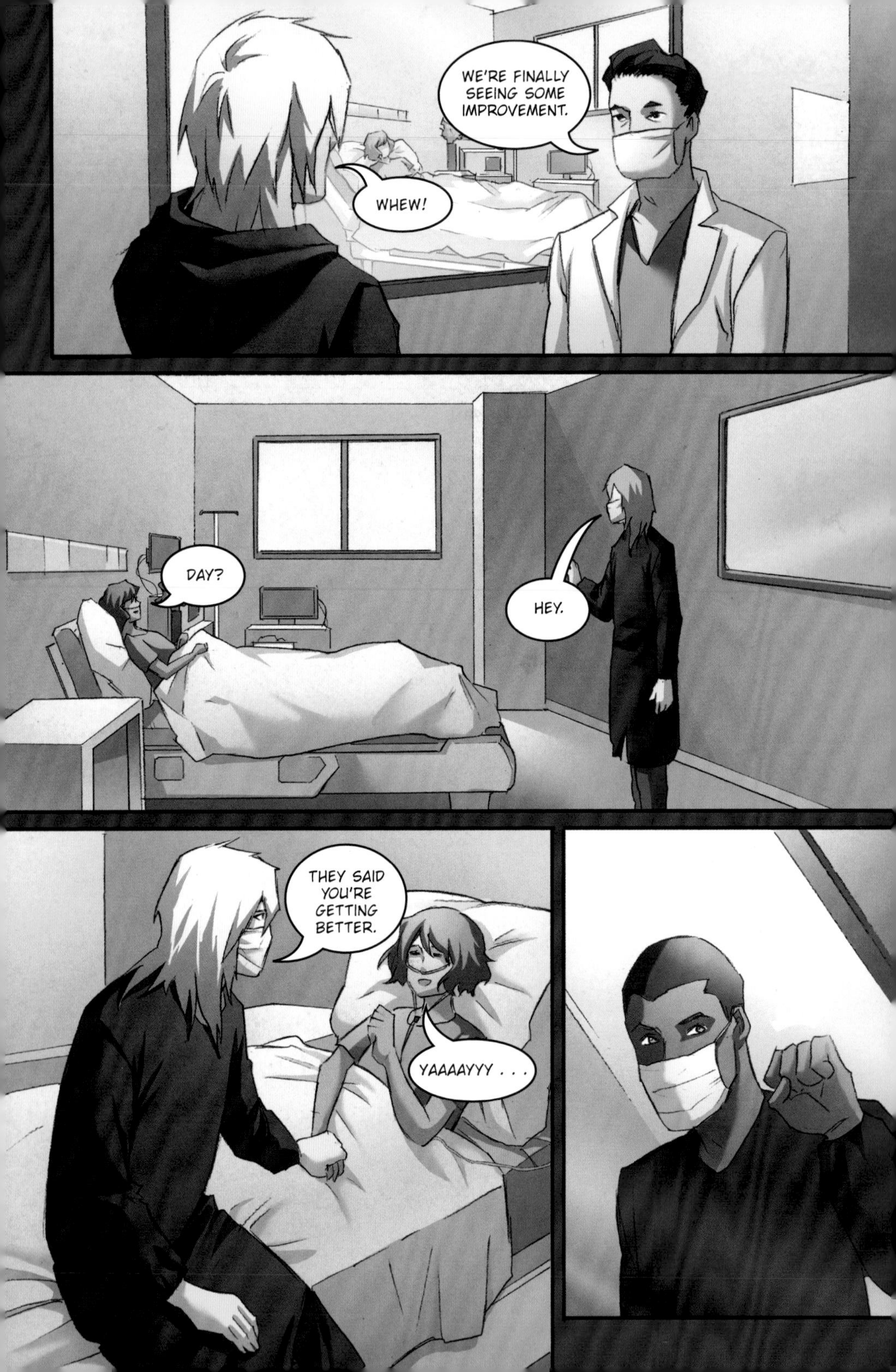
WE'RE FINALLY SEEING SOME IMPROVEMENT.
WHEW!
DAY?
HEY.
THEY SAID YOU'RE GETTING BETTER.
YAAAAYYY . . .

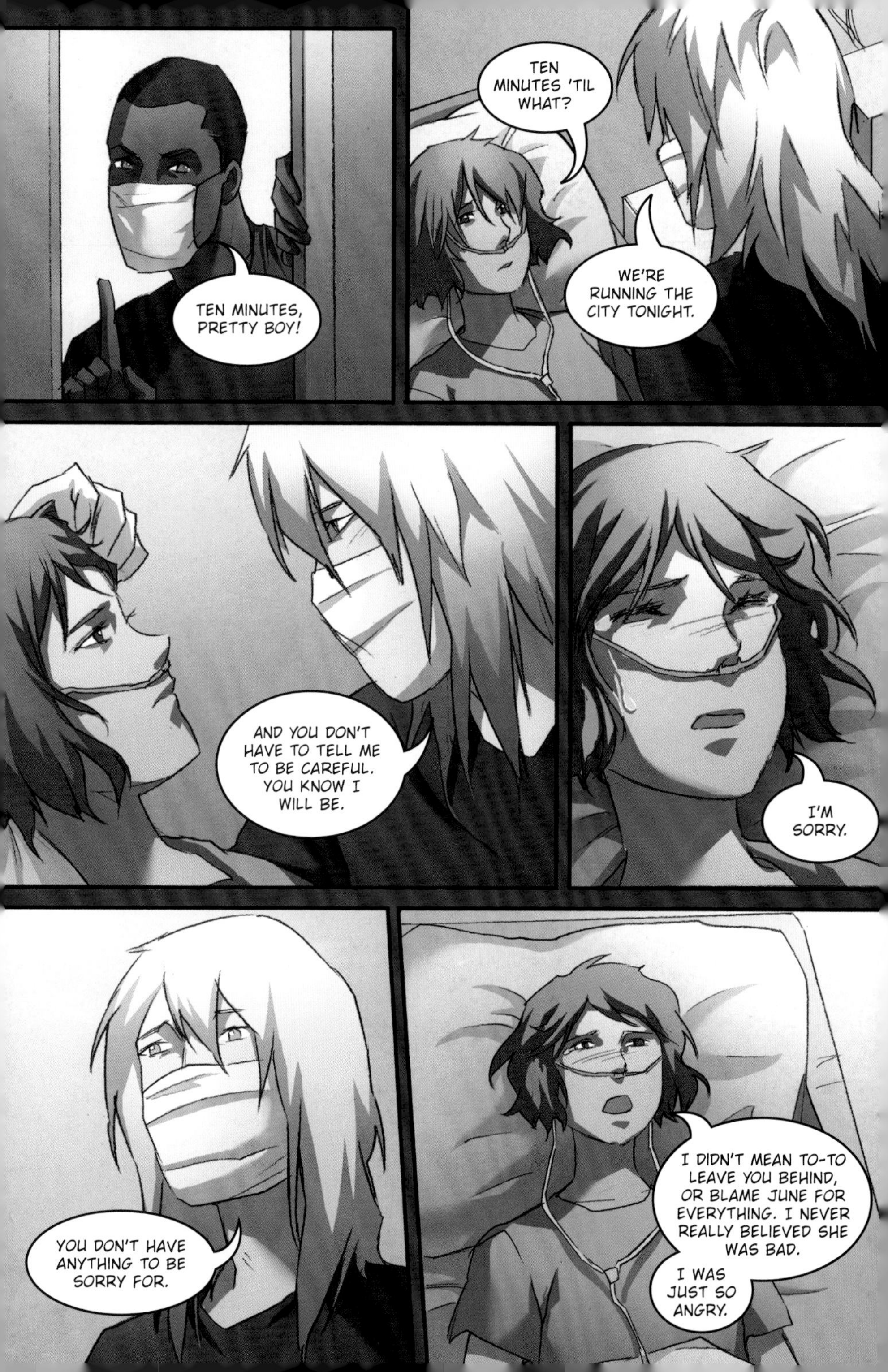
TEN MINUTES, PRETTY BOY!
TEN MINUTES 'TIL WHAT?
WE'RE RUNNING THE CITY TONIGHT.
AND YOU DON'T HAVE TO TELL ME TO BE CAREFUL. YOU KNOW I WILL BE.
I'M SORRY.
YOU DON'T HAVE ANYTHING TO BE SORRY FOR.
I DIDN'T MEAN TO-TO LEAVE YOU BEHIND, OR BLAME JUNE FOR EVERYTHING. I NEVER REALLY BELIEVED SHE WAS BAD.
I WAS JUST SO ANGRY.

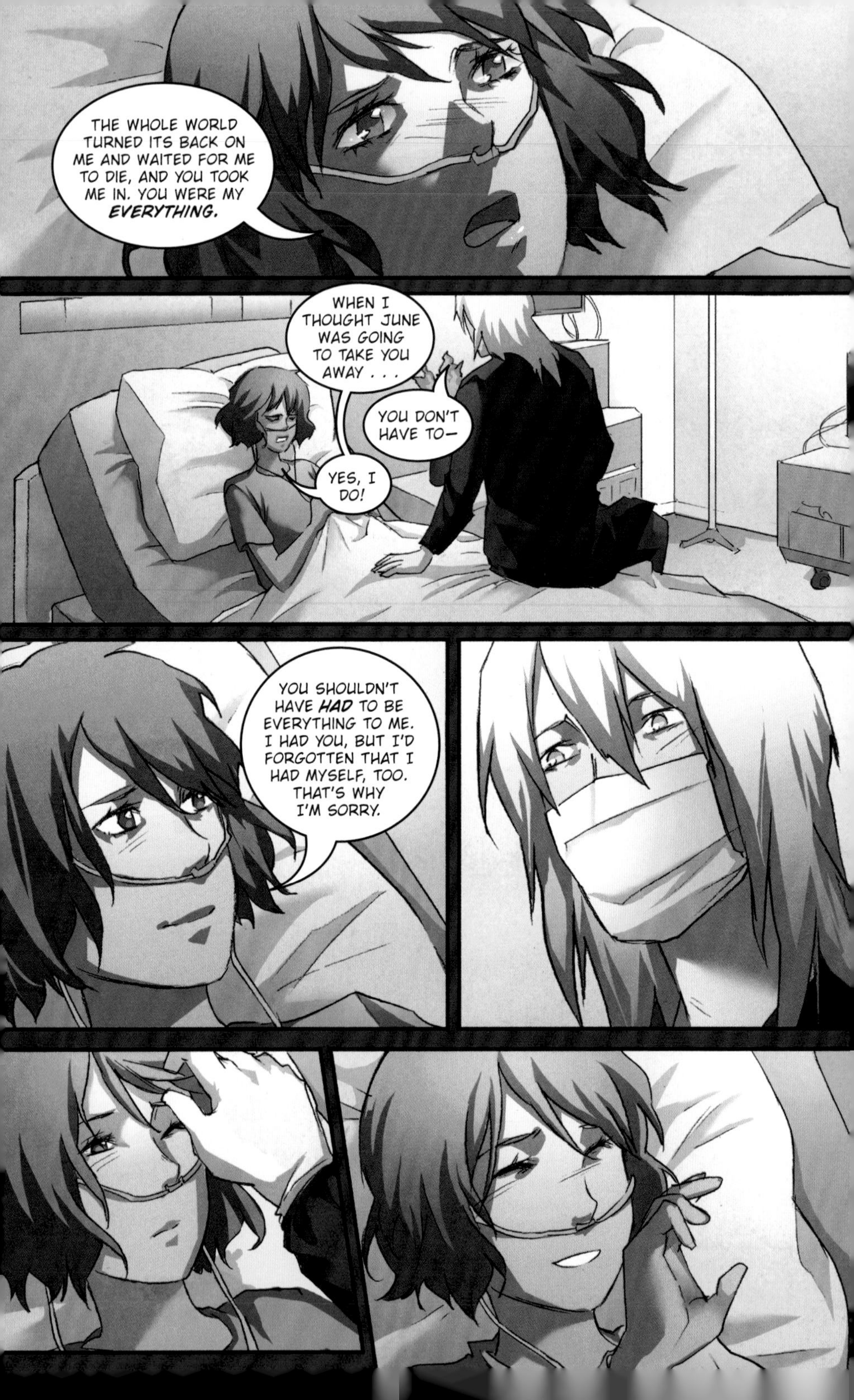
THE WHOLE WORLD TURNED ITS BACK ON ME AND WAITED FOR ME TO DIE, AND YOU TOOK ME IN. YOU WERE MY *EVERYTHING.*
WHEN I THOUGHT JUNE WAS GOING TO TAKE YOU AWAY . . .
YOU DON'T HAVE TO—
YES, I DO!
YOU SHOULDN'T HAVE *HAD* TO BE EVERYTHING TO ME. I HAD YOU, BUT I'D FORGOTTEN THAT I HAD MYSELF, TOO. THAT'S WHY I'M SORRY.

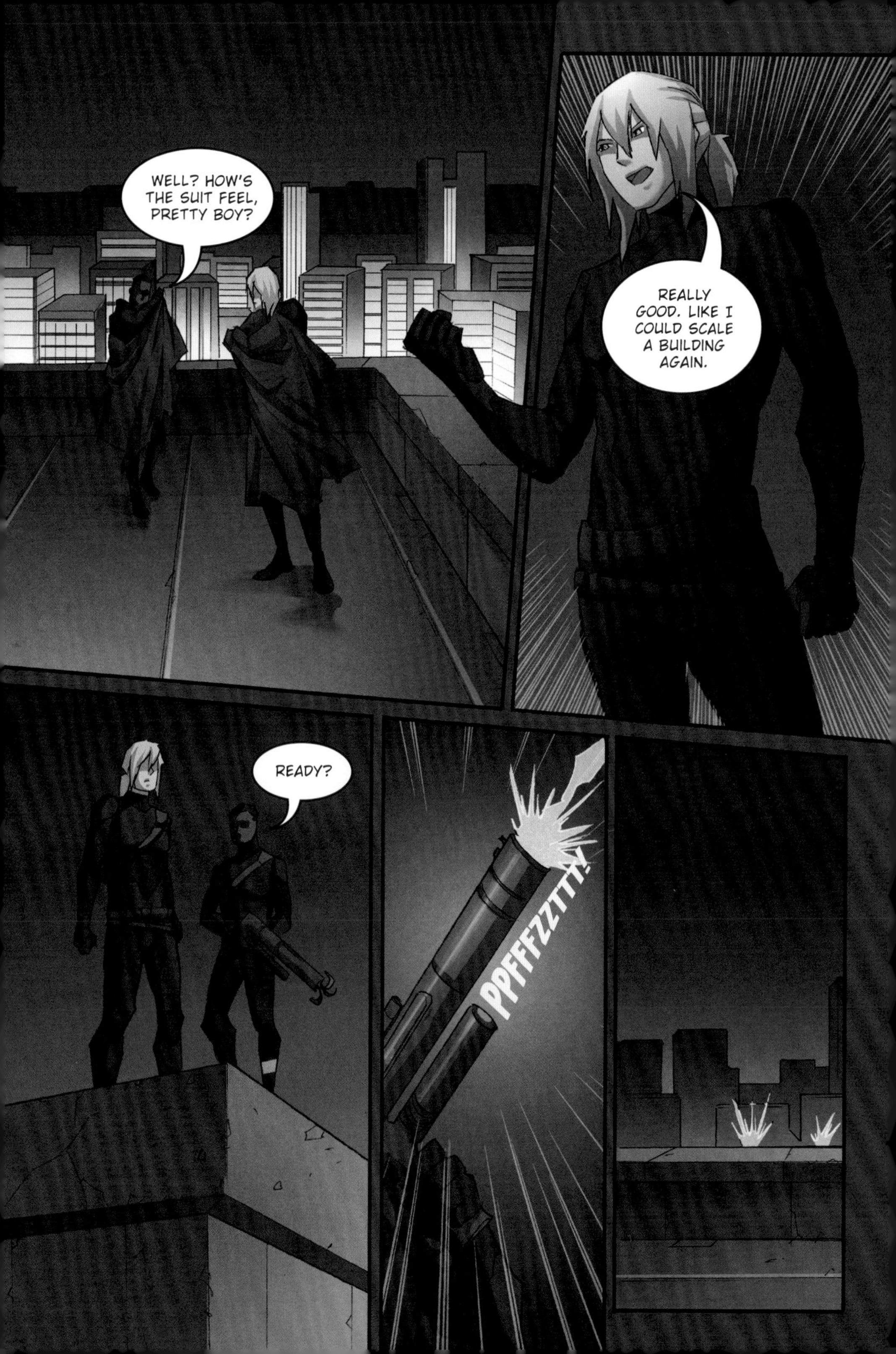
WELL? HOW'S THE SUIT FEEL, PRETTY BOY?
REALLY GOOD. LIKE I COULD SCALE A BUILDING AGAIN.
READY?
PPFFFZZZTTTT!

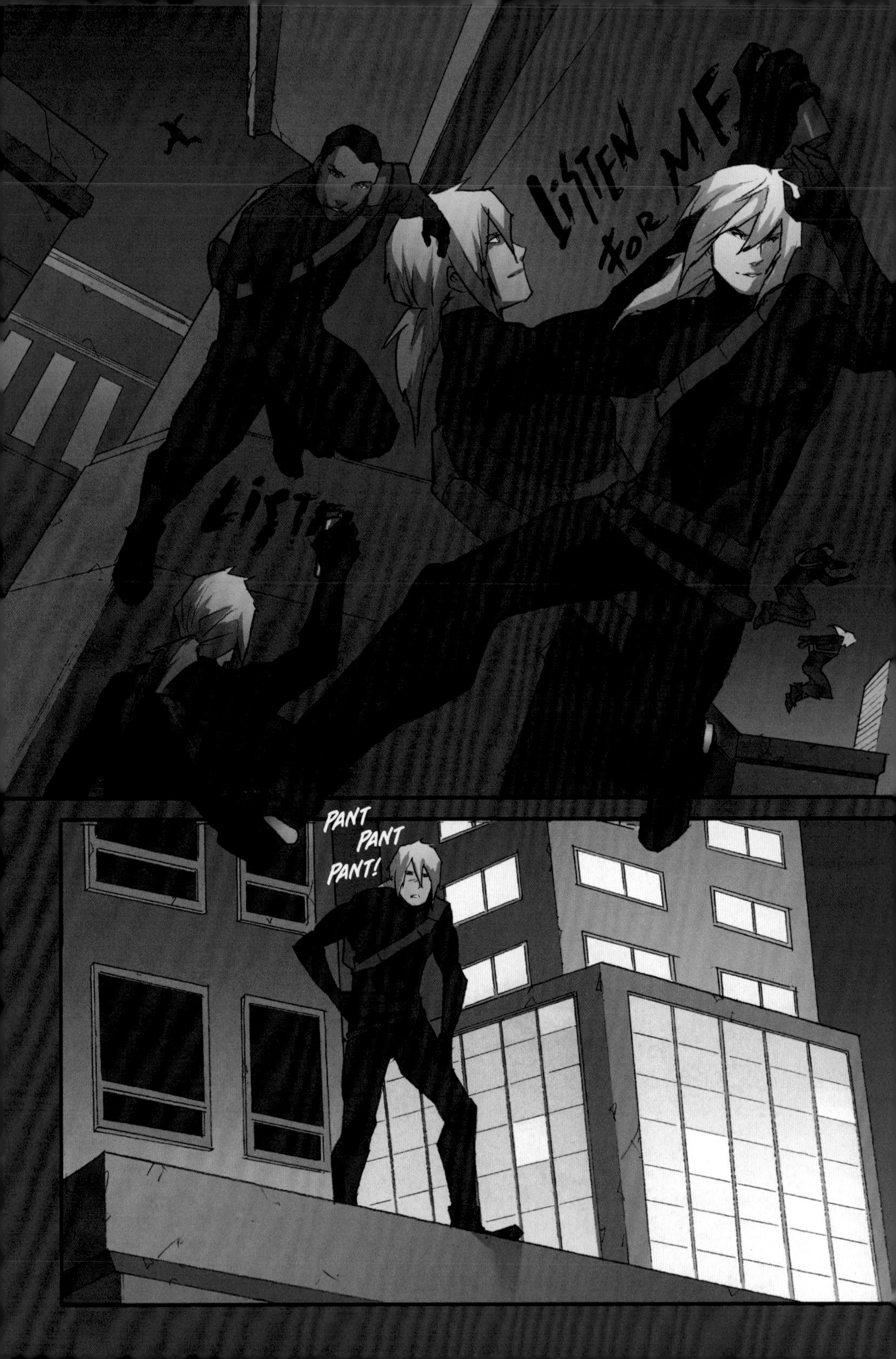
LISTEN FOR ME
LISTEN
PANT PANT PANT!

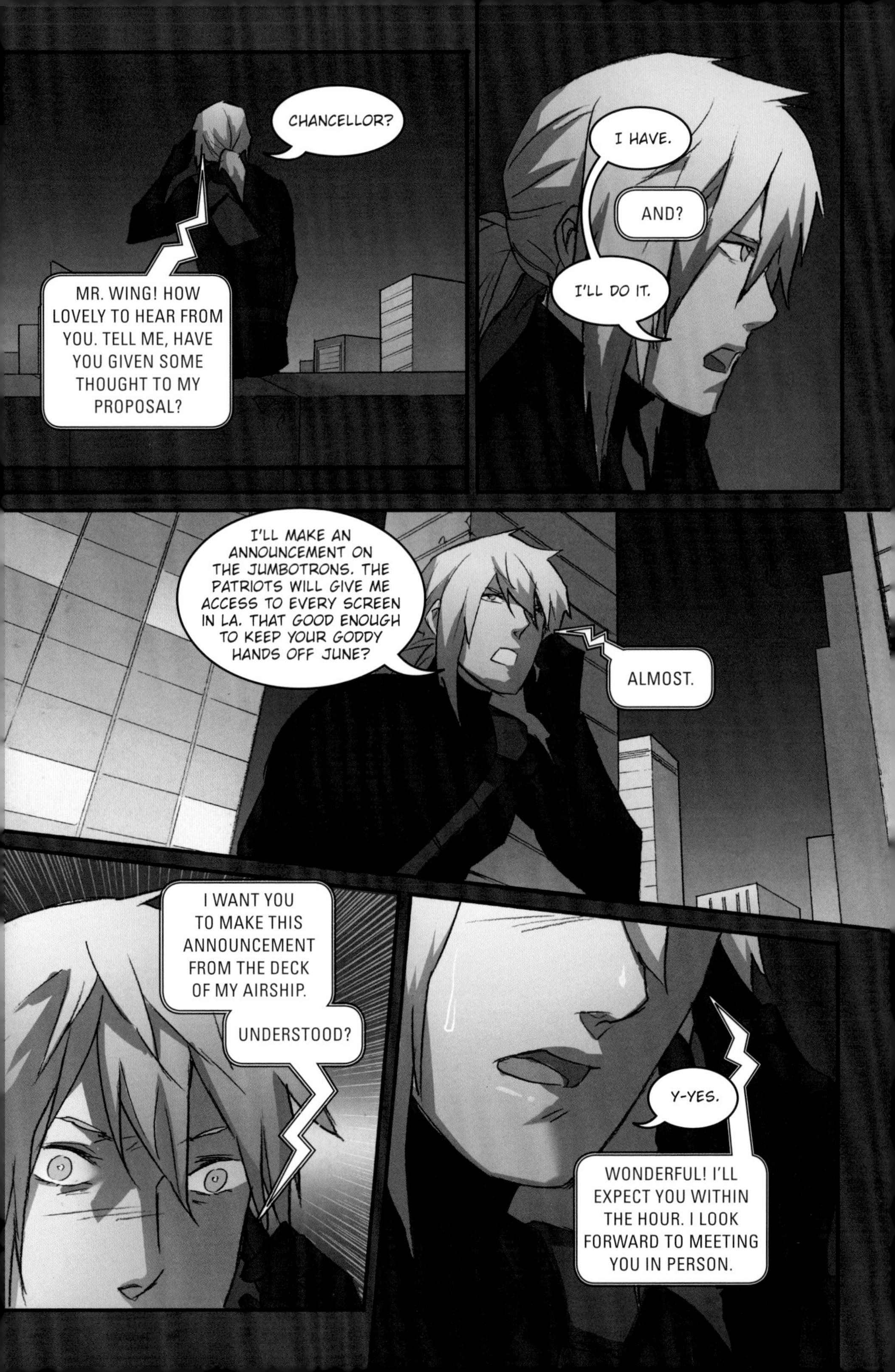
CHANCELLOR?
MR. WING! HOW LOVELY TO HEAR FROM YOU. TELL ME, HAVE YOU GIVEN SOME THOUGHT TO MY PROPOSAL?
I HAVE.
AND?
I'LL DO IT.
I'LL MAKE AN ANNOUNCEMENT ON THE JUMBOTRONS. THE PATRIOTS WILL GIVE ME ACCESS TO EVERY SCREEN IN LA. THAT GOOD ENOUGH TO KEEP YOUR GODDY HANDS OFF JUNE?
ALMOST.
I WANT YOU TO MAKE THIS ANNOUNCEMENT FROM THE DECK OF MY AIRSHIP.
UNDERSTOOD?
Y-YES.
WONDERFUL! I'LL EXPECT YOU WITHIN THE HOUR. I LOOK FORWARD TO MEETING YOU IN PERSON.

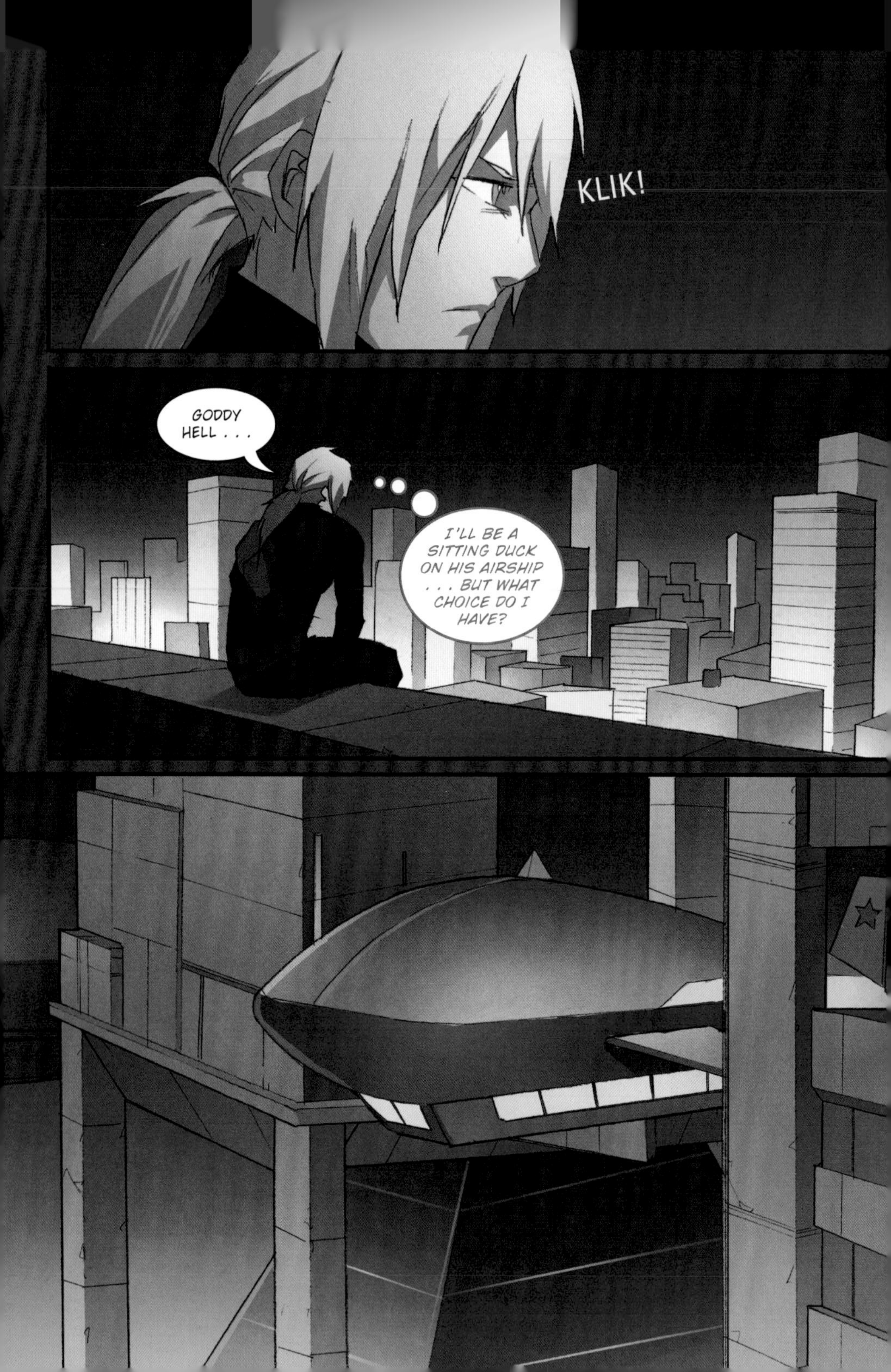
KLIK!
GODDY HELL . . .
I'LL BE A SITTING DUCK ON HIS AIRSHIP . . . BUT WHAT CHOICE DO I HAVE?

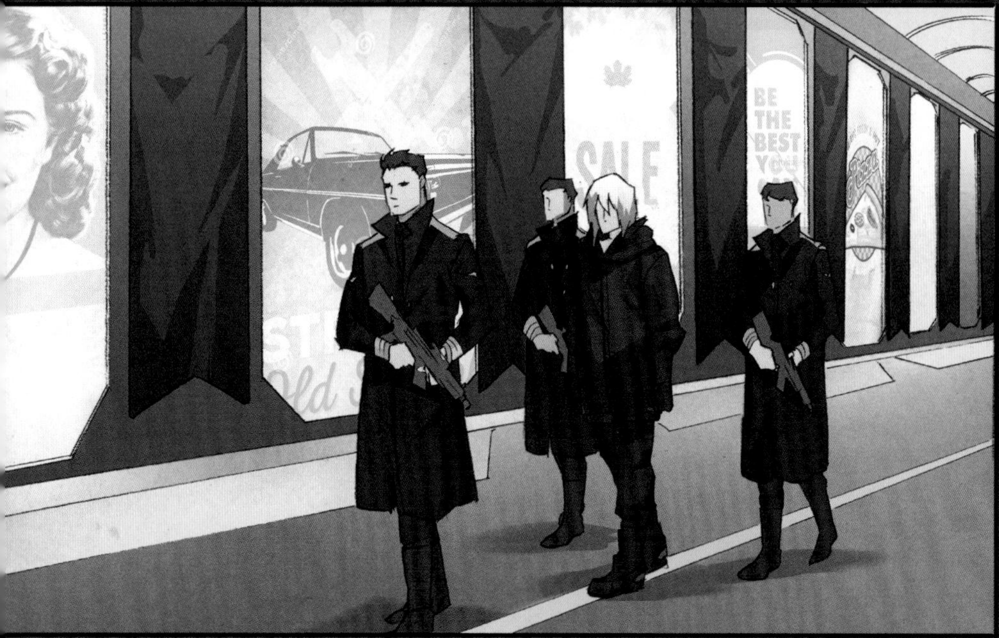
SALE
BE THE BEST

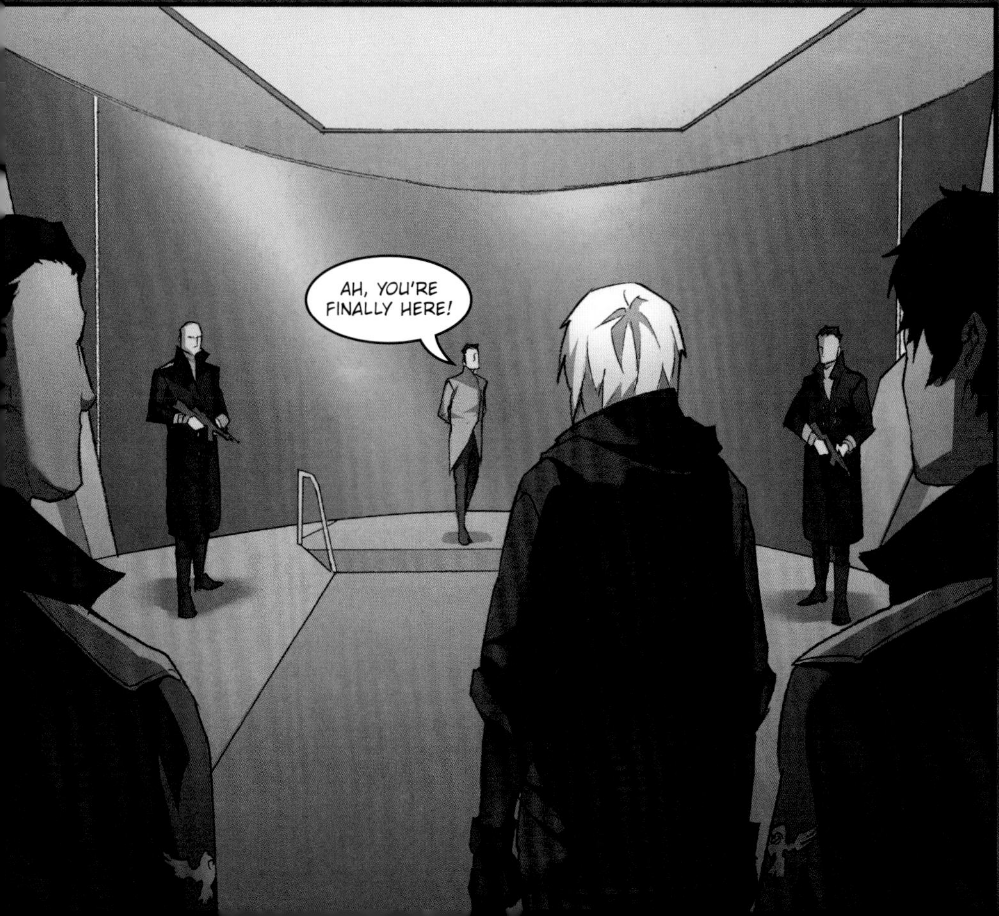
AH, YOU'RE FINALLY HERE!

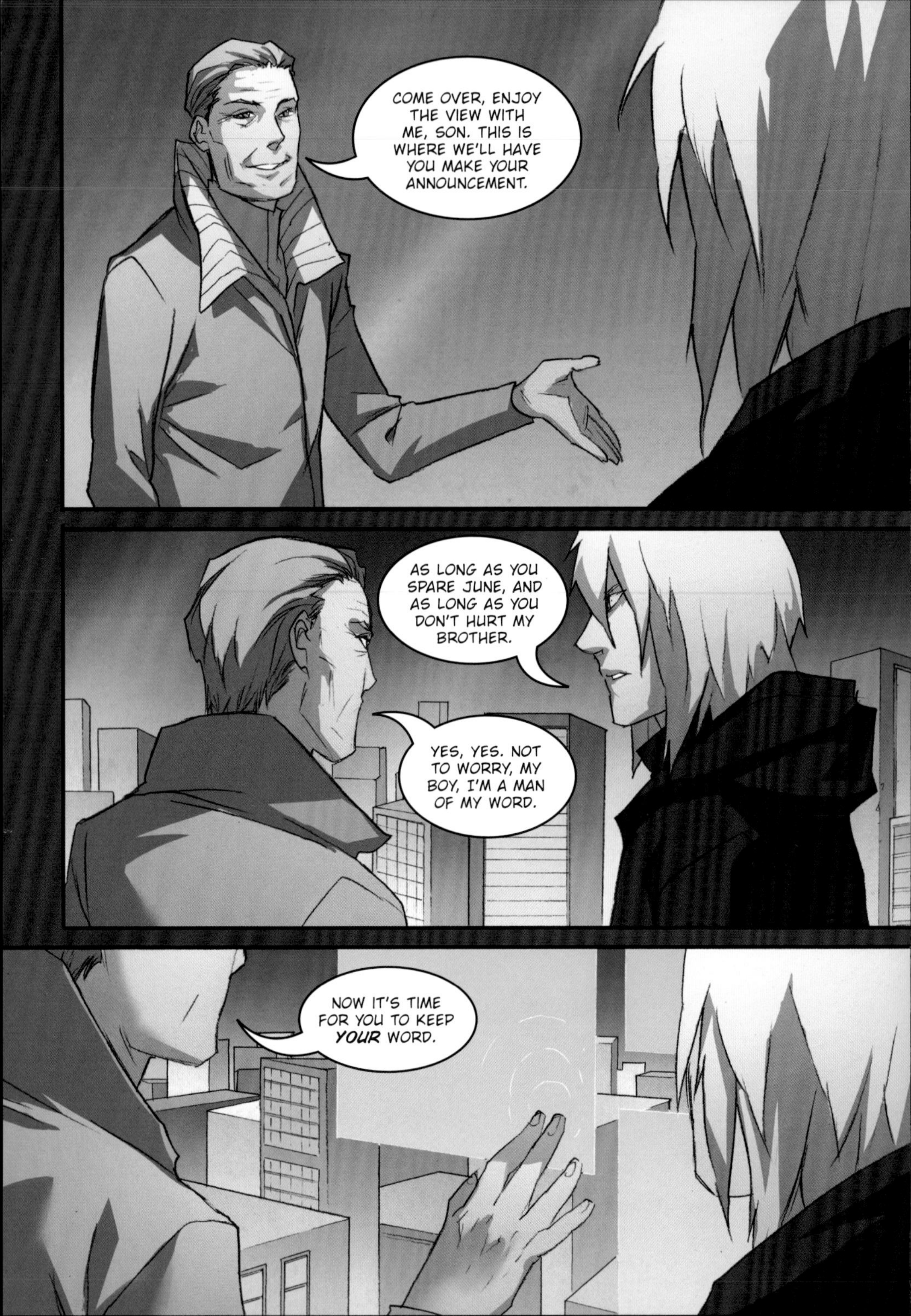
COME OVER, ENJOY THE VIEW WITH ME, SON. THIS IS WHERE WE'LL HAVE YOU MAKE YOUR ANNOUNCEMENT.
AS LONG AS YOU SPARE JUNE, AND AS LONG AS YOU DON'T HURT MY BROTHER.
YES, YES. NOT TO WORRY, MY BOY, I'M A MAN OF MY WORD.
NOW IT'S TIME FOR YOU TO KEEP ***YOUR*** WORD.

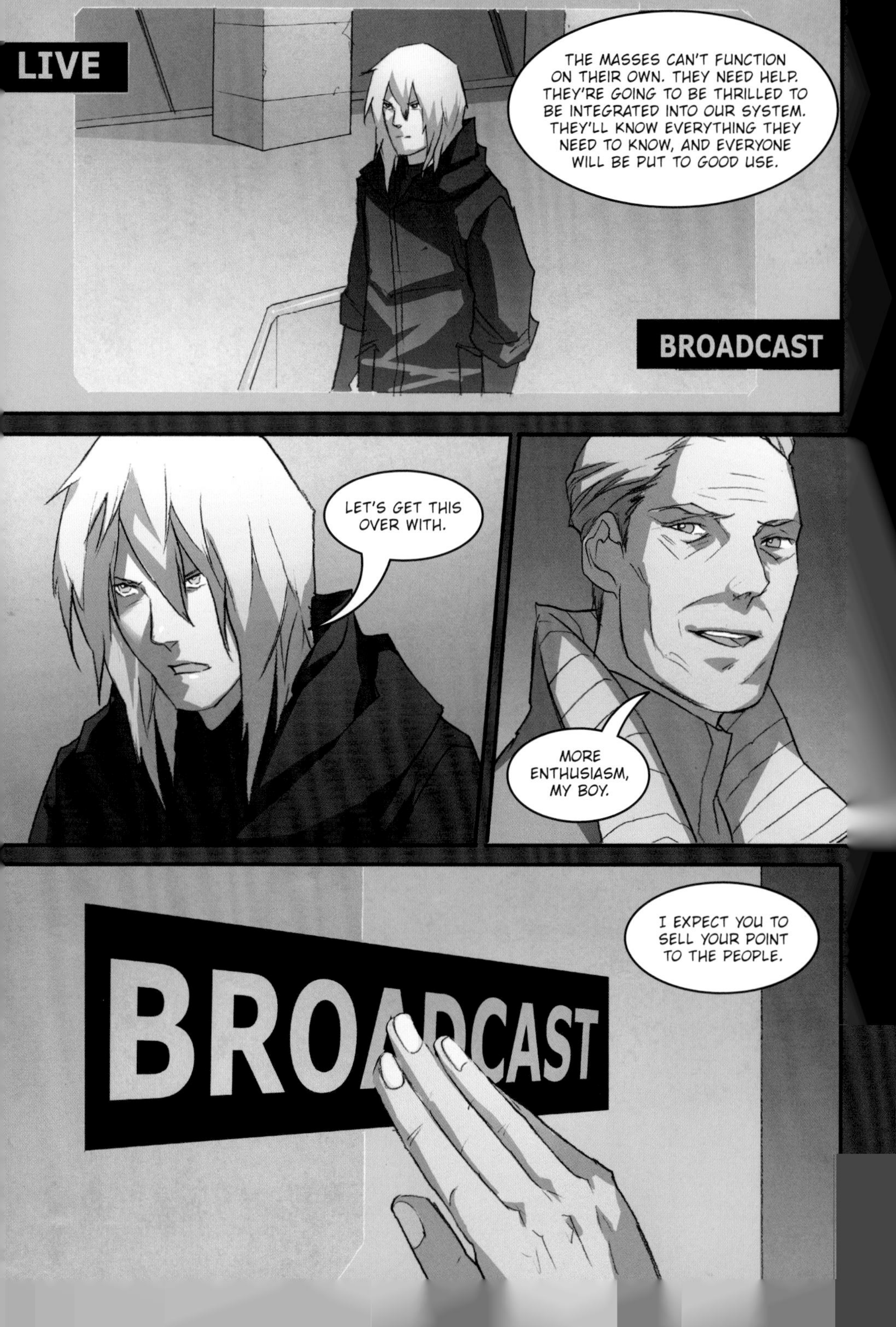
LIVE
THE MASSES CAN'T FUNCTION ON THEIR OWN. THEY NEED HELP. THEY'RE GOING TO BE THRILLED TO BE INTEGRATED INTO OUR SYSTEM. THEY'LL KNOW EVERYTHING THEY NEED TO KNOW, AND EVERYONE WILL BE PUT TO GOOD USE.
BROADCAST
LET'S GET THIS OVER WITH.
MORE ENTHUSIASM, MY BOY.
BROADCAST
I EXPECT YOU TO SELL YOUR POINT TO THE PEOPLE.

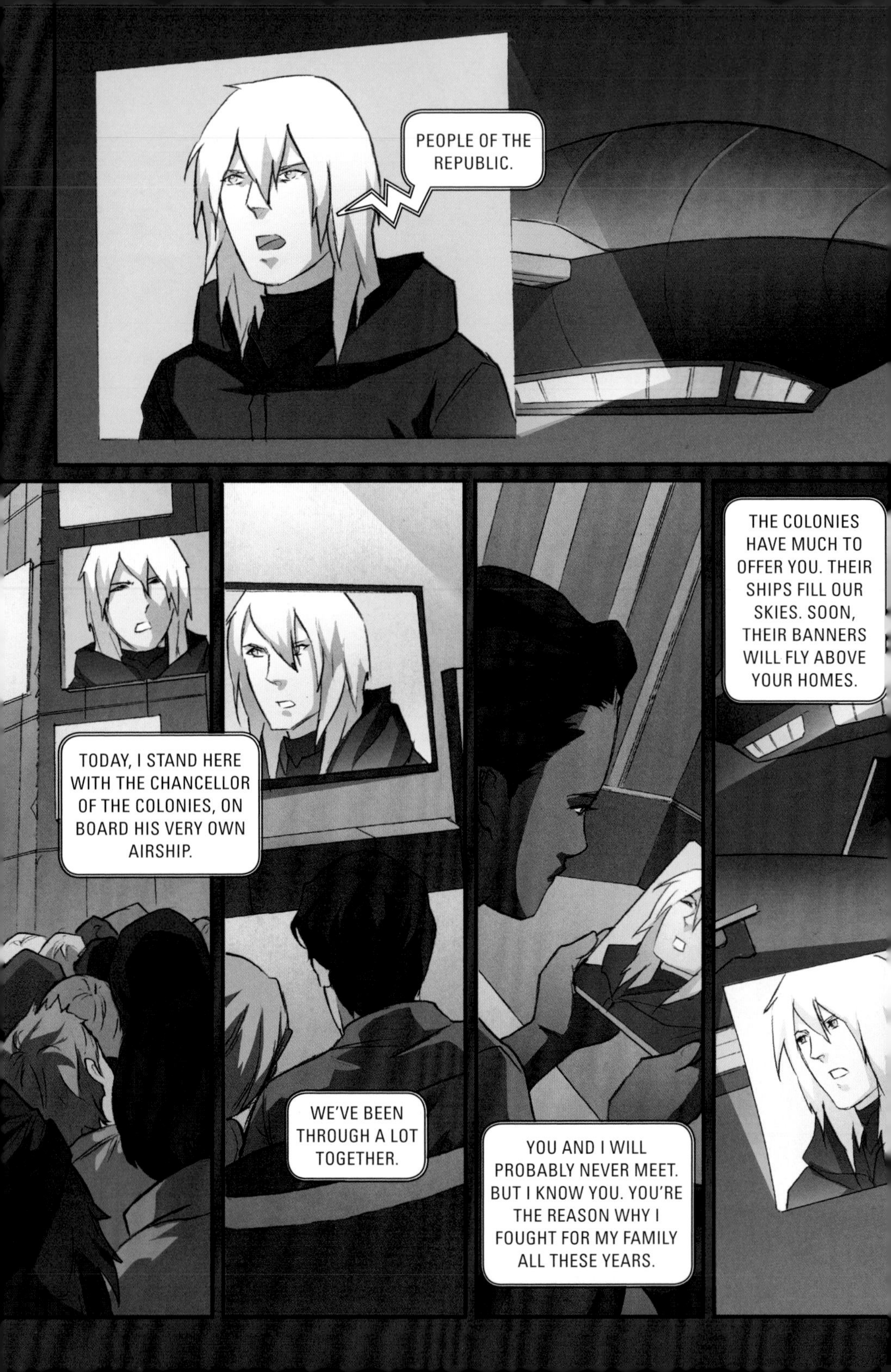
PEOPLE OF THE REPUBLIC.
TODAY, I STAND HERE WITH THE CHANCELLOR OF THE COLONIES, ON BOARD HIS VERY OWN AIRSHIP.
WE'VE BEEN THROUGH A LOT TOGETHER.
YOU AND I WILL PROBABLY NEVER MEET. BUT I KNOW YOU. YOU'RE THE REASON WHY I FOUGHT FOR MY FAMILY ALL THESE YEARS.
THE COLONIES HAVE MUCH TO OFFER YOU. THEIR SHIPS FILL OUR SKIES. SOON, THEIR BANNERS WILL FLY ABOVE YOUR HOMES.

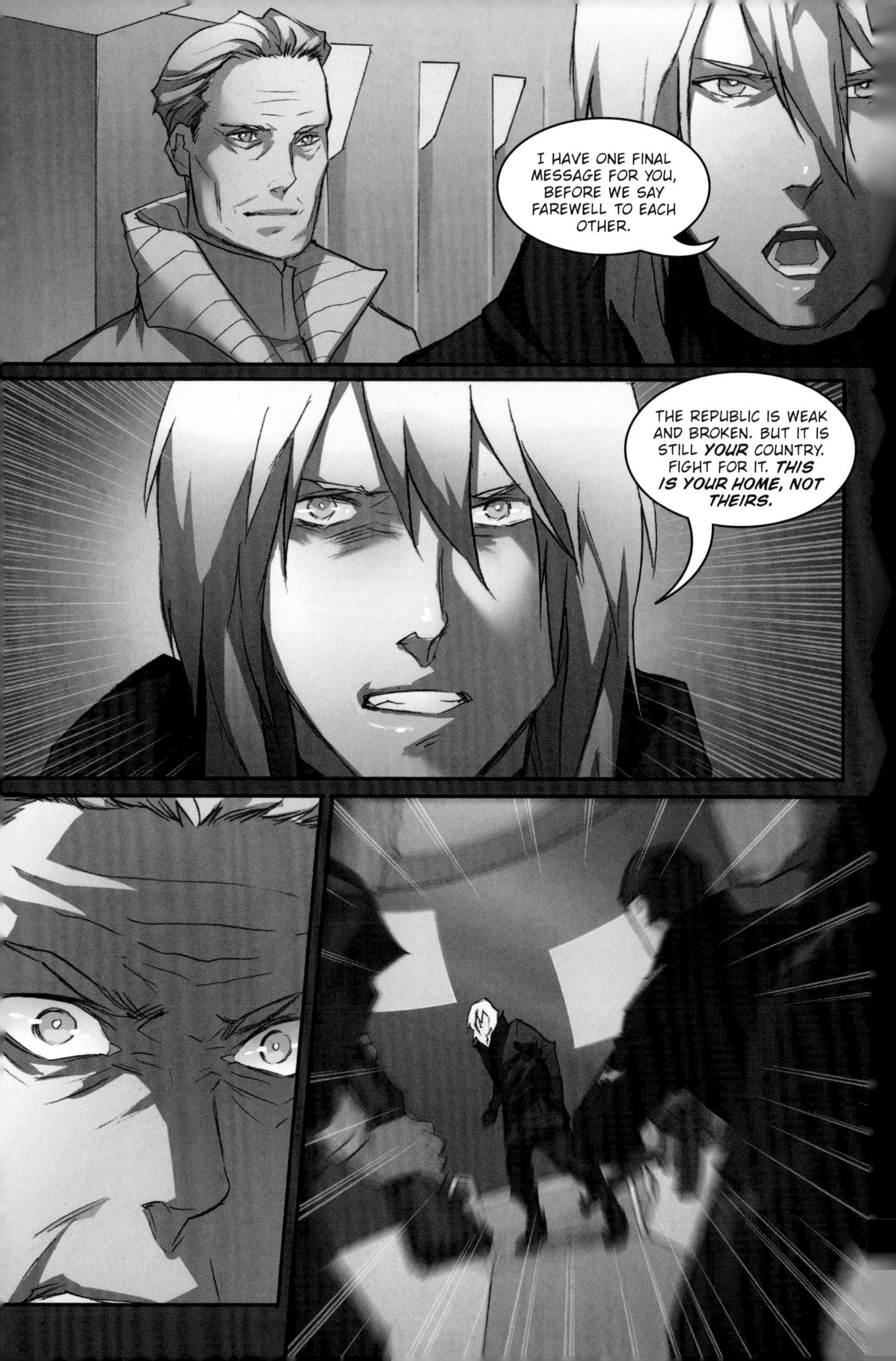
I HAVE ONE FINAL MESSAGE FOR YOU, BEFORE WE SAY FAREWELL TO EACH OTHER.
THE REPUBLIC IS WEAK AND BROKEN. BUT IT IS STILL ***YOUR*** COUNTRY. FIGHT FOR IT. ***THIS IS YOUR HOME, NOT THEIRS.***

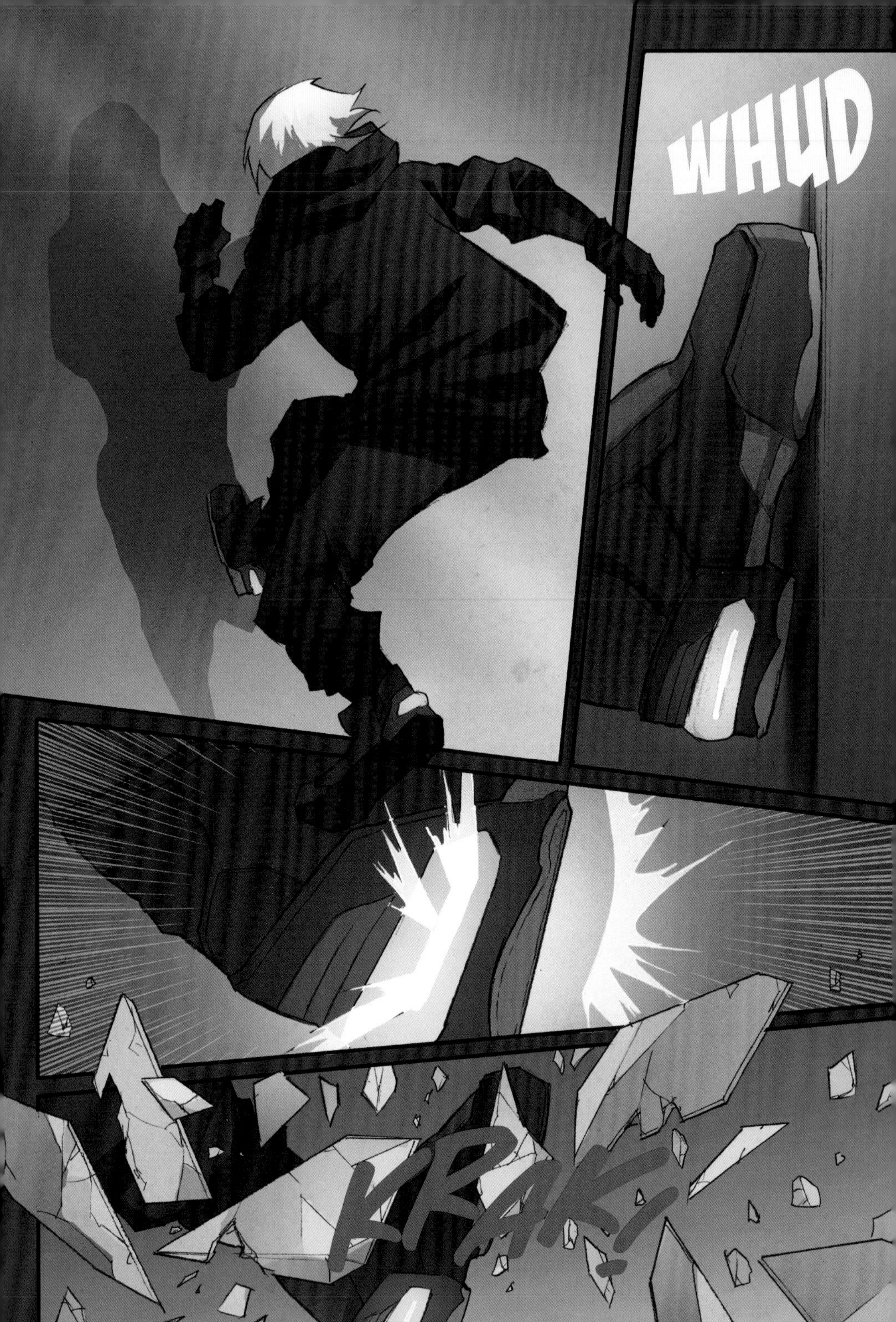
WHUD
KRAK!

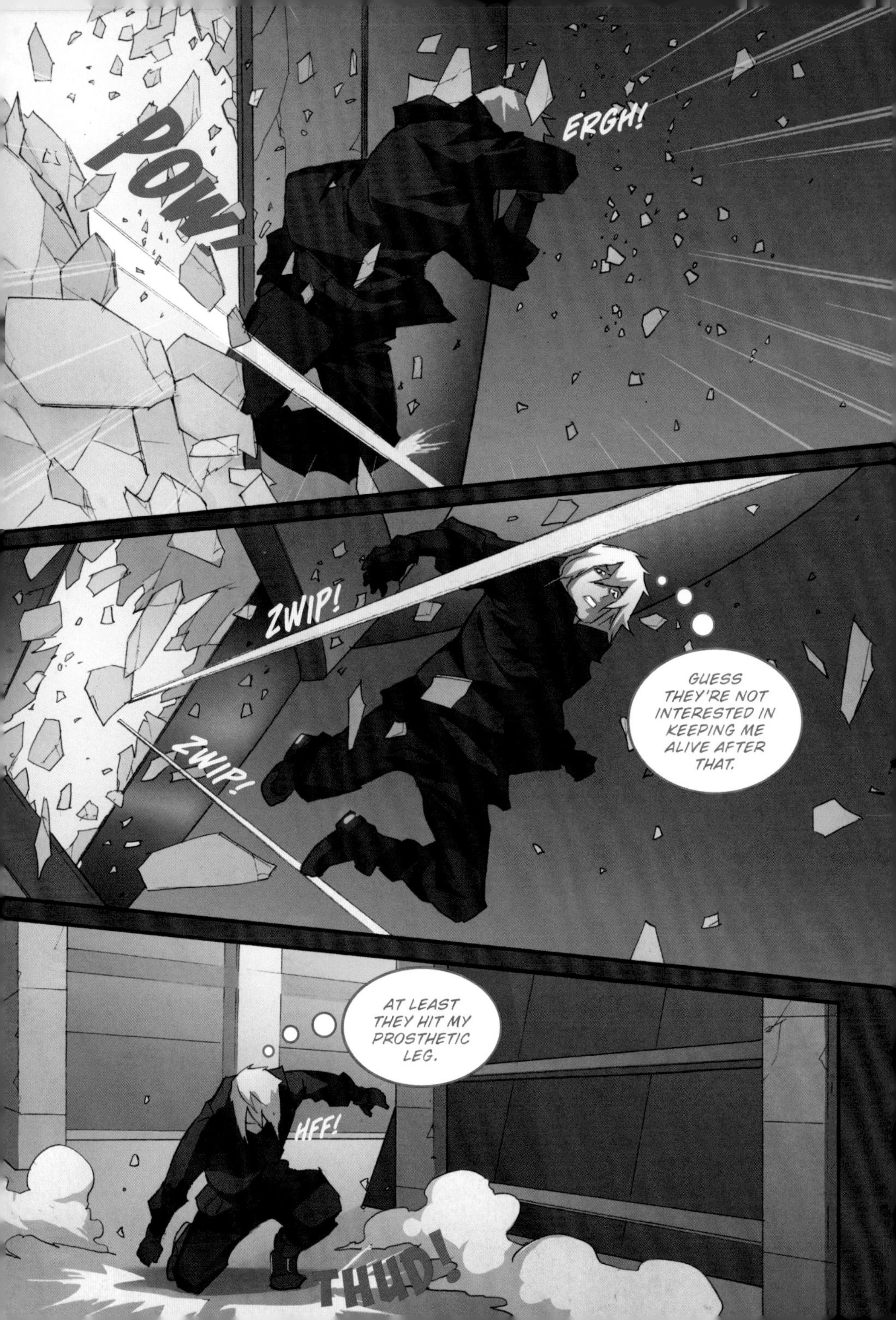
POW!
ERGH!
ZWIP!
ZWIP!
GUESS THEY'RE NOT INTERESTED IN KEEPING ME ALIVE AFTER THAT.
AT LEAST THEY HIT MY PROSTHETIC LEG.
HFF!
THUD!

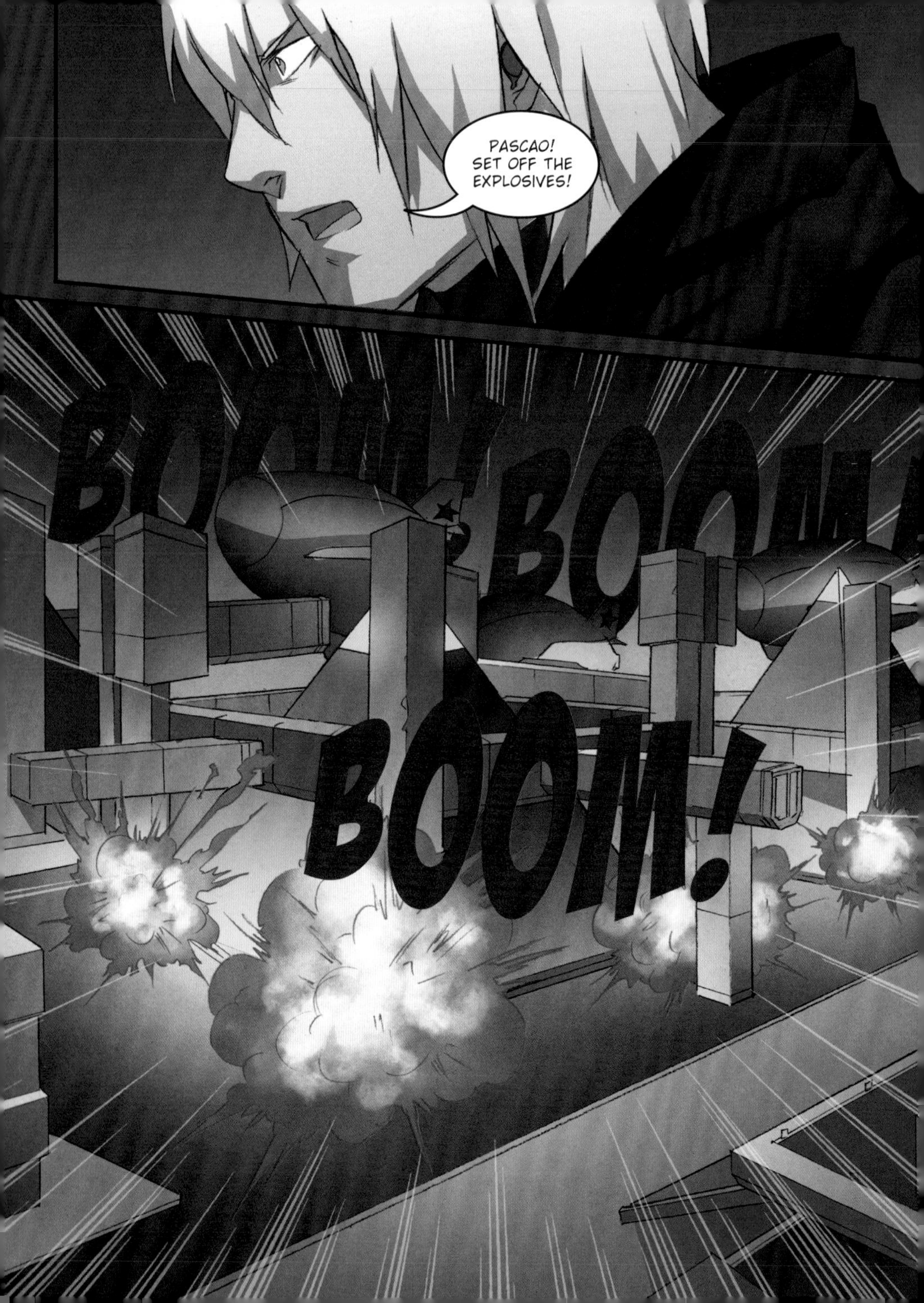
PASCAO! SET OFF THE EXPLOSIVES!
BOOM! BOOM!
BOOM!

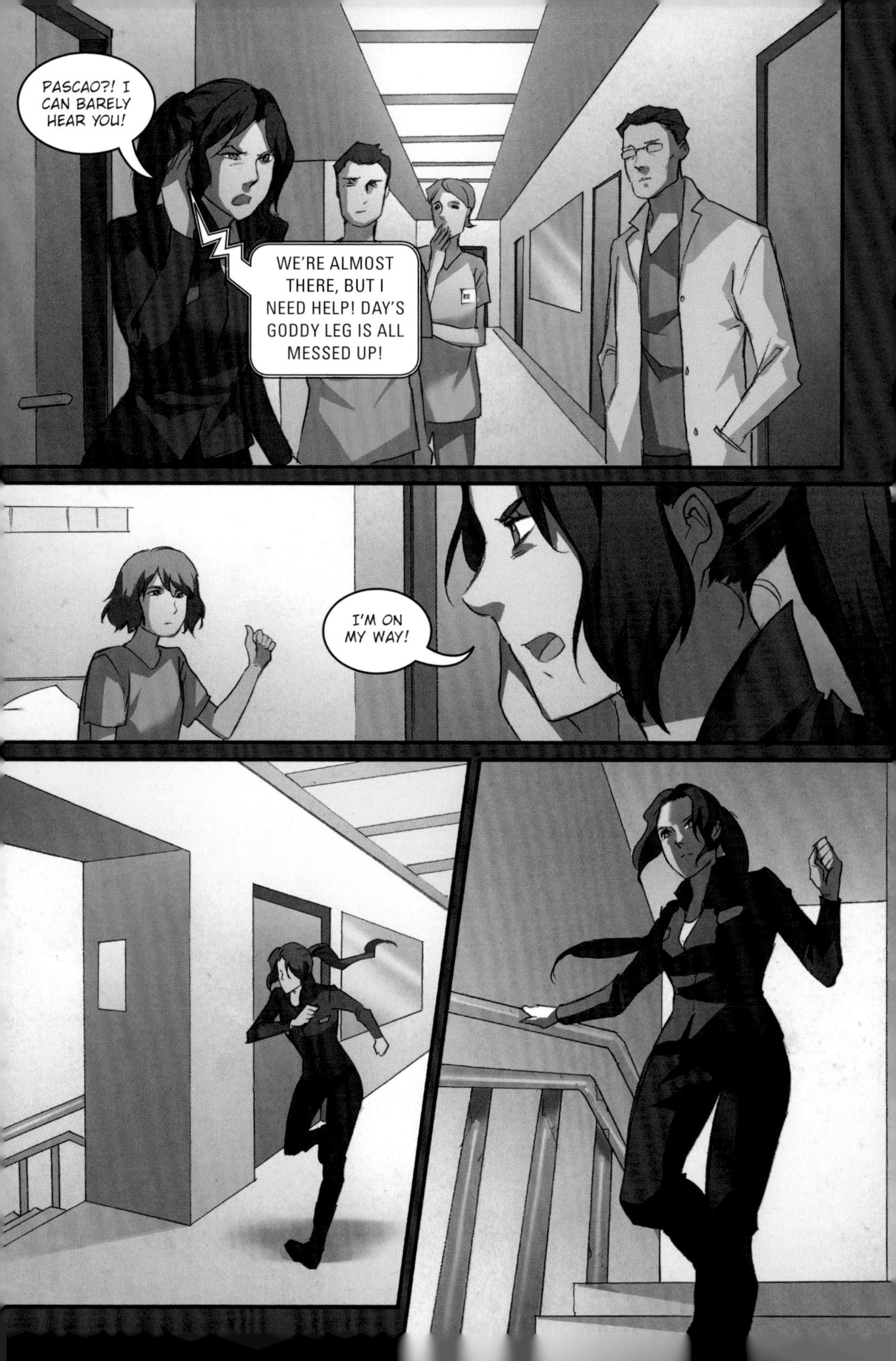
PASCAO?! I CAN BARELY HEAR YOU!
WE'RE ALMOST THERE, BUT I NEED HELP! DAY'S GODDY LEG IS ALL MESSED UP!
I'M ON MY WAY!

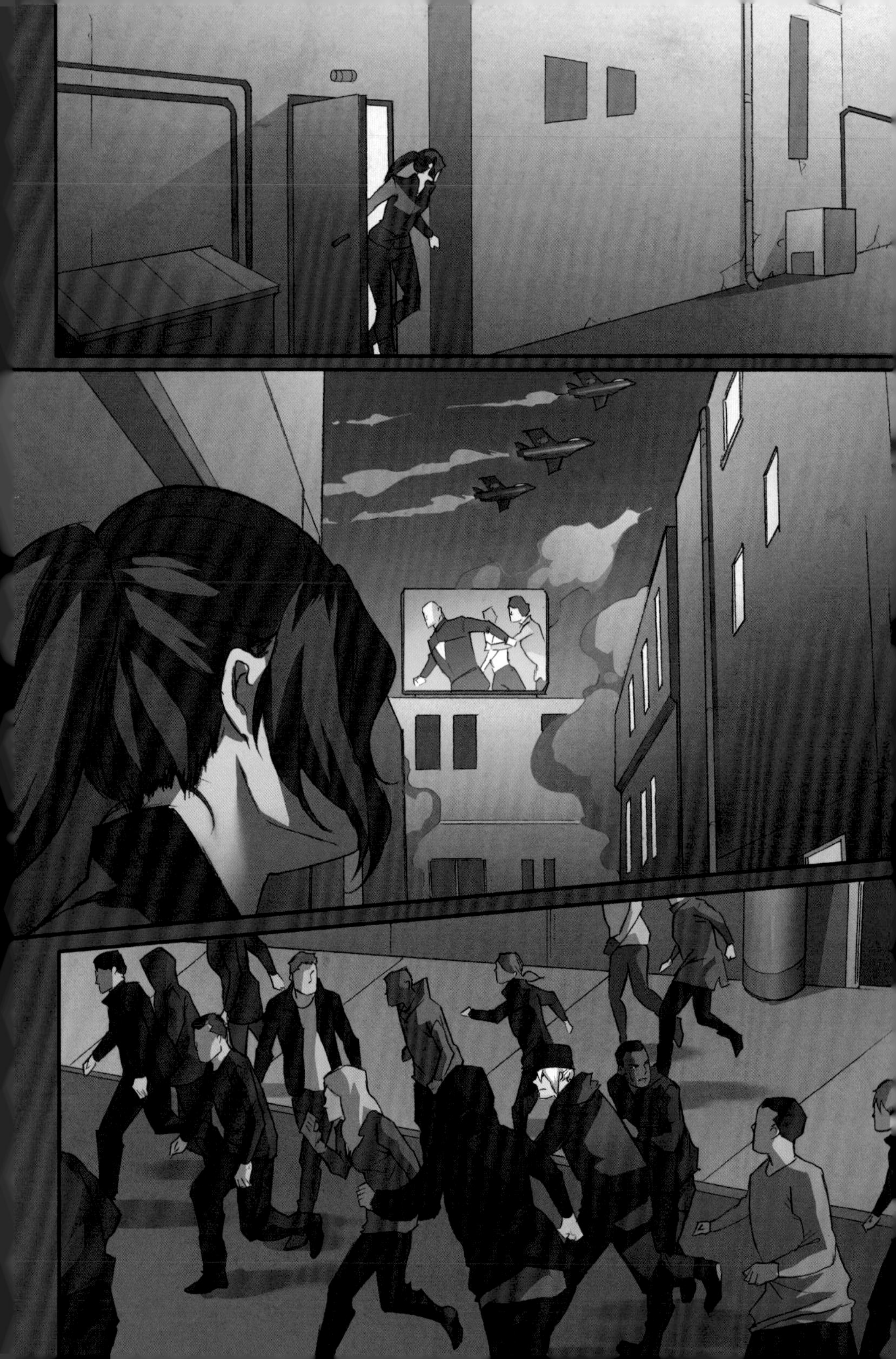

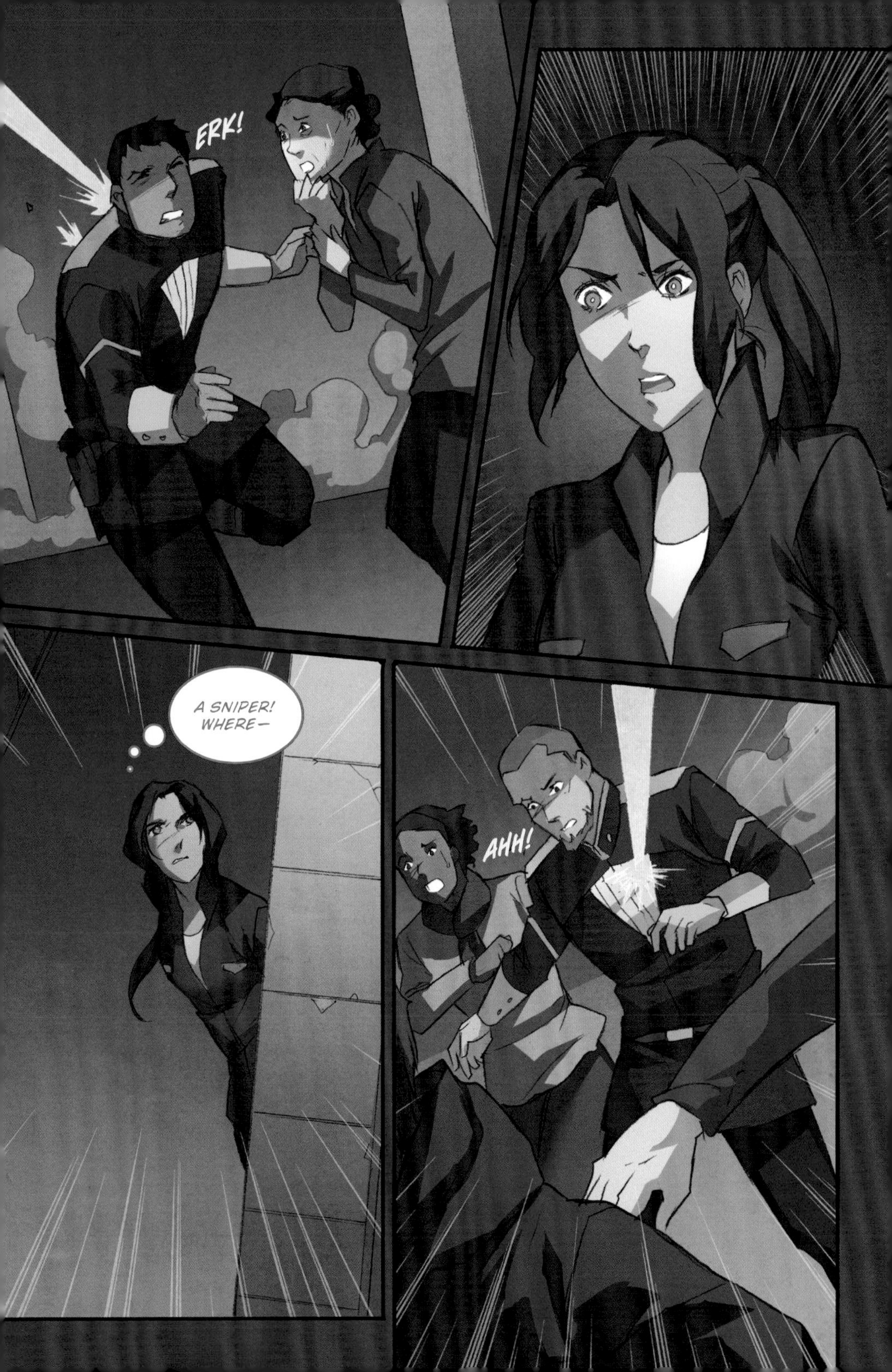
ERK!
A SNIPER! WHERE—
AHH!

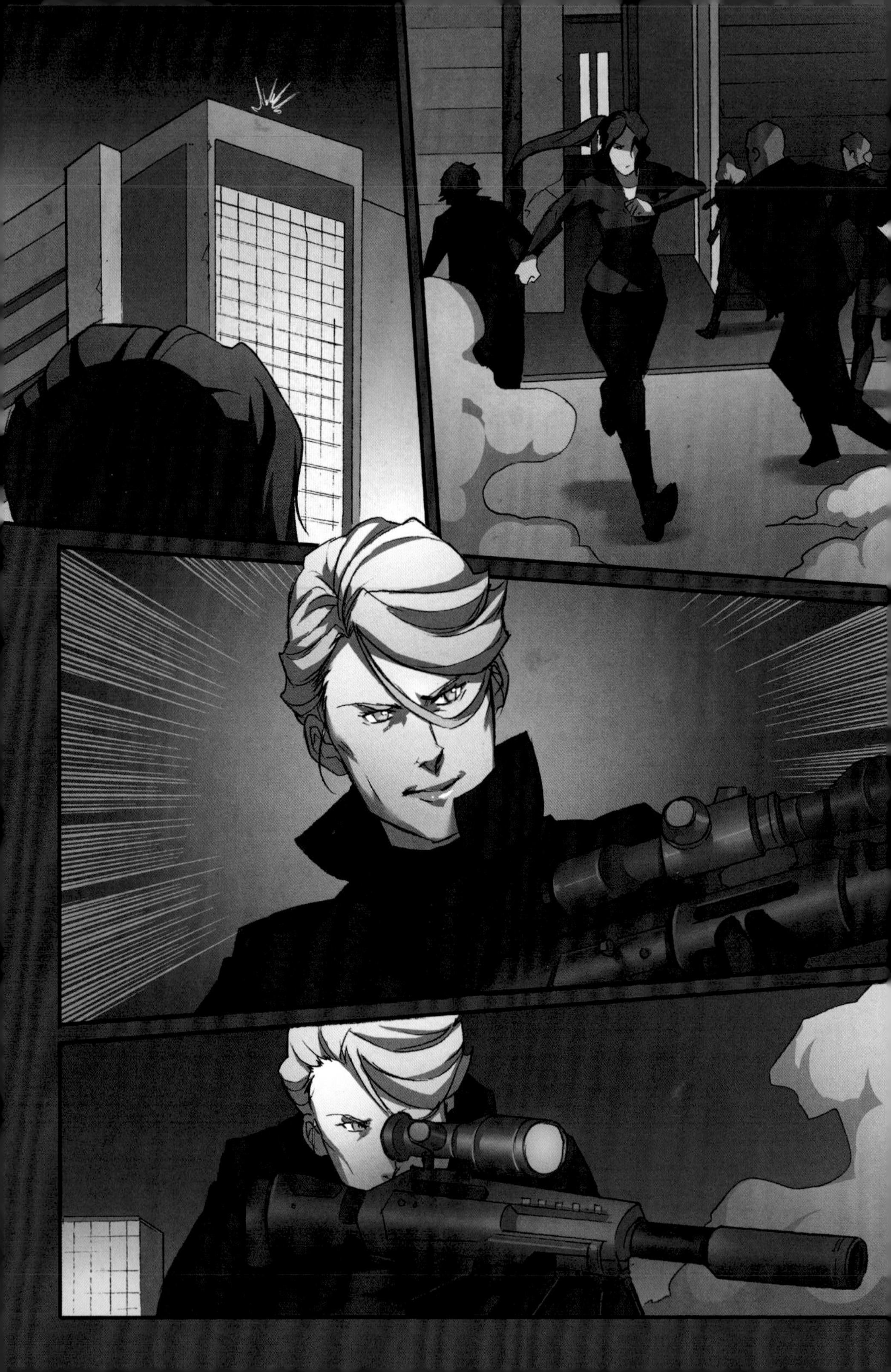

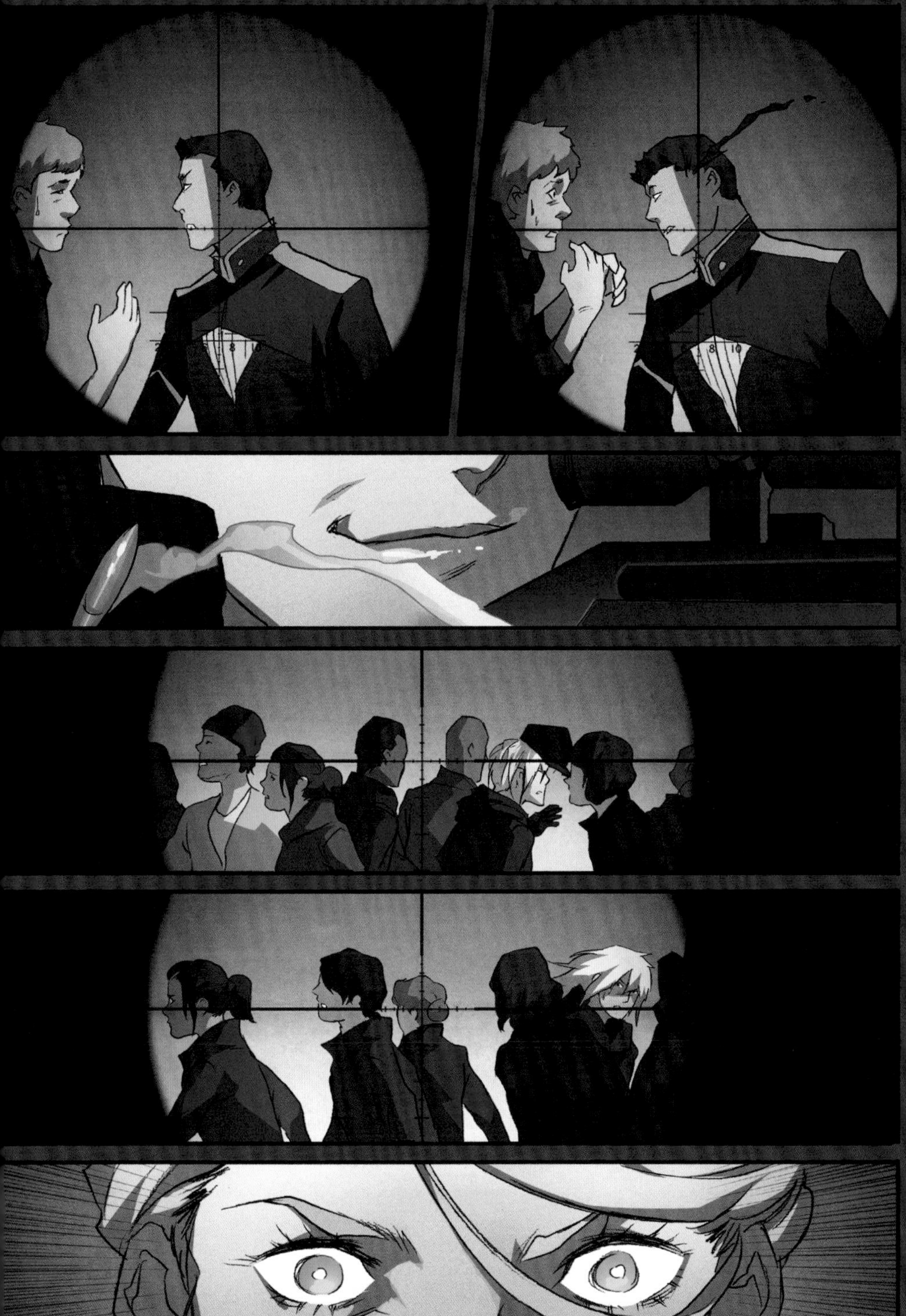

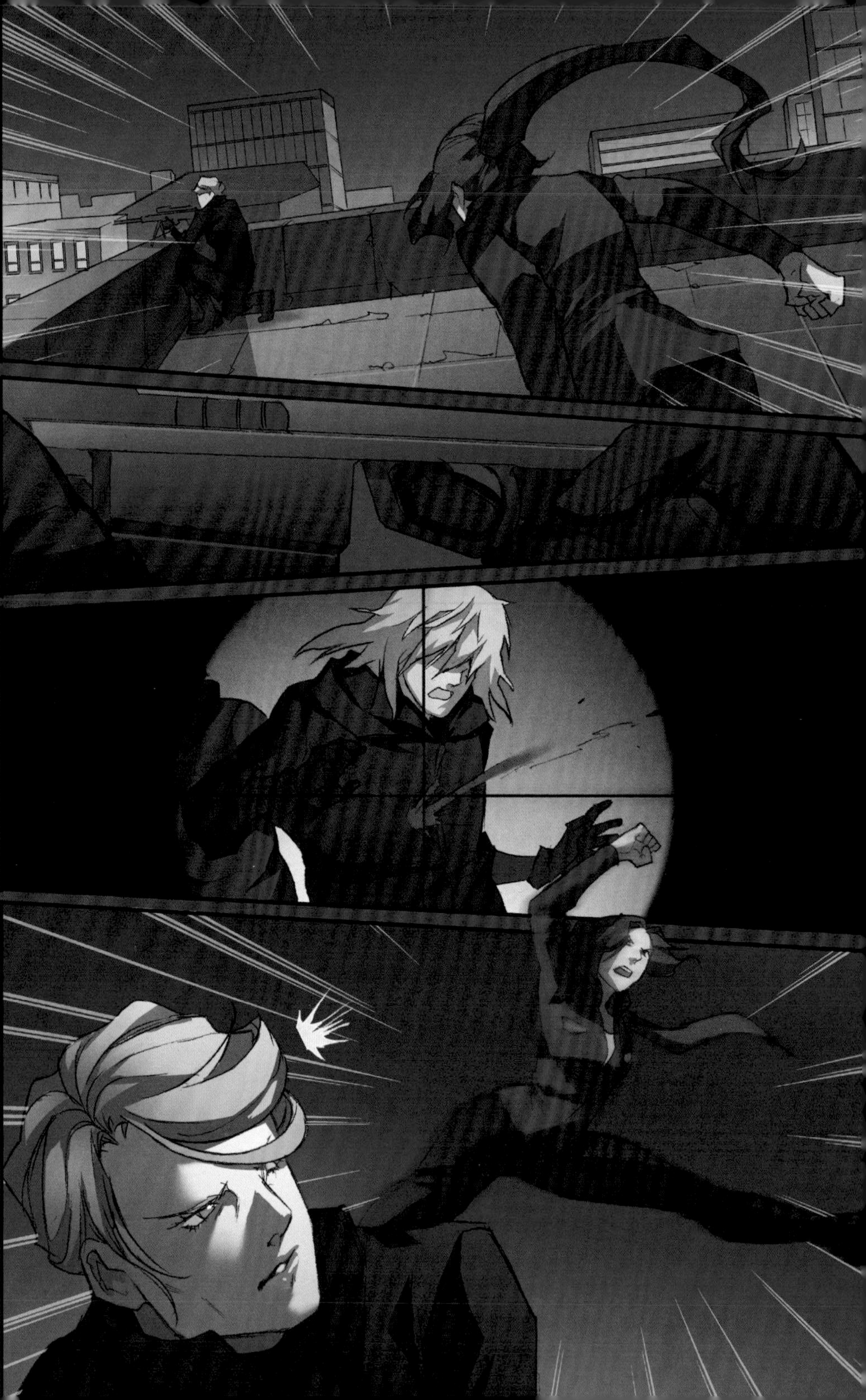

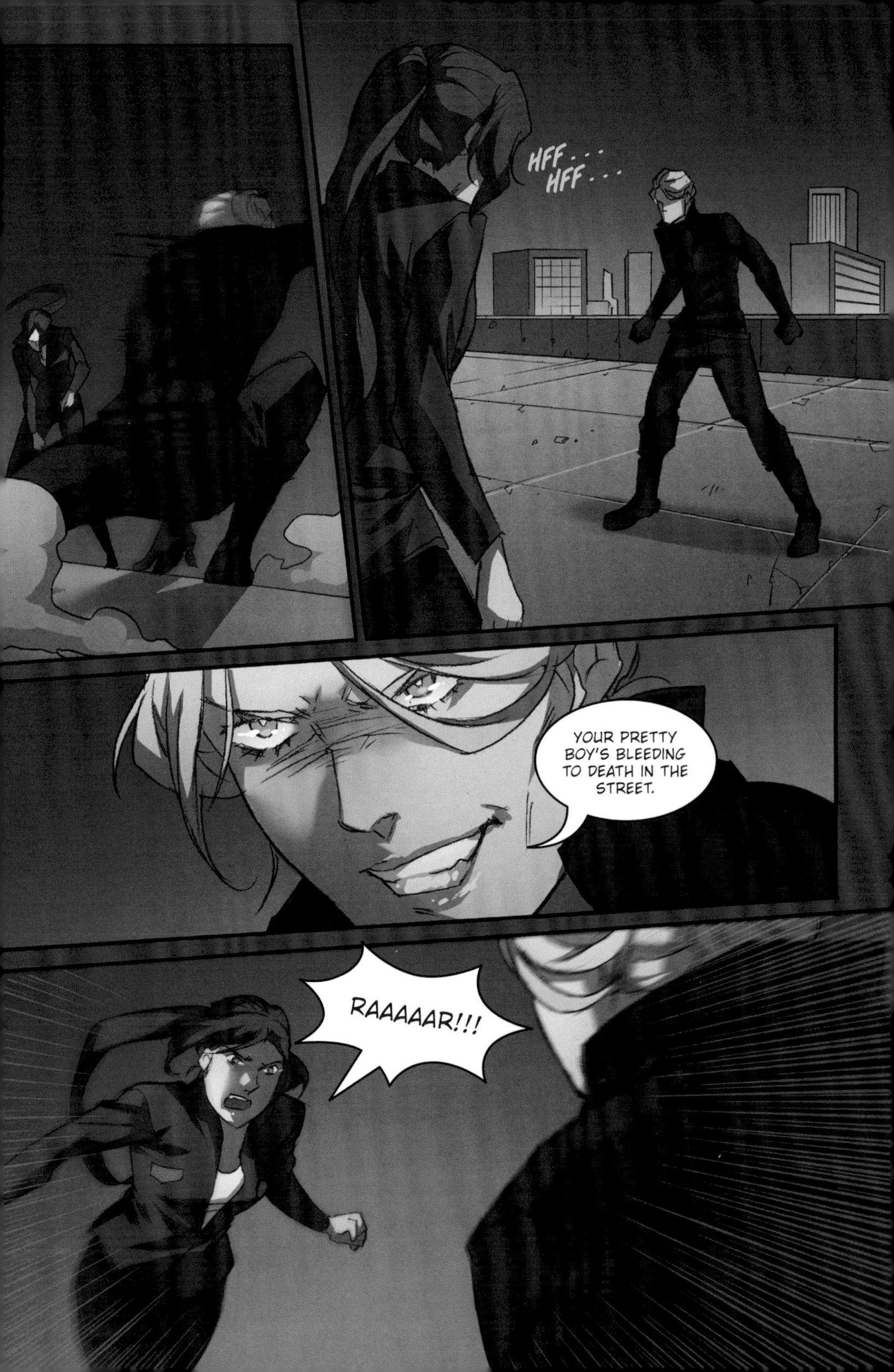
HFF . . .
HFF . . .
YOUR PRETTY BOY'S BLEEDING TO DEATH IN THE STREET.
RAAAAAR!!!

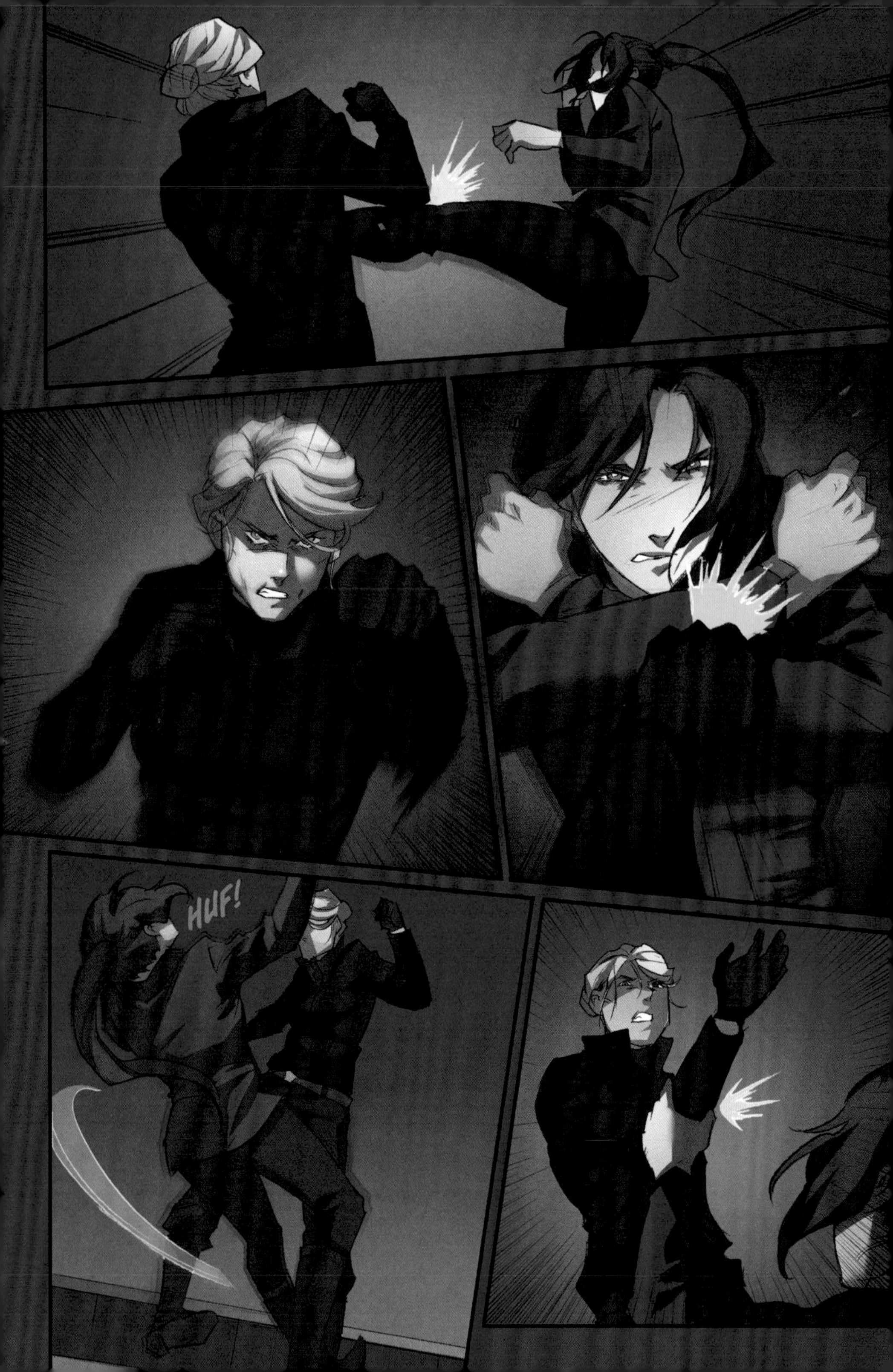
HUF!

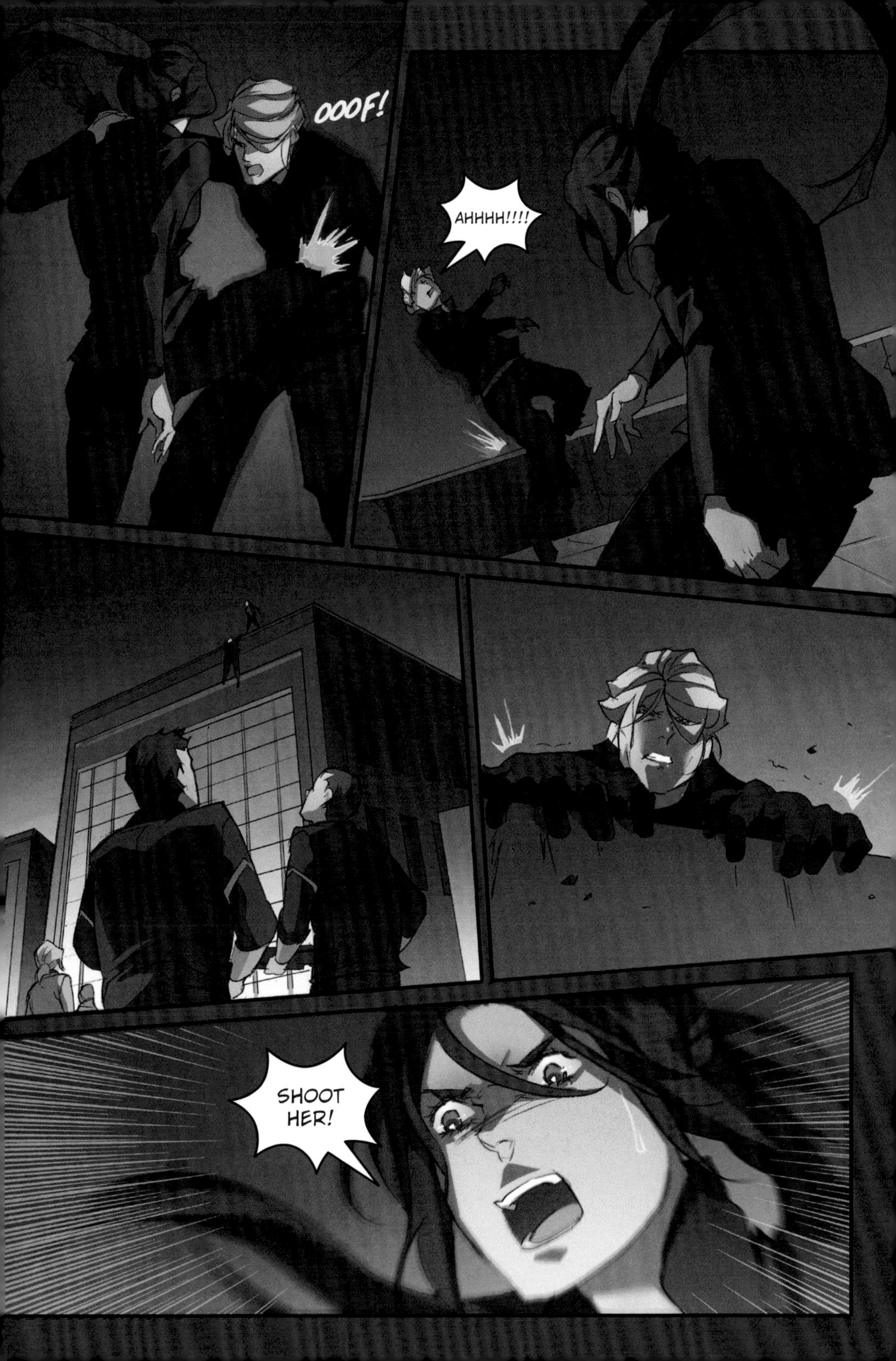
OOOF!
AHHHH!!!!
SHOOT HER!

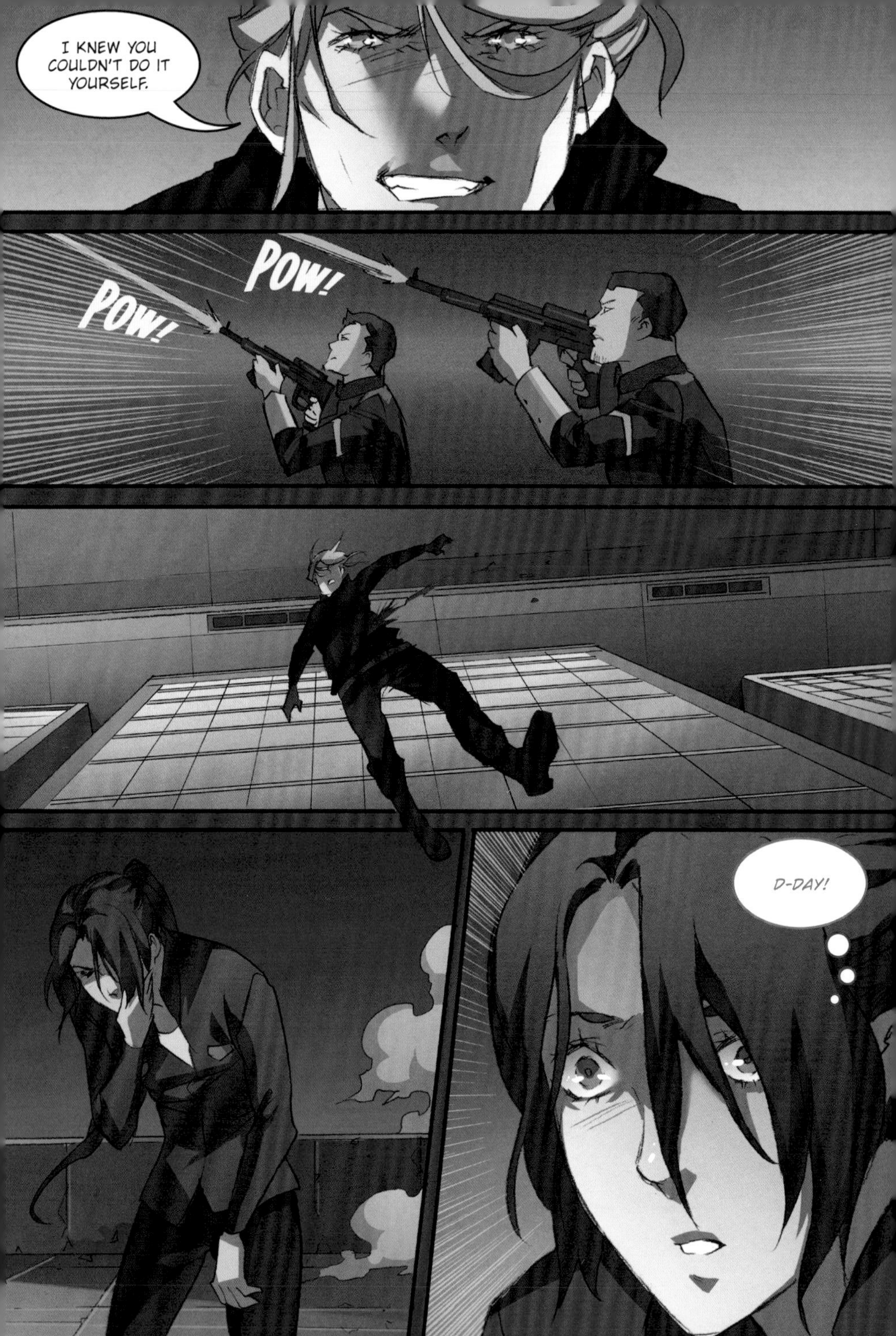
I KNEW YOU COULDN'T DO IT YOURSELF.
POW!
POW!
D-DAY!

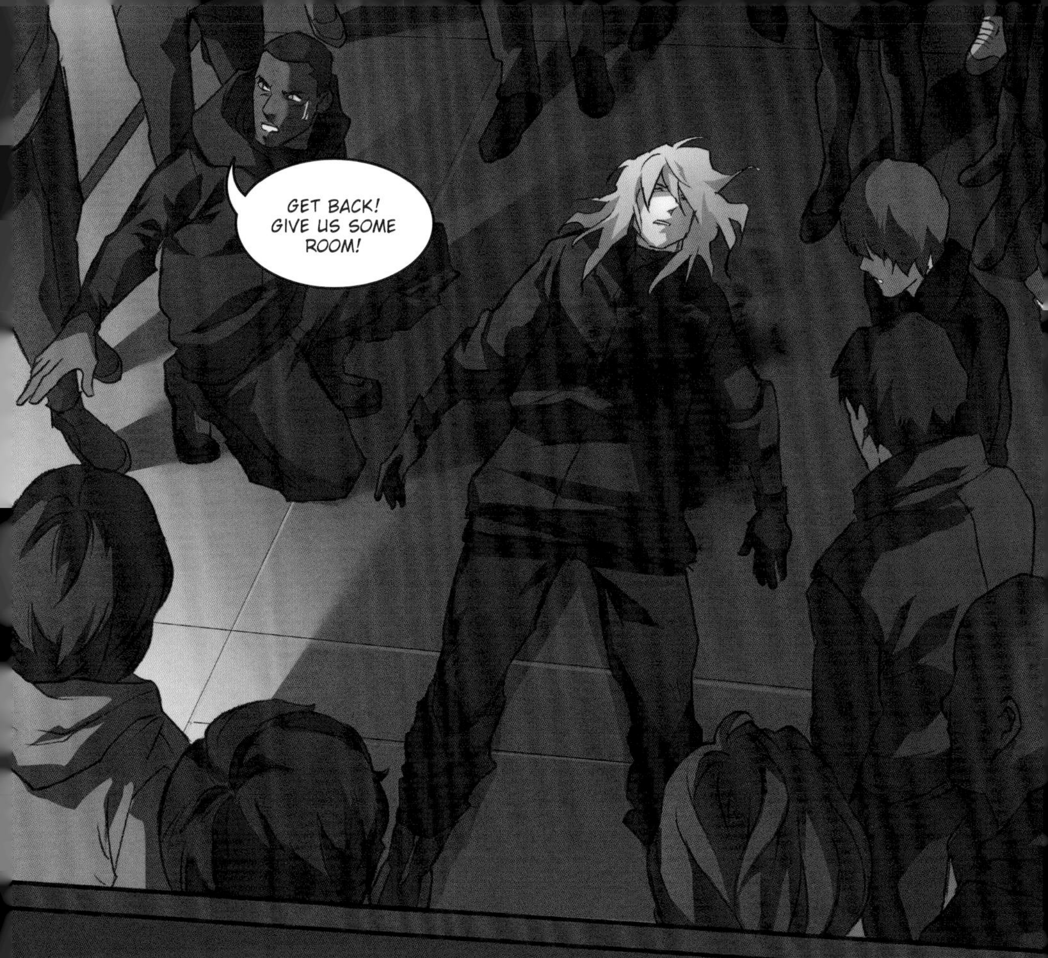
GET BACK! GIVE US SOME ROOM!

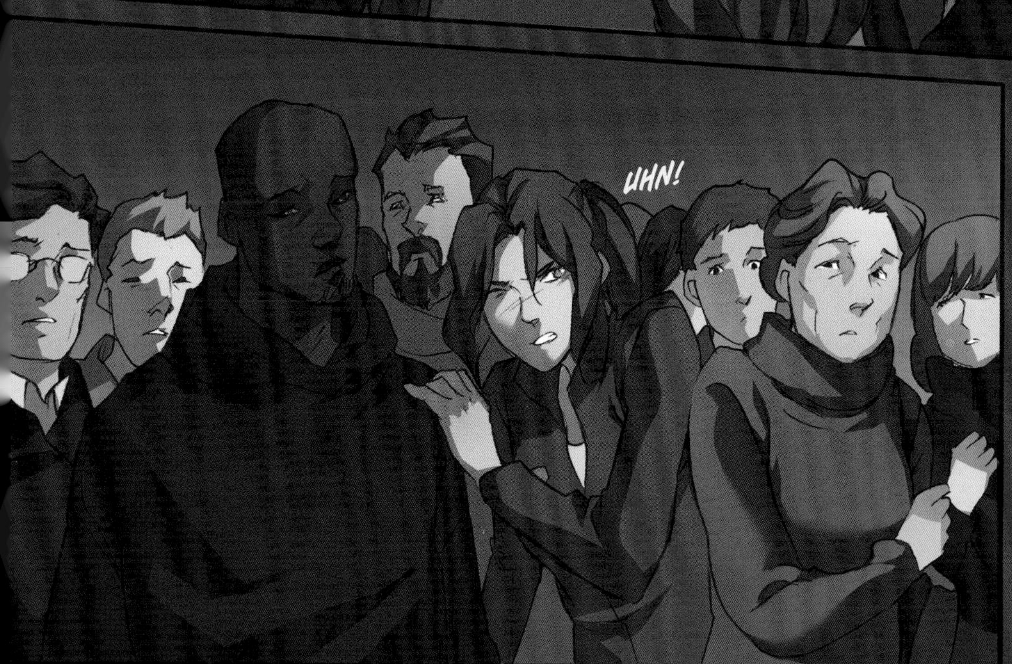
UHN!

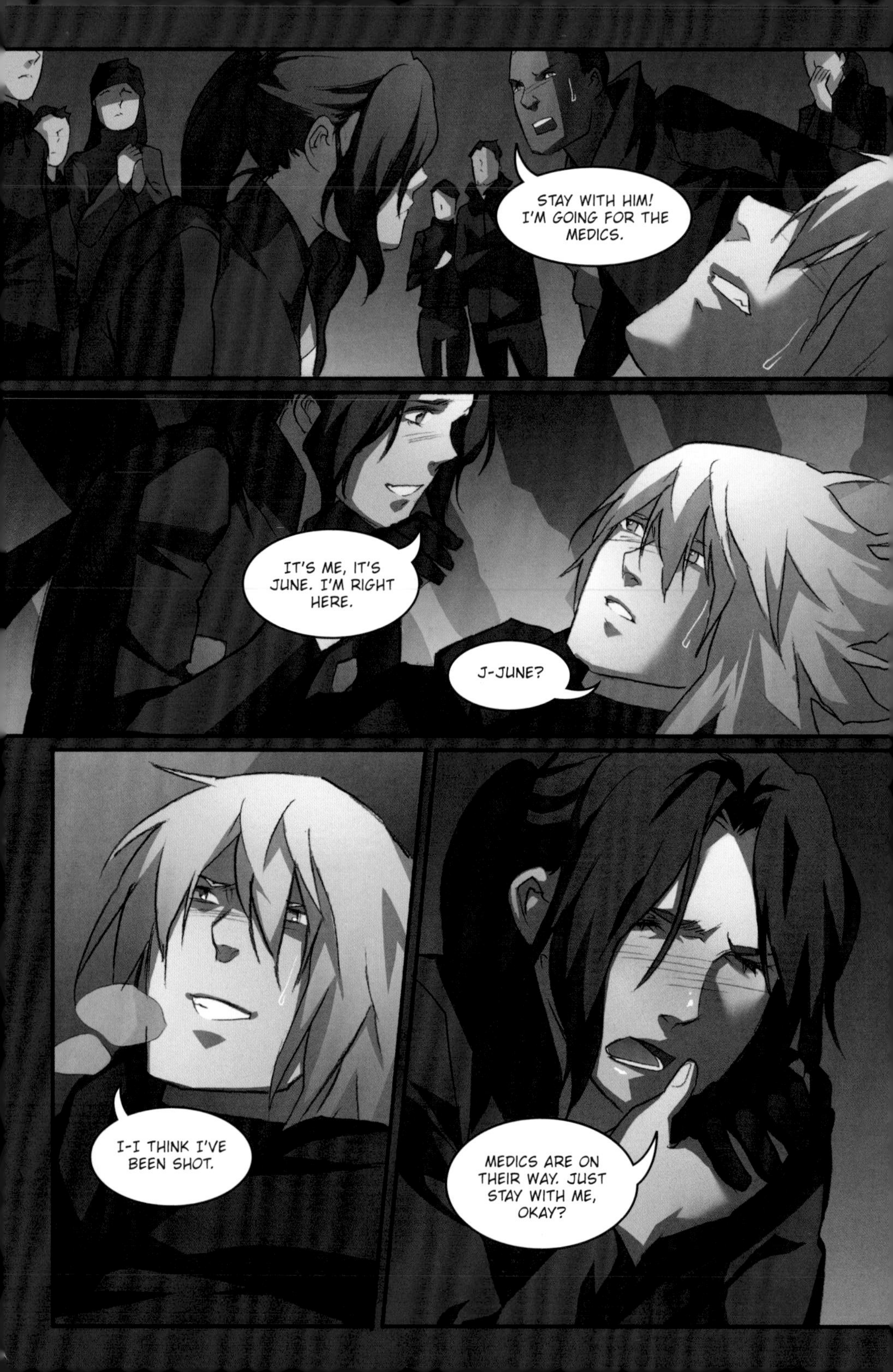
STAY WITH HIM! I'M GOING FOR THE MEDICS.
IT'S ME, IT'S JUNE. I'M RIGHT HERE.
J-JUNE?
I-I THINK I'VE BEEN SHOT.
MEDICS ARE ON THEIR WAY. JUST STAY WITH ME, OKAY?

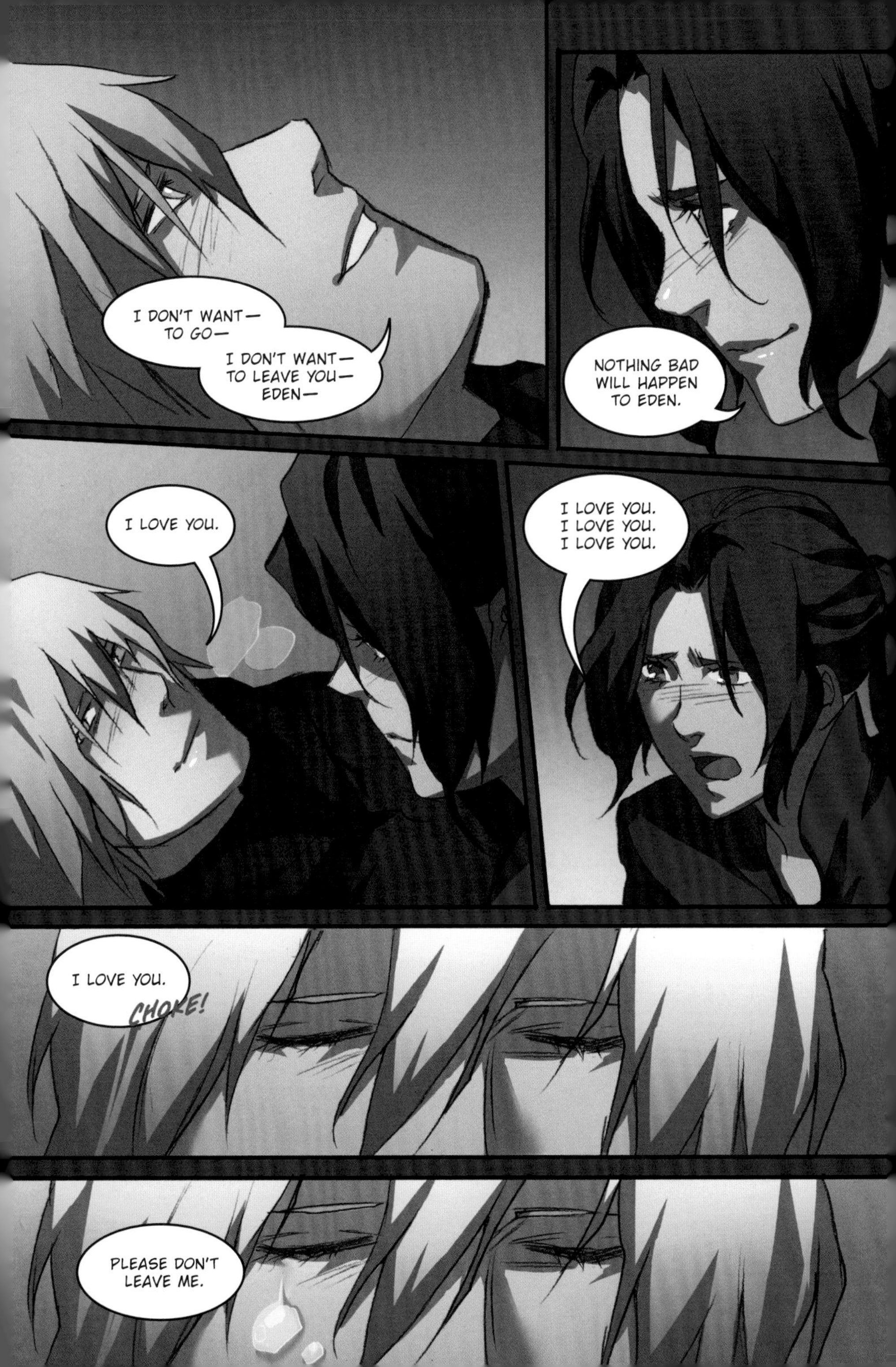
I DON'T WANT—
TO GO—
I DON'T WANT—
TO LEAVE YOU—
EDEN—
NOTHING BAD
WILL HAPPEN
TO EDEN.
I LOVE YOU.
I LOVE YOU.
I LOVE YOU.
I LOVE YOU.
I LOVE YOU.
CHOKE!
PLEASE DON'T
LEAVE ME.

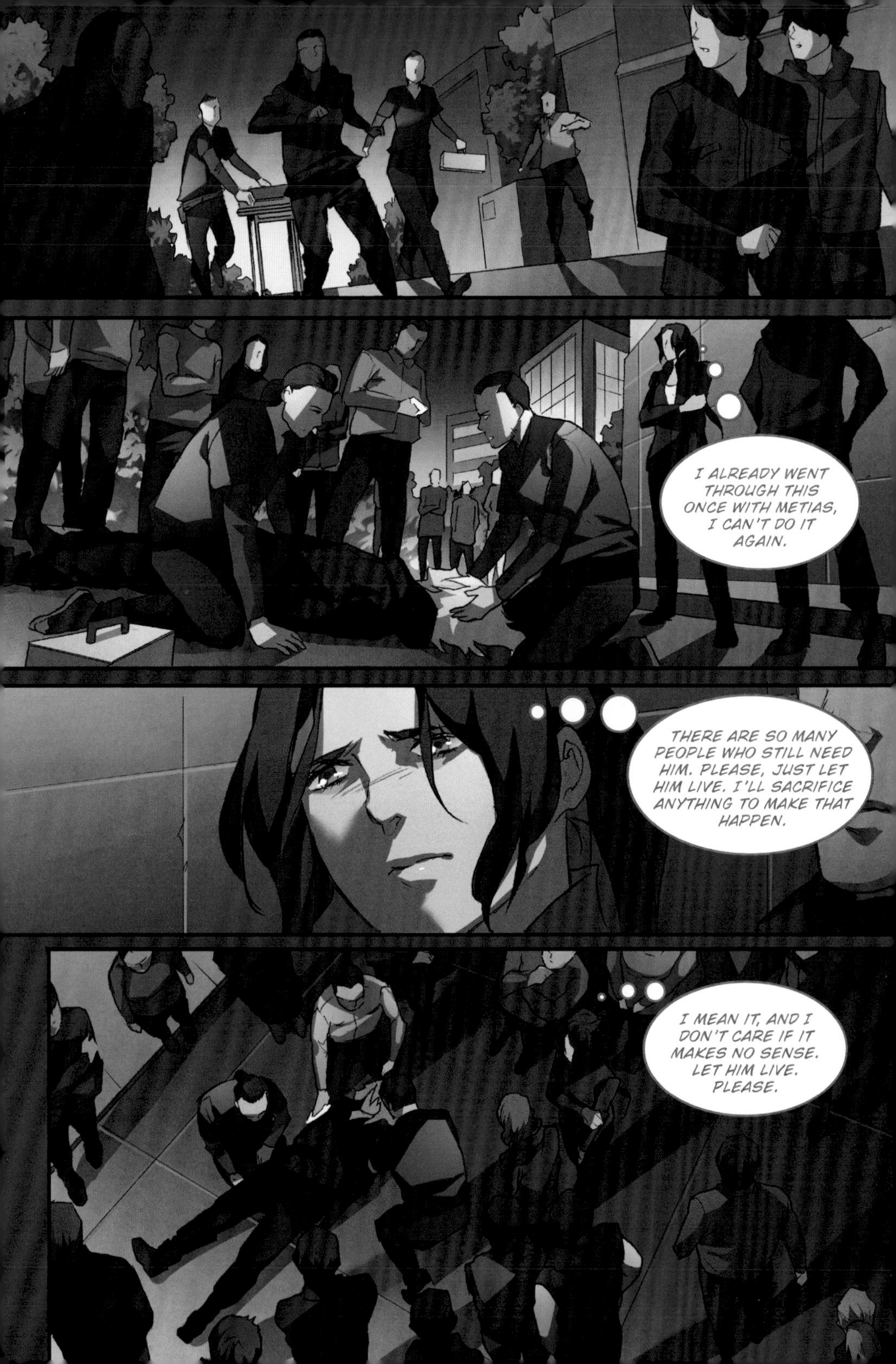
I ALREADY WENT THROUGH THIS ONCE WITH METIAS, I CAN'T DO IT AGAIN.
THERE ARE SO MANY PEOPLE WHO STILL NEED HIM. PLEASE, JUST LET HIM LIVE. I'LL SACRIFICE ANYTHING TO MAKE THAT HAPPEN.
I MEAN IT, AND I DON'T CARE IF IT MAKES NO SENSE. LET HIM LIVE. PLEASE.

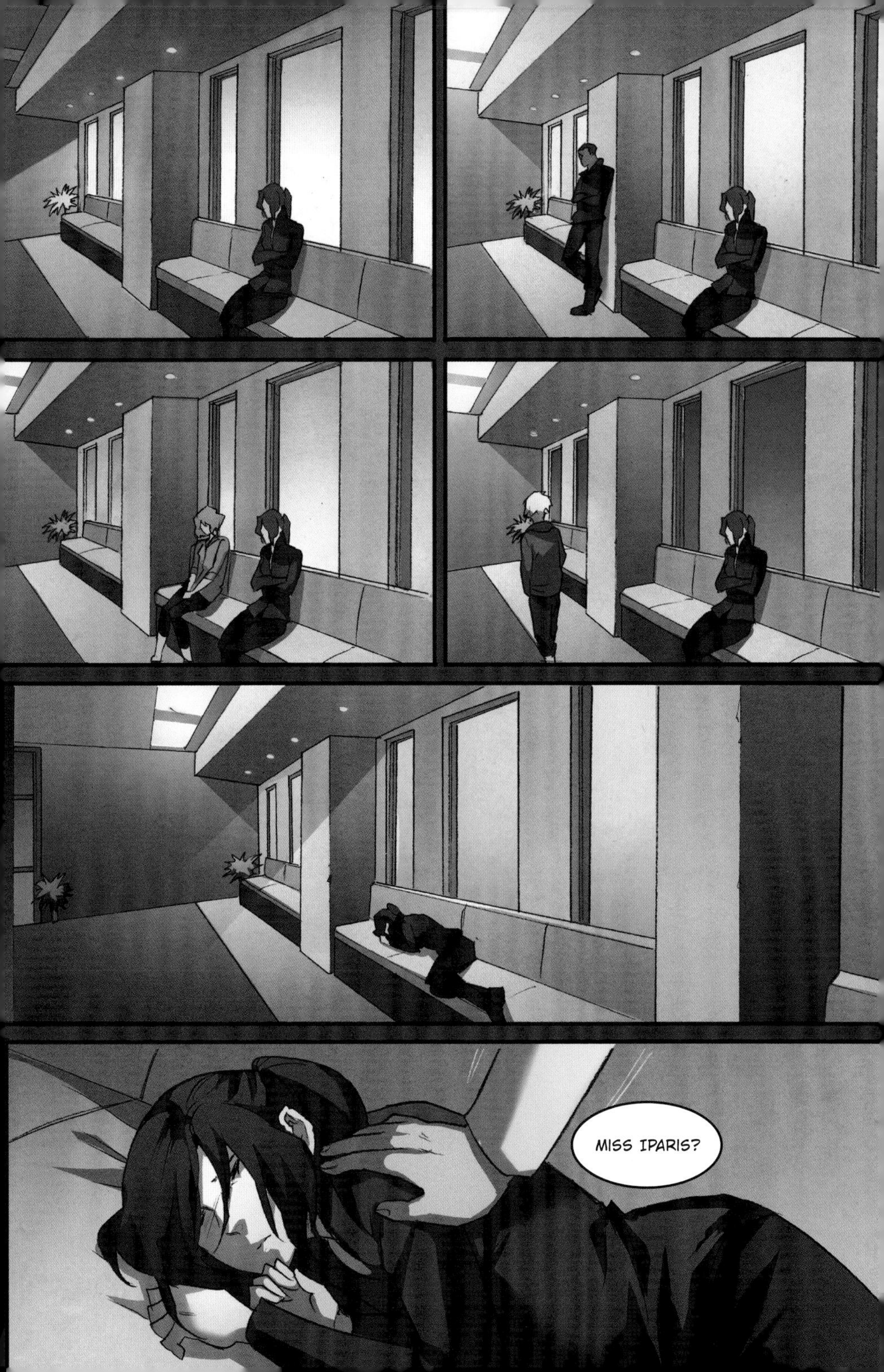
MISS IPARIS?

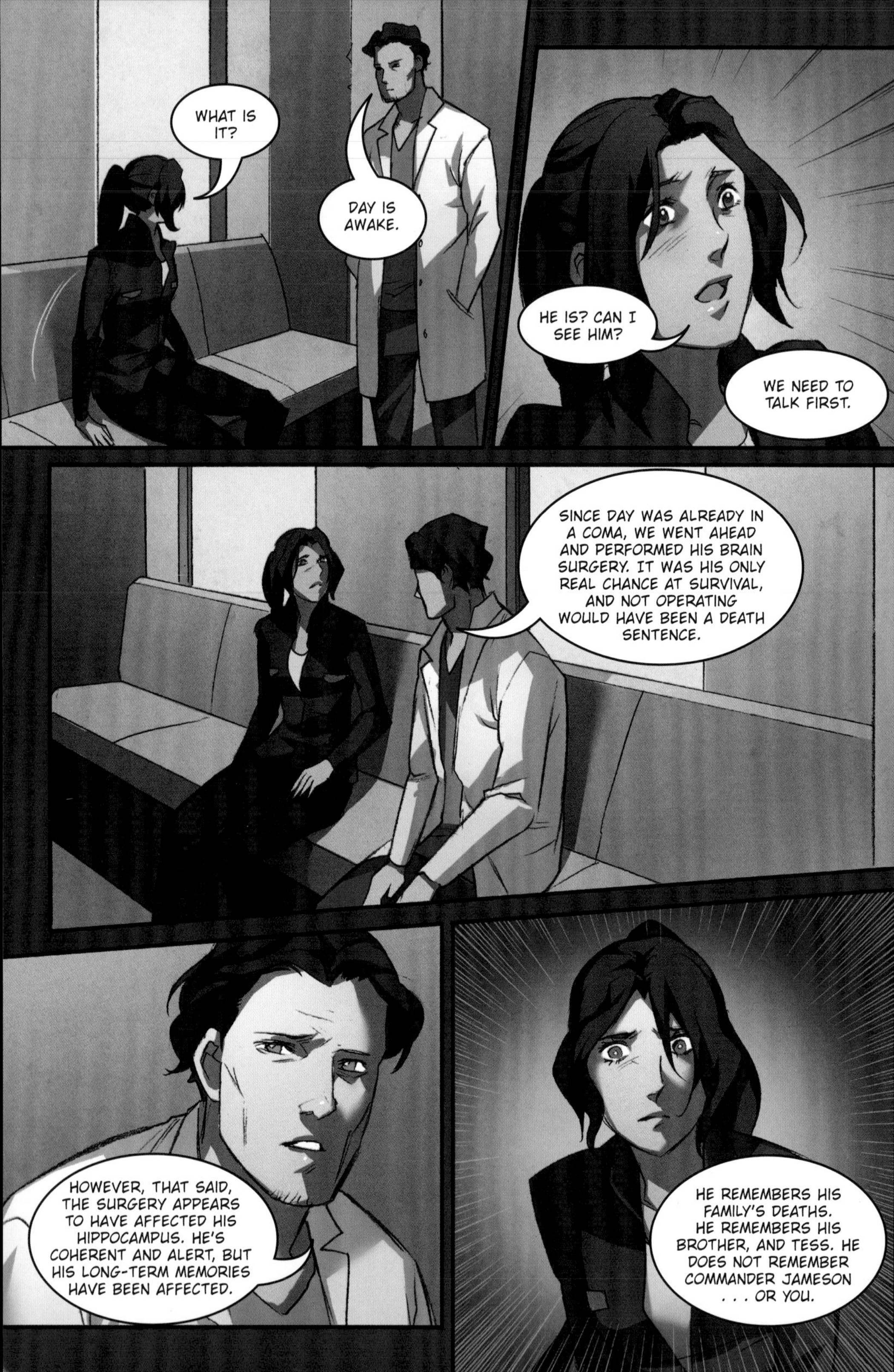
WHAT IS IT?
DAY IS AWAKE.
HE IS? CAN I SEE HIM?
WE NEED TO TALK FIRST.
SINCE DAY WAS ALREADY IN A COMA, WE WENT AHEAD AND PERFORMED HIS BRAIN SURGERY. IT WAS HIS ONLY REAL CHANCE AT SURVIVAL, AND NOT OPERATING WOULD HAVE BEEN A DEATH SENTENCE.
HOWEVER, THAT SAID, THE SURGERY APPEARS TO HAVE AFFECTED HIS HIPPOCAMPUS. HE'S COHERENT AND ALERT, BUT HIS LONG-TERM MEMORIES HAVE BEEN AFFECTED.
HE REMEMBERS HIS FAMILY'S DEATHS. HE REMEMBERS HIS BROTHER, AND TESS. HE DOES NOT REMEMBER COMMANDER JAMESON . . . OR YOU.

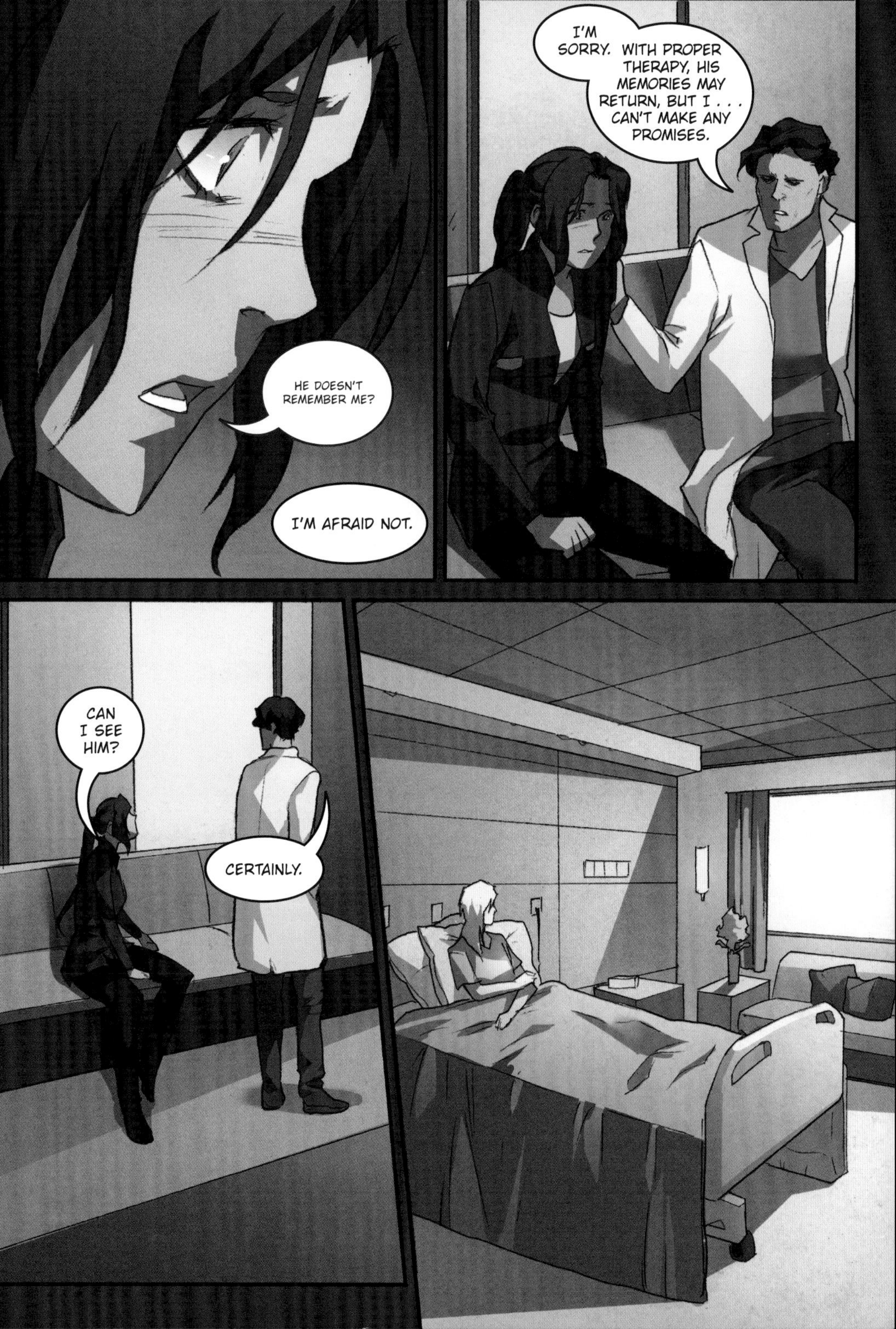
HE DOESN'T REMEMBER ME?
I'M AFRAID NOT.
I'M SORRY. WITH PROPER THERAPY, HIS MEMORIES MAY RETURN, BUT I . . . CAN'T MAKE ANY PROMISES.
CAN I SEE HIM?
CERTAINLY.

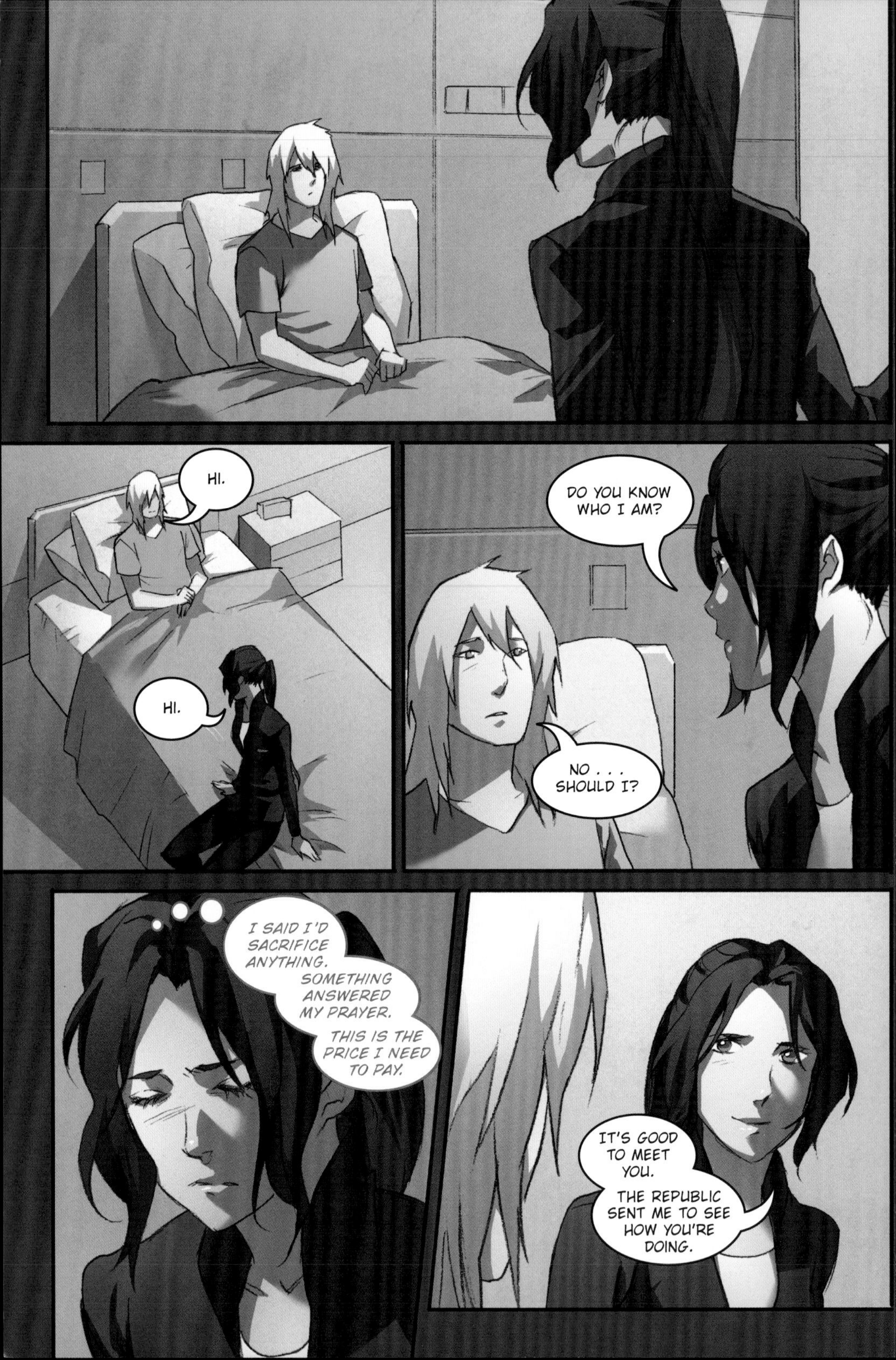
HI.
HI.
DO YOU KNOW WHO I AM?
NO . . . SHOULD I?
I SAID I'D SACRIFICE ANYTHING.
SOMETHING ANSWERED MY PRAYER.
THIS IS THE PRICE I NEED TO PAY.
IT'S GOOD TO MEET YOU.
THE REPUBLIC SENT ME TO SEE HOW YOU'RE DOING.

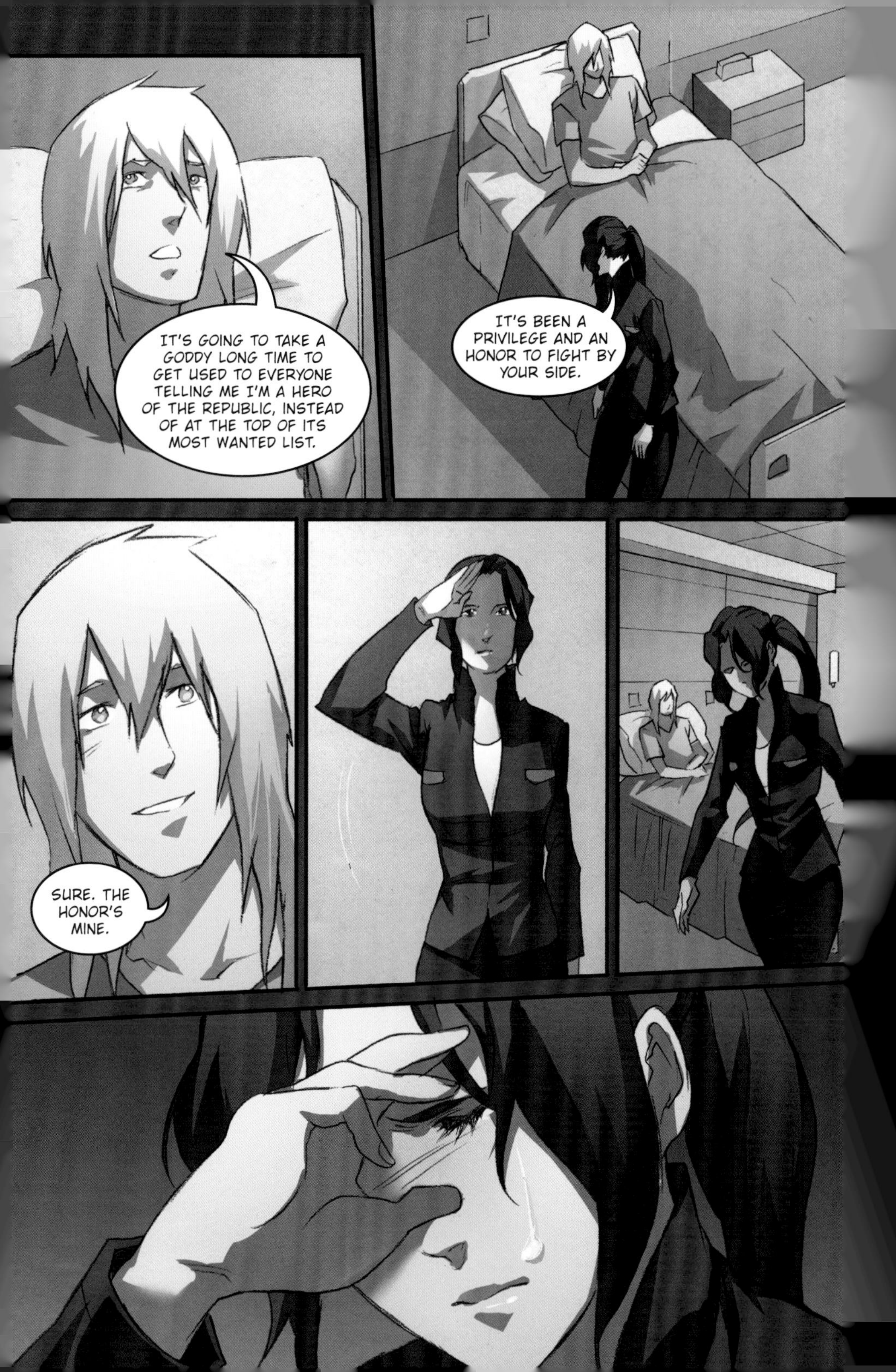
IT'S GOING TO TAKE A GODDY LONG TIME TO GET USED TO EVERYONE TELLING ME I'M A HERO OF THE REPUBLIC, INSTEAD OF AT THE TOP OF ITS MOST WANTED LIST.
IT'S BEEN A PRIVILEGE AND AN HONOR TO FIGHT BY YOUR SIDE.
SURE. THE HONOR'S MINE.

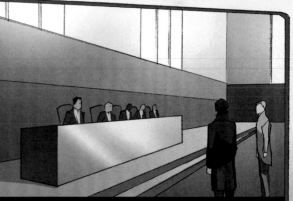
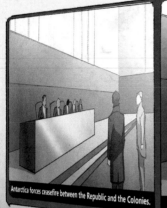

Antarctica forces ceasefire between the Republic and the Colonies.

Antarctica forces ceasefire between the Republic and the Colonies.

President Ikari approves Republic-Colonies peace treaty based on transfer of new plague cure.

Daniel Altan Wing and brother to leave tonight for Ross City, Antarctica.

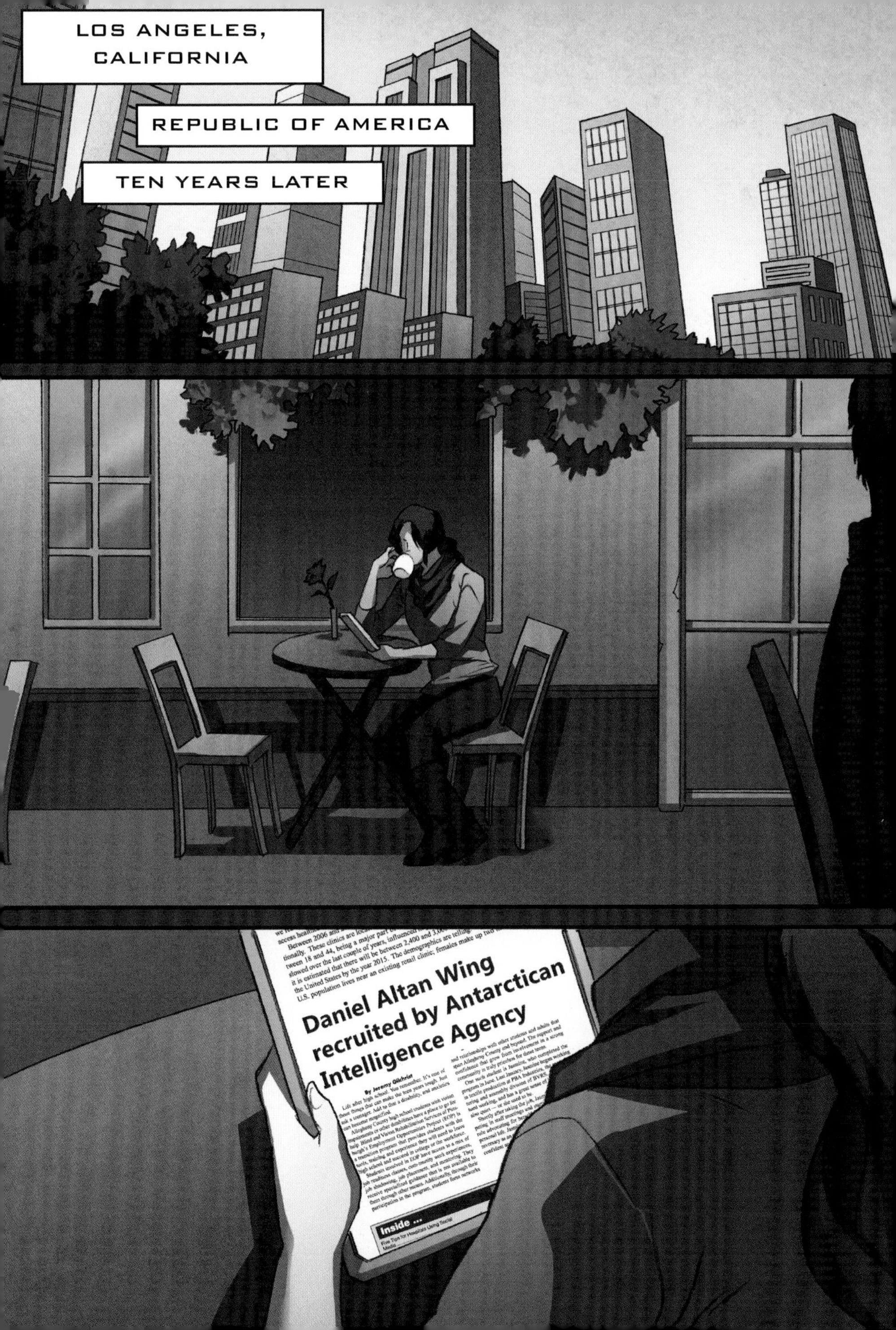
LOS ANGELES, CALIFORNIA
REPUBLIC OF AMERICA
TEN YEARS LATER
Daniel Altan Wing recruited by Antarctican Intelligence Agency
Inside ...

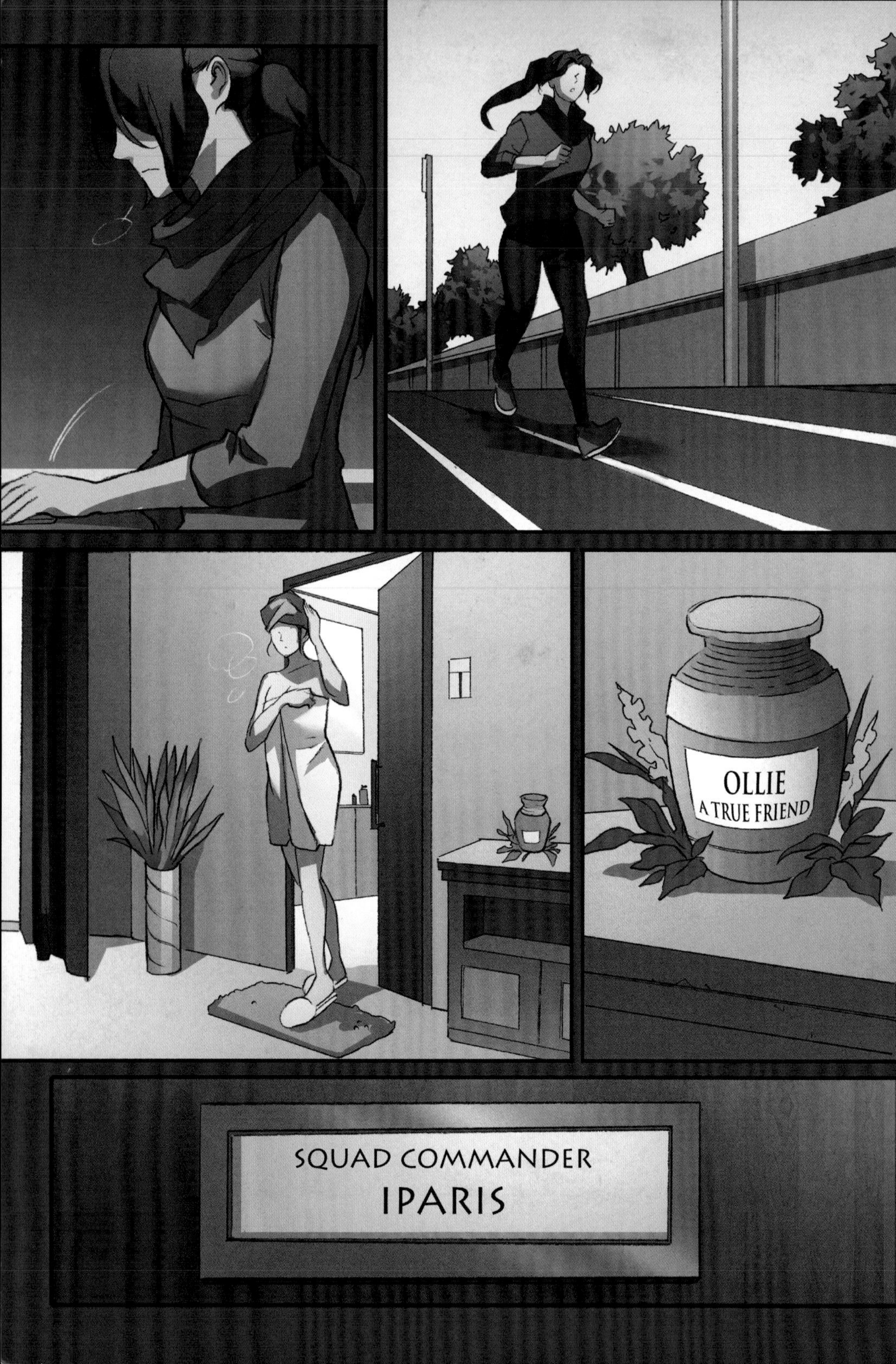
OLLIE
A TRUE FRIEND
SQUAD COMMANDER
IPARIS

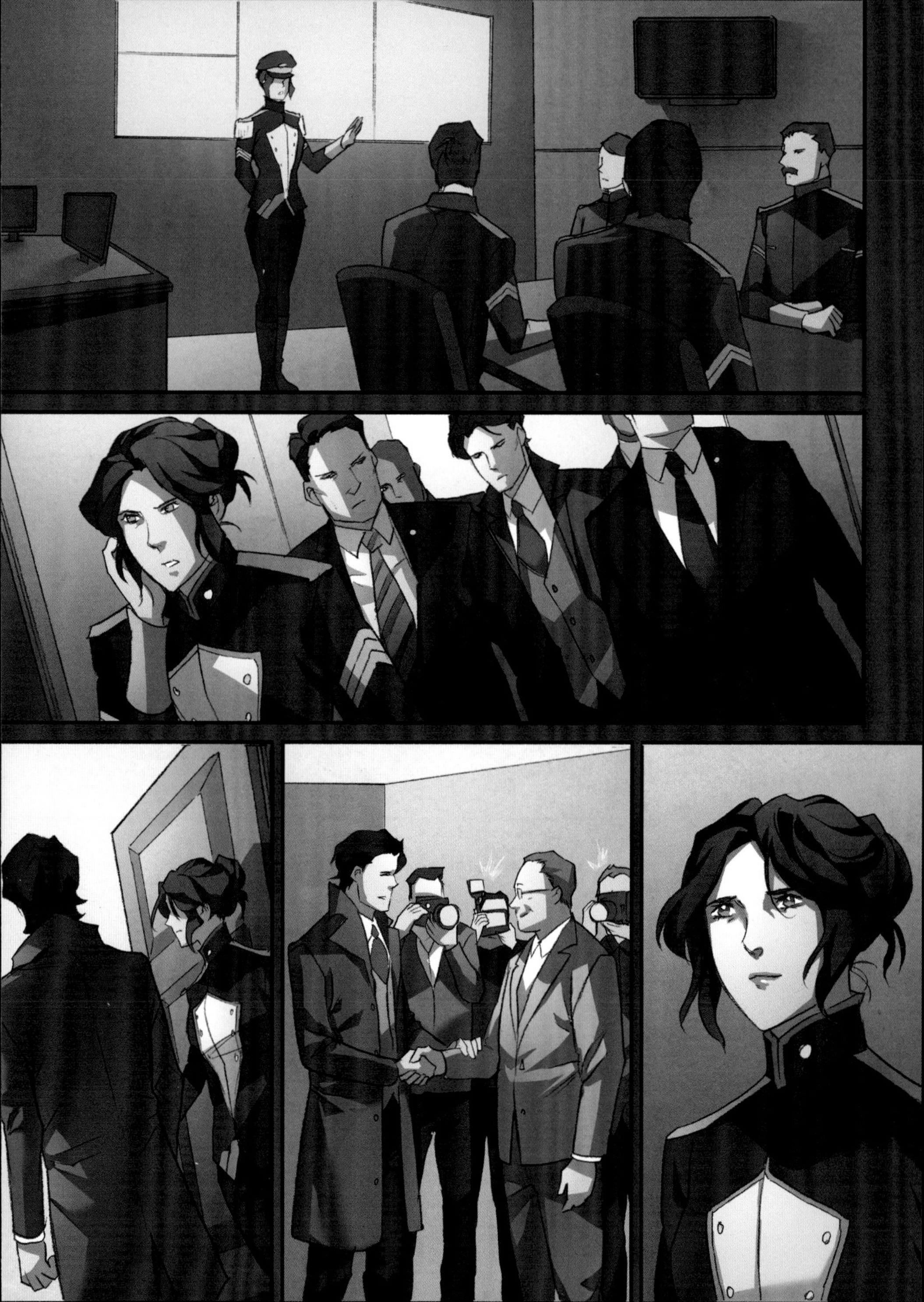

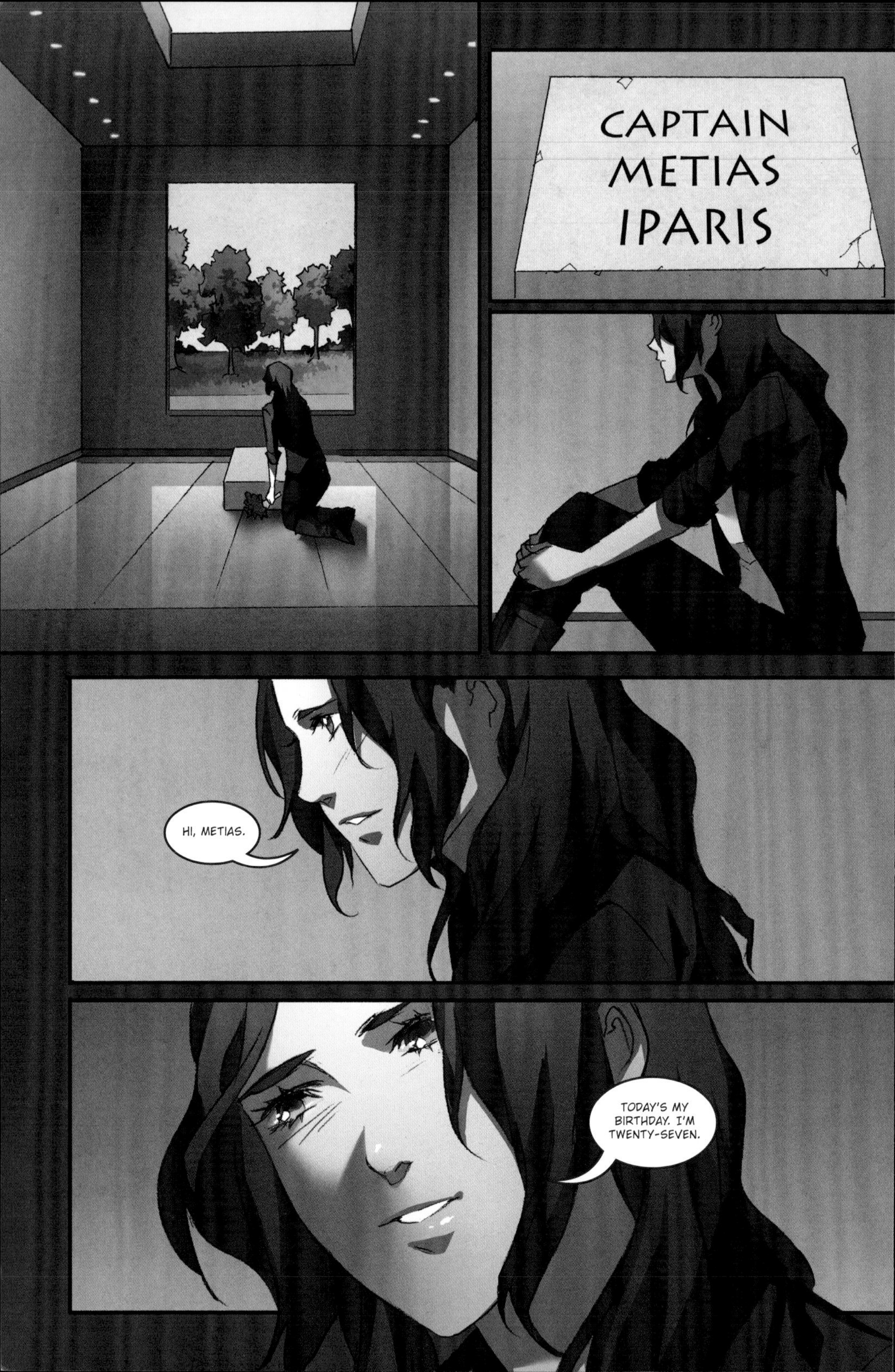
CAPTAIN
METIAS
IPARIS
HI, METIAS.
TODAY'S MY BIRTHDAY. I'M TWENTY-SEVEN.

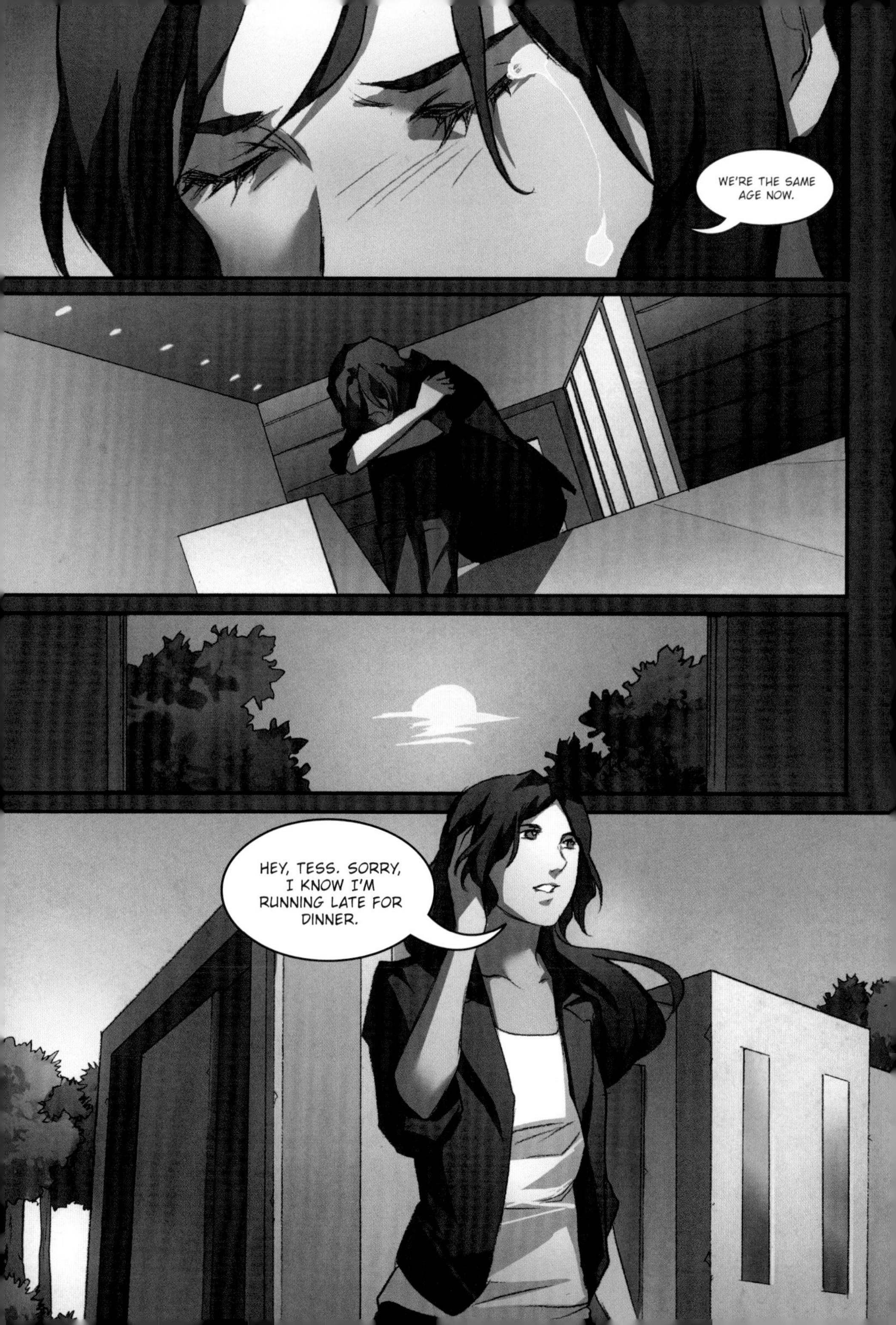
WE'RE THE SAME AGE NOW.
HEY, TESS. SORRY, I KNOW I'M RUNNING LATE FOR DINNER.

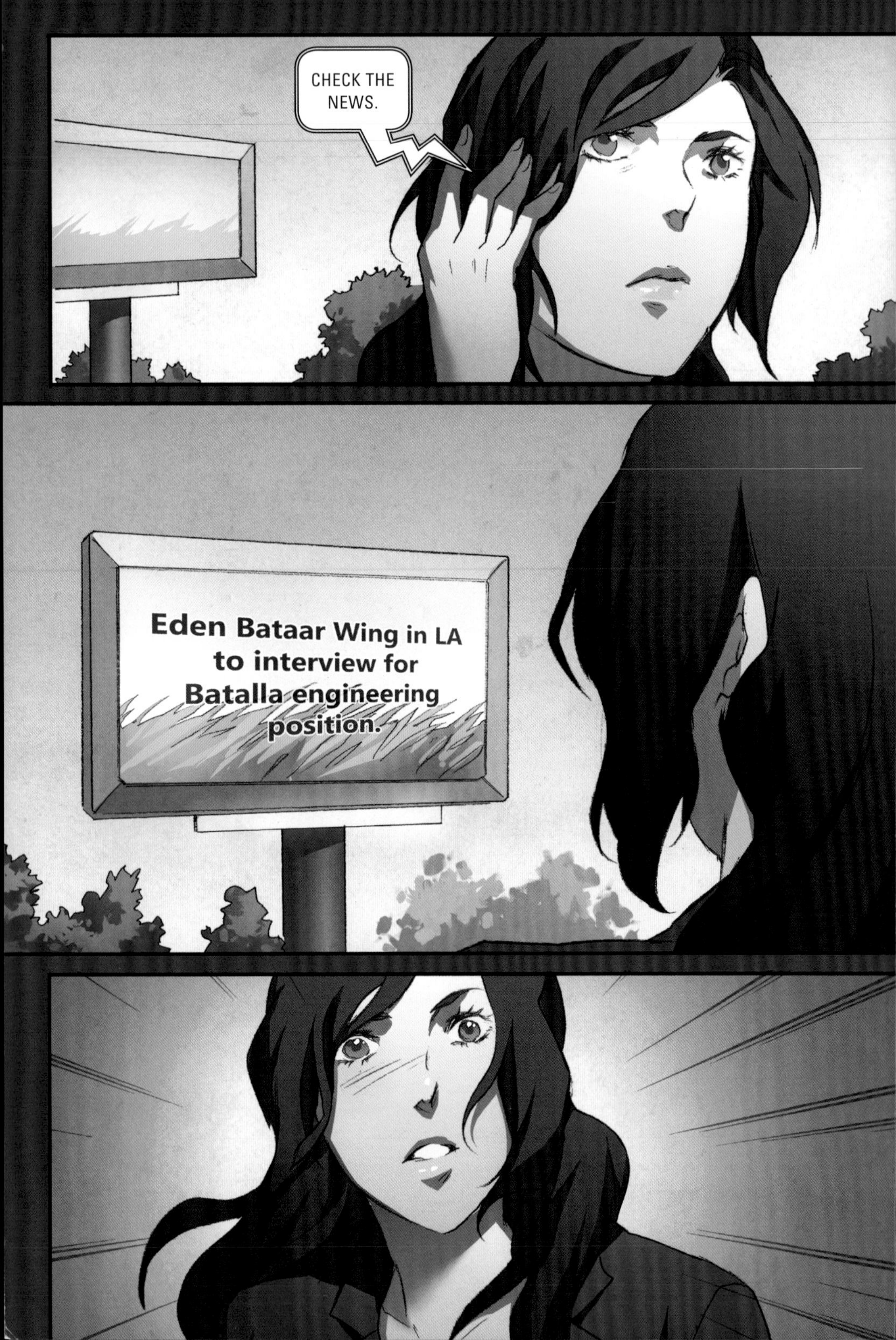
CHECK THE NEWS.
Eden Bataar Wing in LA to interview for Batalla engineering position.

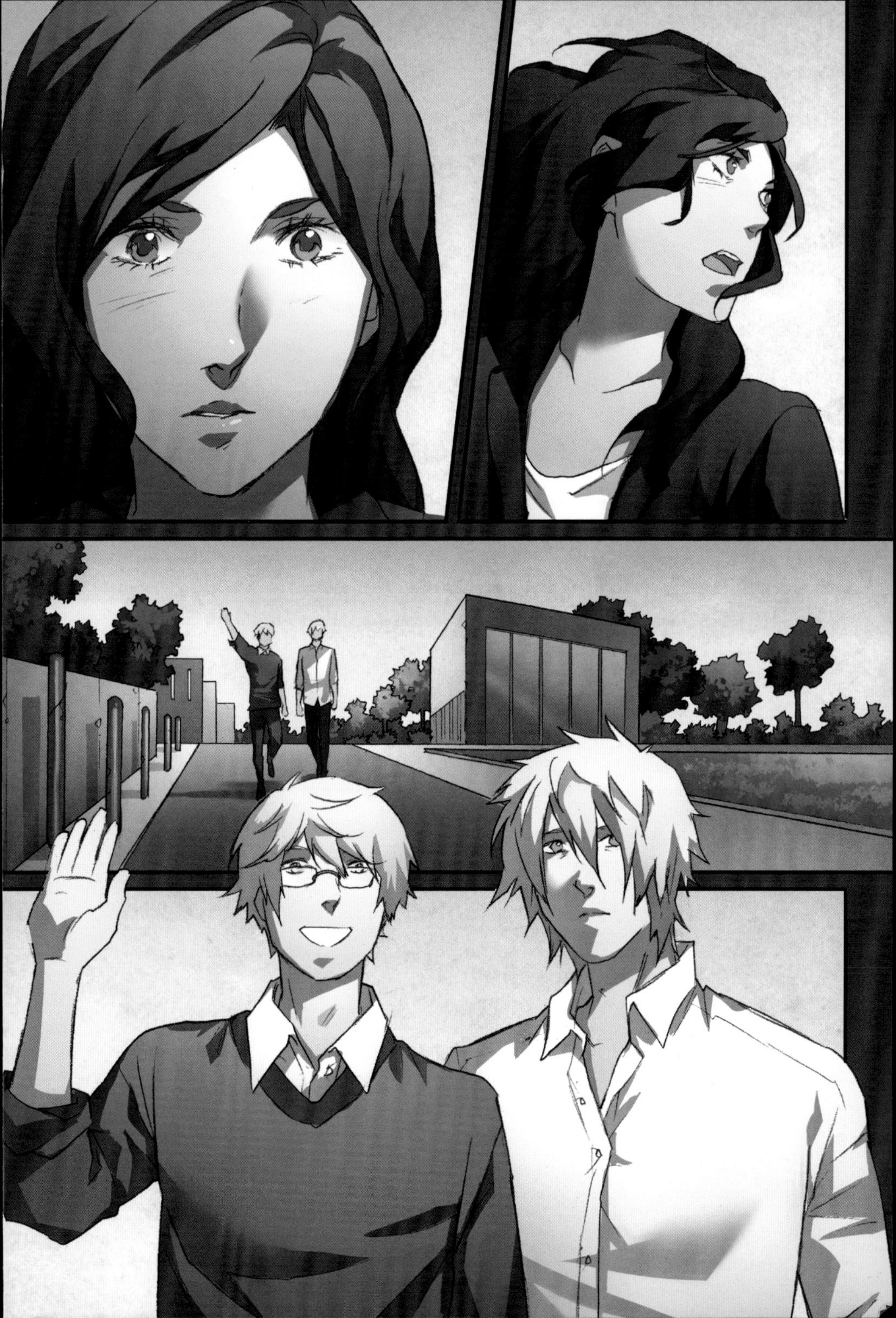

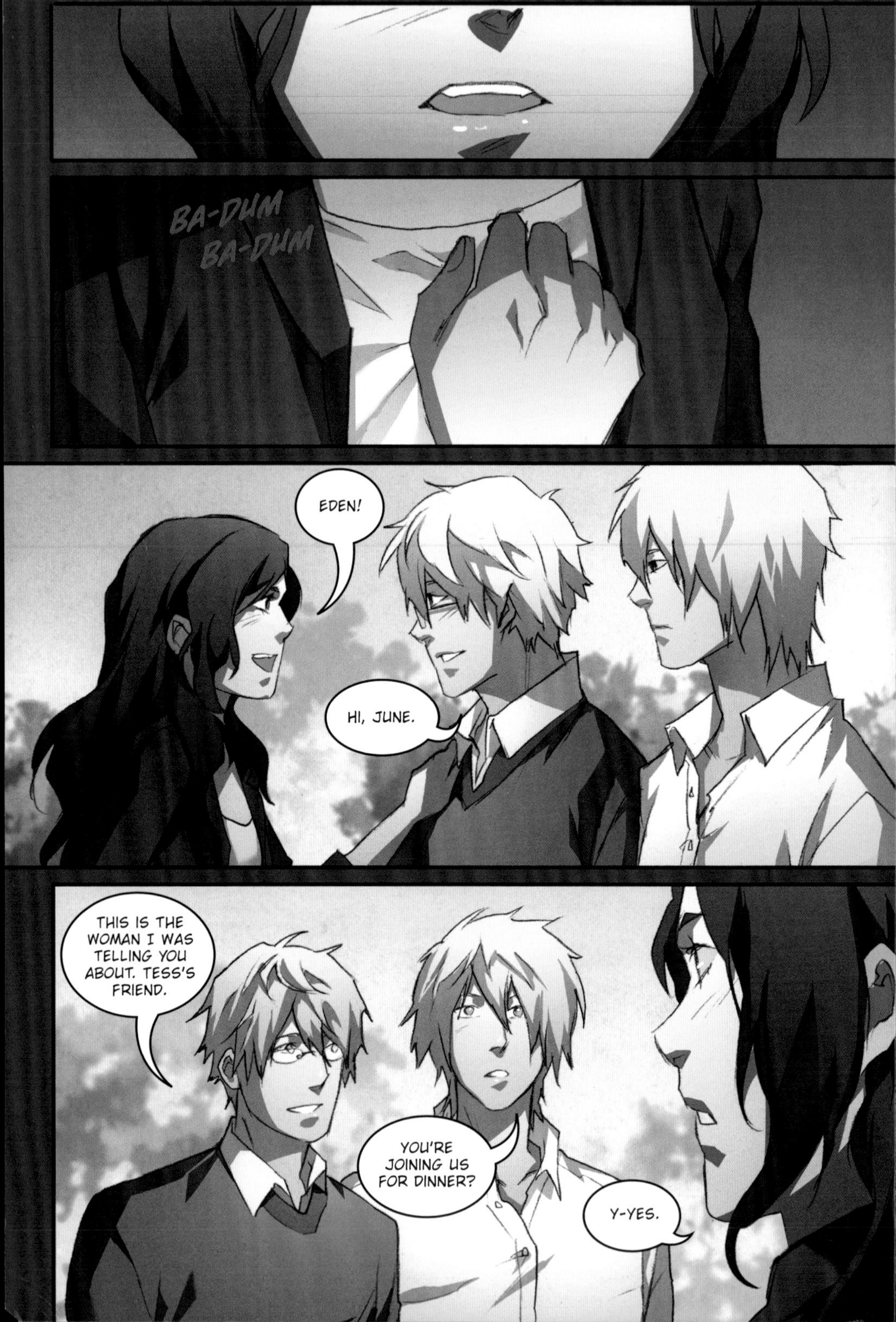
BA-DUM
BA-DUM
EDEN!
HI, JUNE.
THIS IS THE WOMAN I WAS TELLING YOU ABOUT. TESS'S FRIEND.
YOU'RE JOINING US FOR DINNER?
Y-YES.

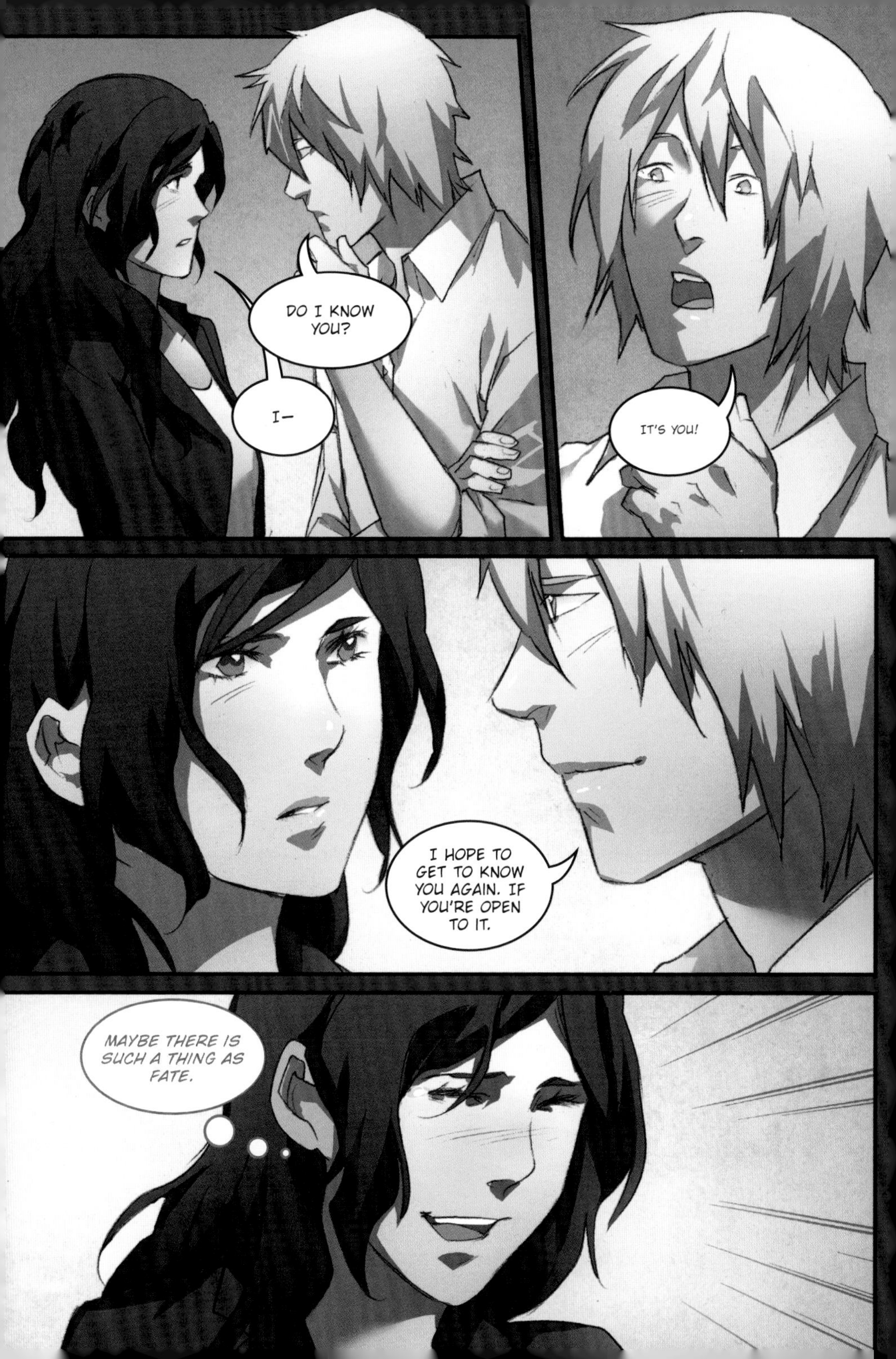
DO I KNOW YOU?
I—
IT'S YOU!
I HOPE TO GET TO KNOW YOU AGAIN. IF YOU'RE OPEN TO IT.
MAYBE THERE IS SUCH A THING AS FATE.

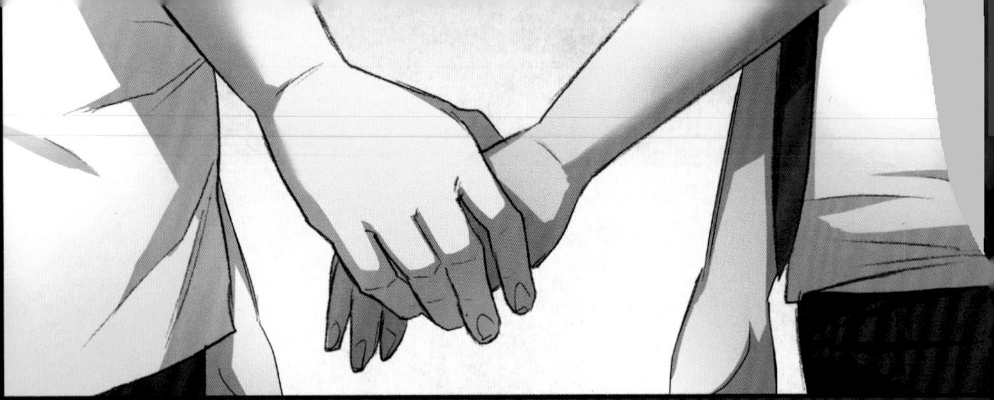
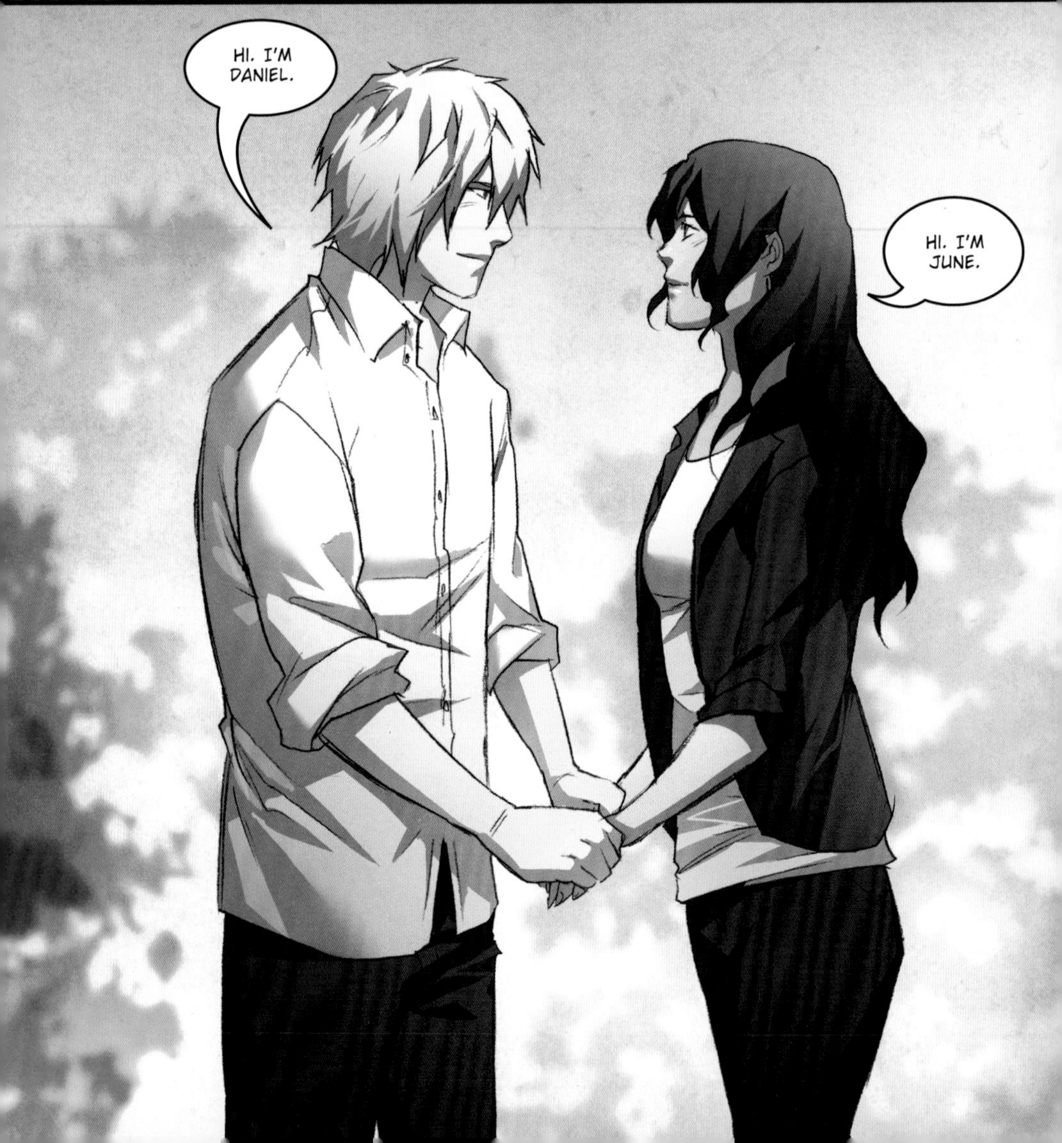
HI. I'M DANIEL.
HI. I'M JUNE.